Selma Lagerlöf (1858-1940) was born on a farm in Värmland, trained as a teacher and became, in her lifetime, Sweden's most widely translated author ever. Novels such as *Gösta Berlings saga* (1891; *Gösta Berling's Saga*) and *Jerusalem* (1901-02) helped regenerate Swedish literature, and the school reader, *Nils Holgersson's Wonderful Journey through Sweden* (1906-07), has achieved enduring international fame and popularity. Two very different trilogies, the Löwensköld trilogy (1925-28) and the Mårbacka trilogy (1922-32), the latter often taken to be autobiographical, give some idea of the range and power of Lagerlöf's writing. Several of her texts inspired innovative films, among them *Herr Arnes pengar* (*Sir Arne's Treasure*), directed by Mauritz Stiller (1919) and based on *Herr Arnes penningar* (1903; *Lord Arne's Silver*), and *Körkarlen* (*The Phantom Carriage*), directed by Victor Sjöström (1921) and based on Lagerlöf's *Körkarlen* (1912). She was awarded the Nobel Prize for Literature, as the first woman ever, in 1909, and elected to the Swedish Academy, again as the first woman, in 1914. Having been able to buy back the farm of Mårbacka, which her family had lost as the result of bankruptcy, Lagerlöf spent the last three decades of her life combining her writing with the responsibilities of running a sizeable estate. Her work has been translated into close to 50 languages.

Linda Schenck grew up in the United States, and has lived in Sweden since she was a young adult. Her professional life has been devoted to translation and interpretation. She has translated five novels by Kerstin Ekman and works by Annika Thor, with *A Faraway Island* receiving the Mildred L. Batchelder Award in 2010. She has previously translated the first two novels in the Löwensköld trilogy, *The Löwensköld Ring* and *Charlotte Löwensköld*.

Some other books from Norvik Press

August Strindberg: *Tschandala* (translated by Peter Graves)
August Strindberg: *The Red Room* (translated by Peter Graves)
August Strindberg: *The People of Hemsö* (translated by Peter Graves)
August Strindberg: *Strindberg's One-Act Plays* (Translated by Agnes
   Broomé, Anna Holmwood, John K Mitchinson, Mathelinda
   Nabugodi, Anna Tebelius and Nichola Smalley)
August Strindberg: *The Defence of a Madman* (translated by Carol
   Sanders and Janet Garton)

Kerstin Ekman: *Witches' Rings* (translated by Linda Schenck)
Kerstin Ekman: *The Spring* (translated by Linda Schenck)
Kerstin Ekman: *The Angel House* (translated by Sarah Death)
Kerstin Ekman: *City of Light* (translated by Linda Schenck)

P. C. Jersild: *A Living Soul* (translated by Rika Lesser)

Selma Lagerlöf: *Lord Arne's Silver* (translated by Sarah Death)
Selma Lagerlöf: *The Löwensköld Ring* (translated by Linda Schenck)
Selma Lagerlöf: *Charlotte Löwensköld* (translated by Linda Schenck)
Selma Lagerlöf: *The Phantom Carriage* (translated by Peter Graves)
Selma Lagerlöf: *A Manor House Tale* (translated by Peter Graves)
Selma Lagerlöf: *Nils Holgersson's Wonderful Journey through Sweden*
   (translated by Peter Graves)

Hjalmar Söderberg: *Martin Birck's Youth* (translated by Tom Ellett)
Hjalmar Söderberg: *Selected Stories* (translated by Carl Lofmark)

Elin Wägner: *Penwoman* (translated by Sarah Death)

Anna Svärd

by

Selma Lagerlöf

Translated from the Swedish
and with an
Afterword by Linda Schenck

Series Preface by Helena Forsås-Scott

Norvik Press
2016

Originally published as *Anna Svärd* in 1928.

This translation and afterword © Linda Schenck 2016.
Series preface © Helena Forsås-Scott 2015.
The translator's moral right to be identified as the translator of the
work has been asserted.

Norvik Press Series B: English Translations of Scandinavian Literature,
no. 68

ISBN: 978-1-909408-28-9

Norvik Press gratefully acknowledges the generous support of the
Barbro Osher Pro Suecia Foundation towards the publication of this
translation.

Norvik Press
Department of Scandinavian Studies
University College London
Gower Street
London WC1E 6BT
United Kingdom
Website: www.norvikpress.com
E-mail address: norvik.press@ucl.ac.uk

Managing editors: Elettra Carbone, Sarah Death, Janet Garton,
C. Claire Thomson.

Layout: Marita Fraser
Cover design: Sture Pallarp

Contents

Anna Svärd

PART ONE

PART TWO

PART THREE

~

Lagerlöf in English
Series Preface

In the first comprehensive biography of the Swedish author Selma Lagerlöf (1858-1940), Elin Wägner has provided a snapshot of her at the age of 75 that gives some idea of the range of her achievements and duties. Sitting at her desk in the library at Mårbacka with its collection of classics from Homer to Ibsen, Lagerlöf is also able to view several shelves of translations of her books. Behind her she has not only her own works and studies of herself but also a number of wooden trays into which her mail is sorted. And the trays have labels like 'Baltic Countries, Belgium, Holland, Denmark, Norway, England, France, Italy, Finland, Germany, Sweden, Switzerland, the Slavic Countries, Austria-Hungary, Bonnier [her Swedish publisher], Langen [her German publisher], Swedish Academy, the Press, Relatives and Friends, Treasures, Mårbacka Oatmeal, Miscellaneous Duties'. Lagerlöf's statement, made to her biographer Elin Wägner a few years previously, that she had at least contributed to attracting tourists to her native province of Värmland, was clearly made tongue-in-cheek.

How could Selma Lagerlöf, a woman born into an upper-middle-class family in provincial Sweden around the middle of the nineteenth century, produce such an *œuvre* (sixteen novels, seven volumes of short stories) and achieve such status and fame in her lifetime?

Growing up on Mårbacka, a farm in the province of Värmland, at a time when the Swedish economy was predominantly agricultural, Selma Lagerlöf and her sisters learnt about the tasks necessary to keep the self-sufficient household ticking over, but their opportunities of getting an education beyond that which could be provided by their governess were close to non-existent. Selma Lagerlöf succeeded in borrowing money to spend three years in Stockholm training to become a teacher, one of the few professions open to women at the time, and after qualifying in 1885 she spent ten years teaching at a junior high school for girls in Landskrona, in the south of Sweden. Mårbacka had to be sold at auction in 1888, and Lagerlöf only resigned from her teaching post four years after the publication of her first novel, establishing herself as a writer in a Sweden quite different from the one in which she had grown up. Industrialisation in Sweden was late but swift, and Lagerlöf's texts found new readers among the urban working class.

Lagerlöf remained a prolific author well into the 1930s, publishing chiefly novels and short stories as well as a reader for school children, and she soon also gained recognition in the form of honours and prizes: an Honorary Doctorate at the University of Uppsala in 1907, the Nobel Prize for Literature, as the first woman, in 1909, and election to the Swedish Academy, again as the first woman, in 1914. Suffrage for women was only introduced in Sweden in 1919, and Lagerlöf became a considerable asset to the campaign. She was also able to repurchase Mårbacka, including the farm land, and from 1910 onwards she combined her work as a writer with the responsibility for a sizeable estate with a considerable number of employees.

To quote Lagerlöf's most recent biographer, Vivi Edström, she 'knew how to tell a story without ruining it'; but her innovative literary language with its close affinity with the spoken language required hard work and much experimentation. 'We authors,' Lagerlöf wrote in a letter in 1908, 'regard a book as close to completion once we have found the style in which it allows itself to be written.'

Her first novel, *Gösta Berlings saga* (1891; *Gösta Berling's Saga*), was indeed a long time in the making as Lagerlöf experimented with genres and styles before settling for an exuberant and innovative form of prose fiction that is richly intertextual and frequently addresses the reader. Set in Värmland in the 1820s with the young and talented Gösta

Berling as the hero, the narrative celebrates the parties, balls and romantic adventures throughout 'the year of the cavaliers' at the iron foundry of Ekeby. But it does so against the backdrop of the expulsion of the Major's Wife who has been the benefactress of the cavaliers; and following her year-long pilgrimage and what has effectively been a year of misrule by the cavaliers, it is hard work and communal responsibility that emerge as the foundations of the future.

In *Drottningar i Kungahälla* (1899; *The Queens of Kungahälla*) Lagerlöf brought together a series of short stories and an epic poem set in Viking-age Kungälv, some distance north of Gothenburg, her aim being to explore some of the material covered by the medieval Icelandic author Snorri Sturluson in *Heimskringla*, but from the perspectives of the female characters. The terse narrative of *Herr Arnes penningar* (1903; *Lord Arne's Silver*), set in the sixteenth century in a context that highlights boundary crossings and ambivalences, has a plot revolving around murder and robbery, ghosts, love and eventual punishment. The slightly earlier short novel *En herrgårdssägen* (1899; *The Tale of a Manor*) similarly transcends boundaries as it explores music and dreams, madness and sanity, death and life in the context of the emerging relationship between a young woman and a man.

A few lines in a newspaper inspired Lagerlöf to her biggest literary project since *Gösta Berling's Saga*, the two-volume novel *Jerusalem* (1901-02), which also helped pave the way for her Nobel Prize later in the decade. The plot launches straight into the topic of emigration, prominent in Sweden since the 1860s, by exploring a farming community in the province of Dalarna and the emigration of part of the community to Jerusalem. The style was inspired by the medieval Icelandic sagas, but although the focus on emigration also establishes a thematic link with the sagas, the inversions of saga patterns such as bloody confrontations and family feuds become more prominent as the plot foregrounds peaceful achievements and international understanding. Yet this is first and foremost a narrative in which traditional structures of stability are torn apart, in which family relationships and relations between lovers are tried and often found wanting, and in which the eventual reconciliation between old and new comes at a considerable price.

Lagerlöf had been commissioned to write a school reader in 1901, but it was several years before she hit on the idea of presenting the geography, economy, history and culture of the provinces of Sweden through the narrative about a young boy criss-crossing the country on the back of a goose. While working on *Nils Holgerssons underbara resa genom Sverige* (1906-07; *Nils Holgersson's Wonderful Journey through Sweden*), Lagerlöf doubted that the text would find readers outside Sweden; paradoxically, however, *Nils Holgersson* was to become her greatest international success. Once perceived as an obstacle to the ambitions to award Lagerlöf the Nobel Prize for Literature, *Nils Holgersson* is nowadays read as a complex and innovative novel.

Körkarlen (1912; *The Phantom Carriage*) grew out of a request from The National Tuberculosis Society, and what was intended as a short story soon turned into a novel. The narrative about a victim of TB, whose death on New Year's Eve destines him to drive the death-cart throughout the following year and who only gains the respite to atone for his failures and omissions thanks to the affection and love of others, became the basis in 1921 for one of the best-known Swedish films of the silent era, with Victor Sjöström as the director (Sjöström also played the central character) and with ground-breaking cinematography by J. Julius (Julius Jaenzon).

The First World War was a difficult time for Lagerlöf. While many of her readers, in Sweden and abroad, were expecting powerful statements against the war, she felt that the political events were draining her creative powers. *Kejsarn av Portugallien* (1914; *The Emperor of Portugallia*) is not just a novel about the miracle of a newborn child and a father's love of his daughter; it is also a text about a fantasy world emerging in response to extreme external pressures, and about the insights and support this seemingly mad world can generate. Jan, the central character, develops for himself an outsider position similar to that occupied by Sven Elversson in Lagerlöf's more emphatically pacifist novel *Bannlyst* (1918; *Banished*), a position that allows for both critical and innovative perspectives on society.

Quite different from Lagerlöf's war-time texts, the trilogy consisting of *Löwensköldska ringen* (1925; *The Löwensköld Ring*), *Charlotte Löwensköld* (1925) and *Anna Svärd* (1928) is at once lighthearted and serious, a narrative *tour de force* playing on ambivalences and multiple interpretations to an extent that has the potential to destabilise, in retrospect, any hard and fast readings of Lagerlöf's *œuvre*. As the trilogy calls into question the ghost of the old warrior General Löwensköld and then traces the decline of Karl-Artur Ekenstedt, a promising young minister in the State Lutheran Church, while giving prominence to a series of strong and independent female characters, the texts explore and celebrate the capacity and power of narrative.

Lagerlöf wrote another trilogy late in her career, and one that has commonly been regarded as autobiographical: *Mårbacka* (1922), *Ett barns memoarer* (1930; *Memories of My Childhood*), and *Dagbok för Selma Ottilia Lovisa Lagerlöf* (1932; *The Diary of Selma Lagerlöf*). All three are told in the first person; and with their tales about the Lagerlöfs, relatives, friends, local characters and the activities that structured life at Mårbacka in the 1860s and 70s, the first two volumes can certainly be read as evoking storytelling in the family circle by the fire in the evening. The third volume, *Diary*, was initially taken to be the authentic diary of a fourteen-year-old Selma Lagerlöf. Birgitta Holm's psychoanalytical study of Lagerlöf's work (1984) read the Mårbacka trilogy in innovative terms and singled out *Diary* as providing the keys to Lagerlöf's œuvre. Ulla-Britta Lagerroth has interpreted the trilogy as a gradual unmasking of patriarchy; but with 'Selma Lagerlöf' at its centre, this work can also be read as a wide-ranging and playful exploration of gender, writing and fame.

With the publication over the past couple of decades of several volumes of letters by Lagerlöf, to her friend Sophie Elkan (1994), to her mother (1998), to her friend and assistant Valborg Olander (2006), and to her friends Anna Oom and

Elise Malmros (2009-10), our understanding of Lagerlöf has undoubtedly become more complex. While the focus of much of the early research on Lagerlöf's work was biographical, several Swedish studies centring on the texts were published in connection with the centenary of her birth in 1958. A new wave of Lagerlöf scholarship began to emerge in Sweden in the late 1990s, exploring areas such narrative, gender, genre, and aesthetics; and in the 1990s the translation, reception and impact of Lagerlöf's texts abroad became an increasingly important field, investigated by scholars in for example the US, the UK and Japan as well as in Sweden. Current research is expanding into the interrelations between a range of media in Lagerlöf, performance studies, cultural transmissions, and archival studies. As yet there is no scholarly edition of Lagerlöf, but thanks to the newly established Selma Lagerlöf Archive (Selma Lagerlöf-arkivet, SLA, accessible at litteraturbanken.se) a scholarly edition in digitised form is underway.

By the time Lagerlöf turned 80, in 1938, she was the most widely translated Swedish writer ever, and the total number of languages into which her work has been translated is now close to 50. However, most of the translations into English were made soon after the appearance of the original Swedish texts, and unlike the original texts, translations soon become dated. Moreover, as Peter Graves has concluded in a study of Lagerlöf in Britain, Lagerlöf 'was not well-served by her translators [into English]'. The Norvik Press series 'Lagerlöf in English' aims to remedy this situation.

Helena Forsås-Scott

PART ONE

Selma Lagerlöf

THE JOURNEY TO KARLSTAD

I

Whatever you may think about Thea Sundler, you must admit that she knew better than anyone else how to handle Karl-Artur Ekenstedt.

Take, for example, Charlotte Löwensköld, who would also have liked to persuade him to travel to Karlstad to be reconciled with his mother but who, in her attempts to do so, reminded him of everything his mother had meant to him. In the end she had even tried to intimidate him by saying that if he continued to be ungrateful to his mother he would never be able to preach well again.

She seemed to want him to return, like the prodigal son, and beg and plead to be restored to favor in his childhood home. This was a useless tactic considering his frame of mind, and the success he had been having with his sermons, such success that the entire congregation adored him.

Thea Sundler, by contrast, used a completely different approach in convincing him to return to Karlstad. She inquired whether what she had heard was true, that dear Mrs. Ekenstedt always expected to be asked forgiveness for even the slightest offense anyone committed against her. If so, and if she was so particular with others, then surely she was ready and willing herself …

Well, he had to admit she was like that. At the very instant his mother realized she had insulted someone, she was eager to make it up to them, and be reconciled.

Next, Thea reminded him of the time dear Mrs. Ekenstedt

had made that hazardous journey to Uppsala during the snowmelt, just to give him the opportunity to ask for her forgiveness. Thea went on to express her surprise that he, a Christian clergyman, was less disposed to be charitable than a woman of the world such as his mother.

Karl-Artur found it difficult to see what she was getting at. He simply stood and stared at her.

And so Mrs. Sundler said that this time it was dear Mrs. Ekenstedt who had offended him. And if she was as upstanding a person as he claimed, then surely he could not doubt that she was now lying there, bedridden, regretting her words, and longing with all her heart for the chance to beg his forgiveness. And since her illness prevented her from coming to him, it was his obligation to go and see her.

This was very different from what Charlotte had said to him. It would not mean going back to his parental home as a lost son, but entering it victorious. And so he went not to humbly beg apology but to be forgiving. It is impossible to say how much this thought appealed to him and how grateful he was to Thea, who had made him see it that way.

So as soon as he had finished at church on Sunday and had a meal at the organist's, he headed back to Karlstad. Indeed, he was so eager that he traveled all night. He stayed awake imagining the beautiful reunion he was going to have with his mother. There was no one who could make such an encounter as lovely as she could.

He arrived in Karlstad at about five in the morning, but instead of going directly home, he took in at the inn. He had no doubt whatsoever about how his mother would be feeling about him, but he did have his doubts about his father. It wasn't at all impossible that he would refuse to let him in, and Karl-Artur did not want to run that risk in the presence of the coach driver.

The innkeeper was standing on the steps, and he recognized Karl-Artur as a former resident of Karlstad as soon as he appeared. He may have heard one or two things about a breach in relations between him and his parents, owing to the fact that the young minister had taken it into his head to marry a peddler woman. He addressed Karl-Artur with gentle, sympathetic words, and Karl-Artur appeared so composed and content and responded so cheerfully, that the innkeeper had the impression that there must be nothing to the rumors about a family argument.

Karl-Artur requested a room, washed off the travel dust and prepared and dressed with care. When he came back out he was wearing his soutane, his clerical collar and his black stovepipe hat. He had put on his professional garb to indicate to his mother the pious and priestly frame of mind in which he was coming to see her.

The innkeeper offered him breakfast, but he declined. He had no desire to postpone the delightful moment when he and his mother would fall into one another's arms.

He walked rapidly along the streets, heading for his childhood home by the Klara river. He was feeling exactly the same high level of pleasant anticipation he used to feel when he came home for a holiday while he was studying at Uppsala.

Suddenly, however, he stopped stock still, looking as alarmed as if he had been slapped right across the face. He was so close to the Ekenstedt residence that he could see it, and all the shutters and doors were closed.

In his astonishment, his first thought was that the innkeeper must have sent a messenger to his parents to alert them of his arrival, and that they had closed the house up tight to keep him out. He went fiery red with indignation and turned right back.

But it only took a moment for him to start laughing at himself. It wasn't even six in the morning, and the house was always closed up at that hour. How absurd of him to have imagined that the shutters were closed and the doors locked just to keep him out. He walked back to the gate, opened it, and sat down on a bench in the garden to wait for the people of the house to wake up.

Still, he could not help interpreting it as an ominous sign that his home had been closed when he arrived. His mood had turned. The great sense of confidence that had buoyed him up all night had fled.

He sat looking at the lovely flowerbeds and the fine lawn. He looked at the large, handsome house as well. Then he thought about her, the woman who governed it all, and who was so esteemed and honored, and he said to himself that it would not be possible for her to apologize to him. Soon his thoughts had carried him so far that he was unable to imagine what Thea Sundler and he had been thinking. In Korskyrka it had seemed to him that it would be natural, and a given, that the colonel's wife would have had second thoughts, but sitting there he realized it was utter nonsense.

He was so firmly convinced that he felt like turning around and leaving at once. In fact he stood up to leave. He was eager to get away before anyone saw him.

But just as he was about to open the gate he realized that this was probably the last time he would be visiting his parental home. If he left now, it would be never to return.

So, leaving the gate half open, he turned to walk around the yard and bid the place farewell.

Heading for the front of the house, he found himself under the big, beautiful trees by the riverbank. No, he would never walk here again, never again admire the beautiful view. He looked long at the rowboat pulled up on the shore. He had assumed that no one paid it any attention now that he no longer lived there, but he noticed that it had been tarred and painted, just as nicely as in the days when he used it.

He hurried over to a little vegetable patch he had been in charge of as a child, and found it, too, just like in the past, with the very same vegetables planted as he used to grow there. And he realized that all this was his mother's doing. She saw to it that the little children's garden was maintained. It must have been at least fifteen years since he had tended it.

He searched under an astrachan for unripe apples, putting one in his pocket although it was green as a cabbage and so hard he couldn't bite into it. And he sampled the gooseberries and currants, although they were past their prime.

He walked over to the outbuildings and to a garden shed where he had always kept a little spade, a rake and a wheelbarrow. He looked in, but hadn't really needed to wonder. All three were right where he had left them. No one had been allowed to dispose of them.

Now it was probably so late that he ought to hurry if he intended to escape unseen. But he kept remembering things he wanted to see one last time. It all had new value for him now: 'I had no idea how much I cared about all this,' he thought.

At the same time, he was ashamed of his childish feelings. He would not have wanted Thea Sundler, with her admiration for the heroic words he had uttered just a couple of days ago about being free of both his home and his parents, to see him now.

Ultimately, he began to suspect that what was keeping him was a covert wish that someone would see him and let him in. And the moment he realized this, he instantly decided to leave.

He was already outside the garden, standing at the gate, when he heard a window open in the closed-up house.

It was impossible to resist; he had to turn around. The colonel's wife's bedroom window had been opened wide, and there was his sister, Jaquette, leaning out to inhale the fresh morning air.

It only took a second for her to notice his presence, and she immediately began to wave and nod. Involuntarily, he responded in kind. He nodded and waved back, pointing to the closed front door. Jaquette vanished from the window, and a couple of minutes later he heard the creaking of latches and locks. The door opened, his sister came out onto the steps and opened her arms to him.

He was ashamed, thinking of Thea Sundler, and of himself as well, since at that instant he did not believe that his mother would ask his forgiveness. Although he did not belong there any more, he could not help running to Jaquette. He took her hands and pulled her close and was so grateful she had opened the door for him that his eyes filled with tears.

She was terribly happy. When she saw him weeping she embraced and kissed him.

'Karl-Artur, Karl-Artur, thank the Lord you have come!'

He had completely convinced himself that he would not be admitted. This generous reception took him so much by surprise that he was hardly able to get his words out:

'Tell me, Jaquette, is Mamma awake? May I speak with her?'

'Of course you may speak with dear Mother. She has been better the last few days. She slept very soundly last night.'

She walked up the staircase before him and he followed, somewhat more slowly. He would never have believed that he could feel so happy to be in his home once again. He put a hand on the shiny bannister, not for support but to stroke it.

Once upstairs, he expected someone to come toward him and show him back down to the door. But nothing happened. He had a sudden insight. Apparently his father had not informed the rest of the family that they had definitively broken off relations. No, he had been unable to do so, because of his wife's illness.

Yes, he realized that this had to be the explanation, and he walked on feeling somewhat calmer.

How lovely the rooms were! He had thought so in the past as well, but they had never seemed as beautiful as today. The furniture was not, as elsewhere, standing stiffly against the walls. These rooms were relaxed and pleasant. She, the mistress of the house, had left her mark on everything.

They had to pass through an anteroom to reach the bedroom door. Jaquette signaled to him to wait, passing into the room on her own.

He ran a hand over his brow, trying to remind himself of why he had come. But he could think of nothing but the fact that he was at home and was going to be allowed to see his mother.

Jaquette came out to get him. When he saw his mother lying there so pale, with bandages around her forehead and arm, he felt as if he had been stabbed in the chest, and he fell to his knees at her bedside. She gave a cry of joy, threw her good arm around his neck, pulled him to her in a long embrace, and kissed him.

They looked into each other's eyes and rejoiced. At that moment there was nothing keeping them apart. All had been forgiven.

He was not prepared to see his mother looking so weak and fragile, and he was nearly unable to restrain his emotions. Very tenderly, he asked how she was feeling. She could hardly fail to notice how much he cared about her.

This was the best possible remedy for her illness, and she pulled him to her a second time.

'Never mind. All's well now. I've forgotten how I felt.'

From this reply he knew that she loved him as before. And at the same time he knew that everything he had mourned as lost a few minutes ago had been returned to him. He could again consider himself a son of this splendid household. He could wish for nothing more.

But at the very moment he felt happiest, he was overcome with uneasiness. He had certainly not accomplished the mission of his journey. His mother had not apologized to him, nor did she appear to intend to do so.

He felt a deep temptation not to be bothered about the apology. And yet it was quite important to him. If the colonel's wife admitted that she had treated him unjustly, he would have a completely different status in this home, and his parents would have to change their view on his marriage to Anna Svärd.

He also felt completely confident and even slightly audacious after having been so well received by his mother. 'I had better get the matter out of the way at once,' he thought to himself. 'There is no knowing that Mamma will be this kind and gentle another day.'

Until that moment he had remained on his knees, now he got up and sat down in the chair next to the bed.

He found it somewhat awkward to have to set his own mother straight. But soon he had an idea that quite pleased him. He remembered that in the old days, when he or his sisters had committed some offense their mother was expecting them to apologize for, she had always addressed the guilty party with these words: 'Well, my child, isn't there something you want to say to me?'

So in order to approach the difficult subject in a playful

manner, he furrowed his brow and lifted his index finger, smiling throughout so his mother would know he was speaking in jest, and said:

'Well, dear Mother, isn't there something you want to say to me?'

The colonel's wife did not seem to have the slightest idea what he was getting at. She just lay still, looking quizzically at him.

His poor sister, by contrast, had been standing there joyously witnessing the happy reunion between her mother and brother. But now she looked terrified, and raised a discreet hand in warning.

Karl-Artur was absolutely sure that the colonel's wife would be delighted with his little joke and respond in kind the minute she realized what he was getting at. He was not about to heed any warning, but went on:

'Mamma, I am sure you have realized that I was quite angry with you last Thursday for having tried to keep me and my fiancée apart. I would never have believed my dear mother could be so cruel to me. I was so upset that I departed without wanting to see you again, Mamma.'

The colonel's wife lay just as still as before. Karl-Artur could not discern the slightest trace of anger or displeasure while his sister, on the other hand, appeared increasingly agitated. She came stealthily closer and behind the bed-head she pinched her brother's arm hard.

He must have known what she was trying to tell him, but he was so sure that he knew better than Jaquette how to tackle their mother that he just went on as before:

'Indeed, Mamma,' he said, 'last Friday morning when Papa and I parted company, I assured him that I would never darken his doorstep again. Still, here I am. I wonder whether the wisest woman in all of Karlstad might understand what I have come for.'

Here he paused. He was certain, having said so much, that his mother would pick up the train of thought naturally. She did not, however. She merely shifted a bit higher on the pillow, not taking her eyes off him for a moment, staring so hard that he found it almost painful.

He could not help wondering whether his mother's mind had been affected by her illness. She was usually quick to interpret insinuations. But since she was not doing so now, he simply had to go on:

'I had really intended never to see you again, Mamma, but when I told a friend about it, she asked me if you, Mamma, weren't precisely the person who always expected an apology for even the slightest offense, and then she asked me whether it wouldn't be so that you, Mamma, would…'

That was as far as he got. Jaquette interrupted him once more. She took him decisively by the arm and shook it.

That made the colonel's wife break her long silence at once:

'No, Jaquette, do not interrupt him,' she said. 'Let him proceed!'

When he heard his mother say those words, Karl-Artur had a presentiment that his mother might not be entirely pleased with him, but he disregarded it. It couldn't be possible that she found him hard and unloving. Hadn't he broached the subject playfully? She couldn't have wished for a gentler manner.

No, their mother had probably just wanted to prevent Jaquette from continuing to disturb him. In any case, he had now spoken for so long that it was best to come to the point.

'This friend of mine, Mamma, was the person who urged me to come back. She told me that it was my duty to come to see you, Mamma, since you were unable to come to me. Do you remember, Mamma, the time you traveled all the way to Uppsala to give me the opportunity to beg your forgiveness? She told me that she was so certain that Mamma would admit, that you, Mamma…'

How difficult it was to rebuke one's own mother! The words seemed to be sticking in his throat. He stuttered, he coughed, and in the end there was nothing for it but to go silent.

A soft smile crossed the colonel's wife's lips. She inquired as to the name of the friend who believed so unconditionally in her.

'It was Thea, Mamma.'

'Was it not Charlotte who believed I was lying here longing

to beg your forgiveness?'

'No, Mamma, not Charlotte but Thea.'

'I am pleased to hear that it was not Charlotte,' said the colonel's wife.

Having said that, she shifted higher onto her pillow and drifted back into silence. Karl-Artur did not speak either. He had already said what he came to say to his mother, although by necessity not as eloquently as he would have liked. Now there was nothing to do but wait.

While doing so, he considered his mother. Surely she was lying there struggling with herself. To admit to her only son that she had been unfair would not be easily done.

In due course, she asked another question:

'You're wearing your cassock?'

'Mother, I wanted to show you the frame of mind in which I came.'

A new smile crossed her lips. He was frightened when he saw it. It was vicious and spiteful.

It suddenly seemed to him that the face on the pillow looked as if it had been carved in stone. The words for which he was waiting refused to come. He found himself in a state of great anxiety over the impossibility of her saying that she regretted her behavior and apologizing.

'Mamma!' he cried, putting all the admonition and anticipation he possessed into that word.

A change occurred. The blood went to her face. The colonel's wife sat straight up in bed, raised her strong arm and shook it at him.

'It has come to an end!' she cried. 'God's patience has come to an – – – ' That was all she managed to utter. The last word died on her lips, inarticulate and faint, and she fell back onto her pillow. Her eyes rolled up in her head, so only the whites were visible. Her hand fell to the quilt.

Jaquette shouted for help and ran out of the room. Karl-Artur flew to his mother.

'What has come over you? Mamma, Mamma! Do not take it so hard, please!'

He kissed her lips and brow, as if to kiss the life back into her.

Prostrate over her, he felt a hand seize him by the neck. A hand on his coat collar, and as if he had been a tiny pup, the strong hand lifted him out of the room and tossed him to the floor.

He heard his father say, in a terrifying voice:

'So you are back. You wouldn't be satisfied until you had finished her off entirely, would you?'

II

At half past seven that same Monday morning the doorbell at the mayor's residence rang, and his elderly, experienced housekeeper hurried to the vestibule to open the door.

The man outside was Karl-Artur Ekenstedt, but the housekeeper thought to herself that had she not lived so many years in Karlstad, known him from boyhood and seen him as an adult, she would never have recognized him. His face was bluish-red, and his beautiful eyes so puffed and bloodshot they looked as if they might pop out of their sockets.

As the housekeeper had been in the mayor's service for so long, and seen many such situations, and was quite accustomed to such matters, she thought to herself that young Ekenstedt looked like a murderer, and she would have preferred not to let him in. However, he was the son of Colonel Ekenstedt and his kind wife, and hence she had no choice but to ask him to come in, and sit down and wait. The mayor was out for his usual morning constitutional, but breakfast was served at eight, so he would surely be back by then.

If the very sight of young Ekenstedt had frightened her, she was certainly not calmed when she noted how he walked past her without a word or a greeting, as if he had not seen her at all.

It was clear that things were not well with him. All Beate Ekenstedt's children were generally nicely-mannered and modest. Something terrible must have happened to this son.

He went through to the mayor's office, and she saw him sit down in the rocker, but not for long. Soon he was standing at the mayor's desk, rifling through his papers.

Then she had to go out to the kitchen to check the clock, so the mayor's breakfast eggs would not be too hard-boiled. She also needed to set the table and start the coffee. But she could not get young Ekenstedt out of her mind. Every minute or two she rushed through the rooms to check on him.

Now he was pacing back and forth in the mayor's office. He walked from the window to the door and back again, talking to himself throughout.

Is it strange that she was frightened? The mayor's wife and children were in the country visiting relatives, so the rest of the staff had been given time off. Thus she was all alone in the house and bore full responsibility.

What was she going to do with the young man in the mayor's office who looked half crazed? What if he destroyed some of the important documents on the desk? Yet she couldn't abandon her duties altogether to keep watch over him.

Then the wise old woman realized she could ask Karl-Artur if he wouldn't like to come into the dining room for a cup of coffee while he waited. He did not refuse; he followed her directly. This pleased her very much, since as long as he was sitting with a cup of coffee in front of him he could hardly do any harm.

He sat right down in the mayor's seat, and drained the coffee cup she filled in a single gulp without seeming to notice that it was scalding hot. Then he reached for the pot she had left on the table, poured a second cup and drank that too. Adding neither sugar nor cream, he just gulped down the scalding coffee.

When he finished that cup, he must have noticed the housekeeper standing on the other side of the room, watching him. He turned to her:

'It was very kind of you, ma'am, to make me such fine coffee,' he said. 'It was probably my last coffee ever.'

He spoke so softly that she could only just hear him. It was as if he were confiding a deep secret in her.

'Oh, I don't doubt that Mrs. Forsius at the parsonage in Korskyrka makes you very good coffee,' the housekeeper replied.

'Indeed she did,' he answered, with a peculiar little laugh. 'But, you see, I shall never go there again.'

There was nothing strange about that. Young pastors were often moved from one parish to another. The housekeeper began to feel less worried.

'I suppose they actually make good coffee at almost any parsonage you might be sent to,' she said.

'Do you think, ma'am, that they also make good coffee in prison?' he asked in an even softer tone of voice. 'I imagine I will have to do without coffee and sweet rolls altogether, there.'

'But Sir, surely you are not going to jail. Why in the world would you?'

He nearly turned his back on her.

'I do not wish to answer that question,' he replied.

Once again he focused his attention on the table. He buttered a slice of bread, added some cheese, and ate as if he had never seen food before, taking large, greedy bites and swallowing them without chewing. The housekeeper began to wonder if his only problem was that he was starving. She went back to the kitchen to get the mayor's eggs. Karl-Artur wolfed them both down quickly and then devoted himself to the bread and butter again. While eating eagerly, he began to speak once more.

'There are many of the dead out walking the streets of Karlstad today.'

He said this very calmly and indifferently, as if he were mentioning the lovely weather. But the housekeeper couldn't help feeling frightened, and he must have noticed.

'Do you find my conversation peculiar, ma'am? Well, I can only agree that there is something odd about my seeing the dead. I have never seen them before, of that I am certain, I have never seen them before what happened to me at seven this morning.'

'Aha,' said the housekeeper.

'You see, ma'am, I felt such a cramping around my heart. I was going to walk into town from home, but I couldn't manage it, and just held onto our garden fence for dear life. At that very moment I saw Dean Sjöberg from the Cathedral approaching, holding his wife by the arm. They were walking the way they always used to when they came to have Sunday dinner with us. And of course they already knew what I had done, and they told me to come here, to the Mayor's, to admit my guilt and resign myself to my punishment. I answered them that I could not do so, but they insisted.'

Karl-Artur interrupted his story to pour himself another cup of coffee and drink it down. He turned a penetrating gaze on the housekeeper, as if to see how she was reacting to what he had to say.

But the housekeeper merely said with great aplomb:

'Well, lots of people have seen the dead, so I don't think you really have to…'

He was notably relieved by her answer.

'Precisely my own thought. I am the same man I have always been, except for this one thing.'

'Yes, that's true,' said the housekeeper, thinking it was best to agree with him and look calm, but she was certainly beginning to wish the mayor would come home.

'I have nothing against bowing to their will,' said Karl-Artur. 'But I am of perfectly sound mind, so I know that the mayor will simply laugh at me. I do not deny that I have a grave sin on my conscience, but it is not one for which I can be remanded into custody and convicted.'

With that he closed his eyes and leaned back. The slice of bread in his hand fell to the floor, his face was distorted, as if he were suffering terrible pangs of torment, but then, strangely, he quickly became himself again.

'My heart clenches up,' he said. 'Is it not remarkable that it cramps right up as soon as I say I cannot do it?'

He rose from the table and began pacing back and forth.

'I will do it,' he said, having now forgotten entirely that the housekeeper was standing there listening to him. 'I *want* to do it, and I shall tell the mayor that I have done something for which I am prepared to be punished. I shall tell him that I have committed manslaughter. I shall invent something. I must tell him I did it intentionally.'

He walked up to the housekeeper.

'Just think, my seizure is over!' he said, looking very pleased. 'It passed as soon as I said that I am prepared to serve my time. I am so relieved.'

The wise old housekeeper was no longer afraid of him. She had been seized with compassion. She took his hand and stroked it.

'But, Sir, surely you understand? Sir, you must not take responsibility for something you did not do.'

'Oh yes, I must,' he said. 'I know it is the right thing to do. And I do so very much want to die. I want to show Mamma that I love her. I will be so happy to meet her again on the other side, when we are reconciled.'

'But that will never happen,' said the housekeeper. 'I will tell the mayor.'

'Oh, no, you mustn't do that,' said Karl-Artur. 'Why should I not be convicted by a judge? I have committed murder, after all, although not with a knife or a firearm. Jaquette knows how it happened. Do you not think, ma'am, that cruelty and lack of love are more harmful than steel or lead? Papa knows too, and can bear witness. I do believe I will be convicted, I am not innocent.'

The housekeeper never had to answer. To her great relief, she heard the front door open and the familiar steps coming up the stairs.

She rushed out into the vestibule, hoping to have time to utter a word of warning to the mayor, but Karl-Artur was right on her heels. He seemed anxious to begin his confession immediately, but he was interrupted.

'Ah, so you are back in town,' the mayor said. 'I am so sorry to hear about your mother.'

At once he extended a hand in greeting, but Karl-Artur kept his right hand behind his back. He turned toward the wall, saying in a trembling voice, but still loud enough to be heard:

'I have come to request that you arrest me, good Sir. I am the one who killed my mother.'

'Damned if you are!' the mayor exclaimed. 'As far as I know the colonel's wife is not dead. I just met the doctor…'

Karl-Artur tottered back. The housekeeper thought he was going to fall, and opened her arms to catch him. But he regained his balance. Grabbing his hat, he rushed out into the street without another word.

The first person he saw was their family physician, whom they had known for years, and he ran toward him.

'How is Mamma?'

The doctor looked disapprovingly at him.

'How fortunate that we met, you scoundrel. Don't you dare go back home again. What on earth came over you? How could you have the temerity to lecture someone who is so ill?'

Karl-Artur did not need to hear any more. He rushed away from the doctor and right back to his childhood home. As he approached, he saw his married sister, Eva Arcker, by the gate.

'Eva,' he cried, 'is it true? Mamma lives?'

'Yes,' she said softly, 'the doctor believes she will survive.'

He wanted to run through the gate. His only thought was to rush in, throw himself at his mother's feet and beg for her mercy. But Eva stopped him.

'You mustn't go in, Karl-Artur. I have been standing here a long time waiting for you. She has had a terrible stroke. Dear Mother would not be able to speak with you.'

'I can wait as long as needs be.'

'I ask you not to enter not only for Mother's sake,' said Eva, raising her eyebrows, 'but for dear Father's as well. The doctor says that Mother will never be the same again. And now Father cannot abide the thought of seeing you. We cannot know what might happen if he encountered you. Return to Korskyrka! That is the best thing you can do.'

His sister's words upset Karl-Artur. He was convinced that she was exaggerating both their father's wrath and the risk to their mother's condition if he were to see them.

'You and your husband have always wanted to turn Papa and Mamma against me,' he said. 'And this is your golden opportunity. Make the most of it!'

He turned on his heel and left.

III

The thing about us human beings is that we do not like things to break. Even if something like a clay pot or a china plate breaks, we gather the pieces, put them next to each other, and try to paste and glue them back together.

That was something like the way Karl-Artur Ekenstedt spent his journey home to Korskyrka.

Well, not the entire journey, because it must be recalled that he had not slept a wink the previous night nor had he, owing to upsetting circumstances, had enough sleep all the previous week. So now his body made its unyielding demands and, in spite of the bumpy farmers' carts in which he traveled, and in spite of all the coffee he had imbibed at the mayor's, he slept sitting up for most of the journey home.

But during the brief periods when he was awake, he tried to gather the bits and pieces of himself so that the Karl-Artur Ekenstedt who had traveled the same route only a few hours earlier and who had then been shattered in Karlstad could be made whole again and used anew.

Some people might be of the opinion that it was nothing but a miserable clay pot that had been broken, on which it was hardly worth expending either effort or glue. But we must, I suppose, forgive Karl-Artur for not being of that opinion himself. He felt an accident had happened to a vase of the finest, costliest, hand-painted porcelain, richly gilded.

In some peculiar way it gave him good assistance in his repair work to think about his sister Eva and her husband, to become upset with them and to keep reminding himself of all the times they had displayed their envy and complained about how unfair Beate Ekenstedt was being.

The more he thought about the grudge Eva had so long borne him, the more convinced he became that she had not been telling the truth. Surely his mother was not in as bad a state as she had implied, nor his father so embittered against him. This was all just a trick Eva and Arcker had been planning. They hoped to take advantage of this most recent mistake of his, which was incredibly serious – he would not deny it – to keep him away from his home forever.

Just as he drew the conclusion that everything would have worked out beautifully if Eva had not shown him the door, he was overcome by fatigue and remained asleep until the cart stopped at an inn.

During another of his wakeful spells he thought about Jaquette. He did not wish to be unfair to her. She was not jealous like Eva. She was kind, and she cared for him. But was she not quite simpleminded? If she had not disturbed him during his significant conversation with his mother, he might have said roughly the same things, but he would certainly have worded them differently. It is not easy to put things right with someone standing behind your back the entire time tugging you by the arm and whispering to you to watch your words.

He found it very useful to think about Jaquette and about how foolish and unintelligent she was. And soon he fell asleep thinking about her as well.

It was with some reluctance that he thought about Thea Sundler now and then, too, and how she had contributed to his misfortune. After all, she was his dearest friend. There was no one in whom he could place greater trust, and yet perhaps she had not actually seen enough of the world to be an advisor in whom he could be completely confident. She had been wrong about his mother lying there waiting for an opportunity to apologize to him. What had led Thea to that error of judgment was her high opinion of him, and it resulted in her causing these unfortunate events to occur. The colonel's wife could have died, and he could have gone mad. He had been well on the way.

All in all, he avoided thinking about his visit to the mayor's residence and his conversation with the housekeeper there. He felt as if thinking about it would shatter him once again, and he would have to begin his repair work anew.

Yet another time during a short wakeful period he thought about the fact that the very horror and grief he had displayed might help him. His mother would probably hear about it, and she would realize how much he loved her. She would be moved, she would send for him, and they would be reconciled.

He wanted to believe that things would end up that way. Every day he would pray to God that things would end up that way.

It may be irreverent to say this, but Karl-Artur was reasonably well back in form by the time he returned to Korskyrka around eleven that evening. He found it surprising that he had recovered from such a terrible emotional upheaval as intact as he was. He was still sleepy, and when he stepped out of the cart by the parsonage gate and paid the local driver, he thought how good it was going to be to stretch out on a bed and sleep for as long as he could.

However, as he was about to enter his rooms, the housemaid came to tell him that the pastor's wife had some supper waiting for him in the dining room. He would have preferred to go right to bed, but he knew that the pastor's wife meant well and had been thinking that after traveling all day he would need a proper meal, so he accompanied the housemaid into the main building.

He probably would not have done so unless he was sure there was no one in the house who would ask him about his journey. But he knew that the old couple would have gone to bed hours ago and Charlotte was gone.

Walking through the entry, he almost tripped over a box or the like, just inside the door.

'Oh, do take care, Sir!' the housemaid said. 'Those are Mrs. Schagerström's moving crates. We've been wrapping her things in straw and bed linens all day long.'

Still it had not occurred to him that Charlotte had come from Stora Sjötorp in person, not to mention that she might be spending the night at the parsonage. He walked calmly into the dining room and sat down.

For quite a while he was undisturbed. He had time to eat his fill, and was just about to clasp his hands in a prayer of thanks, when he heard footsteps. They were heavy and shuffling, and he thought it must be the pastor's wife coming down to inquire about his trip. He did not dare rush away, which was his inclination.

A moment later the door opened, slowly and quietly, and someone entered. It would have been bad enough if it had been the pastor's wife. But instead it was Charlotte. That was the worst thing that could have happened. He had not been betrothed to her for a full five years for nothing; he could guess what he was in for. He knew her and could imagine what a scene she was going to make when she heard that Beate Ekenstedt had had a stroke! She would tell him off properly. He was terribly tired, but was going to have to listen to her for hours. He decided instantly to go on being as insolently polite to her as he had been of late. That was always the best way of keeping her at a distance.

However, before he had a chance to open his mouth, Charlotte had moved far enough into the room for the two tallow candles on the table to light up her face. He could see that her eyes were red-rimmed with weeping and that she was deathly pale. Something horrible must have happened to her.

The first thing that came to mind was that she regretted her marriage. And yet it was highly unlike her to show such feelings so clearly. And surely her former fiancé would be the last person she would confide in on such a matter.

Ah, yes! He had heard a couple of days earlier that her sister, the wife of Doctor Romelius, was seriously ill. He believed he knew what had happened.

Charlotte pulled out a chair and sat down at the table. She began speaking in a strangely harsh and expressionless voice, the kind of voice you use when you have made up your mind that you are not, under any circumstances, going to burst into tears. She did not look at him; one might have imagined that she was sitting there talking to herself.

'Captain Hammarberg was here an hour ago,' she said. 'He had been to Karlstad, and left there a little later than you did this morning. But he traveled in a coach drawn by two horses, which accounts for his arriving so much earlier. He said he had passed you on the road.'

Karl-Artur shifted his chair back from the table. From his head down to his heart he felt a ferocious stabbing pain.

'When he was passing the parsonage,' Charlotte continued in her stiff monotone, 'he noticed that the lights were on in the pastor's study, and thus thought he was still awake. So he disembarked from the coach, anticipating the pleasure of telling the pastor how his curate had behaved that morning in Karlstad. He loves spreading such stories.'

Stab after stab, running down from his head through his heart. All the pieces he had spent the day gathering and reassembling were falling apart again. Now he was about to hear how his fellow human beings judged his actions.

'We hadn't shut the front door,' said Charlotte, 'since we were expecting you any time, and so he was able to walk right into the study unhindered. But my uncle had just gone to bed, and so the person Captain Hammarberg met was not the pastor but me. I was sitting there writing a letter. I had no intention of going to bed until I heard about your trip to Karlstad. And that was how I came to hear it from Captain Hammarberg. I believe he took even greater pleasure in telling his story to me than he would have to my uncle.'

'And you, Charlotte, took no less pleasure in hearing it, I imagine,' Karl-Artur interjected.

Charlotte made a little parrying gesture. That insignificant comment did not merit a reply. It was the kind of thing people say in a moment of dire need when they still want to look self-assured. She continued to speak.

'Captain Hammarberg did not stay long,' she said. 'He departed as soon as he had told me that you delivered a stern sermon to your mother and that she then had a serious stroke. Oh, and he mentioned your visit to the mayor as well. Oh, Karl-Artur, Karl-Artur!'

Having come so far, she abandoned her tranquility. She put her handkerchief to her eyes and sniffled.

But as human beings, we do not like it when others cry over us. Nor do we like thinking about how someone has just been sitting listening to a witty, amusing account of how foolishly and preposterously we have behaved. And so Karl-Artur could not help saying something to the effect that Charlotte, now married to someone else, needn't worry so much about him and his family.

She did not respond to this comment, either. It was natural for him to defend himself that way, and nothing to be bothered about.

Instead, she fought back her tears in order to be able to say what she had been wanting to say all the time.

'When I heard all that, I initially felt determined not to talk to you this evening. Of course I knew you would prefer to be alone. But there is something I need to say to you without delay. I will not detain you long.'

He shrugged his shoulders, looking submissive and miserable. After all, they were sitting there together. He had no choice but to hear her out.

'I need you to know that the whole series of circumstances is my fault,' said Charlotte. 'I was the one who persuaded Thea – about your entire trip to Karlstad – It was I – you didn't want it but I did – and now if your mother dies, it will have been me and not you…'

She was unable to say any more, she felt so unhappy and guilty.

'I ought to have been patient,' said Charlotte the moment she was able to master her emotions again and speak. 'I ought not to have sent you off like that. You were still feeling bitter toward your mother. You had not forgiven her. That was why things developed as they did. But I ought to have known that it was doomed to fail. All of it, all of it is my fault.'

She rose at once and paced the floor for a few moments, her hands tearing at her handkerchief. In the end she stood in front of him.

'That was what I wanted you to know. It is all my fault.'

He said nothing, just extended his hands and took hers, holding them for a few moments.

'Charlotte,' he said very softly and gently, 'just think how many conversations you and I have had in this room, at this very table. We have disputed and argued here, but we have also had many fine moments. And this will be the last.'

She stood there next to him. She had no idea what was happening. He sat there stroking her hand, and speaking kindly to her, more kindly than he had addressed her in years.

'Charlotte, you have always been noble-minded and wished to help me. There is no one as generous as you, Charlotte.'

She was dumbstruck, unable even to contradict him.

'I have rejected your generosity time after time. I have not been willing to see it. And yet you come to me tonight, Charlotte, wanting to bear all the responsibility.'

'Well, but it is true,' she said.

'No, Charlotte, it's not true. Say no more! It is my own self-righteousness, my harshness. Charlotte, you only meant well.'

He lay his head on the tabletop and wept. But he never let go of her hand, and she felt the tears drop onto it.

'Charlotte,' he said. 'I feel like a murderer. There is no hope for me.'

With her free hand she stroked his hair, but she did not yet speak.

'I had such pain in my heart in Karlstad, Charlotte. I believe I was out of my senses. Then, as I journeyed home, I tried to keep it at bay. But I see that it cannot be done. I will have to bear it.'

'Karl-Artur,' Charlotte asked, 'What happened? How did it happen? I have only heard through Captain Hammarberg.'

Karl-Artur had never heard Charlotte speak in such a gentle, motherly fashion. He was unable to resist her, and began immediately to tell his tale. He felt as if he was atoning by leaving out nothing, glossing over nothing.

'Charlotte,' he finally said, 'how could I be so blind? What was deluding me?'

She did not answer that question. But the mercy in her

heart enveloped him and assuaged his pain. Neither of them thought about how peculiar it was for them to be speaking the truth in this way, in greater intimacy than ever before. Nor did they move; he sat the whole time at the table, and she stood leaning over him. They talked about everything. He asked her if she believed he could continue as a clergyman.

'You needn't worry about Captain Hammarberg and what he might say.'

'It's not Captain Hammarberg I am thinking about, Charlotte. I just feel so lamentable and rejected. You cannot imagine, Charlotte, how I am feeling.'

Charlotte decided not to answer.

'Well, you just go in and have a word with Reverend Forsius tomorrow!' she said. 'There is no one as wise or as pious as he. And he may very well tell you that you will be a better minister now than you were before.'

That was a good piece of advice. It gave him peace of mind. And the same was true of everything she was saying. It was doing him good. He no longer felt rebellious or suspicious.

In the end he gave her hand a gentle kiss.

'Charlotte, I have no desire to speak about the past, but let me still say that I cannot understand myself! Why did I abandon you, Charlotte? No, I am not making excuses, but it is as if I am driven to do what I do not want to do. Why have I thrown my mother into the lap of death? Why did I lose you, Charlotte?'

A terrible struggle evinced itself in Charlotte's expression. She walked to the darkest corner of the room. She might have informed him of the reason, but she did not wish to. This was a sacred moment. Nothing that could be interpreted as vengeful must appear on her face.

'My dearest Karl-Artur,' she said, 'in a few weeks I shall be going away. Schagerström and I intend to accompany my sister Marie-Louise to Italy, where she will be treated for the weakness in her chest and be able to go on living and take care of her children. Perhaps that was the reason this all had to happen.'

Having said that, she walked back to the man she loved

and stroked his hair one more time.

'God's patience has not come to an end,' she said. 'I know that it is everlasting.'

A HORSE AND A COW, A MAID
AND A FARMHAND

I

Who was she, to be chosen above all the other poor peddler women, for a life of prosperity and advancement?

Well, it was true that she was clever at making money, and economical, never spending more than she had to, and shrewd and cunning, able to entice people into buying things they needed and things they didn't need. Still, she did not believe she deserved to advance above all her old friends.

So, who was she, to have a person of high station turn his eyes on her?

Each morning when she woke up she said to herself: 'Is it not a miracle? Sure, it is a miracle just as great as those described in the Bible. They ought to preach about it in the churches.'

At that she clasped her hands, pretending she was sitting in a church pew. She imagined people all around her, and a pastor at the pulpit. It was like a traditional church service, except that the pastor's subject was unusual. He spoke of nothing but the poor women from Dalarna who had to plod the roads peddling their wares, suffering so many dangers and hardships. Like someone who was very familiar with these matters, he spoke of their poor accommodation, how little they earned and how often they went without a meal so as not to reduce the paltry earnings they wanted to take back home. But now, said the pastor, he was pleased to be able to tell his beloved listeners that God, in his mercy, had taken one of these tired wanderers in hand. She would never again have to wander the rural roads come rain or come shine. She would be marrying a man of the cloth and moving into a parsonage that had a horse and a cow, a maid and a farmhand.

When the pastor had said all this, the atmosphere in church brightened considerably. Everyone in the congregation was pleased to hear that one of those poor women was going to be made honorable and prosperous. Those who were sitting near Anna Svärd nodded in her direction and smiled.

She blushed with embarrassment, but the worst was yet to come, for now the pastor turned and spoke directly to her:

'Who are you, Anna Svärd, to have been chosen above all the other poor girls who peddle their wares, for a life of prosperity and advancement? Do not forget that it is not on your own merits, but simply mercy and grace, and do not forget all those who have to live by the sweat of their brows to earn their keep!'

Oh, yes, that pastor spoke so beautifully that she would have liked to stay in bed all day listening to him. But when he got as far as talking about the other girls, tears came to her eyes, and she threw off the quilt – if she was being shown such generosity that she had a quilt over her rather than just some old sack or an old rag rug – and jumped out of bed.

'Madwoman,' she shouted to herself. 'What's the point of weeping over things you are only imagining?'

The only thing she could do to help her former fellow wanderers was to head home as early as mid-September. She turned her back on the autumn markets that were just about to begin in many places. It was a sacrifice, but she was determined to forgo them, leaving them to the women with whom she usually competed. She did not wish to stand in the way of them, they who were never going to have gentlemen to marry. She thought about Karin from Risgården farm, who came from Medstubyn like herself, about Annstu Lisa and all the others who would be pleased not to have her near them at the markets, taking away their customers.

She knew that when she returned home no one would be able to imagine why she had been so foolish as to abandon the markets. Nor would she be able to explain it to them. But she had to do something for Our Lord, now that he had been so generous with her.

Still, there was nothing to keep her from stocking up on goods before leaving Karlstad. Nor was there anything preventing her from stopping in at every single cottage she passed as she went north, to see if she could sell something. But when the people were done haggling with her and she had her pack tied tightly to her back again and her hand on the door latch, she found herself unable to resist turning back toward the people in the cottage to bear witness to the miracle that had befallen her.

'I thank you all, and there are many of you here,' she said. 'You'll not be seeing me again. I'm to be married.'

If the cottagers hastened to congratulate her and to ask what kind of man she was marrying, she went on with great solemnity:

'It is a miracle so great they'd ought to preach about it in the churches. For who am I to have had such a fine stroke of fortune? I'm a´marryin' a pastor and movin' into a parsonage. I'll have a horse and a cow, a maid and a farmhand.'

She was quite certain they would make fun of her when she left, but she did not mind. She just had to display her gratitude; otherwise her good fortune might be taken from her.

Once, she was at a farm where she had been unable to persuade the woman of the house to buy anything, in spite of her being a wealthy widow who managed her own funds. She found herself telling the woman that she really ought to buy something today since it was her very last chance, after which Anna Svärd went silent and secretive.

The parsimonious woman of the house was curious. She just had to ask Anna Svärd why she planned to stop peddling.

And the lovely young woman from Dalarna answered that it was a great miracle. Yes, a miracle just as great as those described in the Bible. But that was all she said, and so the woman of the house just had to ask more questions.

Anna Svärd merely sealed her lips and was so completely the old Anna Svärd that the parsimonious woman of the house just had to buy both a silk headscarf and a hair comb so that she could find out that God in his mercy had taken the poor peddler woman in hand in her insignificance, and she was going to marry a pastor and be able to live at a parsonage with a horse and a cow, a maid and a farmhand.

When she left that farm, she was thinking that she had discovered a good sales tactic, and that she would use it many times. And yet she did not. She was afraid it might bring misfortune upon her. One must not abuse what is sacred.

Instead, she found herself giving the little girls in the cottages pins with glass gems as gifts, for nothing. Never before had it crossed her mind to give anything away. It was a way of repaying some of the goodness of Our Lord.

Yes, who was she, to have prosperity coming at her from every direction? Was it because she had forgone the autumn markets and left them to her former wandering mates that people in the cottages were so eager to buy her wares? Wherever she stopped as she walked the roads along the Klarälven River, it was the same thing. Nice to see you! As soon as she opened her sack they came running, both adults and children, as if they imagined she had the sun and the stars for sale. Before she was halfway home, she noticed that her store of goods was running low.

One day when all she had left in her sack were a dozen combs made of animal horn and a few packs of ribbon, and was feeling annoyed that she had been unable to carry twice as much from Karlstad, she ran into old Karin from Risgården farm, coming from the north. Her sack was so full it was bulging. Karin was sullen and surly, having sold nothing for the last couple of days.

So Anna Svärd bought all the goods that were weighing down Karin's sack, offering her into the bargain the news that she was to be married.

Anna Svärd felt she would never forget the heather-covered hillside where they were sitting transacting their affairs. This was certainly the most memorable moment of her trek homewards. Karin from Risgården's face turned as purple as the heather, and later she even pressed out a tear or two. And when Anna Svärd saw the old woman crying, she remembered that it was none of her own doing that she had been elevated above all the other poor peddler women, and she paid her a bit more for the goods than they had at first agreed.

Sometimes, when she reached the top of a hill, she would lean against a fence to support her sack, and let her eyes follow the birds of passage as they flew south. If there was no one nearby to laugh at her, she would cry out to them to carry her greetings to the man for whom they knew she wished she had wings, like them, so she could fly to him.

Yes, who was she, to be chosen above so many others to have her heart put at the disposal of another, so it had begun to speak the ancient language of longing and love?

II

Anna Svärd was finally so close to the end of her homeward journey that Medstubyn was in sight. She stopped, first and foremost to check that it was still safe and sound, beside the Dala River, that the farms were still there, as close together as always, with their low, gray outbuildings, that the church was still on the little point south of the village, as ever, and that the birch groves and pine forests had not been swept off the earth in her absence, but were also still where they belonged.

Once she was certain of all that, it began to seem as if she, like so many before her, was so exhausted she would be unable to complete the final stretch to reach her destination. She needed a walking stick so badly she had to break a post off an old fence, and even so she was still just dragging forward, one step at a time. The sack on her back weighed her down so much she was bent double. She often had to stop to catch her breath.

Although her progress was very slow, she eventually entered the village. Perhaps she had been hoping to encounter Old Berit, her mother, or some good friend who would give her a hand with her sack, but she did not meet a single soul.

A few people did see her trudging along, and immediately began to wonder what would become of her mother, with her daughter returning home worn and haggard, as she appeared to be. Mother Svärd was nothing but a poor soldier's widow with no money and no cottage of her own, who would never have been able to make ends meet for herself and her two children without the help of Erik from Jobsgården farm, her brother-in-law, a wealthy man who had given them a little room attached to the cowshed on his farm, squeezed in between the stable and the cowshed. Berit was industrious, and took her chores and her weaving seriously. She was one of those people of many skills, the kind of person a village cannot manage without. Still, she had had to put all her energy into her work, day and night, to make ends meet with two children, and she was quite worn out. Surely she had hoped that things would be easier now that her daughter had begun peddling. Hopefully Anna was not so very ill! It did not bode well, though, her coming home at a strange time of year. Well, poor people always have their troubles!

Anna Svärd made her way forward between the piles of firewood, piles of logs and logging equipment that stood between the many buildings on Jobsgården farm, until she reached the cowshed. For once, her mother was at home, sitting in the middle of the room spinning flax. You can imagine how upset she was to see the door open and her daughter enter, nearly bent double and supporting her weight on that walking stick. Neither did Anna Svärd take any measures to prevent her mother from being frightened out of her wits. She said good day very softly, as if she could hardly force out the words. She sighed and groaned, turning her face away so as not to have to look the elderly woman in the eye.

Well, what was Old Berit to think? She was used to seeing her daughter walking erect, as if she were carrying no burden at all. She imagined the worst, and pushed her spinning wheel aside.

Anna Svärd just continued her groaning and sighing as she

crossed the floor to the table under the window, placing her sack on the tabletop. When she had loosened the straps, she rubbed at the small of her back. She tried to straighten up, but could not. Just as bent and bowed as when she had entered the room, she walked to the fireplace and sat down on the hearthstone.

Well, what was Mother Svärd to think? Her daughter's sack was just as full as it had been when she left home the previous spring. Had she sold nothing all summer? Had she been ill, had she gone and got herself into some kind of trouble? She was so frightened, thinking of what she was about to hear, that she did not dare to ask.

But Anna Svärd must have been of the opinion that her mother would be unable to absorb her great news correctly unless she had first felt more miserable and down at heart than ever in her life, so she asked, in a pitiful tone of voice, whether her mother, who was rested, would be so kind as to open her sack for her.

Of course Mother Svärd was ready to help her in any way she could, but her hands trembled, and it took her quite a while to untie all the knots and undo all the buckles so she could inspect the contents of the sack. But when she had done so Old Berit, although she had experienced one thing and another in her day, had to admit that what she saw made her head spin. For what was she to think about all the things she pulled up out of the sack? She found neither buttons nor silk headscarves, nor papers of pins. The first thing she pulled out was a small ham, under which was a big bag of brown beans and another bag, just as big, of split peas. She did not find a single packet of ribbons, not one embroidery ring, not the smallest strip of cotton, nothing of the kind a peddler woman ought to have in her sack. All she found was oatmeal and rice, coffee and sugar, butter and cheese.

She felt as if her hair was standing on end. After all, she did know her daughter, and she was not the kind to come home with a load of fancy food. Had she lost her mind, or what was happening?

The old woman was about to run and fetch her brother-in-law to ask him to figure out what was going on, until fortunately she looked in the direction of the hearth and saw her daughter sitting there laughing. She realized then that Anna had only been fooling her, and she thought she really ought to show her the door. At the same time, she did not want to throw her out, at least not until she had heard the story behind all this, because it was just as unusual for her daughter to play practical jokes as it was for her to be wasteful.

'Who on God's green earth did you bring all this home for, then?'

'For you, I s'pose.'

Mother Svärd had been hoping against hope all the time that one of the women in the village had asked her daughter to bring home all this fine food. Now her head was spinning again.

'Madwoman! I can't believe you've carried that load for my sake.'

'Well I'd sold all my goods on the way home, and it felt so strange to be walking the roads with an empty sack. I just had to fill it up with whatever I could lay my hands on.'

But Old Berit, accustomed as she was to eking out her flour with straw or bark, and who was seldom in grand enough circumstances to have a little milk to pour over her watery porridge, was not satisfied with that explanation. She sat down on the hearthstone next to her daughter and took her hand.

'You must tell me what has happened.'

And finally Anna Svärd must have decided she was sufficiently well prepared. She released her important news.

'Well, you see mother, it's a miracle. A miracle just as great as any of those described in the Bible. They'd ought to preach about it in the churches.'

III

Mother and daughter agreed that the first person who ought to hear the great news was Erik from Jobsgården.

He was not only their closest relation, he had always had a kind eye to Anna Svärd, and had often said that if his niece could just find herself a bridegroom, he would see to it that she had a fine wedding.

They went to see him early that afternoon, and found him sitting at the hearth, clearing his pipe of the ash from that awful haircap moss he smoked instead of tobacco. At that time of year, when none of the young men who had gone south to work had yet returned, there wasn't a single pouch of real pipe tobacco to be had in Medstubyn.

Anna Svärd could see at once that he was feeling moody, but she was neither deterred nor frightened. She simply thought that as soon as he heard her great news, he would be cheerful again.

Erik from Jobsgården was tall and of fine bearing with dark hair, regular features and deep, blue eyes. Anna Svärd resembled him so closely she might have been his daughter. Nor were the similarities merely superficial. Erik had also wandered the roads as a peddler in his youth. He had been shrewd and cunning, just like her, and good at making money. When his own children grew up he had wanted to send them off on the same route, but none of them had had a talent for the trade. Anna Svärd, in contrast, had both a yearning and a natural aptitude, and her uncle often boasted about her and praised her more than his own children.

But this time, when she walked into his farmhouse, he certainly neither boasted about her nor praised her.

'How mad can you be?' her uncle shouted the moment he saw her. 'How could you come home now? Turning your back on all the big autumn markets!'

But she, who had experienced such a great miracle and been chosen for prosperity and advancement above all the other poor peddler women, and even above all the girls who grew up alongside her in Medstubyn, did not feel it was proper and fitting to come and tell of her engagement right out, as if she were expressing her gratitude after a meal. No, she had to prepare the way a bit, for the news to be given the reception it deserved.

She therefore said nothing yet about her adventure. She merely answered that she was tired of wandering the roads and was yearning to come home.

'You must never tire of it,' said Erik, and went to tell her all about how he had pursued his trade and how much he had earned.

Anna Svärd listened without interrupting him, but when he was finally quiet she tried to prepare him a bit for what was coming. She groped around her bag until she found a pouch of tobacco and proffered it to him.

But the fact was that Erik had lent Anna Svärd a bit of money three years before, when she set up her trade. Each of the previous autumns she had come to see him right away and reported on her earnings and made a repayment on the loan. Now here she was with no money, just a pouch of tobacco. He was happy to have it, of course, but he still looked quite cantankerous as he accepted it.

Anna Svärd knew him almost as well as she knew herself. And she realized that he started to worry when she offered him tobacco. She had never given him a gift before. Perhaps her sales had not gone well. Was she now turning up with tobacco because she had no money to pay him?

He sat down shifting the pouch from one hand to another without so much as a thank you.

'I was just wanting to give you something for once, since you helped me get started,' said Anna, making a new effort to get to her grand news, 'since the fact is that I am not going to be carrying on my trade any more.'

Her uncle still sat passing the pouch. He looked ready to toss it right in her face. Was she abandoning the trade? He had no idea what she was talking about, but one thing he did understand – that she had no money to give him just then, nor was she going to have in the future.

'For you see, I am going to be married,' Anna Svärd went on. 'We wuz thinkin', Mother and I, that you ought to be the first to know.'

Erik set down the pouch. Now there was not a single chance he would ever see the debt repaid. And not only that, he might also have to see to it that his niece had a fine wedding. He cleared his throat as if he were about to speak, then had second thoughts.

Mother Svärd was really feeling sorry for him. He looked like all the misery of the world had come over him at once. She wanted him to know what kind of a marriage her daughter was making.

'Never would I have imagined, when you sent her off with her peddlin' sack three years ago, that she was heading for such great luck. She'll be marryin' a pastor down in Värmland. She'll be movin' into a parsonage, where there is a horse and a cow, a maid and a farmhand.'

'Yes,' said Anna Svärd, lowering her eyes modestly, 'it is a great miracle. It is as if little as I am, I am destined to be better off than even you, Erik.'

And yet the old man did not seem especially impressed with this information. He looked from mother to daughter, his mouth forming an unpleasant sneer.

'Ah, a pastor,' he commented. 'No better than a pastor. Well, niece, when you came in here on your high horse and gave me a pouch of tobacco I thought you must have gone and got engaged to a prince.'

'Good heavens above,' cried Mother Svärd, 'you don't think she's pullin' your leg, do you?'

'No, I do not think she's pullin' my leg,' he said. 'Even tho' folks down south are such comedians and jokers, as anybody knows who has peddled their wares there. Neither do I wonder that she, who is so young, could let herself be duped. But you and me, Berit, we'd best not let it go to our heads. You go out to the kitchen and ask them to fix your daughter some food for her journey, so you can send her back off in the morning! Two months from now and not a day before, she may come back 'ere.'

Mother and daughter rose, both extremely shocked, and moved toward the door. There, though, Anna Svärd stopped and said hesitantly:

'That money I'm owin' you, I've got it with me today. But perhaps you'd rather not have it till December?'

Her uncle gave her a look that pierced bone and marrow.

'Come on then!' he said. 'Have you grown up so much that you can fool your old Uncle Erik? Don't go off and marry, child! Stick to peddlin' your wares! It'll make you so rich you can buy up all of Medstubyn.'

IV

When they returned from Erik's Anna Svärd wanted them to go see Mother Ingborg at the Risgården farm so she could be the next to find out about the great miracle. But Old Berit wasn't having that.

Although Risgården was right next to Jobsgården, and although the contact between the neighbors had never officially been broken off in a way that became public knowledge, it was certainly not what it ought to have been.

Mother Ingborg at Risgården was a widow, and in spite of the fact that she owned the finest farm in Medstubyn, she had plenty of worries, because there was no man on the farm, and she had to hire all her outdoor help. It was her greatest wish and main effort to keep the farm until her sons were grown up, when all her worries would vanish like smoke. And the person who helped her most in this respect was her sister Karin from Risgården. All the village knew she was the one who brought home the money Ingborg needed to pay wages and taxes. But Karin's peddling had not gone so well since Anna Svärd had taken up the trade. And it was clear that the people of Risgården had begun to resent their neighbors at Jobsgården, especially Anna Svärd and her mother.

But when Mother Svärd expressed these reservations, her daughter told her it was about time that their hostilities came to an end, and that was precisely why she wanted to go in and talk to Ingborg at Risgården. Old Berit didn't have to come along if she didn't want to, but Anna was going to see her in any case.

And so she had her way, and Mother Svärd went along. She thought she might end up serving some purpose.

Anna Svärd was amazed when she entered the main room at Risgården farm. She hadn't been there for several years, and had forgotten how lovely it was. Every inch of the walls that was not blocked by the grandfather clock or the cupboard was covered with murals from the Bible. On the long wall in front of her she saw Joseph riding in a barouche pulled by a team of four, with a coachman and a servant, on his way to meet his father Jacob, and over the big window there was a small Virgin Mary curtseying to an Angel of the Lord in a gold-ornamented uniform and a three-cornered hat. Anna Svärd took both these signs as good omens. She liked being reminded of people who had been raised up out of their humble stations by the miraculous power of God.

Mother Ingborg of Risgården was tranquil and beautiful. She was a person with a gift for knowing how to make her surroundings lovely. She was almost always busy with some detailed handiwork. Now she sat with a white mitten stretched over her left hand, embroidering a pattern of flowers and leaves on it.

Although some guardedness may have been noticeable, she otherwise welcomed Old Berit and her daughter in the traditional way, walking over, shaking hands, and inviting them to have a seat on the bench under the window. She then sat back down at the table and continued her embroidery.

A short silence arose, and Anna Svärd thought Ingborg must be thinking that her visitors probably expected to be offered coffee, but she had no intention of giving them anything. Why should she treat the people who were depriving her sister of her income to coffee?

When a suitable amount of time had passed, Anna Svärd started the conversation by saying that as she walked back home she had met Karin on the roads, and she therefore wanted to look in on them at Risgården farm to send Karin's greetings and to let them know she was well.

'We're very pleased to know that she is well,' said Ingborg. 'Being in good health is the very most important thing of all.'

'Indeed, it's important to everyone,' Mother Svärd hastened to confirm, 'and all the more important for those who peddle their wares on the country roads.'

'Quite right, Berit,' said Ingborg.

After this the conversation came to a standstill, and Anna Svärd found herself thinking that Ingborg must be wondering whether she might have to offer the women coffee after all. But she was still unable to make the offer. All they had come here for was to bring her sister's greetings. That wasn't enough to merit coffee.

Anna Svärd said next that she would not have come in the mid-afternoon and disturbed Mother Ingborg at her work if her only reason for coming was to bring greetings. But, you see, Karin had been on her way south with a whole sack full of goods, while she, Anna, had been coming up north and had no goods left in her sack. And so she bought up Karin's whole stock, and when they parted ways Karin had been hurrying to Karlstad to spend the money on new stock she knew she would be able to sell at the autumn markets.

The two sisters shared the trait of blushing violently when they were upset. And now Ingborg sat there listening, her face the color of a heath in bloom. That was the only indication that the news had particularly moved her. She said no more than a few words about how fortunate Karin had been to bump into Anna and get her whole stock sold.

'And sure the luckier one was Anna, who got a new sackful of stock, being as she was heading homewards and had nothing left,' said Old Berit.

It wasn't easy to keep the conversation going. Another silence followed, and Anna Svärd sat thinking to herself that Ingborg must be wondering whether she shouldn't offer the women a cup of coffee after all. But she didn't really want to. That young lass from Jobsgården farm had really only come by to boast about having been able to lend a helping hand to the older peddler woman from Risgården. No, she could not bear to put on a pot of coffee for her sake.

Then Anna Svärd went on to explain that this was not at all the only reason for her visit to Risgården. In fact, what had happened was that when she made that purchase she had ended up with something that didn't belong to her. It was all done in great haste, and they had simply taken everything that had been in Karin's sack and put it in Anna's. But the next day when Anna was spreading out her goods in a farmhouse, she had noticed a five daler bill folded into one of the silk headscarves.

At that, Anna Svärd put her hand into her bag and pulled out a five daler bill, smoothed it and set it on the table in front of Ingborg from Risgården. Mother Ingborg's face turned an even deeper shade of purplish red.

'But what on earth could have possessed my sister to be so careless with her money?' she asked. 'I can't imagine how she could have left five whole dalers loose in her sack. Perhaps it isn't hers at all.'

'I s'pose that's not impossible,' said Anna Svärd. 'That five daler bill may have been folded into the headscarf when she bought it. I'm inclined to believe, myself, that she didn't know it was there.'

At last Ingborg set down her handiwork. She looked at Anna Svärd in astonishment.

'But if you do not think that Karin knew about the bill, you could have just kept it. In fact you'd bought the whole contents of her sack.'

'Well, I do know it's not mine,' said Anna Svärd. 'And so I'd like to ask you to hold it in safekeeping, till Karin comes home.'

Ingborg of Risgården farm did not answer this at all, and Anna Svärd sat thinking that now she must really be wondering whether she ought not to ask the women to stay for coffee after all, no matter how little she cared for them.

She had just barely finished thinking that thought, when Ingborg had made up her mind.

'I'd have gladly invited the both of you for coffee,' she said, 'but I'm ashamed to admit that I have no real coffee in the house, so all I can offer you is a cup of hot rye-chicory.'

She rose and went out into the kitchen. The coffee was eventually brought in, and they each drank a cup or two, but Ingborg from Risgården was still a bit guarded. She served them the best things she had to offer, but the two women still had a feeling she was doing so reluctantly.

Not until they were all finished did Anna Svärd give her mother a little sign, and the old woman began straight away:

'Anna's a bit embarrassed to tell you herself. But the most amazing miracle has happened. She's to marry a pastor down in Värmland.'

'I can hardly believe my ears,' exclaimed Ingborg. 'Getting married? That must mean she won't be…'

She broke off, being too well-mannered to go on, not wanting the two women to see that the first thought that came into her mind was that this might be personally advantageous to her.

But Mother Svärd replied to that which had not been said outright:

'No, she will never again peddle her wares. She'll be living at a parsonage. She's going to have a horse and a cow, a maid and a farmhand.'

Ingborg of Risgården farm lit up. Her face reflected the enormity of the news.

She rose and curtseyed.

'Goodness gracious me! Why didn't you say so in the first place? Would I be serving the future wife of a pastor rye coffee? You just wait right here, and I'll look and see whether I can rummage up a bag of proper coffee beans after all. Sit right down back, please, I beg of you!'

THE WIFE OF THE COUNTY SHERIFF

When Anna Svärd had been at home for a couple of weeks, she and her mother paid a visit to the homestead of Mr. Ryen, the county sheriff, just north of Medstubyn, and asked for a word with his wife. Both Erik from Jobsgården and Ingborg from Risgården knew why they were going, and approved. Ingborg was now their dearest friend, and had been very eager to send them there; in fact the whole scheme might very well have been her idea.

And so they arrived at the home of the sheriff, and presented themselves at the kitchen entrance, as Old Berit preferred, in spite of Anna Svärd's opinion that the future wife of a pastor ought to enter through the front door. From the kitchen they were shown into a little room off the kitchen, where the sheriff's wife was busy sorting the clean laundry, which was spread out on a large drop-leaf table. She raised an eyebrow when she saw them, and did not look particularly pleased. The story about Anna Svärd marrying a pastor had reached her ears, of course, and she was no more fool than that she immediately realized why the women had come.

Still, of course, she received them politely. She greeted them, shook their hands and offered them seats, making them feel comfortable enough to take their time in asking what they had come to ask.

Anna and Mother Svärd had decided in advance that the elder of them would direct the conversation. Ingborg from Risgården had told them it was more suitable, and had also urged Old Berit not to be too roundabout but to get right to the point.

And so Anna Svärd sat listening quietly while Old Berit explained that they had come to ask whether it would be possible for Anna to spend a few months in the county sheriff's home, to learn how to run a household. Since she was to be married to a pastor down in Värmland, she needed to be taught how the gentry do things.

Mrs. Ryen was small and nimble, with sharp little eyes, but she was not unpleasant looking, in fact she was quite pretty. She was such a lively person she had trouble sitting still. All the while Berit was talking, she stood there folding and counting a pile of towels. She never lost count, stacking them one dozen at a time. Yet in spite of the fact that she had only been listening with one ear, she was prepared to answer immediately.

'I have heard about this marriage,' she said, 'but it does not please me. And I don't want anything to do with the matter.'

It is not surprising, is it, that the two visitors were so astonished they did not know what to say? Here they were, having done hardly anything but go from one cottage to the next since Anna came home, to have coffee and discuss the matter of the proposal and marriage. Wherever they had gone, people said it was the best news they had heard in days and days, that it was a credit to Medstubyn that a young woman from there was to be elevated to a pastor's wife. Some people had even told Anna Svärd that they used to find her difficult, since she was so much like Erik from Jobsgården, putting money foremost. But now she was a completely different person, now she was bright and cheery, the way a young woman from Dalarna ought to be. Others, in turn, had been especially pleased to hear that Berit would have a home with her daughter in her old age. Everywhere, the same satisfaction had prevailed. And here was the sheriff's wife herself saying that she did not want anything to do with this marriage!

Mrs. Ryen saw them sitting there at a loss, and so she seemed to feel that some explanation was in order:

'This will not be the first time a pretty young woman from

Dalarna marries a gentleman,' she said. 'But such marriages seldom end well. Berit, I propose you advise Anna to give up the idea entirely.'

After hearing those words from the mouth of the wife of the county sheriff, it was as if Anna Svärd awoke from a dream. In the last few days, the young men and women of Dalarna who had trudged south for summer work had begun to return to Medstubyn. Of the young women who had gone, some had found garden work, others had rowed a ferry across Norrström in Stockholm, and many had cleaned bottles at breweries, but none had done anything but work. And when they got home and heard the kind of thing a person could also experience out there in the world, their eyes had glazed over, and they had wanted her to tell her story again and again, of how the young pastor had approached her on the road, what he had said and how she had answered. The young men had reacted in a particular way. Never before had they thought much of her, but now they said that they couldn't imagine how they could have been so blind. And as soon as she was alone with any of them, they were sure to say that if that pastor down in Värmland had second thoughts, she shouldn't worry. Whatever fellow was at her side on the village street at that moment assured her he would be happy to provide a satisfactory replacement.

And here was the sheriff's wife saying that she ought not to marry a gentleman! She found her too common. That must have been her point.

Anna Svärd said not a word. She simply rose, and Old Berit did likewise. The sheriff's wife shook each of their hands as politely as when they had arrived, and showed them out. Whether or not the reason was that she did not want them to have to be seen by the servants leaving dejectedly and in disgrace they did not know, but she walked them all the way through the drawing room and the vestibule, so they would not have to leave through the kitchen door.

Walking homeward, they felt that this rejection by the sheriff's wife was the worst thing that could have happened. If the wife of the minister had told them the same thing, it would not have been important. But the fact was that the wife of the county sheriff had a very high reputation in Medstubyn. People thought of her as the yardstick by which they measured all things. When she saw that a local young man and young woman were suited to each other, she acted as matchmaker, and the matter was settled. And if men from two of the neighborhood farms had fallen out with each other and were threatening legal action, before they knew it the wife of the county sheriff was there, helping them reach a settlement.

In reality, it made no difference. Mrs. Ryen had no power over either Anna Svärd or her mother, but Anna still felt that now that the sheriff's wife didn't want her to marry a gentleman, it was all over.

She felt as if all the despondency she carried around inside after her difficult childhood years was coming over her again, but soon enough it receded, because that very same day she received a letter. She could not read it, but she knew, of course, who it was from. She went around with it unopened in her bag, thinking about the man who had written it. His own parents had also been of the opinion that she was not good enough for him, but he had stood up to them like a man, and surely he would bring the sheriff's wife around as well.

The next day she did what everyone in Medstubyn did when they had the inconvenience of receiving a letter. She went to see Medberg, the church cantor, and asked him to read it to her.

Cantor Medberg was sitting in the schoolroom off his kitchen. In it there was a table so large it filled half the room, and around the table boys were sitting, learning to read the words in a book.

He took the letter from her hand, carefully cut the seal, and glanced at the handwriting. It was precise and clear, no question about that, and he began to read the whole content of the letter in a loud voice.

It did not occur to him to ask the children to leave the room, so they sat there listening to the beautiful words of love her fiancé had written. It was even possible that Cantor Medberg thought it was good for the boys to hear how competently he could articulate a well-written text. It would be futile to ask him to wait to read the letter until another time. He might very well have told her to get out of there and read her letter on her own.

While the cantor was reading, she tried not to think about anything but the words in the letter, but she was unable to keep herself from glancing at the boys. Obviously, they were going to make a joke of it. They sat there, beet-red, cheeks bursting with restrained laughter.

She had felt some worry gnawing at her since their visit to the sheriff's wife. Her previous happiness and confidence were gone. She could hardly blame the boys for laughing. She certainly was not worthy of being written to in that tone.

For a couple of days she went about wondering how to answer. She wanted to tell him that she had realized she was not good enough for him, that his parents had been right and that he should banish all thoughts of her from his mind.

When she had thought her answer through and composed a long letter in her mind, she went to see Cantor Medberg again. She had taken the precaution of coming in the afternoon, after the boys had left. The cantor sat right down at the large table to take her dictation, and everything seemed to be going smoothly. There were no boys sitting there grinning at her. She said her piece without interruption. The cantor wielded his pen with vigor and dash, and in the blink of an eye the letter was finished.

He then read it out to her, and she could not help feeling a bit surprised. For Cantor Medberg had written lots of love letters in his time, and what a love letter was meant to contain, he knew much better than a young woman from Dalarna who was only just now sending her very first one. So he did not bother to write the things a poor inexperienced girl dictated to him. He opened the letter by saying how delighted she was to know that her fiancé was in good health, since good health was the very most important thing of all, about which he went on at great length and so covered an entire page. Then he wrote about her huge longing for him, how every passing day felt like a month, every month like a year. He embroidered on that idea quite extensively as well. He concluded by assuring her fiancé that he could have every confidence in her fidelity, and by urging him never to betray her, for if he did he would have as many nights of misery as there are leaves on the linden, nuts on the hazel, sand on the seabed and stars ad infinitum in the firmament.

When she asked the cantor why he had not written the letter in accordance with her dictation, he asked her back whether she believed him to be ignorant of how a love letter ought to be written. There was no way he was going to write the kind of gibberish she had pieced together. She would do well to recall that she was writing to a pastor.

And so she had to accept his word as law. The letter was folded and sealed and posted as it was. But what was her fiancé going to think when he received it? She felt her unworthiness and humble station more deeply than ever.

For the third time, she went to see Cantor Medberg, asking him if he could teach her to read and write. He did not conceal his reaction, that she was too old to learn such difficult arts, but she persuaded him to allow her to try. She was told to come to his place the next morning along with the young boys.

And so it came to pass that Anna Svärd found herself at the cantor's large table a few weeks later, quill in hand and paper in front of her, copying out: *The early bird catches the worm*.

It was desperately hard work. She held onto the narrow quill for dear life, pressed the point to the paper so hard that the ink splattered out in little drops here and there, creating strange squiggles instead of letters.

It was desperately difficult in other ways as well. Her only aim in acquiring this burdensome knowledge was to be able to tell that man down in Korskyrka that she was unworthy of him and that he should put her out of his mind.

But in spite of the fact that she was striving toward such a sorrowful goal, no one could say that she was doing less than her best. She put all her energy into it, as if the task at hand were to lift a barrel of rye. Every word cost her such effort that she had to set down the quill and catch her breath before beginning on a new one.

'Hold your pen gently, fingers straight,' the cantor said. But she was certain that the goose quill would not allow itself to be held except if she held it so tight her knuckles went white. The boys grinned at each other over her head, and made fun of her. Anna Svärd was so sick of it all that she was about to walk out, when the door opened and the sheriff's wife walked into the schoolroom.

She was herself, quick and nimble, and had come to settle a matter of village business with Cantor Medberg. But when she saw Anna Svärd sitting there with all the young lads, writing with such fervor that the ink was splattering around the quill tip, her interest was triggered.

'Ah,' she said, 'You've not yet abandoned your plans to marry a pastor, I see.'

Anna Svärd did not reply at all, but the cantor muttered something to the effect that if she absolutely had to be able to write to marry a pastor, she was not ever likely to achieve that status.

The boys grinned anew, until the sheriff's wife gave them a look that turned them solemn again at once. Then she leaned over Anna Svärd, looked at the piece of paper with its writing symbols pointing every which way, like the posts in a fence that had collapsed.

'What are you writing?' the sheriff's wife asked her. 'Let me see: "The early bird catches the worm." Just a moment! Lend me your pen.'

She laughed, bent over the table considering, quill feathers to her lips.

'What's your fiancé's name? Ah, Karl-Artur. Have a look at this!' She printed two words in big, round letters.

'Can you read what I just wrote there? It says: Karl-Artur. Try writing that name! I think you'll see that you can do it, if you care for him.'

Once again she put the pen into Anna Svärd's hand. Then she took the cantor out into the kitchen to speak with him.

Anna Svärd sat looking at the lovely name Mrs. Ryen had printed. She wanted very badly to copy it in the same way, but it was impossible. She tossed the pen aside.

In an hour the sheriff's wife and the cantor came back into the room.

It was silent as the grave in there. The boys were no longer grinning, nor were they working in their ABC books. They were all staring at something remarkable that was happening at the table, at the hand of Anna Svärd.

She sat there, smiling and delighted, working away. When the sheriff's wife and the cantor came back in she hurriedly secreted her needlework under the table.

'Out with it now! Out with it!' said the sheriff's wife.

And what they saw was a miracle. Instead of the goose quill and ink, Anna Svärd had taken a needle and thread from her bag and a piece of white fabric on which she had embroidered the letters. They were every bit as well-formed as the sheriff's wife's, and in her pleasure at being able to stitch the name of her beloved, she had ornamented it with a little flowering vine.

Mrs. Ryen regarded this effort, one finger to her nose, as was her habit when she was trying to figure out something important.

'Just look at that! Do you care so much about him?' she asked. 'I didn't know that. I thought you were just keen to have that parsonage and to be a pastor's wife. Well, in that case, you can come and stay with me starting tomorrow, and I will try to make a lady of you yet.'

THE WEDDING

I

One Saturday afternoon about three o'clock Anna Svärd was standing on the steps to the sheriff's home, watching a sledge make its way slowly up the lane toward the farm. It was winter and biting cold, but she did not feel it. Her heart was pounding and her cheeks burning. She knew that he was sitting in that sledge, the man to whom she had been sending greetings with the birds of passage.

Anna Svärd had been at the sheriff's for four months learning how to run a household, and had received a thorough schooling. Mrs. Ryen had made her aware of her posture and her way of walking, her table manners, her way of speaking and responding, her way of saying hello and good bye, her way of laughing and coughing, her way of sneezing and yawning, and thousands of other things. No one could have asked, of course, that she should succeed in making Anna Svärd into a real lady in such a short time, but she had learned her own weaknesses and shortcomings, and when she saw the sledge with her beloved approaching, her feelings were not only of joy. For it was possible that he would no longer like her when he saw her among the gentry. The sheriff and his wife had two daughters, and although they were up-nosed and flaxen-haired, they certainly did know how to behave, and they certainly walked lightly, and talked beautifully! And what lovely clothes they had! If only she could have afforded clothes like theirs! But she was still wearing the folk costume of her parish, and that was her greatest worry. Surely a pastor's wife in Värmland could not go around in colorful garb that made her look like a green woodpecker.

She was also worried because she did not really know why her fiancé had come all this way. Perhaps, in fact, he was coming to break off their engagement. Shortly after Christmas he had sent a letter containing the necessary documents so that the banns could be read for them in church. And once the banns had been read for a couple, people said, they were as good as married. But that gave her no comfort at all.

Everyone in Medstubyn was pleased when the banns were read. Erik from Jobsgården, for example, had not really dared to believe the marriage was going to take place until he heard it announced from the pulpit. But the third Sunday the banns were read, her uncle had solemnly declared that he intended to arrange her wedding. It would be a three-day feast, finer than the village had ever seen, with food and drink, fiddlers and dancing, and all the young people would be invited to stay the night, sleeping on mattresses on the floor. What with his niece making such an excellent match, the wedding had to live up to it. One of the sheriff's daughters had written to the pastor in her name to explain Erik's promise, and the remarkable thing was that his only answer to this letter was that he was coming to see her. Was he having second thoughts after he heard the word wedding mentioned, or why was he coming?

Well, she was unable to sort out her thoughts, and now the sledge was coming up the hill and arriving at the farm. Now she was going to see him again, and that was a great pleasure. In fact, no matter what happened, it would be good and fine to see him.

By the time he stepped out of the sledge, Anna Svärd was no longer alone on the steps; both the sheriff and his wife were there to receive him. And they were the first people he greeted. Then he went over to her, embraced her, and tried to kiss her. But she was embarrassed and evaded his kiss. She couldn't possibly let herself be kissed with people standing all around watching! At the next instant she remembered that among the gentry it was customary to kiss, even in the presence of others, and was annoyed with herself for having behaved foolishly.

As soon as he had unwrapped himself from his travel furs, they all went into the dining room, where the table was set with coffee and lots of cakes and the sheriff's wife's finest china. She was seated next to her fiancé, and as she had been having her afternoon coffee with the sheriff's family daily, she knew how to behave. But suddenly she had forgotten everything she had learned. Without a thought, she filled her cup so full that the coffee ran over and into the saucer. Then she put a piece of sugar into her mouth and sucked the coffee through it. She behaved as if she were having coffee back home with Mother Svärd and Ingborg from Risgården farm, and when she happened to look in the direction of the sheriff's wife, she nearly choked.

She was annoyed with herself once again, but her comfort was that it made no difference. She had a feeling things were not as they were meant to be. Her fiancé was not treating her as he had the last time they met. Surely he had come to break off the engagement.

While everyone was having their coffee, she sat listening to his impressive way of conversing with the sheriff and his wife. It seemed so easy for all of them to exchange pleasantries. He thanked the family for everything they had done for his fiancée over the last four months, and Mrs. Ryen answered that he owed them no thanks at all. Anna was such a good worker and had made herself so useful in the household that they were probably the ones who owed her a debt of thanks, not the other way around.

The sheriff's wife, the daughters and the sheriff himself were all looking pleased and had been speaking in such kind, cheery voices ever since the arrival of her fiancé. They had probably not expected him to be the sort of man he was. Perhaps they had imagined him as hunchbacked or one-eyed. Surely they had thought there must be something wrong with him because he wanted to marry a poor young woman from Dalarna.

She was prepared to forgive them for it, as she had actually forgotten herself what a handsome man he was, perfect in every way. She wondered if they were attentive to the pale sheen of his brow. Or to the lucky fact that he tended to keep his heavy eyelids lowered, since otherwise one would not want to do anything but sit dead still and gaze into those deep, remarkable eyes.

Her fiancé seemed to be enjoying himself with the sheriff and his family. The coffee was cleared away, but still he sat there for a while longer, conversing with them. The conversation was maintained not only by the sheriff and his wife; both daughters said one thing and another. She felt as if they were quite taking him away from her, and with every minute that passed she became more and more unhappy and bewildered.

'These are the people he belongs with,' she thought to herself, 'he no longer cares a whit about me. He can certainly tell now that I am not suitable for him. I haven't a thing to say and neither he nor any of the others even remembers I am here.'

At that very moment he suddenly turned to her. He raised his eyelids and gave her a look she felt just as distinctly as you feel the sun when it breaks through the clouds. He said he would very much like to pay a visit to the parsonage, assuming it was not too far away.

No, it was definitely not far away. All he had to do was walk through the village and turn left. It was just north of the church.

She said those words in such a hostile tone that her feelings were clear to all, and they looked at her in amazement and disapproval.

'I thought you might show me the way,' he said.

'All right, I s'pose.'

She did not want to refuse him, as she could tell that he wanted to speak with her alone, to break it off. But she found it impossible to look pleased. Her heart felt like a dead lump in her chest. He was not himself, not in any way. The others, who had never met him before, could not possibly know how much he had changed.

Once she and her fiancé were on the main road, they walked as far apart as possible. But it was only late February, so the sun had not yet begun to eat away at the high piles of snow that lined either side. This narrowed the available space, making it difficult for Anna Svärd to be as far from her fiancé as she would have liked. The days were getting quite long, so it was still light. A little sliver of moon could be glimpsed in the pale sky as well. She thought it looked hazardously keen-edged up there, as if it had been sharpened. 'Perhaps it is the switchblade that will shred my happiness to bits,' she mused.

She was accustomed to the cold, and seldom wondered what the temperature was. But never in her life had she experienced an evening as cold as this one. With every footstep the snow screeched. 'I'm not surprised it's complaining,' thought Anna Svärd. 'The snow is in pain, because the feet trampling it down are heavy with grief.'

At last they reached the parsonage, and not until then did he break the silence.

'Anna, I do not expect you to object to the proposal I am about to make to the minister. I am sure you, too, feel that I will do what is best for both of us.'

No, she had no intention of opposing him, of that he could rest assured. She would do whatever he wished.

'Thank you for promising me that,' he said.

They went on into the minister's office, where they found him at his desk. It was Saturday evening, and he was probably working on his sermon. He was not disposed to give them an encouraging look as they came and interrupted him.

Anna Svärd's fiancé introduced himself, and the minister's expression changed visibly once he was aware that his visitor was also a man of the cloth.

Anna Svärd was standing silently over by the door, while the two clergymen exchanged a few words about professional matters. But a few minutes later her fiancé approached her, took her by the hand and stood in front of the minister with her.

'Sir,' he said, 'I see that you are a very busy man, and I hasten therefore to bring up the matter at hand. I am sure,

Sir, that you do not find it difficult to identify with the love and desire of a younger man. Not until the day before my departure did I have the thought that it would be wonderful not to return to Korskyrka alone. The idea pleased me greatly. But was there any chance of making it reality? The little home I had prepared for my wife and myself was nearly ready. Good friends promised to urge the painter and carpenter to hurry, so we would be able to move in toward the end of next week. So that was not an obstacle.'

Anna Svärd noticed that the expression on the face of the minister was quite unsympathetic. He seemed fully prepared to put forward objections, but her fiancé did not give him an opportunity to speak.

'I left home last Tuesday, and I ought certainly to have been here in Medstubyn by Thursday or Friday, but all my calculations were foiled by unfortunate circumstances. Exhausted teams of horses, inebriated local drivers and melting ice on the rivers all prevented me from arriving until this very afternoon. But, Sir, does that really have to defeat all the hopes I have so dearly housed? The foremost objection would be, I assume, that my fiancée has so much looked forward to the large wedding her uncle has promised on the occasion of our union. I can understand that she took pleasure in the idea, but I cannot for a moment imagine that she would not forgo a feast in order to be able to return with me. I therefore ask you, Sir, to be so kind as to wed us in church tomorrow, after the service.'

The minister held back his answer for a moment. He knew his congregation, knew how many of the parishioners were already looking forward to the big three-day celebration, and he feared their censure if he accepted the change.

'My dear young friends,' he said, 'please be so good as to take the advice of an old man and relinquish this idea. You see, Doctor Ekenstedt, this marriage has been the subject of much discussion in the village. No one expected it to be concluded in this humble, hurried manner. Everyone has been hoping for a large wedding.'

Her fiancé made a deprecatory gesture.

'Let us be frank, Sir. You know as well as I what a large wedding brings in its wake. Drunkenness, gluttony, fighting, immorality. I would never have accepted such a thing. My original reason for coming here was to avert the idea of that kind of celebration. I can only find that the best and most appropriate way of accomplishing that aim is to bring to fulfillment the plan I have had the privilege of putting forward to you.'

The minister looked up and down the room, as if seeking a way out, an escape from this stubborn young brother of the cloth. At last his eyes fell upon Anna Svärd. His face brightened, he clearly thought he had found his solution.

'But Doctor Ekenstedt, you have not yet told me how your fiancée feels about this plan which, in my view, is somewhat precipitate.'

Karl-Artur answered without a moment's hesitation:

'Before I entered this room my fiancée promised me that she would approve of my arrangements.'

Anna Svärd could not help a slight gesture of surprise, and the minister noticed.

'But Anna, are you also really completely aware of the nature of these arrangements?' he asked, turning directly to her.

Her face went bright red. There was one thing she had entirely understood during this conversation. Her fiancé wanted to marry her. She had nothing to worry about. He had not found her too common and coarse. He still wanted her to be his wife.

And yet at the same time she was displeased and upset. Why had her fiancé not asked her out there on the road whether she was prepared to marry him the very next day?

'He does not care for me the way I care for him,' she thought. 'If he did he would have begun by asking how I wanted things to be.'

But although she felt hurt and offended deep down inside, she did not want to make her fiancé look bad in front of the minister.

'Oh, Father Pastor, I'm sure you know that I mean to go

along with 'im, wherever in the world he wants to take me,' she replied.

'Well, if that's the way it is, then of course I am at your service, Doctor Ekenstedt,' the minister said.

II

The sheriff's wife was sitting in her parlor, one finger on her nose, which meant she was trying to figure something out.

The fact was that she had come to care for Anna Svärd, and it pained her to think that the young woman would be deprived of the fine wedding to which she had been looking forward. And so Mrs. Ryen had begun that very Saturday evening to put everyone both in her own home and in the whole village of Medstubyn to work to do what they could about the matter. The special bridal folk dress, which was stored at Risgården, was mended and brightened up, and on Sunday morning Ingborg from Risgården and her sister had come to the sheriff's home to dress Anna Svärd for her wedding in the ancient, traditional manner. The wedding procession, arranged on the slope outside the church, was long and impressive, thanks to the sheriff's wife. Two fiddlers walked at the head as they entered the church. The sheriff, Cantor Medberg, Erik from Jobsgården, the deacons, the lay assessors and all their wives walked behind the bride and groom. Bringing up the rear were the young men and women of Dalarna, all in parish dress. It had all been lovely and solemn. Endless preparations would hardly have given better results.

It had not been possible to arrange a feast at Jobsgården farm, so instead the sheriff's wife had arranged a small wedding party at their home. Fortunately, she had already planned and prepared for a small gathering for Anna Svärd's fiancé and his new relations that day, so she had been able to bring a larger one off quite well. Moreover, the guests were all sensible people, and had realized that there would be no question of a sumptuous meal.

But had she known how dull the party was going to be, she would certainly not have followed her well-meaning instinct. Although all the guests were normally talkative people, that evening they seemed to have nothing to say. She did her very best, as did her husband and their daughters. The bridegroom also made an effort to keep the conversation going. But there was something heavy in the air. Perhaps people were thinking about the big wedding, with all its pomp and pleasure, of which they had been deprived.

As for the bride, she refrained from speaking entirely. She sat all evening, her heavy eyebrows drawn together, staring straight ahead. She resembled a person accused of a crime and waiting for judgment to be passed.

'This marriage is certainly not off to an auspicious start,' thought the sheriff's wife. 'I wish I knew what Anna Svärd is brooding about. Could it be missing the big wedding at Jobsgården farm that's making her look so downhearted?'

To make the time pass, the sheriff's wife turned to Doctor Ekenstedt and asked if he wouldn't be so kind as to say a few words to the guests. He acceded immediately to her wish, and so she sat there listening to him. He spoke freely and eloquently, but she could not deny that his words frightened her. 'Good grief, what is he saying?' she thought to herself. 'This young man is heading out onto ice that is too thin.'

Her astonishment continued to grow. 'What on earth does he mean?' she wondered. 'Does he wish to live a life of poverty in the imitation of Christ? And is that the reason he has sought out a wife who, like him, will turn up her nose at wealth, who knows that the only true happiness is doing the deeds of the good Lord among one's fellow men?'

The sheriff's wife, who knew very well that the young bride had spent the entire period of their engagement dreaming of a parsonage with a horse and a cow, a maid and a farmhand, could not deny that her head was spinning.

'What an awful misunderstanding!' she thought. 'Anna Svärd knows nothing of all this. Wherever will it end?'

The more she listened the clearer it became to her what

kind of man he was, the man before her. 'Our dear Anna Svärd finds herself in the hands of a fanatic,' she thought. 'He has taken a wife from the peasant class in order to have a woman at his side who is accustomed to hard labor and who is able to look after her own home. He is one of those young men who wish to live the life of a peasant farmer. It is no longer fashionable to be a gentleman.'

Her eyes wandered from one listener to the next. What was Erik from Jobsgården farm thinking, who never spent a farthing unless he had to? What was Old Berit thinking, who had been waging a life or death struggle against poverty all her life? What was Ingborg from Risgården thinking, who fell asleep every night with a head full of worries about her farm? And what was the young man's new wife thinking, who had wandered the road with her peddler's sack for three years, about all this preaching?

'I am sure they are at least as horrified as I am,' she thought, 'but there they sit, looking completely unperturbed.'

She realized that these people were not taking the young pastor seriously. Talking about the blessings of poverty was one of his official duties. It was a beautiful speech, and uplifting to listen to, but none of them believed for a moment that he intended to practice what he preached. Why should it upset them? They knew very well that some pastors were poor, and none of them imagined that this young man had already been assigned to a fine parish, but surely he would be able to offer his wife far greater comfort than she was used to. He was, after all, from a good family, and sons of good families never starve to death in Sweden.

The sheriff's wife, on the other hand, who knew that he meant what he was saying, and that the life upon which his wife was about to embark would be a trying and difficult one, wondered what attitude to take. 'These two young people hardly know each other,' she thought, 'and because Anna Svärd cannot write, they have not been able to become acquainted by letter, either. They are still as much strangers to one another as when they met on the road for the first time. Would it not be wise of me to open the bride's eyes a bit? She is a decent person, but she certainly has no propensity for self-sacrifice. I have truly come to care for her. Can I allow her to enter into this marriage without forewarning her of what to expect?'

After some consideration, however, she decided not to become involved in their business. Had they not already been man and wife, she would certainly have been obliged to intervene. But things being as they were, she found it wisest to leave them to themselves.

However, once the party was over, the guests had departed and the daughters of the house had accompanied the bride up to the guestroom, where the bridal bed had been prepared, the young bridegroom himself came and requested a word with his hostess.

After this discussion, which surely lasted at least half an hour, Mrs. Ryen went into her bedroom and took her Bible from the nightstand. Thus armed, she walked upstairs and entered the guest room, where her daughters had just released Anna Svärd from all her bridal finery and helped her into bed.

All she needed was one quick look at Anna Svärd to see that her thick eyebrows were still pulled tight and her dark eyes still staring straight ahead as if anticipating some awful event. When she saw the sheriff's wife enter with the Bible under her arm she nodded gravely, as if to say: 'So I will be proven right after all. I have been waiting for this all evening.'

Mrs. Ryen took her time. She trimmed the candles, sent her daughters off to bed, put on her spectacles and leafed through her Bible. When she had found the passage she was looking for, she told Anna Svärd that there were a few words in the Scriptures she would very much like to read to her, now that she had entered into holy matrimony.

Anna Svärd sat up in bed and clasped her hands. She undoubtedly found it unnecessary for Mrs. Ryen to quote Scripture to her. She knew that this was the prologue to being told something difficult. And she would have preferred not to have to wait.

The sheriff's wife began reading from I Corinthians 13:

'Love is patient, love is kind. It does not envy, it does not boast, it is not proud. It does not dishonor others, it is not self-seeking, it is not easily angered.

'It keeps no record of wrongs. Love does not delight in evil but rejoices with the truth.

'It always protects, always trusts, always hopes, always perseveres.'

Mrs. Ryen, perhaps recalling her own wedding night, read these remarkable words emotionally, and Anna Svärd could not keep from being swept along. The words seemed to have been drawn from her own heart. Never had she heard anything quoted from the Bible that was so right and true.

When the reading was done, Anna Svärd repeated the last verse to herself.

'Perhaps you would like to hear it again?'

'Yes,' said the bride, so moved she could barely whisper the word.

Her eyebrows were suddenly not so tightly pulled. Her eyes stared less hard. The sheriff's wife began to hope that she might accomplish her mission without too much resistance.

'I declare,' she said to herself, 'Anna Svärd is anything but foolish. She heard her husband's exhortation a while ago. Perhaps she has already realized how it all fits together.'

When she had read the beautiful passage about love once again, she closed the Bible.

'If things do not turn out exactly as you had expected,' she said, 'bear those words in mind!'

Those dark, melancholy eyes turned toward the speaker. Those could merely have been suitable words to say to any new bride. But they might also have been the introduction to the terrible things to come.

The sheriff's wife hastened to explain:

'You see, my dear, if you care for someone with the right kind of love, you are not concerned about how your life takes shape in terms of worldly things. You have not, after all, married horses and cows or maids and farmhands.'

Mrs. Ryen found Anna Svärd's behavior extremely odd. An intimation of that kind ought to have put her in a state of extreme anxiety. But she said not a word and moved not a muscle. The explanation would have to continue.

'Do not think, my child, that I would interfere in your affairs without being asked. Your husband came to see me a short time ago, when you had already come upstairs, and spoke frankly with me about your future together. I then asked him whether you really already knew all this, and he replied that you had known it from the very outset.'

At that point Anna Svärd really did say a few words:

'What am I supposed to have known?' she asked, in a voice of utter indifference. The terrible thing she was expecting did not seem to be of that nature.

'Do you not remember,' Mrs. Ryen asked, feeling the need to raise her voice, as if she were speaking to someone who was not quite awake, 'do you not remember how he has spoken to you about living your life in imitation of Christ? He said it this evening as well.'

'Yes, but …'

'I suspected right away that you hadn't really understood. And when I explained that to your husband, he asked me to explain to you right away what you have ahead of you. He asked me to tell you that he does not have a parsonage. He is a curate, and his annual salary is one hundred and fifty dalers. Until now he has had free lodging and meals at the parsonage, but now that he is married, he will, instead, be given certain quantities of grain, butter and milk. I am sure it will suffice, but only just, and what with your very high expectations…'

Anna Svärd asked a question, on hearing this. The sheriff's wife understood that she was merely asking out of consideration for her, since Anna Svärd did not seem the least bit personally interested in the matter. She asked where they would live.

'Your husband received a small inheritance last autumn from an aunt who passed away,' said Mrs. Ryen. 'It was only a thousand dalers and a set of furniture. However, he invested the money in a cottage with a kitchen and one more room. And surely that will be enough for the two of you. But, you see, there are no outbuildings, no fields or meadows. You will be doing your own cooking, lighting the fire and baking, taking care of your own cleaning and, well, your own everything.'

The sheriff's wife wondered whether Anna Svärd was simply feigning indifference, and whether the storm that must be brewing inside her would break out when her husband arrived. But there was no indication to that effect. That strong, solid young woman simply sat there watching all her hopes be dashed without showing the smallest sign of regret.

'I am very sorry I lured you into teaching me how to run a household,' she said.

'That is the least of it,' said Mrs. Ryen. 'It has been a pleasure to teach you, since you are so quick to learn. We are very fond of you, as I am sure you have realized, child. This is the first unpleasant moment I have spent on your account.'

Anna Svärd did not acknowledge these kind words with so much as a thank you, and the sheriff's wife began to be slightly upset.

'Perhaps you're comforting yourself with the thought that your husband will soon have a higher position. But I wouldn't be so sure of that, either. He says, at least, that he wishes always to remain poor. Or if you are recalling his wealthy parents, perhaps I ought to tell you that he had quarreled with them over you and can expect neither help nor any inheritance from them.

'I am sorry for Mother,' said Anna Svärd. 'She probably thought we would be able to take care of her for the rest of her life.'

'If the minister at Korskyrka should die,' the sheriff's wife went on relentlessly, 'your husband will be sent to some other parish as curate, and that is the very worst part, because if that happened you would not be able to accompany him, but would be left alone in your cottage. And the minister at Korskyrka is seventy-six years old; he is not likely to live much longer.'

'All right, I understand that things will be difficult for us,' said Anna Svärd as indifferently as ever.

'And because you are facing such an uncertain future,' said Mrs. Ryen, 'I believe that your husband is quite right in his suggestion. That is, he asked me to ask you … He found it difficult to do it himself. He wanted me to suggest to you that…'

She was interrupted by a brusque movement on the part of her listener. Anna Svärd had turned to face her. She sat leaning forward, listening. Now she was wide awake. All her drowsiness had vanished. Mrs. Ryen's cheeks flared red.

'My dear child,' she said, 'I feel a bit intimidated by the way you look at me. But I feel that his reluctance is well founded. Surely it would be wise of you not to start a family. Well, I am certain you understand what I mean.'

Anna Svärd had sunk back down to the pillow. She was not weeping, but she was wringing her hands, and her face was desperately contorted.

'I knew it,' she said. 'I was expecting it. He does not care for me any more.'

'My dear,' said the sheriff's wife. 'Do not take it that way. Your husband is not like the rest of us. He is an entirely different kind of person, you see. He does love you, I know that, but people of his kind regard themselves as serving God by forgoing the things they most desire.'

'How can you say that he loves me when he sends you to deliver such a message?' cried Anna Svärd shrilly. 'Could you not tell from his whole way of being that he has tired of me? Well, he will no longer have to have anything to do with me.'

She threw off her quilt, pulled her stockings and shoes toward her and began to dress.

'My dear,' said Mrs. Ryen placatingly, 'I assure you that you are wrong. Your husband told me that he bears a great love for you. Ever since he saw you on his arrival here he has been battling down his affection. He has not dared to speak with you about it.'

She stopped herself. Anna Svärd finished dressing as quickly as if escaping from a fire.

'I don't believe a word of it,' she shouted. 'Could he possibly care for me if he saw to it that we had that kind of wedding? I do not know what he wants with me.'

The sheriff's wife saw how fast her hands were moving, and

how wild her eyes were, shining out from that pale face. Mrs. Ryen did not walk from the room, no, she ran.

She found Karl-Artur Ekenstedt in the dimly lit dining room. He was on his knees, deep in prayer. She rushed up to him, grasped his arm and gave him a shake. He stood up, red with embarrassment.

'I was praying to God to help Anna take your message in the right spirit.'

'This,' said Mrs. Ryen, 'is no time for praying,' shaking his arm again. 'Doctor Ekenstedt, if you do not hurry upstairs to Anna and demonstrate to her that you love her as a man is meant to love his wife, I think we shall have to go searching for her in a hole in the ice on the Dala River tomorrow.'

A NEW HOME

Anna Svärd was surely a woman made to go peddling her wares from a sack. She had the right eye for what a customer would want. It had never happened that she bought any merchandise for her sack that she was unable to sell. If she came into a home in which no one wanted to buy anything, she simply left without being unpleasantly pushy. If she found herself among customers who enjoyed driving a bargain, she let them have their way and looked convincingly unhappy, so they would imagine they had made a good deal. Moreover, she was completely honest. She never offered anyone a length of fabric that was moth-eaten or had gotten wet. If a silk headscarf had been in her bag for so long that it had split at the folds, she would voluntarily display the defect and sell the cloth for as good as nothing.

There is not the least doubt that Anna Svärd would have made a small fortune if she had continued in the trade. But from the day she met Karl-Artur Ekenstedt on the road, a great change had come over her. She had in no way become less shrewd, less calculating, less on her guard. The thing was, though, that these qualities, which had helped her earn her living in the past, had since that moment been put to use in the service of love. She wondered many times how she could have been so eager to earn money before. Was she really the same person who had stood at market stalls, pleased to see every customer who approached? Was she the Anna Svärd who had wandered the roads without a thought about anything but how her income was piling up? It was all very strange and incredible. But in those days she had not known what the most important thing in life was.

The newlyweds stayed in Medstubyn for a couple of days, but early on the Wednesday morning they departed, and on Friday afternoon the sledge dropped them in Korskyrka, pleased and content, to take possession of their little home on the slope above the village.

After several pointed comments from the sheriff's wife Karl-Artur had refrained from keeping Anna unaware of what awaited her. He asked whether she recalled, having been in Korskyrka last summer, a couple of little cottages on the hillside just above Doctor Romelius' yard. And she, who had actually crisscrossed the parish quite thoroughly for three summers in a row, immediately remembered two ramshackle buildings that looked as if they might collapse at any moment. She had never been inside either one, since of course a peddler has no reason to visit a hovel where the inhabitants could not even afford to have their broken windows repaired. But because she liked to be well-informed, she had been sure to find out who owned them, so she knew that one of them housed an old soldier who got by on a pension of twenty dalers a year, and the other a poor girl everyone called Matts the crofter's Elin, who had ten younger siblings to support and feed.

She did not know, however, that Karl-Artur had bought all ten of those children at a poorhouse auction to keep them from being spread to the winds, and of course she knew nothing either of the fortunate change in their circumstances that had resulted. A number of the most influential women in the village had made an arrangement to see to the needs of the children. Their cottage had been repaired, and the children fitted out with clothing and supplied with foodstuffs. All would have gone splendidly if their eldest sister had not suddenly up and died. It had truly seemed as if that poor young woman, who had worked so hard, now knew her siblings had clothing, a cellar full of potatoes and a little larder stocked with flour and herring, a repaired cottage floor where the rats could no longer creep up through the cracks, and windows that no longer had to be crammed with rags, and so she felt she therefore no longer had any remaining obligations in this world, and had lain down for a well-earned rest.

This had, though, placed a great burden on Karl-Artur. The wonderful women who had taken the children in hand soon found them a new nursemaid, an old woman who had worked at the parsonage for many years, and who took excellent care of them in some respects, but she was old and could hardly be expected to keep an eagle eye on ten unruly youngsters. Karl-Artur would personally have been happy to help her keep his wards in line, but that was not an easy job for him to take on as long as he was living at the parsonage. Which was why, when he came into that little inheritance, he hurried to acquire the old soldier's cottage, which was just next to the cottage where the ten children lived, and have it repaired.

So that was where the newlyweds were to live. The young curate assured his wife that it had been improved beyond recognition. Generally speaking, he felt he had made a good bargain. He had acquired a nicely-situated home, small and unpretentious, and with a good lookout over the large brood of children.

Anna Svärd who, at the time, was concerned with nothing but knowing that her husband loved her, had laughed it all off and inquired no further. What should she have done otherwise? After all, they were married now, and she had promised to share his lot, for better or for worse. Moreover, she had great confidence in her own capabilities. She knew that if everything should turn out for the very worst, she would be quite able to earn her keep and provide for her husband as well.

On their journey homeward, as they approached Korskyrka, Anna Svärd told her husband that where she came from it was customary, the first time a newlywed couple entered their home, for them to fall to their knees on the threshold and pray to God to sanctify the house and their life within its walls. Karl-Artur found it a lovely custom, and said they would follow it. But upon their arrival it was forgotten.

This was not because Anna Svärd was overwhelmed by the cottage when she caught sight of it. No, it stood there, quite as she remembered it. It had definitely not been transformed into a manor house. The repairmen had even forgotten to put in a new set of steps, leaving the same unstable stone that had passed for a step in front of the door in the old soldier's day. She was still convinced that she would have thought twice before entering a hovel like that to peddle her wares. She said so to her husband, teasingly, and they both laughed and were in the best possible spirits.

It was absolutely nothing to do with the accommodation that caused them to forget to fall to their knees at the threshold and pray to God to bless their new home. Rather, the reason was that at the very moment the sledge came to a halt, the door sprang open and a fat little woman stepped out onto the loose stone step to welcome them.

It was not for nothing that Anna Svärd had been in and out of almost every home in Korskyrka selling her wares over the last three summers. She knew every single person in the parish by name, and yet she was still having trouble recognizing this woman. However, it only took her a couple of seconds to realize that it could be no one but Mrs. Sundler, the organist's wife. The last time Anna Svärd saw her she had had long lovely curls around her face, but now her hair was as short as a boy's, which changed her appearance.

Of course it had to be Mrs. Sundler; Karl-Artur had been talking about her throughout their journey. She had helped him to purchase the cottage, and had arranged for the carpenters. In fact the entire marriage was her creation. The two of them would not be sitting there in the sledge, so content and so divinely happy, if it had not been for her. Thus it was perfectly natural for Mrs. Sundler to have come to their little home to heat up the rooms and to welcome them, having been so instrumental in their becoming a married couple.

Mrs. Sundler opened her arms to them, enclosing them both in an embrace. With a great deal of emotion, she went on about how glad she was to see them, explaining that her deepest hope was now fulfilled, and how wonderful it was that Karl-Artur, too, was now seeing his dream of a plain little cottage and a simple wife come true, a dream he had harbored as long as she had known him.

With Mrs. Sundler making this little speech, their intention of praying to God to bless their home was completely forgotten. Both were, from that moment on, entirely preoccupied with the organist's wife.

When, at last, she released them from her embrace, she opened the door and accompanied them into a narrow passageway running straight across the cottage and dividing it in two.

While they were removing their overcoats and hanging them in the passageway, Mrs. Sundler was saying that something had told her they would be arriving that evening. She had just barely had time to pack her coffee pot and hurry over to the little sparrows' nest as she liked to call Karl-Artur's home in her thoughts, and set the table for coffee when she heard the jingle of the approaching sledge. She couldn't tell them how happy she was to be there to welcome them, so they did not arrive at an empty house.

However, it was not so much what Mrs. Sundler was saying that gave Anna Svärd pause, as the great change Karl-Artur underwent at the moment she appeared. He was no longer as lively and carefree as he had been while they were traveling. Now he became anxiously eager to please Mrs. Sundler.

His young wife felt that he was not entirely happy about Mrs. Sundler's being there just when they were going to take possession of their new home, but she imagined that he was immediately reminded of all she had done for them and struck with remorse.

He began telling his wife again how Thea, whose name he mentioned in every breath, had helped him with everything. She was the one who had thought of the hooks here in the passageway so they would have somewhere to hang their overcoats. Wasn't that kind? He opened the door to the right and invited his wife to come in and have a look. Had she not known better, she would not have thought that this was the kitchen she was meant to live in and run. He seemed only to have brought her into it to admire all Mrs. Sundler's arrangements.

The kitchen occupied fully half of the cottage, and she found it much larger than she had anticipated. It must have been three times as large as the room by the cowshed at Eriksgården where she grew up. The walls smelt of paste and lime, as new places do, and she supposed that was what made it feel less than homey. It was also quite bare and not exactly what she had dreamt of. Her thoughts had seen the main room at Risgården farm, with its big brown and blue cupboard fixed to the wall, the tall grandfather clock painted with roses and a four-poster bed with hand-woven curtains around it. She had also been wishing for a Joseph in a splendid golden carriage on the wall between the cupboard and the bed, and a Virgin Mary curtseying to a gold-plated angel of the Lord over the windows. But it was vanity to wish for those things. She should be satisfied with what there was.

There was, indeed, a plentiful sufficiency, all supplied by Mrs. Sundler. She had procured it all: the table over by the window, and the chairs around it and the water barrel by the door and the wood box by the stove. Hearing her husband speak, Anna might have thought that Mrs. Sundler was the first human being ever to realize that a kitchen needed pots and pans, whisks and ladles, a coffee pot and tubs, spoons and knives. Even if it was not Mrs. Sundler herself who had boxed off a little corner for a larder, and who had hung a shelf on the wall for the pots and pans, it was thanks to her that all those things were there.

One of the first things Anna Svärd noticed in the kitchen was a narrow bed-settle over in the secluded far corner of the room, as if it was ashamed of itself. It had a wooden seat that was open, and the bed was made up. It was all neat and nicely done. The only problem was that it was narrow as a coffin, and Anna Svärd could plainly see that there was no trundle bed to pull out. No, there was no way of making it wider. Once you had wriggled down into it, you probably had to lie there all night worried about getting stuck and being unable to get out the next morning.

That settle preoccupied her. She tried to listen to her

Selma Lagerlöf

husband's description of everything Thea had done for them. She had attended a couple of auctions on their behalf and bid on housewares and furniture, acquiring them at remarkably low prices. But he had already told her all this on their journey and her mind was also full of that settle. As the bed had been made, she assumed one of them was expected to sleep in it. And there were only two to choose between.

Thea had not only set out coffee and cookies for them, there were also bread and butter, cheese and a couple of eggs. Anna Svärd could not deny that it all tasted delicious, but Karl-Artur made it sound as if he had not had anything proper to eat since the last time he was at Mrs. Sundler's. The sheriff's wife in Medstubyn was otherwise renowned for her cuisine, but her husband had dismissed from his mind everything in the world, including his wife, just to ingratiate himself with Mrs. Sundler. It was as if he had somehow offended her and needed to get back into her good books.

When Karl-Artur had sampled each of Mrs. Sundler's creations, praised them lavishly and fussed over her sufficiently, he rose from the table to go into the other room, walking right past the settle bed, and Anna wondered to herself whether he was going to praise it, too, but he did not mention it.

Walking across the passage, they entered a room not quite as large as the kitchen, but still fairly spacious. Peeking in, his wife felt that she would just like to run away, because it was a room fitted out for the gentry. If the kitchen was empty, this room was full: a desk, a book cupboard, a sofa with a coffee table, a chest of drawers, a bed, and many other things as well. So this was the furniture he had inherited from his aunt. The wood was dark and highly polished, the chairs and divan upholstered in silk. Wherever she looked, from the mountings to the inlays, there was a lovely sheen.

This room was wallpapered, had long curtains at the windows, and a tiled stove rather than an iron range. A large, gold-framed mirror hung over the divan, there were a chandelier with candles hanging from the ceiling and silver candlesticks on the desk. The room would have fit right in at the Ekenstedts' home in Karlstad.

The bed in this room, like the one in the kitchen, was made up for the night. It, too, was a single bed, and not a very wide one, either.

Yes, one thing was perfectly clear. This was to be his room, the place where he would both sleep and work. She was meant to spend her days in the kitchen, and her nights as well. He would live the life of a gentleman, and she would be kept as his maid.

Her husband continued his praise. When he left to be married, the tiled stove in this room had not been quite finished and the furniture had not yet been in place. Thea Sundler had arranged it all in his absence. And what a fine job she had done with this room, how lovely it was! One could hardly believe one was in a little peasant cottage! Could there be a more elegant room in the entire village?

He tried to urge his wife, too, to praise Mrs. Sundler. But her mind was fully preoccupied with her own thoughts, and she said nothing.

The other two were so busy exploring the various drawers and drop-leaves of the desk that they did not notice her tiptoeing out. She went back to the kitchen, took a candle from the table to light her way into the passage so she would be able to find her overcoat and her hat. She was perfectly calm. There was no uproar inside her as there had been on their wedding night. She had no intention of harming anyone. All she wanted to do was to get herself to the home of some people in the village who had given her a place to sleep last summer when she was peddling her wares in Korskyrka, to spend the night. She had to show that man in there and his Thea that she expected the place of a wife and not of a servant in this household.

While looking for her coat she noticed a third door in the passageway. There was no key in the lock, but that caused her no puzzlement. She took the key from the kitchen door, inserted it cautiously into the lock, and it turned. She found herself looking into a little room, hardly more than a storage area really, with a little window in one wall but no source of heat. Still, the room did not feel cold, because the heat from the tiled stove in her husband's room kept that wall warm as well. The walls were undecorated, just painted white with a few hooks up here and there. Presumably it was intended to serve as a closet.

But at the very back she saw something that surprised her greatly: a proper bed of state. There it stood, with lovely red curtains around it, made up with a puffy down mattress and pillows, sheets with a wide lace border, in a word everything she might have wished for.

Having examined this miracle for a few moments, the clergyman's young wife removed her coat and hat once more, returned the borrowed key to its hole, and went back into the kitchen.

She was alone there for a few minutes, until the others must have noticed her absence. Quickly, they both came back in.

'Where did you disappear to?' Karl-Artur asked. 'Are you tired after our journey? Are you ready for bed?'

'I came in here to try out the bed that is to be mine. As you can imagine I was afraid there wouldn't be room for me.'

She looked a bit vexed, but was laughing as well.

'Well, how is it?' asked Karl-Artur, laughing too.

'It was like a cow feels when she's put into a box meant for a calf. There was too little room both the long and the short way. I might be all right lying on my side. But that will be a problem, too, since I think I'll have to toss off the bedclothes and get up just to be able to turn over.'

Her voice still showed no sign of anger, and her husband went on laughing. She could tell he was a bit embarrassed, and laughing to cover his discomfort.

'Well, husband, you can laugh, but you must remember that I have been traveling in a sledge for three days and I am feeling both bent and stiff.'

Karl-Artur walked over to the settle and looked at it.

'All right, you take the bed in my room!' he said. 'I'll see whether there is room for me in this box.'

'You must be mad! You've not gone and got married so you

can sleep a whole night with your feet hanging over the edge of the bed. No, I'm considering whether I might lie on the floor. It wouldn't be the first time, but I'm still a bit uncertain. It'll get cold over here by the middle of the night when the fire dies down. I wouldn't want to catch my death now that I finally have a home of my own.'

Her husband appeared to be completely at a loss. He cast a pleading glance at Mrs. Sundler, but his good friend was sitting tapping the table top and pretending she didn't mean to eavesdrop on husband and wife discussing their concerns.

'You'd need to have animal hides both underneath and on top,' his wife went on, 'to be able to sleep on this floor on a cold winter's night, and since all we own is one, I thought I'd ask you, husband, whether you'd mind if I went to see a family here in the village who housed me last summer, and ask them if I could spend the night there. Why don't you ask Mrs. Sundler, who has made so many other fine arrangements for us, whether that might not be the best solution.'

The man and his wife both turned toward Mrs. Sundler for her good advice, but she sat silent. You could see that this was a matter in which she simply did not wish to intervene.

Anna Svärd extended her hand to her husband.

'Farewell, then,' she said.

Karl-Artur's cheeks had gone a bit red, and the look he shot Mrs. Sundler was not overly kind.

'No, this just will not do,' he said. 'Thea, can you not help me figure something out? It must be possible for me to sleep on the divan in my room. I have slept on it many a time, when I used to visit the cathedral dean. So then Anna could sleep in the bed, couldn't she? We must make do with what we have. That settle you acquired for Anna is really impossible. Let's carry the bedding into the other room.'

Mrs. Sundler squirmed on her chair when Karl-Artur addressed her so firmly, but she made not a sound. Anna Svärd, in contrast, was not slow in responding.

'Are you mad?' she asked again. 'You can't really imagine I would let you sleep the night on that elegant silk upholstery! There's nothing but loose straw under the sheets on that settle, and we can't be dragging straw into the best room, which Mrs. Sundler has arranged so elegantly for you. No, I think I'd better be off.'

She extended her hand once more to say good-bye. He brushed it brusquely aside, but at the same time he appeared so doubtful and uncertain that she began to feel sorry for him.

'It's kind of you to want to make it possible for me to sleep in your room,' she said a bit more gently. 'But I'm sure you see that it can't be done. Back in Medstubyn and at the inns it didn't matter that we shared a room. But here in Korskyrka everyone knows, of course, how much better than me you are. So here I will have to sleep alone in the kitchen, like people's maids do.'

'But Anna,' he cried, brushing off her hand once more as she extended it to him. That was all he could manage. She was really very curious to see whether he would let her go, and yet she did not wish to drive him to extremes. None of this annoyed her nearly as much as it might have done, since she knew very well she held the trump card. She was actually tempted to burst out laughing.

She approached Mrs. Sundler.

'It would look quite odd, don'tcha think, if I left, and you stayed on here?' she said. 'In a village like this even the walls have eyes, and people know everything that happens. Don'tcha think it would be best if you brought this monkey business to an end?'

At last Mrs. Sundler came to life.

'Why Mrs. Ekenstedt, whatever do you mean?' she asked.

'Never in my wildest dreams did I think my uncle's words about people down south being such comedians and jokers would come true so soon,' Anna Svärd replied. 'You just stand here listening to my husband and me having an argument and being at odds with each other because there's nowhere for me to sleep. And yet you've known all along that there is a curtained bed right in this house, already made up with bolsters and cushions, as fine as anyone might want. I call that a good joke.'

Karl-Artur simply stared. He turned to Mrs. Sundler for an

explanation, and she had her reply worked out.

'I have been battling with my feelings,' she said. 'A bed was delivered to the cottage yesterday evening, a wedding gift from the parsonage. But I thought Mrs. Forsius would want to give it to you herself. It seemed most appropriate to me to lock it up. But now that you have already seen it, Mrs. Ekenstedt…'

She rummaged a key up out of her skirt pocket and gave it to Anna Svärd.

Late that night Anna Svärd awoke with a feeling she had forgotten something important. And she had. She remembered that she and her husband had neglected to ask God's blessing over their home.

'Well, the Good Lord will have to forgive us,' she thought. 'Mrs. Sundler is to blame.' With that, she turned over and went back to sleep.

THE EARLY BIRD

Anna Svärd woke up early the next morning, at first light. But instead of getting right out of bed she lay there having a little conversation with herself.

'I wonder if the pastor's young wife is lying abed waiting for their good maid to carry in the coffee and freshly-baked bread?' she mumbled to herself with a laugh, and was in the best possible morning mood.

She stayed in bed for a few minutes more. Time after time she raised herself up and looked in the direction of the door.

'I'm surprised there's not a peep from the kitchen though it is nearly six o'clock. I suppose I'll just have to get dressed and see what's going on.'

Her husband was still asleep, and his young wife pulled on her clothes as quietly as possible so as not to wake him. Then she tiptoed out in her stocking feet across the passage and entered the kitchen, where she began by putting on her shoes.

Having done that, she looked around with a pair of eyes that widened with astonishment.

'I've been through things both bad and good in my day,' she said, 'but I've never seen the like. The kitchen maid and the housemaid both oversleeping! You might have thought, otherwise, that they'd be especially on their toes the first morning. What lazyboneses they must be, the two of them. Neither wood nor water has been carried in. And the fire's gone out in the range, that's the worst thing of all. Mark my words, it has to have been Mrs. Sundler who hired the domestics, since she arranged everything else around here. In which case, what could I expect?'

In the midst of all this lamenting she seemed to have an insight, and struck her brow.

'Stupid me. I deserve a good thrashing. Ought to've known from the very first that they're out in the cowshed doing the milking.'

She went out into the passage and onto the loose front step, where she gazed at her surroundings.

'Ah, I see, I see,' she muttered, taking stock of a little enclosure with a woodshed, an earth cellar, a well and nothing more. 'I'd really like to see the expression on the pastor's young wife's face when she gets a look at all these outbuildings. Well, that one must be the cowshed and barn. The newlyweds will probably have trouble affording enough cows to fill that big cowshed.'

She stepped down from the stone step, walked a pace or two, only to stop and rub her eyes.

'I can't for the life of me figure out where the farmhand sleeps. And not a stick in the woodbox. In any case he must be in the stable grooming the horses by this hour. Well, what can I say? It's fortunate that Anna Svärd came along. Without her the pastor's young wife would be at a complete loss.'

A moment later she was in the woodshed, had found the axe stuck in the chopping block, and was chopping firewood as fast and vigorously as if she did it every day. But after a few good chops the axe stuck in a knotted log and she had to pull and twist it for quite a while to get it out.

As she struggled, she heard footsteps outside the shed, and a tall boy stepped into the doorway.

'Wonder what he's doing here?' thought Anna Svärd. 'Before you can say jack rabbit the whole village will know that the pastor's young wife has to split her firewood herself. How am I gong to explain to the lad that it's not the pastor's young wife doing the chopping, but just Anna Svärd?'

When she had freed the axe and lifted it to chop the next log, the boy approached.

'I'll do that chopping for you,' he said.

She gave him a quick look, saw that he was skinny and pale, with a yellowish hue to his skin, and shook her head.

'Don't be mad,' she said. 'You can't be more than nine years old.'

'I'm fourteen,' said the boy, 'and I've been chopping wood since the day I was born, I've already done our chopping this morning.'

He pointed, indicating a nearby cottage, where a thin column of smoke could be seen rising from the chimney.

His offer was very tempting, but Anna Svärd did not lose her usual sense of caution.

'You'll want to be paid, I s'pose?'

'Yes, I'll want to be well paid,' the lad grinned, 'but just how I want to be paid I won't tell you until the job is done.'

'I'll just go on chopping my own wood, then, thanks.'

For a few minutes she worked steadily, but then she had a bit of bad luck and the axe got caught in another knot.

'It's not money I'll be wanting,' the boy said.

She looked at him once more. His mouth was tightly pursed and his eyes were squinting. Although he looked canny and older than his age, he certainly did not look unkind. Suddenly she understood that he must be one of those ten children of whom her husband had taken custody. 'He's one of our own, you might say,' she thought to herself. 'So he can hardly expect to be paid.'

'All right, then, you can chop. Afterwards you can come into the kitchen for some bread and butter.'

'Thank you,' said the lad, 'but we've got food at home. Almost more than we can eat.'

'So what in the world am I supposed to give a great man like you, then?'

The boy already had the axe above his head, but now he couldn't contain his secret any longer.

'I s'pose you've brought your sack with you? Do you think you might come over to our place and let me and my brothers and sisters have a look at what's in it?'

'You must be mad after all! You don't really imagine, do you, that a woman who's married the pastor can go around with a peddler's sack?'

Suddenly she heard footsteps. A young girl came in. She,

too, had skin of a yellowish hue, and she looked troubled. It was easy to see that the two of them were brother and sister. Eagerly, she approached her brother.

'What did she say? Can we have a look in her sack?'

They had planned it all. Those poor, penniless children in Crofter Matts' cottage, who had never had anyone come peddling, were longing to get a glimpse of the riches she had displayed in other homes.

'She says she cain't go round peddlin' now that she's married to a pastor.'

The girl looked as if she were about to burst into tears.

'I'll fetch your water and milk for you,' she said persuasively. 'I'll light the fire in your range.'

Anna Svärd did some quick thinking. Of course she did have her sack, but it was full of nothing but her own clothes. She had to figure out some way to satisfy these children's need; it was vital if they were to become good neighbors.

'Well,' she said. 'As I've told your brother, the pastor's young wife can't go around peddling her wares. But if you do a good job of the chopping, and you run home and bring back a lit stick to get my stove going, I promise to see to it that a woman by the name of Anna Svärd brings her sack around your place later.'

And around eleven that morning a pretty young peddler woman from Dalarna with a big, black leather sack on her back really did come around Crofter Matts' cottage. She came in through the door, stopped and curtseyed, and asked if there was anyone there who was interested in examining her wares.

It did not take a minute for the ten children to surround the peddler. The two oldest ones, who seemed to recognize her, were jumping with joy and trying to explain who she was to the younger ones. The old woman who had been looking after the children was sitting on a bench by the window spinning wool. She looked up when the peddler entered, saying a few words to indicate that in their cottage there lived no one but some impoverished children who would not be able to purchase anything. But she broke off when she saw the peddler wink.

'The children asked me to come, since they have such a vast amount of money to spend,' the peddler said.

She walked over to the table, turned her back to it, shifted her sack to the tabletop and loosened the straps. Then she walked over and took the older woman by the hand.

'You'll recognize Anna Svärd, I'm sure, ma'am. You bought both a comb and an embroidery frame off me last summer.'

The old woman stood up, blinked a couple of times and curtseyed so deeply it would have done even Mrs. Forsius, the pastor's wife, proud.

The peddler went over to her sack and began undoing the straps and buckles. The children stood around her, breathless with anticipation, but they had a great disappointment in store. The sack was full, not of goods for sale, but of straw.

No one could have been more upset and astonished than the peddler woman herself. She clapped her hands and moaned. She had not opened her sack since last night, she said, and during the night someone must have taken the opportunity to steal away with all her lovely silk headscarves and buttons and ribbons and lengths of cotton fabric, replacing it all with nothing but straw. Well, it had struck her that the sack felt remarkably light when she shouldered it that morning, but she certainly could never have imagined anything like this, because the people who had given her lodging had looked as solid and reliable as a gold coin.

The children stood there, upset and disappointed. The peddler went on lamenting her fate. Imagine anyone doing something so vicious: taking all her pretty things and filling the sack with that awful straw!

She felt around in the straw, shifting it aside to check that none of her wares might have been left behind.

At the very bottom she found a small silk headscarf, a woolen scarf and a box that still contained a dozen little breastpins set with bright glass.

She was inconsolable at not having anything else left. She said that since all the rest was gone there was no point saving those little things. So if the oldest girl would accept the silk headscarf she would be pleased to give it to her, and the woolen scarf to the oldest boy. The little ones could share the breastpins among them, and perhaps the old woman could use the box they were in. She would be glad to give it to her, had no need for it herself.

Oh yes, the little cottage was filled with joy.

A VISION IN CHURCH

Anna Svärd entered her kitchen humming a folk tune, a cattle-call. But she broke off suddenly. While she was in the neighboring cottage Mrs. Sundler had arrived, and was seated on the narrow settle bed, waiting for her.

It would be a wild exaggeration to say that she was welcome. Quite apart from their little clash the previous evening, the pastor's young wife had quite a lot to accomplish that morning. A cartload of her clothing, and the simple wedding presents from neighbors and friends in Medstubyn, plus her loom and spinning wheel had arrived a short time before, and she had not yet had a chance to unpack all those things and put them in their places.

On top of that, she couldn't even ask her husband to keep their guest company. Shortly after breakfast Karl-Artur had gone to the parsonage to catch up on all the work he had neglected, and was not expected back until about two o'clock.

It is not easy to understand the reason, but at the very moment Anna Svärd caught sight of Mrs. Sundler both her speech and her gestures became very coarse. The four months she had spent at the sheriff's home, and which had actually refined her substantially, were entirely forgotten. Perhaps the pastor's young wife felt instinctively that in the case of Mrs. Sundler fine manners would do her no good. It is also possible that it pleased her to have the other woman think that she was very foolish, very inexperienced and, in a word, that she had no sense of decorum.

Mrs. Sundler came toward her enthusiastically. She explained that she had been at home all morning until she realized how difficult things must be for Mrs. Ekenstedt, who surely had her hands full in her new home, to also have to make her husband's dinner. But she would be happy, oh so happy, to have him dine with the organist and herself. In fact, he was welcome for dinner for the next few days, until things were in order at home and they had had time to stock up on provisions from the local farmers. Oh, and she would be happy to be of assistance with that as well. Would Mrs. Ekenstedt not like to send Karl-Artur to them for dinner, beginning today?

While Mrs. Sundler was holding forth, the pastor's young wife started to remove the packaging from a bundle of hand-woven linen Karin from Risgården farm had given them as a wedding gift, and when she found herself struggling with a particularly stubborn knot she simply bit it off with her teeth. This caused a tremor to pass through Mrs. Sundler, but she refrained from commenting.

'It would only be for these early days, until you get things arranged,' she hastened to emphasize.

The pastor's young wife looked up from the linen, walked over to Mrs. Sundler and stood in front of her, feet wide apart and hands over her stomach.

'I'll tell him, ma'am, that you're expectin' 'im,' she said.

Mrs. Sundler hurried to express her pleasure at having her little suggestion so kindly accepted, as it was meant. Anna Svärd remained standing in front of her in the same position as she went on:

'But somethin' else I'll tell him, ma'am. If he cain't eat the food his wife cooks, she's no prouder a woman than that she can take her wares and go out peddlin' and manage on her own.'

Mrs. Sundler had raised her arms and was holding them up as if to defend herself. She looked as if she were expecting the other woman to strike her.

'I s'pose it's not the done thing to speak one's mind to the gentry,' said Anna Svärd.

But she had no reason to be concerned. Mrs. Sundler was quick to compose herself and now did her best to smooth things over and make excuses.

'Oh, that's not at all what I meant, my dear Mrs. Ekenstedt! I am quite certain that you prepare precisely the kind of meals Karl-Artur would want. I only meant well by my suggestion. Let us never speak of the matter again.'

There was now silence in the room. Anna Svärd began measuring the linen, but using her left arm as a measuring rod. She could not possibly have indicated more clearly to Mrs. Sundler that she really had no more time for her.

'You see, I was thinking, my dear Mrs. Ekenstedt,' Mrs. Sundler began very softly, 'about what very good friends you and I are going to become. I have been looking forward to it. I am afraid you might imagine, Mrs. Ekenstedt, that I consider myself on a higher rung of the world than you. But you could not be more mistaken. My parents were very poor people. Mama worked herself to the bone from dawn to dusk, and as for me I would have had to take a position as a simple serving maid had not Baron Löwensköld of Hedeby invested a bit in my education, so that I could become a nursery maid. Mama worked for his parents for fifteen years, and once upon a time she had done him a great personal service, which he wished to repay. And Karl-Artur is, of course, the nephew of that man who helped me up in the world. My mama always told me to do my very best to serve and aid the Löwenskölds, wherever I encountered them, and to me Karl-Artur and his wife are one and the same person.'

'Twenty-seven, twenty-eight, twenty-nine, thirty!' Anna Svärd muttered to herself. When she got to thirty she stopped measuring for a moment and directed a remark toward Mrs. Sundler.

'If it was true you thought of us as one and the same person, I s'pose you might've asked me to dinner, too, since you invited him.'

Mrs. Sundler rolled her eyes up toward the ceiling, as if there might be someone up there to bear witness to what a kind, pious woman she was.

'Oh, Mrs. Ekenstedt, you do make things difficult,' she said in a light but lamenting tone of voice. 'You seem to always imagine the worst in a person. I do assure you that I did not leave you out from unkindness, though it may have appeared that way. You know, today is Saturday, Mrs. Ekenstedt, and we will be having our usual Saturday fare: creamed carrots, herring and gruel. And with Karl-Artur coming that didn't matter. He comes and goes in our home as he pleases. But the first time I have you in my home, Mrs. Ekenstedt, I would not want to offer you such a simple repast, would I?'

She gave Anna Svärd a pleading look, and the thought that came into Anna's mind was that she was slippery as a serpent. She wriggled out, however firmly you thought you had her in your grip.

'I find this difficult to approach, Mrs. Ekenstedt, but there is something you ought to know. There can never be a proper relationship between us until you have a perfectly clear picture of how things are. At the same time, I am reluctant to tell you. Ah, how I wish Karl-Artur had told you all these awful things himself. But he does not appear to have done so.'

Anna Svärd had finished measuring the linen, but she started over again. Her measurements might have been disturbed and she could not be certain of the results. So as not to lose count again she refrained from replying to what Mrs. Sundler had just told her, but that did not deter her.

'I imagine, Mrs. Ekenstedt, that you do not care for me meddling in your affairs in this way, but I cannot help doing so, I consider it my obligation. However, I do so wish that you would meet me half way with your confidence! I do not even know if Karl-Artur has told you about his mother and the close relationship between the two of them. But I am sure you do know, at least, that Karl-Artur's dear mother did not approve of your union. Shortly after the funeral of the wife of cathedral dean Sjöborg, Karl-Artur and she had words on the subject, and Karl-Artur may have been a bit overly forceful when his mother was feeling very weak – well, in any case she had a stroke in the end. And I am sure, Mrs. Ekenstedt, that you can imagine how he accuses himself of having caused this misfortune. In fact I believe that at one point he intended to break off his relationship with you to accommodate her, but he was told that it would have served no purpose. The colonel's dear wife has largely recovered now, you see, and is quite well, but she has entirely lost her memory. No matter what Karl-Artur would be prepared to sacrifice to please her, it would serve no purpose. What's done is done.'

From the very moment Mrs. Sundler told her that Karl-Artur's behavior had caused his mother to have a stroke, she no longer had to worry about not having Anna Svärd's full attention. The bundle of linen fell to the floor and was left lying there. Anna Svärd sat down without a word facing Mrs. Sundler and staring at her.

'Ah, I see it was as I feared,' said Mrs. Sundler. 'You were left completely in the dark, Mrs. Ekenstedt, as to the unhappy things Karl-Artur goes around pondering. He would naturally have wanted to spare you for as long as possible. And perhaps I should not have told you, either. You looked so happy just a few moments ago. Perhaps it would have been best, Mrs. Ekenstedt, for you not to know.'

Anna Svärd shook her head.

'Now you've given me such a fright,' she said, 'would ya please just come out with all the awful things you've been storing up at once?'

Mrs. Sundler felt herself start every time Anna Svärd addressed her in her dialect. After all, she was married to a pastor now and ought to be able to speak like someone other than a rural peasant. Karl-Artur would certainly have to help her become accustomed to speaking more appropriately. This was no time to be thinking about such things, however.

'Ah, where shall I begin?' she asked. 'Well, I must first tell you that one Sunday in September, just a month after the day of that misfortune, Karl-Artur saw his mother in church. He saw her sitting in a pew under the balcony, where the light is fainter than elsewhere in the church, but he still recognized her perfectly. She was dressed as usual in a tight-fitting brimless little cap that tied under her chin, and to be able to hear better she had loosened the straps and freed up her ears. He had seen her this way many a time in the church in Karlstad, and this little gesture alone made him sure it was she. She held her head tilted upwards, so as to see him better, and he even seemed to see in her face the same expression of joyful expectation his dear mother always showed in anticipation of hearing him speak or preach.

'He found himself amazed that she had been able to make such a long journey so soon after her serious stroke, but he had no doubt whatsoever that he was seeing her. And, you can imagine Mrs. Ekenstedt, he was so overjoyed he could barely go on with the sermon. "Mother is well again," he thought. "She has come because she knows how unhappy I am. Now everything will be all right." And so he said to himself that he would have to preach twice as eloquently as usual that Sunday.

'It is not surprising that he failed to do so. He did not dare look in his mother's direction for fear of becoming distracted. Still, not for a moment was he able to forget that she was there in church, and his sermon came out both short and incoherent. When he was done he stepped down from the pulpit and glanced in her direction. He did not see her, but that did not worry him a bit. He quite simply thought that dear Mrs. Ekenstedt had tired of listening to the long service and would be waiting for him outside.

'Forgive me, Mrs. Ekenstedt, for going on at such great length, but I want you to understand that Karl-Artur was completely persuaded that he had seen his mother. He was so certain that when he did not see her outside he went about asking people where she had gone. No one had seen her, but still he did not despair, thinking that she had gone on to the parsonage before him. Not until he failed to find her there either did he begin to wonder if he might have been mistaken. Although he was very upset, it never occurred to him that there was anything peculiar about the whole matter.'

Until that point Anna Svärd had simply been sitting quite still, staring Mrs. Sundler straight in the face. At this point she interrupted the story to ask a question.

'Don't tell me the colonel's wife had died?'

Mrs. Sundler nodded. 'I understand your thought, Mrs. Ekenstedt,' she said. 'I will get back to that in due course. But first I would like you to know that Karl-Artur has a very fine relationship with the couple at the parsonage. That has not always been the case. Last summer, before his mother's misfortune took place, Karl-Artur's sermons were so wonderfully brilliant and moving. He was on the verge of inspiring a great evangelical movement. People in these parts idolized him. They would have been prepared to relinquish their worldly possessions to gain a seat in heaven. But the minister and his wife were not pleased. You know they are very old, Mrs. Ekenstedt, and old people want things to stay as they have always been. Well, after his mother's misfortune Karl-Artur was frightened, he no longer had confidence in his inspiration, and turned to Pastor Forsius for advice. And he went on preaching very beautifully, but now also extremely cautiously. His former ardor was gone. The evangelical movement he might have given rise to died out. Many people mourned it, but the old couple at the parsonage were content. And Karl-Artur became like a son to them. I have heard Mrs. Forsius say that they would never have gotten over the loss of Mrs. Schagerström, who had lived with them at the parsonage for many years, if Karl-Artur had not so lovingly filled the vacuum. But of course, Mrs. Ekenstedt, the question is whether all this has been good for Karl-Artur. I am personally pleased that he will be beyond the sphere of influence of the parsonage, now that he has a wife and a home of his own. No, I am not saying this to curry your favor, Mrs. Ekenstedt, but merely so that you will see what hope Karl-Artur's true friends are placing in you.'

Truth be told, it looked as if all this might be too much for Karl-Artur's young wife. Her eyebrows were so tightly drawn you could practically see her mind working away behind them. She was obviously doing her best to follow, but it was a great effort.

'Well, aren't you going to tell me what he said in church?' she asked.

'Quite right, Mrs. Ekenstedt,' said Mrs. Sundler. 'I shall not dwell on his relationship with Mr. and Mrs. Forsius. It is quite sufficient for you to know that they care for Karl-Artur and only want what is best for him. But in spite of this he did not tell these good friends that he believed he had seen his mother in church. He is extremely reluctant to speak of her. It is also conceivable that he kept silent because he still harbored some slight hope that she had sought refuge with us, in my house, you see. It was quite irrational, but his dear mother was an unpredictable woman. And so shortly after dinner he came to see us, but of course she was not there either.

'However, I want you to know, Mrs. Ekenstedt, that we were extraordinarily pleased, both my husband and I, to see Karl-Artur. Oh, clergymen have such a tremendous burden in the autumn with all the catechetical meetings and all the new parishioners to register that we hadn't seen him in weeks. I think, though, that he enjoyed being in our home. At least he stayed all afternoon. My husband remained in the sitting room with us the entire time, and we had the most innocent amusements in the world, we made music, sang and recited poetry. I hope you don't mind my saying so, but they have no idea about such things over at the parsonage, and I believe it gave him some recompense for his disappointment over his mother. After supper we fell into very intimate conversation about all the things we cannot possibly know regarding what it is like on the other side – I am sure you know, Mrs. Ekenstedt, to what I am referring – during the course of which Karl-Artur came to tell us that the very same day he had believed himself to have seen his dear mother in church. We continued talking for a long time about what it could have been, and it was almost midnight before he went home. On Monday, though, he had to go on with his catechisms, and although he had had such a nice time with us I did not see him again all week. He may have thought, of course, that he ought to stay in with the old couple when he had a free evening. No one in the world is as considerate as Karl-Artur.'

Anna Svärd was frowning even more deeply by this point, and she looked quite bewildered. But she let the speaker continue uninterrupted.

'As I was saying, I hadn't seen him, nor had I given a second thought to the story he told us about his mother. But the next Sunday I happened to bump into him on the way to church, and said to him, in jest, that I hoped he would not be seeing his dear mother this Sunday again, as it might disturb his sermon. Well, Mrs. Ekenstedt, I had a feeling he was not pleased by my words. He answered quite brusquely that his conclusion was that a woman who had been passing through the parish and who resembled his mother had been in church for part of the service, and that he really did not want to imagine it might have been otherwise.

'I had no chance to reply. We met other parishioners and the conversation turned to everyday matters. During the service, however, I sat there worrying that I had been wrong in saying those words. I tried to comfort myself with the thought that Karl-Artur could not possibly have paid my comment, made lightly, much heed. But you can imagine, Mrs. Ekenstedt, what a fright I took when he interrupted himself right in the middle of his sermon and just stood staring in the direction of the balcony. In just a second he resumed speaking, but from then on he was strangely distracted and incoherent. And oh, he had been discussing such a captivating subject. But now he was unable to pick up the thread of his discourse. I cannot tell you how frightful it was.

'He came to see me that afternoon, deeply distressed, telling me explicitly that it had been my words that caused him to see his mother a second time. Earlier in the week he had had no such expectations. Of course there is no knowing for certain about these matters, but it did seem to me that he was being terribly unfair. In that case it would also have been my fault that he saw her the first time. And on that Sunday I hadn't seen him in weeks.'

Anna Svärd had been sitting drawing a fingernail up and down her apron, tracing its stripes up and down, up and down in silence. Now, however, she made a remark.

'I wonder how he could think his mother would possibly appear to him unless she was dead!'

'That is precisely what I said to him. I assured him that he had let his eyes deceive him again, as last time, and that his dear mother who, as far as we know, was alive and well, could not possibly have appeared to him. But he claimed that it was none other than his mother he had seen. He had recognized her, and she had sat there nodding at him. You can imagine, Mrs. Ekenstedt, that he was extremely overwrought. He said that if this was going to go on he might just as well give up the cloth at once, because when he found it so frightening and so upsetting to see her, he then had no idea what he was saying. He believed that his mother was appearing to him out of vengeance, and he reminded me that his former fiancée had once threatened him that he would never again be able to hold a good sermon until he was reconciled with his mother. Her prediction was now being fulfilled.'

There was no denying that Karl-Artur's young wife followed every word being said with the utmost attention. And, wise person that she was, she was entirely on her guard, fearing that the other woman would try to make her believe something that was not true. But as Mrs. Sundler got deeper into her story, Anna Svärd found herself somehow numbed. It was not that she became sleepy, but she became less suspicious, less particular about the details.

'This cannot be anything but the truth,' she said to herself. 'She couldn't possibly be sitting here making it all up.'

'Goodness, Mrs. Ekenstedt, what was I to say or counsel?' Mrs. Sundler asked. 'I could do no more than stand firm on the whole thing being his imagination, a kind of hallucination. That was the only possibility. How could his dear mother have been in our church, and above all how could he imagine that such a loving mother would want to come here and hurt him? In that way, I gradually calmed him back down. Fortunately, my husband was out walking, and Karl-Artur and I had time to talk through all these difficult, sensitive matters before he returned home. When Mr. Sundler returned he played lovely music for Karl-Artur, which is always good for him. Remember that, Mrs. Ekenstedt. During the week that followed he came to see me a number of times, always wanting me to persuade him that the vision he had seen in church was nothing but his imagination. I did believe he was completely convinced when we parted ways the next Sunday morning, but he must not have been, because that day he saw his mother for the third time.

'And you know, Mrs. Ekenstedt, that was when I began to be truly concerned. People were saying that Karl-Artur's preaching was not up to what it had been during the summer. They commented that he was not merely more circumspect and guarded; they also found him incoherent and uninteresting. Oh, Mrs. Ekenstedt, that was a terrible time. Just think what a setback this was for such a gifted speaker! Suddenly he had far, far fewer listeners than last summer, and just imagine what a disappointment that must have been to him! An astute, educated man such as he is could hardly really have thought the supernatural was at play, but on the other hand he could absolutely not doubt the testimony of his own senses. He must have feared that he was losing his mind.'

Mrs. Sundler spoke with real feeling. There were tears in her eyes. There was no doubt that she had been extremely worried indeed. Anna Svärd found herself more and more caught up in the story. All those words were spinning around her like a finely meshed, invisible trap. Soon she was unable to see the matter in any other light than Mrs. Sundler's. She would have been utterly incapable of putting up any resistance, or of being as rude as she had been at the beginning of their conversation. Yes, something was ensnaring her.

'But what do you think it was?' she asked.

'I shall tell you the truth, Mrs. Ekenstedt. I do not know. Perhaps it was his guilty conscience expressing itself, perhaps it was his mother's thoughts that somehow evoked his hallucination. But he finds it so humiliating and horrifying. He does not think he can prevail over it of his own free will. He has prayed to God endless times to spare him these visions, but they still return. He saw his mother the fourth Sunday as well.'

His young wife looked extremely alarmed. It was as if she had personally seen the image of the colonel's wife appear out of a dark corner in the room.

'He came to see me that afternoon,' Mrs. Sundler went on, 'to say that he planned to write to the bishop and renounce his calling. He could no longer bear making a fool of himself in front of the entire congregation, having had to do so four Sundays in a row. Of course I understood his feelings very well, but somehow I still managed to prevent him from resigning, at least for the moment. What I did was to advise him to begin writing out his sermons again, so he would not lose track of what he was saying. And he has truly followed my advice since then. He has not preached once without a written manuscript. But, Mrs. Ekenstedt, you would not believe what a difference it has made. When Karl-Artur reads written sermons you would not recognize him. Still, it was very helpful to him, because the vision ceased to appear. Perhaps this was because he felt calmer. Who knows?'

Anna Svärd asked a question.

'But do you think he will ever be free from imagining those things?'

'That, Mrs. Ekenstedt, is precisely what you are going to help him with. Karl-Artur came to see me last year at Christmas time to tell me he had come into a small inheritance from his aunt, the wife of cathedral dean Sjöborg, who died when you were in Karlstad last autumn. It was only a thousand dalers and a suite of furniture, but now that he had that money to live on, he planned to leave the service of the church. But when I heard about his inheritance I suggested that, instead, he act on his old intention to live the same life as a simple laborer. I also counseled him to take the opportunity to be united with the bride God had chosen for him. You see, Mrs. Ekenstedt, I thought he might do something great and uplifting and thereby be released from his pangs of conscience. He might make himself a model for us all. He might show us the way to achieving a good and holy life. If there were something he could do in order for the Kingdom of Heaven to come to us even in this world, perhaps God would ward off those visions that were threatening to be the ruin of him.

'To begin with he hesitated, but as I went on speaking he soon began to embrace the plan with as much enthusiasm as I felt for it. I do believe he went to see the old soldier, Berg, that very evening to ask about purchasing his cottage. And since then the thought of at last living his life in the footsteps of

Christ has buoyed him up. I don't know how many times he has said that as soon as he was married to you, as soon as he moved here, to his humble dwelling, he expected to be able to preach without a written sermon again. He thought the vision would then cease to disturb him.

'But, my dear Mrs. Ekenstedt, there is one thing, and a very difficult one indeed, that must be said, although you may already have drawn that conclusion yourself, and that is that Karl-Artur must not become mired down in worldly affairs. I know better than anyone how much he has been looking forward to living here with you in this little cottage. He considers you his guardian angel, thinks you will protect him from all evil. He grieved deeply that he could not write to you about all of this, but of course he could not write such things in a letter that would be read aloud to you by others. Therefore it was only in me, Mrs. Ekenstedt, he was able to confide the tender, passionate feelings that filled him at the thought of his young bride from the far north who was going to walk by his side and aid him in showing humanity the way to righteousness.'

Mrs. Sundler's voice had taken on a mysterious, compelling tone, and Anna Svärd sat still, as if bewitched.

'Yes, my dear Mrs. Ekenstedt,' Mrs. Sundler began again, 'when Karl-Artur left for Medstubyn, he was firmly convinced that the two of you would live in a holy union, as brother and sister. He was afraid that if anything resembling ordinary worldly pleasure was mingled with your life, the vision would return. Can you understand that? Can you understand that you have not married an ordinary man, but a man of God's elect? And can you understand me and my behavior now? I had no idea, of course, that Karl-Artur had deviated from his intention. I had arranged everything in these rooms according to his instructions.'

Mrs. Sundler's voice was no longer gentle and ingratiating. It had become commanding and accusatory. When Anna Svärd thought of her wedding night, she experienced real pangs of conscience.

'But no one told me any of all that you just explained to me.

All I heard was that he was poor.'

'That, too, is true, Mrs. Ekenstedt. But underneath that, there were all the things I have told you now. Karl-Artur did not know you very well. Perhaps he may not have felt it was right to speak to you in confidence in the home of strangers. And so he pleaded poverty. I can certainly understand that. But I imagine that you now see matters in a different light. It is so very important for Karl-Artur to be saved. That vision *must* not come back.'

His young wife was so entangled and ensnared in this tightly-spun web that she would have followed Mrs. Sundler anywhere. And so she opened her mouth to make the pledge that was being asked of her.

'Yes, for my own part I do promise,' she began but then she stopped short.

Mrs. Sundler had risen quite suddenly and was looking out the window, and what she saw made such a shimmer of joy transform her unattractive features that she looked nearly beautiful.

Anna Svärd rose as well, and saw that the person Mrs. Sundler saw approaching outside the window was Karl-Artur.

And suddenly it occurred to her that it might not be the Good Lord who was demanding that vow of her, but merely Mrs. Sundler, and so she left it unsaid.

THE SUNDAY HAT

I

Who was she to imagine that she was wiser than such a learned man as Karl-Artur, she who had never progressed as far as the ability to read a book, she who had been in the tutelage of Procentor Medberg for an entire autumn without learning to write as simple a thing as: *The early bird catches the worm*.

Indeed, who was she to dare to claim that this entire spectacle around Karl-Artur was nothing at all? It was neither pangs of conscience nor a punishment; it was nothing, plain and simple.

As she was sitting listening to Mrs. Sundler she had been miserable and confused, but no sooner had that stranger departed than she realized how all the pieces fit together.

But still. She knew very well what an ignorant creature she was, and thus she said not a word to her husband concerning her conclusions. Imagine if she had! Though of course she would never be so presumptuous. After all, she was nothing but a poor peddler woman.

Later that afternoon Karl-Artur went into his study to work on the next day's sermon, and she was left alone. So she went to her larder, so well stocked thanks to Mrs. Sundler, and took out a covered knitting basket. In it she put some of her husband's dirty clerical collars and headed off to the organist's.

Not a word did she say to Mrs. Sundler, either, about what

she thought she had reckoned out. Mrs. Sundler would certainly have been the last person in whom she would have wanted to confide what was on her mind. Anna Svärd had, to say the least, just as much respect for Mrs. Sundler's wisdom as she had for her husband's.

All she did was to request that Mrs. Sundler be so kind as to help her a bit with the collars. Her husband had asked her to starch and iron a few for him, but she had simply no idea how to proceed. She had been working on them for a couple of hours, but one just wouldn't lie straight and another refused to lie flat. She needed a lesson.

Mrs. Sundler said how pleased she was that Mrs. Ekenstedt had come to ask her for help with this little difficulty. Ironing clerical collars was indeed an art, she was not sure she was much of an expert herself, but she would do her very best. So they had moved in the direction of Mrs. Sundler's kitchen and washed and ironed collars until Anna Svärd had the knack of it.

When they were finished Mrs. Sundler said she would like to make them a cup of coffee, but Anna Svärd declined, because she needed to get home. So Mrs. Sundler suggested a glass of cordial instead. She had some very nice cordial, even wealthy Mrs. Schagerström had praised it, and it would be refreshing after their exertions. Anna Svärd had not said no, and Mrs. Sundler had gone to the basement to get the bottle. And while her hostess was downstairs, her guest slipped out into the vestibule, took Mrs. Sundler's special Sunday hat down from its hook, carried it into the kitchen and stuffed it into a large kettle on a shelf that was so high up no one could look inside and see what it contained.

When Anna Svärd was ready to leave, Mrs. Sundler accompanied her out through the vestibule and into the evening air, but never did it occur to her to check that her Sunday hat was still in its place. In a part of the world where people were so honest it was considered superfluous to lock the door when one went out, no one ever had a thought of things being stolen or even hidden.

Anna Svärd set off for home, very pleased with what she

had done. She expected it would take Mrs. Sundler quite a bit of hunting to locate that Sunday hat of hers. She felt that in her rightful wifely capacity she had done what was in her power to enable her husband to give his sermon undisturbed the next day, and to spare him another fright.

The next morning as she walked alongside her husband to church, she continued to be pleased with herself. She had no more guilty conscience for having hidden the hat than a hunter feels when he has set a trap for a wolf. For who was she? She didn't come from here, from Korskyrka, where everyone was enlightened and well educated. She was Anna Svärd from Medstubyn, and what people in Medstubyn believed and held true was what she had learned; it was this wisdom that guided her.

She was quite pleased with everything that morning. Her husband led her into the church through the pastor's entrance, via the sacristy, where the old pastor's wife took her in hand, and the two of them sat together at the very front of the chancel, in the parsonage pew. She wished that someone from back home could have been there to see her, because she knew that neither the sheriff's wife nor Karin from Risgården farm would ever be raised to a status as high as she now held.

She looked around the congregation for Mrs. Sundler, but saw her nowhere. Once she was completely sure, she leaned forward in the pew and prayed along with the pastor's wife and all the others. She appealed to God to go on helping her so that Mrs. Sundler would not think of looking for her hat in the big copper kettle. If she just failed to find that hat, Anna Svärd was quite sure that she would not come to church. Surely the wife of a poor organist would not have more than one Sunday hat, and if it went missing she would have to stay at home.

After that, Anna Svärd sat watching people as they gradually arrived, but she was not at all happy to see that the church did not fill up completely. There were empty seats in every pew. Still, a moment later she was laughing to herself.

'Here you are, Anna Svärd, starting to behave like a real

pastor's wife already!'

That brought to her mind all the other pastors' wives before her who had sat in this very pew waiting to see their husbands walk to the pulpit. What thoughts might have been in their minds? Could they have been unnerved and upset to anticipate their husbands going up there to speak the word of God? Well, she was far below all of them, and yet she dared to send a sighing appeal to all the pastors' wives of the past.

'Help me, all of you who know what it is like to sit here waiting anxiously, so the woman I am thinking about won't be able to come to th'church this Sunday!'

She grew increasingly uneasy as the service progressed and the moment approached for the sermon to begin. She jumped in her seat every time the church door opened to a latecomer.

'I s'pose that's the organist's wife coming after all,' she kept thinking to herself.

But Mrs. Sundler was not there, nor did she come. The first part of the service drew to a close, the hymn preceding the sermon was sung, and Karl-Artur walked up the steps to the pulpit. Mrs. Sundler was nowhere to be seen.

It was Shrove Sunday, and in the epistle for the day Anna recognized the beautiful words about love which Mrs. Ryen had read to her on the night of her wedding. That could be nothing but a good omen, could it? And when Karl-Artur, after a fine opening, went on to address that very part of the text, she felt convinced that Our Lord and the pastors' wives from the past must have heard her prayers. Surely Mrs. Sundler would not come now, and she herself would be able to sit there calmly in the parsonage pew and listen to the man she loved sing the praises of love itself.

Well, who was she? She had no idea of what counted as a good sermon but – she could have sworn it – she had never heard anything so beautiful. And she was not the only person there who was listening with pleasure. She saw how people were turning their heads and staring up at the preacher. Some moved closer to the person next to them in the pew, giving him a nudge to urge him to pay attention.

'Listen up! This is what I call a real sermon.'

And indeed it was. She vowed that if she had ever before heard any human being speak like that, well, let them turn her into a block of granite. Sitting there in the chancel, she could see how soft and solemn the expressions on the faces in the pews were becoming. A couple of young women's eyes began to sparkle like stars.

At the very moment when it was at its best, there was a slight motion in the church. Mrs. Sundler crept in. She was evidently embarrassed about arriving late. She walked on tiptoe, more or less pressing against the edge of each pew row to make herself invisible. But everyone saw her in any case, and looked at her in surprise and disapproval.

She wore no hat on her head, only her everyday cap. It looked old and worn, and she had tried to improve it by tying a big bow in the front.

Just one second later, though, Mrs. Sundler was forgotten, as everyone turned again to look toward the pulpit and to hear the beautiful sermon that was flowing from there.

'He's made such a grand start,' thought Anna Svärd, 'and I don't even think he noticed her coming in. Maybe she won't have any power over him.'

However, less than five minutes after Mrs. Sundler entered the church, Karl-Artur broke off in mid-sentence. He leaned very far forward in the pulpit, staring toward a dark recess in the church. And what he saw there frightened him so badly his face turned white as a sheet.

He looked as if he might pass out, and Anna Svärd started to rise from her seat to rush forward and help him down. But there was no need. Just as quickly as it had come over him it passed, and he straightened up and began to speak once more.

However, it was no longer a pleasure to listen to him. The young clergyman had completely lost his train of thought. He said a few words that had nothing to do with where he had left off, went totally silent again, changed his subject but only to say something that made no sense at all. The congregation became restless in their seats. Many people looked scared or unhappy, which undoubtedly further contributed to the increasing bewilderment of the man at the pulpit. He wiped perspiration from his brow with his large clerical handkerchief and raised his hands above his head in what appeared to be a desperate prayer for guidance.

Anna Svärd had never felt so sorry for anyone before.

She would have liked just to walk away. Did she really have to sit here and see her husband's suffering? But before she stood up, she threw a sidelong glance at Mrs. Forsius, the wife of the old pastor, who just sat there, unmoving, her face devout and her hands clasped. No one would ever have known, from looking at her, that things were not as they ought to be in that church.

That was how a pastor's wife was supposed to behave. She shouldn't run out. She should sit still, hands clasped and face devout, whatever happened.

So Anna Svärd also stayed in her seat. She just sat there, immobile and solemn, until the postlude had been sung and Mrs. Forsius rose to go.

That gave her time to settle her mind. She was able to pull herself together and recall that she was a poor, ignorant peddler woman from Dalarna.

Back home in Medstubyn, everyone who grew up there believed that the world was full of evil trolls who could fool people and make them see things that weren't there. Here in Korskyrka perhaps no one had ever heard of such a thing.

Back where she came from, anybody could tell you all about Finn-Lotta, a nasty troll who was going to be burnt at the stake. Blindfolded, she was taken out to the place where the bonfire was readied, but before they tied her to the stake she requested a final opportunity to see the earth and sky. So the executioner removed the blindfold, but at that very moment everyone became aware that the courthouse was in flames. So they all ran off from Finn-Lotta to help rescue people and put out the fire, and the old woman broke free and got away. But there had been no real courthouse fire. It was just that troll who had fooled the assembled crowd.

Back where she came from, people knew other things as

well. They could recount the time Erik from Jobsgården farm had a stand at the market but hadn't sold a thing, because at the stand next to his was a troll who could swallow burning straw and exhale fire, and who fooled the customers at the market, making all Erik's bright, shiny knives, sharp-toothed saws and fine, well-honed scythes appear to be nothing but rusty rubbish. Her uncle sold not so much as a three-inch nail until he realized the trick the troll was playing on him, and drove him out of the marketplace.

Back where she came from, any and everyone would have realized that the organist's wife was casting a spell on Karl-Artur, and making him imagine he saw his mother in church. If anybody from Medstubyn had been there today and seen it all happen, that person would have been as certain as she herself was.

But Korskyrka wasn't Medstubyn. Anna Svärd had to remember who her husband was and who Mrs. Sundler was and who she was, and keep what she knew and thought to herself.

She had to be patient when her husband said not a word to her on their way home from church, just walking beside her as if he didn't know of her existence. She thought of all the eyes that were on her, and tried to look the part of a proper clergyman's wife, but without really having the slightest idea as to whether she was succeeding.

Once at home, her husband went straight to his study and shut himself in. He did not give her so much as a hand with laying the table or preparing the meal. Usually he enjoyed playing assistant to her, only pretending of course.

During dinner he sat opposite her without uttering a word. Indeed, she felt like the most evil of sinners. And him sitting there thinking that his sermon had gone awry because he hadn't followed Mrs. Sundler's instructions. She felt like screaming. What if he never wanted to have anything to do with her again?

The sheriff's wife had advised her to roast a few grouse and other types of wild fowl that were so plentiful up north and take them along with her to Korskyrka so she would have food ready to put on the table the first few days. But surely grouse was not considered much of a delicacy down here. Her husband set his cutlery aside after only a couple of little bites.

She dared not ask him a single question during the meal. And the moment they stood up, Karl-Artur mumbled something about a headache and needing a walk, leaving her alone with her miserable thoughts.

II

Is it not peculiar that it should be so difficult to have your wishes granted?

If you were wishing for something that was wrong, it might be understandable, but when the only thing you are asking is that the man who is your heart's desire should come and visit one or two afternoons a week and sit and converse or listen to music with you in your little parlor, well, you certainly ought to be able to have such a wish granted. It would be a different matter if you were absolutely asking to have him to yourself, but you are asking no such thing. You don't mind at all if Sundler joins you. The two of you have nothing to hide. Not you, and certainly not Karl-Artur.

If you had sent Charlotte Löwensköld off to some terrible or cruel fate, if she had had to become a poor schoolteacher or a housekeeper, then perhaps you might have anticipated punishment and disappointment. But now that you had captured her the best catch in all the land, an excellent man with status and a fortune, why should you not then have an opportunity to enjoy the modest little pleasure you had hoped to have for yourself? Why did Mrs. Forsius, the pastor's wife, have to become hostile toward you over it? Because it all fit together. Karl-Artur made his excuses, saying he had catechetical meetings and all sorts of things, but of course it was Mrs. Forsius who had been whispering to him that people had begun to talk about the intimacy of their friendship. Of course it was the gossip that explained why that autumn, week after week passed without his coming.

If you had been the least bit to blame for Karl-Artur having visions of his dear mother in church, if you had worked him up to a pitch afterwards, thinking that it might bring him back to your previous intimacy, well then you would have had good reason to anticipate reversals and unpleasantness. But since all you had done was to try to comfort him and to help him understand, should you not have been given opportunities to aid him in his adversity? Had you deserved for it to be precisely then that your own husband started behaving jealously and making scenes, so that it became nearly impossible to welcome Karl-Artur into your home? Karl-Artur needed a friend and confidante more than ever before, and you asked nothing more, nothing at all more than to be able to aid him.

And if, at that time, in order to assuage your husband's jealousy, you proposed to Karl-Artur that he marry, was there anything worthy of punishment and condemnation? True, you couldn't tell Karl-Artur the real reason, what with him being so detached from the world as he was, he would never understand, but in any case, what could be wrong about having helped him bring the greatest dream of his youth to fulfillment? And that simple peasant girl from up north, should she not have been satisfied to live in his home and see to it that he was dressed and fed? Could anyone possibly have imagined that such an ignorant person could have captivated him, that he would return from his wedding journey head over heels in love and without a thought for anyone but his wife?

It had been a labor of love to assist him in arranging his little home, to consult with him on the acquisition of the furniture and the decisions concerning the repairs. It had been possible to dream many a lovely dream while doing so. But was that any reason to be punished by being made to feel superfluous from the instant his wife crossed the threshold? Who was it, after all, who had made this simple creature a clergyman's wife? Who had seen to it that the most noble, most brilliant, most spiritual of men had become her husband? Yet what gratitude did she demonstrate? When you entered the little house you had arranged yourself, you could clearly feel how the couple who had moved into it just wished you would hurry up and leave.

Not that you had for a moment wished for it, but you could hardly help feeling a bit of malicious pleasure when the vision returned. It was only to be expected, since he ignored the advice you gave him. No, of course you had not wished for it, but you did find it difficult to feel the least bit of compassion.

It was also a source of irritation that someone had stolen your Sunday hat. It was not likely to have been a proper theft. Surely it was just a bit of mischief someone had played to keep her from going to church to hear Karl-Artur preach. It was extremely irritating to think about who that someone could have been. Could it possibly, could it really have been her own husband who had foolishly gotten it into his head to hide her hat?

You knew, of course, that Karl-Artur would arrive to complain, and you expected him just after Sunday dinner, but instead hour upon hour passed without his coming. You had already managed to persuade yourself that he had confided in his wife, that he had sought comfort from her on this matter as well, which had been a secret between yourself and him. You had sat there remembering all your disappointments and ungranted wishes, and you were hardly in the right frame of mind to receive him when he finally walked in. You ushered him in to your little parlor, sat down at one end of the sofa and heard him out, but you were in a strangely downhearted mood. You heard his complaints without being moved by them. You had to grit your teeth so as not to shout at him that you were so tired, tired, tired, that you could not always be soft and submissive, that there was a limit to your patience, that you were not a person who could be picked up and dropped at whim.

You heard him say that he had taken a long walk so as to be able to think through his decision, but that he was still feeling quite befuddled. Then he went on to his usual rant about not being able to bear this persecution, that he would have to resign from the clergy, that it was what his mother was demanding of him.

Under other circumstances you would have done your utmost to comfort him. Today you can barely cope with listening to him. You sit perfectly still, but your fingertips are twitching. You want to strike out and claw at some flesh with your nails. You have no idea whether it is his skin or your own you are longing to strike out at, but you know that it would be a great relief to do such a thing.

He talks and talks, but somehow in the end he notices that you are failing to respond, that you are not displaying your usual empathy with him. He is surprised, and inquires as to your health. And you answer quite brusquely that you feel perfectly fine but that you are surprised to find him still coming to fret. He does have a wife now, after all.

That is how you respond. You say the most foolish thing you could possibly say. Perhaps you had hoped he would object that his wife was too inexperienced and ignorant, that he needed to speak with a refined woman who could follow his train of thought. But whatever you had hoped for, it did not come true.

Instead he looks a bit surprised, says a few words in apology for having come at a bad time, and leaves.

You go on sitting there, perfectly still, the whole time, until you hear him shut the front door. You find it difficult to believe that he is really leaving, you are certain he will come back. Not until the door closes firmly behind him do you spring up, shout, call out. What have you done? Is he gone forever? How could this have happened? He was here, and you rejected him. You did not want to hear his complaints. You advised him to turn to his wife for help. And today of all days, when everything was at stake, when you might have won him forever!

III

Karl-Artur could not, of course, experience that very special sense of well-being and security we all tend to feel as we approach home when, at dusk, he turned back from his visit to Mrs. Sundler. Naturally he did not say to himself, when he saw the little cottage appear at the top of the rise above the doctor's garden, that he now had a little corner of the world where he would always be welcome, where he would always be defended, where he had his definite place and was not in anyone's way. On the contrary, he found himself wishing that he had never taken a wife, never purchased that old cottage, never embarked on the whole adventure at all.

'This is terrible,' he thought. 'Miserable as I feel, I still cannot be alone. I have a wife who has been sitting here bored all afternoon. I must see to it to amuse her. She may be angry and say bitter things. And she truly has the right to do so, but how will I bear her lamentations?'

He walked over the loose step and reached most reluctantly out to open the door. But before his hand could touch it, he pulled it back with a start. From inside, he heard singing, hymn singing, and children's voices.

Almost instantly he felt liberated. The terrible pressure over his heart that had led to his living only half a life since that morning, eased tangibly. Something inside him whispered that he was free to enter without fear. What awaited him inside was precisely what he had not dared to wish for.

A moment later he was opening the kitchen door very quietly and looking in. The room was in almost complete darkness, except for a couple of logs that were still smoldering at the hearth, and before the dying fire sat his wife, with the whole band of children from Matts the crofter's cottage around her.

In spite of the poor light, or perhaps thanks to it, this little group looked charming. The youngest child was on his wife's lap sound asleep. The others were so close around her as they could get, their gazes firmly fixed on her lovely face, singing the hymn "*Now the day is over*".

Karl-Artur closed the door behind him, but did not cross the room. He remained in the dark corner over by the wall.

Into his heart, tormented by anxiety and pangs of

123

conscience, crept once more the healing thought that here was the woman appointed by God to be his salvation. She may not have been as he had first imagined her, but who was he to know? Just look! Instead of sitting there vexed over his absence, she had gone to collect the children he had once rescued from the greatest misery, and passed the time by teaching them hymns. In her behavior he found something both wise and touching. 'Why should I not simply open my heart to her and ask her to help me?' he wondered.

The moment the hymn was finished, his wife rose and sent the children home. Perhaps she had not even noticed her husband's arrival; in any case she left him alone, standing in his corner. Humming the evening hymn she had just been singing with the children, she went to the larder to get out milk and small beer, added some wood to the fire and set into the embers a little three-legged pot to heat the milk to make the milky drink referred to as beer gruel.

She went on about her business in the room, laying the table, putting out butter and bread, moving two chairs to the table by the window.

It was lovely to see his wife moving around in this dusky light. The gaudy colors of her peasant costume, sometimes a bit overwhelming in the light of day, now merged into a warm beauty. The thick cloth rustled like brocade. Karl-Artur suddenly became aware of the meaning underlying all these peasant dresses. They were farming women's way of imitating the silks and satins of ancient queens and noblewomen. With their colorful front panels, their puffed, white sleeves, their caps that nearly entirely hid their hair, one could imagine these dresses being worn by the most prominent women of the land once upon a time.

At the same moment, his wife appeared to him to have been magically uplifted to an heiress of the dignity that had once surrounded burgher women. What others found to be her simple gestures were merely old-fashioned customs from the days when queens lit their own hearths and princesses washed their own garments at the riverside.

When his wife had set out the two cups of gruel, she lit a

tallow candle and put it in the middle of the table, sat down on one of the chairs, and clasped her hands to say grace. In the light of the flame that evening, her face appeared to Karl-Artur to have something noble about it. The wisdom and quiet solemnity of a woman who has had her trials to bear had replaced her previous youthful defiance and self-confidence.

Seeing her this way, it seemed to him not at all impossible to share with her even his most deep and sensitive problems.

'I have been childish to imagine that she would not understand me,' he thought. 'Her naturally noble nature would guide her in the right direction.'

Even before his wife had finished saying grace Karl-Artur had sat down across from her at the table and clasped his own hands in prayer.

They ate in silence. He appreciated her way of eating without talking, as if the meal, the loan from the Lord, were a sacred, life-sustaining act.

As soon as their simple meal was over, Karl-Artur moved his chair around the table so he was sitting at his wife's side, put his arm around her shoulders and pulled her toward him.

'You must forgive me,' he said. 'I was harsh and impatient after church, but I know you understand how upset I was.'

'Don't bother your head about that, my husband! You never need to worry about how you behave toward me. I care for you, no matter what you do.'

At that instant, which must have seemed very solemn to her, Anna Svärd spoke not with her rural accent but in her very best Swedish. This surely contributed to Karl-Artur finding her words extremely beautiful. He kissed her in gratitude.

And this kiss unsettled him a bit. He would really have liked just to go on kissing his wife and thinking of nothing else.

'I love her madly,' he thought. 'She belongs to me, and I to her. I suppose that vision will appear to me every time I enter a pulpit. I will never be a good preacher, but why should I let that prevent me from being happy with my wife in my home?'

His wife seemed to know what he was thinking.

'Now there is one thing, my husband, that you should know,' she said. 'You will never again have to be frightened in church. I am going to see to that.'

Karl-Artur looked amused at her confident assurance. He knew very well that his inexperienced, ignorant wife would not be able to help him, but the empathy she revealed with those words had a calming, liberating effect on him.

'I know that you love me sufficiently to want to bear all my burdens,' he said in a loving tone of voice, kissing her once more.

This was a moment of great and restorative happiness. Love infused its joy and determination into the heart of the young man. He could imagine a future in which he and his wife, always united in this same sweetness, created a paradise on earth in their little home, which would be a model to the entire congregation.

'My dear wife,' he whispered, 'we shall work together. We will be very happy.'

Hardly had he uttered these words, when they heard someone opening the door forcefully and loudly, and footsteps pounding the hall floor.

Anna Svärd rose quickly, and as the visitors entered she could be found clearing the butter dish and the slices of bread from the table.

Karl-Artur was still at the table, mumbling that it was not very nice to be disturbed this late in the evening. But when he saw that their visitors were Sundler the organist and his wife, he rose and moved toward them.

The organist, who was a large, elderly gentleman with a thick head of white hair rising over a face that was always red and puffy, seemed to be even redder and puffier than usual that evening. He had his wife on his arm, and he walked right into the middle of the room with her. Although it was such a cold winter, he did not bother to shut the door behind them. He neither said good evening nor extended a hand in greeting.

It was easy to see that he was terribly upset, but it must also have been that which made him look quite impressive as well. Anna Svärd could see that he was a competent man, as opposed to his wife Thea, who was hanging onto his arm, and who appeared to her to be like an old, worn dishrag. 'She has a good husband,' thought Anna Svärd, 'but she has been dipped into far too much dirt. She can never be really clean again.'

Hardly had she finished this thought, when she noticed that Mrs. Thea Sundler had her Sunday hat on her head.

'Aha,' she said to herself. 'Here it comes.'

She walked toward the door to close it, wondering if the wisest thing wouldn't be just to run away from it all. But, bravely, she summoned up the courage to stay.

The organist came straight to the point. Without mincing words he explained that his wife had been unable to find her Sunday hat that morning when she was getting ready for church. She had imagined it stolen, until earlier that evening when, after a thorough search, they had found it stuffed into a copper kettle on one of the very top kitchen shelves. His wife had then accused the organist himself of having hidden her hat, but of course he knew that he was innocent, unless he had done it in his sleep. What he did remember, however, was hearing that Karl-Artur's wife had visited their home and stayed for several hours on the Saturday. So now he was there to ask a straightforward question and obtain a clear answer.

Anna Svärd stepped forward at once, saying that he was quite right. While Mrs. Sundler was down in the basement getting the cordial, she had sneaked out into the vestibule, taken the hat, and hidden it in the kettle.

While admitting her guilt, she felt herself sinking deeper and deeper. She was sinking in the eyes of the organist, and in the eyes of Karl-Artur. Mrs. Sundler, in contrast, seemed to be squinting at her with a very interested look on her face.

'But why in the name of God would you have done such a thing?' the organist asked in alarm, and Karl-Artur repeated the question shrilly.

'Why in the name of God? What was your point? What were you getting at?'

Anna Svärd realized later that it would have been better for her not to tell the truth, but to make up some excuse. But at the time she was happy to be able to clarify the matter. She forgot that she was no longer in Medstubyn talking with her mother or Erik from Jobsgården farm. She believed that she would be able to crush and destroy that dishrag, Mrs. Sundler.

'I was trying to keep that woman out of church today,' said Anna Svärd, pointing at Mrs. Sundler.

'But why? Why?'

'Because she casts a spell on my husband and makes him imagine things that are not there.'

That dumbfounded all three of them. They simply stared at her, as if she were a corpse risen from the grave.

What was she saying? How could she believe such a thing? How could she even imagine it?

Anna Svärd turned right to Mrs. Sundler. She took a couple of steps in her direction, coming very close.

'Are you denying that you are the one who casts a spell on him? You can ask Mrs. Forsius, the old pastor's wife, in fact you can ask anybody who was at church today, if they have ever heard a better sermon than the one he was preaching. But the minute you walked in, it was lost to him.'

'But Mrs. Ekenstedt, my dear Mrs. Ekenstedt, how could I? And even if I could, why would I want to harm Karl-Artur, who is my own and my husband's closest friend?'

'Somebody like me can never know what a person like you has in mind.'

Karl-Artur took his wife firmly by one arm and pulled her back. He appeared to be concerned that she might throw herself at Mrs. Sundler and strike her.

'Silence!' he ordered her. 'Not another word.'

The organist stood before her, fists raised.

'You watch your words, you peasant lass, you!'

The only person who maintained her composure was Mrs. Sundler. She even began to laugh.

'Now, now, let us not overreact! Mrs. Ekenstedt appears to have a superstitious side. But what would one expect?'

'Don't you see,' asked her husband, 'that she's accusing you of some sort of witchcraft?'

'Yes, of course. I told her yesterday that Karl-Artur sometimes thinks he sees his mother at church, and this is her explanation. All she was trying to do was to rescue her husband by any means she saw fit. Any peddler woman from Medstubyn would probably have done the same thing.'

'Thea!' Karl-Artur exclaimed. 'You're magnificent.'

Mrs. Sundler immediately countered that she was anything but. She was just relieved that their little misunderstanding had been cleared up so readily. Now that it was all over, there was no reason for her and her husband to outstay their welcome. They would be off now, leaving the young newlyweds to their own devices.

And so, with a very pleasant good night to both Karl-Artur and his wife, she left with her husband, still angry and growling, as he had not had a chance to vent his wrath properly.

Karl-Artur walked them to the door. Then he approached his wife, arms across his chest. He made no accusations, but his face displayed disgust.

'He has the look of a man who was expecting heavy cream but was served plain whey,' Anna Svärd thought.

After some time when she could no longer bear the silence, she said a couple of words, in all humility.

'Will you never care for me again?'

'Can you restore my faith in you as the woman God Himself chose for me?' he countered in a broken voice.

He gave her one last, long look of anger and grief. Then he left the room. She heard him walk across the passageway, go into his study and shut the door, turning the lock twice.

THE VISIT

No doubt the old couple at the parsonage would have been thinking that it would not be long until the great pleasure of seeing each other on a daily basis would be denied them. As if to make the most of the precious opportunities they still had, they found themselves spending much more time together than before, in fact sometimes even right in the middle of the day old Mrs. Forsius would enter her husband's study for no special reason. She would sit quietly on the sofa with her knitting, or possibly at a whirring spinning wheel, a task she preferred, while her husband, without allowing himself to be disturbed, continued to arrange his herbarium and draw on his long pipe.

That was how Karl-Artur found them on the Monday he took his wife along for a first visit. The young pastor, who knew the habits of the household, did not bother looking for his hostess in the dining room or the parlor; he went straight to the study, where Mrs. Forsius was sitting weaving a ribbon on a hand loom as the pile of plant-pressing paper rose on her husband's desk, with a light smoke haze floating near the ceiling to contribute to the pleasure of the scene.

Karl-Artur held a short speech of thanks for all the good things he had received from the couple at the parsonage, not least their latest, enormous, gift. The pastor replied in a very kind tone, while his wife was quickly setting aside her hand loom in a corner and making room for the young pastor's new wife next to her on the sofa.

Mrs. Forsius, who dearly loved all kinds of ceremony, wiped a tear from the corner of her eye as she listened to Karl-Artur's well-formulated discourse. But if anyone thought, seeing this, that she was pleased with Karl-Artur's marriage, they would have been sorely mistaken. An old woman with a long marriage and a wealth of life experience behind her could, of course, only lament the marriage of a penniless young clergyman at all, and the poor peasant girl he had chosen did not make things a bit better. No, there was no question she had done everything she could to thwart this madness, but Mrs. Sundler had been determined to see Karl-Artur married, and Mrs. Forsius had been powerless against her.

She could not, however, resist examining this former peddler woman with some curiosity. She looked a bit out of place sitting there on the sofa, and when she was asked a few questions, she replied bashfully and in very few words. That was, of course, just what one might have expected or even desired, but the thing that surprised the pastor's wife greatly was to see how Karl-Artur behaved toward his wife. 'Had I not known better,' she thought, 'I would not have thought he was a newly-married man bringing his wife over here, but a peevish old schoolmaster having to put a poor pupil on display.'

There was a good reason for her concern. Karl-Artur let not a word cross his wife's lips without correcting her.

Time and again he said: 'You must forgive her, dear Mrs. Forsius. Anna can know no better. Medstubyn is a fine place, but compared with Korskyrka it must be about a hundred years behind the times.'

His wife never tried to defend herself. This hardy, energetic woman was so keenly aware of her insignificance in comparison with her husband that it was quite pathetic.

'I see, I see,' thought Mrs. Forsius. 'It is as I anticipated. All is well as long as she keeps her mouth shut and does not stand up for herself, but that day will undoubtedly come.'

Karl-Artur went on at great length about his journey to Medstubyn, the wedding and his new relations. His description was quite humorous, and some of his anecdotes may have offended his wife. One time she dared to object:

'You must be mad! Excuse me, Mrs. Pastor, but as a minister's wife you cannot possibly believe…'

'Anna!' Karl-Artur exclaimed in his strictest voice, and his wife stopped mid-sentence. Her husband turned to Mrs. Forsius.

'My dear Mrs. Forsius, do forgive her. I have told Anna time after time that she must not address you so familiarly. We certainly cannot be expected to behave the way people do in Medstubyn down in our part of the country.'

He went on with his story, though the pastor's wife was only listening with one ear. 'What will become of them?' she worried. 'I had such high hopes that the woman he married would be able to help him in his hour of need!'

The need Mrs. Forsius was primarily thinking about, of course, was his relationship with Mrs. Sundler. Although she knew perfectly well that there was nothing improper about it, she found it very upsetting that vile rumors were being spread about her husband's subordinate. She had done her best to persuade the village gossipmongers that Thea Sundler was too clever to throw herself into an escapade, and that all she really wanted was to be able to sing for Karl-Artur or go for a walk up along the ridge with him at sunset, looking out for clouds with silver linings. But what good had it done? Being Regina Forsius and having held the post of pastor's wife in Korskyrka for fifty years, she could make them hear her out, but moments later the rumor mill was in full swing again.

'There's more to it than that, dear sister! I'm sure we know why Thea was the agent of this marriage. To placate the organist. More to it, more to it! Sister, have you heard that he's going to keep his wife in the kitchen day and night, like a serving maid? And what's more, sister, have you seen that settle bed? More to it, more to it and more! How could anyone have imagined, sister, that it would be a real marriage!'

The old pastor's wife had heard about that settle bed so many times she had made up her mind to have an old four-poster bed they had in one of their guest rooms renovated and to send it to the newlyweds' home. She now thought that although this had quieted the gossip quite effectively, the best cure for those vicious tongues would have been for Karl-Artur to love his wife and to show it.

'I do wonder what Pastor Forsius is making of all this,' she thought. 'When Karl-Artur came to see him on Saturday, he spoke with such enthusiasm about his wife. Who would have imagined? I certainly hope Thea Sundler has not been meddling again!'

She was full of compassion for the poor peddler girl from Dalarna, and sat there wondering how she could help her.

By then the newcomer had conquered her timidity sufficiently to dare to raise her eyes and look around the room. Neither the bookcases nor the pastor's herbarium appeared to capture her attention. In contrast, a joyous smile spread over her face at the sight of the hand loom.

'Glory be, a ribbon-weaver!' Anna Svärd exclaimed, honestly looking so happy she might have been about to embrace it.

The fascination exerted by that simple piece of equipment was so great she was unable to sit still. Abandoning her secure seat on the sofa, she dared to stand up and move over to the ribbon-loom, which she examined and admired.

'You can't imagine how many bundles of ribbons I have woven in my day,' she explained to her husband, as if to excuse her own behavior.

Clearly the hand loom had made her feel at home, and the pastor's wife, assuming that a task she enjoyed would make her feel more comfortable still, asked if she would not like to run the shuttle through it.

'You are too kind, Mrs. Forsius. My wife would only muddle up your weaving. There is no question of her accepting your generous offer.'

'Nonsense, Karl-Artur. Of course she shall weave if she pleases.'

Moments later the young pastor's wife was sitting at the hand loom, weaving at a pace that astonished even the old pastor's wife. She and the two men found themselves standing around the loom watching the younger woman's fingers fly like those of a conjurer. There was no way the eye could keep up.

'Gina, my love,' said the pastor, 'it seems to me that you

believed you had mastered the art of ribbon weaving. But now we know how much remains for you to learn before you can call yourself an expert.'

The young wife's face beamed. It was clear that she suddenly felt as if she were back home. She was surrounded by familiar objects, her mother stood at the hearth, outside the window were all the low, unpainted buildings, and she could hear the melodious Dalarna twang of the speech of the others in the room.

After a few minutes' fast weaving the spool was empty. The contented weaver looked up with a sigh. Her eyes sought those of her husband. Was he displeased? Had she behaved rashly now again?

Her husband looked hesitant, but Regina Forsius, the old pastor's wife, leaned forward, fingered the ribbon, nodded approvingly and curtseyed before Karl-Artur.

'Well I never! I am deeply impressed, and give you my most heartfelt congratulations. If only I could use my hands so skillfully! I am absolutely convinced, Karl-Artur, that you have found precisely the wife you need.'

The young pastor made a little face:

'My dear Mrs. Forsius…' he began.

But the pastor's wife interrupted him.

'I know what I am talking about, Karl-Artur, and you mustn't let anyone persuade you that you might have made a better choice!'

Some time later, when the young couple had left, the pastor's wife got up from the sofa and walked over to the desk, curious to ask her husband his impressions from the visit.

The old man, who had moved his piles of plant-pressing paper aside, sat quill in hand eagerly filling a large sheet of paper with neat letters. When his wife leaned over him, she saw that it was a letter to his eminence the bishop in Karlstad.

'What on earth are you up to, Forsius?' she exclaimed.

Her husband stopped writing, set the pen in its little pot of small shot, and turned toward his wife.

'Gina, my love,' he said, 'I am writing to the bishop to

request that he move Karl-Artur to a different parish and send me a new curate. I promised Charlotte to be patient with him, and I have done my very best, but now he will have to go. Consider, my love, how the entire congregation is saying that he is so much in love with the organist's wife that he loses his train of thought entirely the minute she turns up at church.'

The pastor's wife was horrified.

'But Forsius, Karl-Artur is married now; he has bought a home of his own here in the parish. He believes that he will be staying at least as long as you are alive, and has arranged things accordingly. Have you no thought for his wife?'

'My love,' he replied, 'I feel the greatest empathy with that fine young woman who has abandoned her home village to accompany her husband down to ours. It is for her sake that I am writing immediately. If Karl-Artur stays here for many more days, you may be sure that he will reject her, as he has rejected both Charlotte and his mother.'

Selma Lagerlöf

PART TWO

Selma Lagerlöf

PARADISE

I

Karl-Artur Ekenstedt, who had been shifted from parish to parish for a year and a half without ever becoming kept on permanently, came riding down the road one raw and chilly autumn day. The goal of the journey was Korskyrka, where Pastor Forsius had passed away over a month before. His widow, who had always had a soft spot for Karl-Artur and who was probably also under the influence of Mrs. Charlotte Schagerström, had applied to the bishop and chapter to have him appointed temporary pastor in Korskyrka, at least until a new permanent minister could be decided on, and this application had been granted, although not without some hesitation, owing to the fact that Colonel Ekenstedt's son was not exactly a *persona grata* with the higher powers.

The thoughts of the traveller naturally went back to the time, eighteen months earlier, when he, a newly-married man, had been sent away from his wife and home. Actually, he had not been terribly unhappy about having to leave. With unspeakable disappointment he had by chance discovered that the soul of his wife was filled to the brim with unsophisticated superstition, and the contempt and disgust this had triggered in him had made their lives miserable. Today all these unpleasant feelings were gone. After their long separation, he bore no other sentiments toward his wife than love, gratitude and, one might even say, admiration.

'At last,' he thought, 'at last the time has come when we will build that paradise of which I have always dreamt.'

It seemed to him that he had garnered a great deal of useful experience during his nomadic moves from one parsonage to the next. More than ever, he was persuaded that his original plan had been the right one. It was the foolish insistence of human beings concerning the importance of earthly possessions that was the root of most of their misfortune. No, a life in all simplicity, liberated from need, raised above all small-minded desire to outshine one's equals, was the way to win happiness in this world and eternal bliss in the next.

But sermons and urgings were not sufficient to convince people of this simple truth. What they needed was a tangible example, which, more than the most moving words, would encourage them to follow.

When Karl-Artur had thought that far, he closed his eyes. He imagined his wife, and felt suffused with tenderness and enchantment.

When he had left Korskyrka, he had told her she would probably have to return to Medstubyn. She certainly could not come with him; he would be lodged and taking his meals at the parsonage to which he was being posted. The very small salary he would receive, a total of 150 riksdaler, he would send to her, but he thought it would be easier for her to live on this modest amount back at home with her family than here in Korskyrka. Nor did he know if she could possibly live on in their little cottage, alone and without protection.

But his wife had refused to leave.

'I won't be any worse off than other women whose husbands work far away,' she said. 'And you must have a kitchen and a bed to come back to one day when you have a chance.'

That, in itself, was a fine thing, that she was prepared to wait for him there, in spite of her solitude and poverty. But it was no more than many others would have done, and indeed it was not all she did.

Shortly after he left Korskyrka, the old nursemaid who had been looking after Matts the crofter's children had turned in her notice, and the kind ladies who had taken it upon themselves to see to it that the children were cared for had scoured the area for a replacement, in vain. They began to think that their only choice would be to foster out the children one by one. Of course they were not auctioned off; instead agreements were made with good local families, but the impoverished children were still absolutely devastated at the news that they were to be separated. They refused to accept the inevitable, and when the appointed foster parents arrived to collect their wards, they found the cottage empty and the children gone.

Having no idea where to seek the lawless flock, the families naturally went into the neighboring cottage to try to find out. It transpired that all ten children had taken refuge precisely there. They were assembled around Karl-Artur's wife, the poor peddler woman from Dalarna, who explained to the new arrivals that these children had already been bought at auction by her husband, and were thus his property. They were therefore now in their home, where they belonged, and no one was going to take them away without his permission.

Karl-Artur loved imagining this scene over and over again, as it had been recounted to him in long letters from both Mrs. Forsius and Mrs. Sundler. There had been quite an animated altercation, some of the charitable ladies had been called in, and had made it clear to the young woman that if she did not give up the children voluntarily, there would be no further contributions to their maintenance. But Anna Svärd from Medstubyn had laughed at that threat. What kind of contributions did they need? These were children able to work for their keep, as she had done all her life. And before these children, whom the man in her life had taken under his wing, were sent out to strangers, they would have to murder her in cold blood.

Her husband could just hear her resounding Dalarna-accented voice and see her gesticulating. There stood his heroic wife, taking the terrified children's side. How could he feel anything but pride in her?

She had, of course, come out victorious. The children had been left in her care, and indeed it was a great burden to her. The charitable ladies had probably not been very serious about their threat, but his wife no longer permitted the children to accept any charity at all. She had put her honor at stake with her claim that she and they would make ends meet for themselves by the sweat of their brows.

Ah, how he longed to arrive home and thank her, to lavish his tender attention upon her, to eradicate the memory of the suspicion he had once cast upon her in his arrogance.

Suddenly the traveler was awoken from his daydreams. The local driver had had to swerve aside to make room for a fine carriage that was coming toward them, pulled by a team of four black horses.

Karl-Artur recognized both the carriage and its passengers as it passed. How extraordinary that they should be the ones to cross his path just as he was approaching Korskyrka!

Charlotte was sitting on the box driving the team, proud and radiant, with the coachman beside her, arms crossed over his chest. The passengers in the carriage were Schagerström and Mrs. Forsius.

Charlotte, whose full attention was on the team, did not see him, but the pastor's wife and Schagerström acknowledged him. He, in turn, nearly neglected to respond to their greeting. He was bewildered. The sight of Charlotte had confused him. A jolt of joy and pleasure ran through his entire being. But of course he had ceased to love Charlotte long ago.

Recalling the last time they had met, he understood his reaction better. His wife was the woman he loved, but Charlotte was his good friend, his guardian angel. That was what gave him such pleasure when he saw her.

He took this encounter as a good omen, a confirmation of his optimism about the future.

II

No one has ever heard of Adam and Eve having children while they were still in paradise. There are no ancient legends about the young sons of these first human beings running around and playing tag with the lion cubs, or riding on the backs of leviathans and behemoths.

Instead, the children must have come into being after the expulsion, unless it was the fact that they, more than the serpent and the lovely apples of the tree of knowledge, were the reason the parents had to leave the Garden of Eden. That is certainly the kind of thing we can still observe today.

We need look no further than to Karl-Artur Ekenstedt, the man who returned home with such fine intentions, prepared to create a new paradise on earth in the little cottage above the doctor's garden. Although he was completely certain he would be the man for the task, he had failed to take the ten children into account.

For instance, it had never occurred to him that they would be in his home day and night. He had thought that, at least at night, they would be sleeping in their own nearby cottage. But when he asked his wife whether it might not be possible for the children to sleep at their place, she had laughed and scorned him.

'Oh, my husband, I see you must think we have a goldmine to dig in. For surely you would not want the children sleeping in an unheated cottage? And firewood costs money.'

Thus he was forced to accept that his kitchen, once so nicely arranged by Mrs. Sundler, was now furnished with a large bench-bedstead and two settle beds. The little space that remained was occupied by a loom, three spinning wheels, two hand looms, one lacemaking pillow, one yarn swift, one winder and a small table where his wife made hair jewelry. In other words, there was such a surfeit of paraphernalia that it was only just barely possible to navigate through it. But it was all necessary, as his wife and the children made ends meet by taking in orders for lace and watch chains, bundles of ribbons and woven cloth from the people of the parish. Not to mention that they had to make their own clothing.

Every time the beam was pulled on the loom, the whole little cottage shook on its foundation, and when the spinning wheels and the yarn swift and everything else was up and running, the noise penetrated into Karl-Artur's study, so he often felt as if he were sitting adjacent to a flour mill. When he emerged into the kitchen to eat, he often found his meal placed on a board set on top of the children's bench-bedstead, and should he intimate that it might be a good idea to open the door for a few minutes to air the place out, his wife would explain to him that she had already had it open for quite some time while she was sweeping the floor earlier that morning, and that they could certainly not afford to chill the cottage more than once a day, as they had no goldmine at their disposal.

As all ten children were living with him, he also had to accept finding their Sunday clothes, jackets and overcoats, skirts and trousers hanging in the vestibule, where everyone who had reason to come to their little provisional parsonage could see them. Because this kind of thing was not usual in Korskyrka, he told his wife that their clothing would have to be carried up to the attic. To which she responded that there were both mice and moths in the attic. The clothing would be ruined there in a couple of months' time, and she had absolutely no idea how they would ever be able to replace it, as they had no goldmine at their disposal.

His wife was more beautiful than ever, she loved him most tenderly, and she was proud and pleased to have him at home. For his part, he loved her back. There was no doubt that he and she would have been happy together, had it not been for the children.

He had to admit that no one was better with children than his wife. He never once saw her coddle them, nor did she beat them, but she certainly did know how to scold them, and if one of them did not do things properly, she could be quite cross. What she was like seemed to make no difference, however. The little ones were devoted to her. Nor was it only Matts the Crofter's children who adored her. Had there been room in that kitchen, every child in the village would have been there, sitting for hours, following her every move, and waiting patiently for a kind word from her.

Was it not a wonder how she had transformed the ten children from the greatest imaginable lazyboneses into the most industrious worker ants? And although they had to work from dawn to dusk, they were now red-cheeked and plump. It seemed to be their great pleasure in living close to her that made them thrive.

When Karl-Artur had first come home, all ten were prepared to show him the same devotion they gave his wife. Particularly the littlest girl had taken to him for no special reason. She would climb into his lap and stroke his cheek. She had no idea that her fingers were dirty and her nose runny, and could not for the life of her understand why she was lifted roughly down onto the floor. She began to howl.

At that, you should have seen his wife. She stormed over, raised the little girl into her arms and held her close as if to protect her from the enemy, glaring at her husband in a way that alarmed him terribly.

So actually, in spite of his wife being just as beautiful as before, she had also changed a bit. Now that she had so many little ones to order about, she had become just as commanding as the wife of a local councilor. All her humility, girlishness and mischievousness had vanished.

III

No one could say of Karl-Artur that he was spoiled. He paid no mind to what he was served to eat or drink, he was accustomed to working all day long, and he never complained when he had to ride in shaky farmers' traps or preach in ice-cold churches. One thing he found difficult to live without, however, was some semblance of order, of propriety, of well-being and of peace and quiet in which to work.

One morning when he came out into his kitchen for breakfast, he found that the parish cobbler had arrived. He had set up his workbench over by one of the windows, exactly where Karl-Artur preferred to sit. The entire room reeked of leather and wax, and the usual disorder was increased by the presence of bundles of birch bark, bunches of lasts, and jars of grease.

On the table, which had been pulled into the center of the room, his wife had set two individual plates and two large pewter bowls, all full of gruel. The two plates were, of course, for himself and the shoemaker. His wife and the children would, as usual, all spoon theirs from the pewter serving bowls.

Now this was a custom to which he had objected even previously. He had nothing against the gruel itself; their meals were always simple and frugal, as circumstance dictated. But he had asked his wife to see to it that the children had individual plates, explaining that it would be good for them to learn proper manners from the outset.

She merely replied that he must be mad to imagine her having time to wash ten plates three times a day, although she assured him that he, her husband, would always have a plate of his own, to which he was accustomed.

Otherwise he had to admit that the children did behave quite well at the table. They said grace, ate what was put before them, and never tried to eat more than their fair share from the communal bowl. He did not find it particularly difficult to share his table with them, but to now be expected to sit at the same table as the cobbler, that he could not accept. Just one look at those black, waxy fingers was enough to put him off his food.

Without really thinking of what he was doing, he took his bowl, his spoon and a piece of bread and carried it into his study. That room was still a refuge for him, where the air was fresh and the surfaces dusted. Well, he was a bit ashamed to be running away, but he also had to admit that he had not enjoyed a meal so thoroughly in a long time.

A while later, when he carried his bowl back to the kitchen, he found it deathly silent. The shoemaker was eating, his brow deeply furrowed, and his wife and the children sat there, their gazes averted, as if ashamed on his behalf.

On that day he felt uncomfortable in his own home, so a short while later he put on his hat and went out. He walked the road, not quite knowing what else to do with himself. He could not visit Mrs. Sundler, as the organist was in bed with his rheumatism and his wife was nursing him devotedly, not leaving his side night or day. Nor could he go to the parsonage for a chat with Mrs. Forsius. Charlotte had found it unthinkable that her old friend should spend her first winter as a widow alone in the parsonage, and had invited her to spend it at Stora Sjötorp instead.

As he was passing the parsonage he felt a powerful yearning to see the lovely old building that had been his home. He opened the gate and crossed the courtyard, heading for the garden.

It is easy to understand how, walking there among the tall, well-kept hedges, the memory of the last time he walked there with Charlotte came upon him. He recalled their quarrel, how he had explained everything to her, how he would not marry anyone but the woman the Good Lord appointed to be his wife.

And now he was married to the woman Destiny had sent to cross his path on the road, and he was convinced she was the right woman for him and that the two of them together would create a new paradise on earth. Was it all to go wrong now, simply because they had all these children hanging like millstones around their necks? He could not deny that Charlotte would have the right to make a laughingstock of him if he allowed all those great plans to fail, simply because he was unable to cope with a brood of children.

When he arrived home it was time for the midday meal, but before he could even appear in the kitchen his wife was at hand in the study, his meal neatly arranged on a tray. She was kind and cheerful as always.

'You know, my husband, I had been imagining you wanted to eat in the kitchen with the rest of us. If only you had told me, I would have brought your meals in to you from the outset.'

He hastened to reply that he did not mind eating with her and the children. It was the cobbler's black and greasy hands that had put him off. So he proposed that she eat in the study with him. Wouldn't it be nice, for once, for the two of them to have some time alone?

No, she could not agree to that. She had to eat with the little ones, to keep them in line. But she would be happy to sit in here while he ate.

She settled down in his desk chair and they conversed. She told him that the cobbler was planning to leave that evening. And that his schedule was then full until after the new year. The children would not have new shoes for the Christmas morning service as she had promised them.

Karl-Artur realized he had offended the cobbler, and that was the reason he was leaving. But what could he do about it?

At that moment Charlotte's face appeared before him, and he saw her poking fun at him for his inability to rectify even such a small problem.

When his wife had left with the dinner tray, he sat cogitating. Soon he had a solution. He went into the kitchen with a pair of shoes that needed half-soling, and sat down at the cobbler's bench. He asked the shoemaker to show him how to mend the shoes himself. And as the cobbler was not unwilling, Karl-Artur borrowed a big apron from his wife and sat with the cobbler until evening, and tried to understand the man's trade.

He found, of course, that it could not be learned in an afternoon, so he persuaded the cobbler to continue his teaching the next day. And it never occurred to this kind, pleasant man, who had thoroughly enjoyed his afternoon, to refuse.

IV

Sitting at that cobbler's bench was not the only thing he did for the children's sake, it was also because of them that he had to go about in clothes of simple gray homespun, looking like a miller.

He could not deny that they had had a truly fine Christmas. On Christmas Eve the kitchen was scoured spic and span, all the clutter had been removed, the floor covered with clean yellow straw, and a large table with a white tablecloth had been placed in the middle of the room. The children were bathed and had clean, new clothes and new shoes. They were relaxed and happy because Christmas had finally arrived. Parishioners had come to their little home from nearly every house in the village bearing gifts of sausages, butter, bread, cheese and Christmas candles, and because no one could say no to a gift at Yuletide, the pantry was full to bursting, not to mention the twelve stacks of sweet Christmas buns, circular braided loaves and apples garlanding the table.

Karl-Artur led a little Christmas prayer and sang holiday hymns with his wife and children. Afterwards, while his wife stood at the stove stirring the Christmas porridge, he and the children played games, laughing and rolling in the Christmas straw.

Late in the evening he brought out a few small Christmas gifts. The children received ice skates and a sled he had ordered for them, his wife an antique breastpin that had once belonged to his mother. All the presents were received with pleasure, and the house was infused with a sense of contentment.

He had neither expected nor hoped to be given a gift, but just as the evening was about to break up, the two eldest children brought out a heavy roll of fabric. They bore it toward him, with his wife and the other children in procession behind. He realized it was for him.

'The children have so much been looking forward to giving something to you,' said his wife. 'They've been working on it all autumn.'

But all they brought him was a roll of gray homespun. He quickly leaned forward to feel the quality. Everyone knows that there is nothing softer, warmer or stronger than homespun, home-woven cloth, but it is also heavy, thick and gray. And for his entire life Karl-Artur had worn suits of fine, smooth fabric, well suited to his station. It had never entered his mind that he might one day wear a homespun jacket.

Their present upset him terribly, and all he could think

was whether there was any way he could be spared having garments made from that cloth and having to go about dressed like a peasant.

His wife and children stood before him, waiting to be thanked and praised. His silence made them both disconcerted and upset.

Karl-Artur realized how hard they must have worked to acquire the wool, to card it, spin it and weave it. It was easy to imagine how this had taken them the entire autumn. And all the while, doing their carding and winding and weaving, they had enjoyed imagining how pleased he would be, and his words of praise for their homespun cloth. How he would admire them for giving him something of such value, how he would tell them he was looking forward to never freezing again, outdoors or indoors, now that he would have clothing made of homespun. That was what they expected of him.

Oh, what was he to do? If he could not find something nice to say, their entire pleasure in Christmas would be spoiled.

Fortunately, he had inherited some of his mother's ability to cope in uncomfortable situations, and he knew right away what he ought to say. Still, it took him a great deal of effort to utter the words.

'I wonder,' he asked, 'whether Anders the tailor plans to leave his needle in its box right through the holiday season? I must go and ask him. Just think if he could make me something of this fabric before New Year's Eve, so I'd have it to keep me warm when the coldest weeks of the winter arrive.'

How they beamed, all eleven of them, once they realized that it was only his astonishment at their cleverness that had made him look so startled to begin with.

V

Ever since that Sunday in Lent when Karl-Artur had lost his train of thought during his sermon on love, he had stopped even trying to preach without notes. He wrote all his sermons at his desk, and while he was writing he insisted on having total peace and quiet.

So one morning he made his wife and the children promise to neither speak nor sing, as they otherwise often did, because he was going to write his sermon. They managed to keep their promise for all of half an hour, but then the air resounded with roars of laughter.

He waited for at least two minutes before opening the kitchen door to see what was going on.

'Now don't be angry with us, my husband,' said his wife, who was also laughing so hard that tears were running down her cheeks. 'It's just the kitty, being so wild. We did try not to laugh, but I think that just made it worse in the end.'

The laughter died down quickly when he told them in no uncertain terms that their kitchen antics were ruining everything for him and if it were up to him he would move out and never again have to hear their eternal shrieks and laughter.

'See to it that this room stays silent! And I want no one to come in and disturb me before dinnertime,' he concluded, slamming the door shut behind him.

And his wish came true; he was able to work in peace and quiet all morning long. But when dinnertime arrived his wife told him that Mrs. Romelius, the doctor's wife, and Mrs. Schagerström had been to visit them in the kitchen a short time earlier, and had ordered some watch chains and bracelets. She was delighted about their visit. They had placed quite a large order, and Mrs. Schagerström and her sister had been so cheerful and kind.

Karl-Artur knew that Mrs. Romelius had recently returned home, it was said that she was completely cured. There was nothing remarkable about the idea that Charlotte, visiting her sister, would have found a reason to come up to his cottage and see how he was getting on. And yet he found the news utterly overwhelming. He simply stood there, breathing heavily, unable to utter a word.

Charlotte had been there! She had been under his roof, and no one had told him!

He asked with deliberate indifference whether the visitors had not asked to see him.

Yes, of course they had asked about him, more than once, but he had given them those strict instructions that he was under no circumstances to be disturbed.

There was nothing to reply to that. There was no reason to be angry. And he was astonished that he had neither heard them come in nor recognized their voices. He bit his lip and said not a word.

His wife looked searchingly at him.

'You cannot doubt for a moment that I would have liked to invite such fine guests into your study,' she said. 'It really was most awkward to have them here in the kitchen, in all this clutter, but I didn't dare to interrupt you.'

There was, as mentioned, nothing to do or say, but disappointment came over him like a lead weight. If only there had been someone he could blame for this misfortune! He was completely off his dinner, could hardly swallow a single bit.

After dinner, he threw himself down on the sofa in his study, but he was too uneasy to lie still. There was a seething turmoil inside him. Longing and regret surged through his veins.

He put on his overcoat to go out, but felt unable to walk slowly and quietly along the road. He felt like screaming, fighting, brandishing a weapon.

He went to the woodshed, picked up the axe and stood for a few moments, toying with it. Then suddenly he began hacking at the pile of wood that was lying there. Of course it was not his intention to make himself useful, but just to find an outlet for all the fury that was ringing and roaring inside him.

And it did him good. As soon has he had struck a few blows he felt better. He went on chopping for a couple of hours, after which he felt calm and had overcome his pain.

He was standing there, hot and perspiring, resting on the axe, when one of the children appeared in the doorway. Mother was wondering, the child asked, whether he would like some afternoon coffee.

He went along into the cottage, where his wife then served evening coffee to celebrate his woodcutting.

The atmosphere was different than usual inside. Not only had they aired the place out, cleared up the middle of the room, and set a proper table for coffee. No, his wife and children were also seeing him completely differently. So he had the strength to chop wood, he could contribute to the household work like they all did, he was a real man!

All at once he had become the paterfamilias, the center of gravity of the home, to whom they all looked up.

THE FALL FROM GRACE

I

Karl-Artur, who was now in the habit of chopping wood for a few hours every day, noted one morning a shadow passing as he got to work in the woodshed. He looked up, thinking he recognized Thea Sundler, whom he had barely seen all winter. He tossed the axe aside and ran out. Quite right, it was Mrs. Sundler, but she was already outside the gate and hurrying down the slope. He shouted her name, but instead of stopping she merely quickened her pace. He had been working in his shirtsleeves, so he pulled on his coat quickly and followed. He had to find out what was going on here.

All winter the organist had suffered so badly from his rheumatism he could hardly move. To enable him to do his job, the man who usually pumped the organ and the church warden would help him up the narrow stairway to the organ loft. Thea always accompanied him, sitting at his side throughout the service. She never came down into the church proper or the sacristy.

Karl-Artur had begun to suspect that it was more than her husband's rheumatism that was to blame for their never seeing each other. She probably had some other reason for keeping away, and since he truly cared for her, he did not wish to lose this opportunity to request an explanation.

He managed to catch up with her before she had made her way down the slope and turned onto the village street.

'Thea,' he cried, laying a hand on her shoulder. 'Do stop a minute! What's wrong with you? Are you afraid of me?'

Without looking up, she tried to release herself from his grip.

'Let me go!' she mumbled, almost inaudibly.

Karl-Artur did not obey. Instead he stood in the middle of the road, blocking her way. He noticed that her eyes were red-rimmed and she had lost weight. She looked as if she had endured a serious illness, like her husband.

He told her he was not letting her go until she told him why she, his old friend and advisor, never wanted to see him nowadays. What had he done? How had he offended her?

'You?' she asked, a powerful sense of pain in the word, 'You! How can you imagine that *you* offended me?'

'What should I imagine when you refuse to see me?'

She looked up at him, her face expressing endless pain. Karl-Artur looked back, astonished. One would never have called Thea pretty, but her obvious grief gave her plain features an expressive, touching look.

'Let me go!' she moaned. 'I made a vow to Mrs. Forsius. I swore never to see you again. It was on that condition she agreed to your returning here, to your wife and home.'

So saying, she pushed him aside and turned onto the village street. Karl-Artur did not stop her. Her words had been so thought-provoking that he just stood there, perplexed.

The next day Karl-Artur again bumped into Mrs. Sundler. One of the children had developed a temperature, and he walked down to ask Doctor Romelius to come and examine the young patient. But when he arrived, the doctor was occupied with a patient, and Karl-Artur was asked to have a seat in the waiting room. There he found Mrs. Sundler, engaged in eager conversation with an elderly farmer's wife.

When Karl-Artur entered the room she stood right up as if to leave, then changed her mind and sat back down. He bowed silently in her direction without attempting to address her, but after just a few moments Mrs. Sundler turned to him.

'It was a bit awkward for us, Per-Erik's old mother and myself, when you came in, because we had been sitting here talking about you. But actually there was no need for embarrassment, as we had nothing but praise for you, isn't that right, ma'am?'

The large, sturdy farmer's wife gave a pleasant smile.

'Yes, Sir, you could have heard every single word with no shame, Pastor.'

'That's right,' confirmed Mrs. Sundler. 'All we were saying was that we admired your tolerance. You sit there surrounded by ten screaming children day and night, never any peace. We were also saying that you must originally have been meant for greater things than chopping wood and becoming a cobbler to provide for Matts the crofter's children. But that makes it all the more impressive that you press on.'

'Actually, it looks to be doing you the world of good, Pastor,' the farmer's wife hastened to add. 'I've never seen you so hale and hearty.'

'We were also commenting on how sensible it is of you to go around in homespun,' Mrs. Sundler added. 'It makes it very clear to people how firmly you have broken with your past. You want to live a life of poverty, and are even resisting dressing like a gentleman.'

'To begin with,' the farmer's wife said, 'To begin with we all thought the little cottage and the poverty was nothing but show. But you've proven otherwise.'

Karl-Artur felt a powerful sense of vexation rising in him, felt his cheeks burning. He found Thea inconsiderate, and implied with a shake of the head that she ought to change the subject.

'What does it matter that your preaching is not what it once was?' Thea asked. 'I was just saying to Per-Erik's mother that your life itself is one vast sermon.'

'Yes, the life you and your wife are leading is a living sermon to us others,' the farmer's wife confirmed at once. 'When you come into church of a Sunday with the whole flock of children in tow, neatly dressed and ruddy cheeked and as well behaved as you could wish, we old farm women just have to stand quietly and admire them. We know how those children used to run about the village, ragged and wild. You and your wife, Pastor, have done a great deed.'

'Indeed you have,' said Thea, 'and you know, ma'am, that

even if a person had an idea of what they might be able to do to make the burden of the children less heavy, she would hardly be able to voice it. It would just be a shame to disturb something so fine, and which gives rise to such general admiration.'

Karl-Artur had been sitting with his face lowered, but at that he looked right up, an expression of anticipation and hope in his eyes.

The farmer's wife asked: 'Are you telling me, Mrs. Sundler, that there is someone willing to take on the children? No one here in Korskyrka seems to think that they have any other relatives than an uncle, who is a pauper, like their father.'

'What if that uncle of theirs had married into money, a farm of his own and a fine wife? If that were so, it ought not be impossible for him to take over the children if only he knew his brother had passed on.'

'Well, if that were so,' said the farmer's wife.

Then she was interrupted. The doctor opened his door, showed a patient out, and asked the farmer's wife to come in.

Once Karl-Artur and Thea were left alone, there was a moment's silence.

Thea then began to speak in a very different tone of voice than she had been using. Suddenly she was trembling with pure fervor:

'I've been sitting at home praying to God to help you,' she began. 'I knew, of course, that you wished to live in simplicity and poverty, but I would never have dreamt that you would ever be cobbling shoes and chopping wood. It is sure to be the end of you. I should be keeping watch over you, but I am not even allowed to invite you to my home. It's awful, awful.'

Karl-Artur gestured as if to prevent her from continuing, but instead she moved close to him, speaking with great force, as if trying to make the words penetrate deep into his soul.

'Mr. Sundler has a brother,' she said, 'who is the parish organist up in Ekshärad. He's visiting us just now, and yesterday we were chatting, and you and the ten children came up in the conversation. He happened to mention that there is a man in Ekshärad who comes from Korskyrka and who seems to be Crofter Matts' brother. The man has, at least, mentioned a poor brother with several children a number of times, and he does not seem to know that his brother has died. My brother-in-law is going home this afternoon. Shall I ask him to inform the children's uncle that they are living on the charity of you and your wife, or shall I ask him not to mention it?'

Karl-Artur had risen. He stood erect, chest raised, shoulders high. Everything he had suffered through this past winter for the sake of the children went through his mind. To be freed of them, to be freed of them in a good, honest way!

'You never get a quiet moment to think,' Thea insisted. 'Any schoolboy would blush to write sermons like yours are now. You, who used to speak with the voice of an angel, who knew every secret of God's kingdom. Now you know nothing.'

Karl-Artur still said nothing. He had of late begun to feel accustomed to his meager way of life. The children and he were good friends now. He felt a bit cowardly sending them away, not fighting the battle to the end.

'Say something,' Mrs. Sundler begged. 'I need to know. Any minute now the doctor will be finished with Per-Erik's mother. Give me some sign, even a tiny one!'

He gave a laugh. As if there were more than one possible answer! As Thea spoke he felt his bonds break, saw winter ice melt, heard songs of freedom.

He did something he had never done before. He bent down, embraced Thea, and out of the infinite gratitude in his heart he kissed that ugly little woman right on the lips.

II

Who was she, to contradict her own husband, a man so much wiser than she, who could preach the word of God, and admonish and exhort every petty sinner who had fallen into wrongful ways? She would have to believe that what he was doing was also right, now that he had let the children leave them.

When she came to think of it, she did not really know what else her husband could have done, since the children's blood uncle had come to fetch them and look after them. If that uncle had been a poor man, there might have been some reason, but since he turned out to be a well-to-do man with a farm of his own and a kind wife but no children, how could Karl-Artur deny him the opportunity to take his nieces and nephews back home with him?

To begin with she had not wanted to see the man as anything but a fraud, coming to entice the children away from her. But the two eldest siblings had recognized him, as had others. It was just that no one had had the slightest idea that things had gone well for him. When he left Korskyrka, he had been just as impoverished as his brother.

The parish where this uncle was living was way up north, so there was nothing strange about his not having heard that Crofter Matts had died and the children placed in the care of strangers. But as soon as he knew the state of things he made his way to Korskyrka to invite the ten children to join him in his good home.

And that was kind of him, of course. She just had to believe that he was a good, fine man. Neither she nor anyone else could begrudge him taking the children up to Ekshärad.

Karl-Artur had not been a bit mulish about it, but he had spoken so eloquently about the special dispensation of the Lord that had sent this stranger to them to ease the heavy burden they were both bearing, particularly her, of course. He had made her think that because she was expecting a little child of her own come summer, she would not have been able to work as hard for the others as before.

She could not but agree with him about that, and so she had grown ambivalent and found it difficult to know what she really wanted. All the talk of God had confused her. The children were so sweet. Perhaps God wanted them to have a better life than they had with her. And Karl-Artur had clearly been having a difficult time, more difficult than she had realized. She understood that now, from all his eloquence in speaking in favor of allowing the children to go.

The children had shown surprisingly little unhappiness about leaving her. They were excited about seeing the world. Their uncle had horses and cows and pigs and laying hens they would be allowed to care for and feed. And he had a dog that could give you his paw after a meal and imitate the voice of the cantor leading the congregation in a hymn. The children had never imagined they could be so fortunate as to hear a dog singing hymns.

When they had left, she sat down on the loose stone step outside the cottage, and she was sitting there still. She was completely listless. She had not sat still like that with her hands in her lap in the last couple of years except on Sundays and hardly even then. She said to herself that she should be pleased now that she could finally rest up.

Her husband joined her outside. He sat down right beside her, took her hand and spoke of how happy they were going to be now. He believed that the children had been sent to them to try them, and their being taken away now was a sign that God had seen all they had done for the little ones and found it good.

She knew, of course, that she was nothing compared with him, that she knew nothing of God's ways, and that she had not even managed to learn book-reading, but still she grew angry with him. She answered that those children had been sent to her by the grace of God, and that she could not understand what evil she had committed that had resulted in them being taken away from her.

When she answered him thus, her husband rose and went off without a word. She had not called him back to her, nor did she regret it. She was like a bowl filled with bitter bile. It wasn't easy to come close to her without the bile swilling over.

She knew she ought to go inside to clean the cottage and straighten up after the children, but going inside frightened her. She was afraid of the vast emptiness she would encounter there.

Now she was going to be as helpless and forsaken as she

had been early in their marriage, before she took on the brood of children. Since then she had felt secure and at peace. No, how could she have been so foolish as to let anyone take the children away from her?

She sat remembering the trap that had driven them off. The children had loaded on their bundles of clothing and the other belongings it was suitable for them to take along. There was room for some of the littlest ones to ride, while their uncle and the older children were to walk alongside. He had said, laughing, that he would look as if he were one of the many vagrants who rode the countryside with a trap full of kids and bundles.

It had been surprisingly easy for the children to say farewell to her. Their heads had been full of the horse and trap, and of what they were taking along, and the only thing they were really unhappy about was that the kitten refused to be taken. They had hardly shed a tear. Neither had she wept. But the minute they were gone, fear possessed her. She saw their uncle's face in her mind's eye. She was far from certain that he was really as kind and gentle as he had appeared to be in their cottage. He was probably not what he seemed to be, but a vicious, tightfisted man. The children were sure to have a hard life with him.

All this came to her as a certainty, she had no doubt. She wished she could have run after the children and taken them back, but she hadn't been able to bring herself to, and now it was too late. Why had she not done it while there was time? Now that thought plagued her, she imagined the children cold and starving.

Spring was in the air. The snow had melted and the sun was shining down on her, softly and pleasantly, as she sat there. It would not have been long until the children could have moved back into their cottage for the summer, which would have made things easier for Karl-Artur.

She tried to cheer herself up by thinking that she would no longer have to be making meals for more than one person. Nor would she have to sit up half the night darning holes in socks.

If only she knew that they would have their socks darned where they were going! If only she knew that they would be urged to say their prayers at bedtime! The littlest girl was terribly afraid of the dark. If only she knew that someone would be looking after her; she was only six years old and did not dare to go to sleep unless there was someone sitting next to her holding her hand!

THE CUPBOARD

For the first few days after Anna had let the children go, she was too apathetic and full of remorse to even tidy up after them. She was convinced that the children were suffering privations and ill treatment with their relations, and that she and her husband would have an enormous price to pay for having allowed them to move to such disreputable people.

This all came over her without her volition, like a fever. She did her best to fight it, but that was impossible. She had no reason in the world to be so worried, but she could not let go of the thought that the uncle who had come to collect the children had a disagreeable, dangerous face, and she imagined his wife, about whom she knew nothing, as the worst possible witch. She was also certain that the brunt of the penance would have to be paid by the baby she was expecting. It would come into the world deformed or deaf and dumb. Or else she, Anna, would die in childbirth, leaving her child to grow up motherless.

It did her very little good to talk with Karl-Artur about these matters. He believed her neither when she told him that the children were suffering nor when she told him that the two of them were going to be punished. He was extremely gentle with her, that cannot be denied, but the fears she entertained did not seem to him to be worthy of consideration, and so she had to struggle with them on her own.

One morning she believed she had discovered a cure. She set about moving the loom, the spinning wheel and all the other paraphernalia out of the kitchen. She carried the bench-bedstead and the trundle bed, which belonged to the children, back up to their own cottage, which she locked up tight. Then she scrubbed the floor, re-whitewashed the walls, washed and dried all the utensils, and soon found herself sitting in a kitchen just as neat and tidy and as desolate as it had been the first time she set foot in it.

Once she had removed everything that might remind her of her brood of children, she said to herself that she would pretend that everything was as it had been early in her marriage. The children had never been there; they were just a dream she had had. If she could just get away from the thought that they had ever really lived there with her, everything would be all right. Because of course no one went around unhappy and upset about a little dream.

'You know very well,' she mumbled to herself, 'that young newly married women just spend their time thinking of their husbands. Now pull out your knitting needles and your yarn and make him a pair of mittens, so you'll have a project to enjoy! Think of nothing else but how remarkable it is that you are now a pastor's wife and have been raised above all the other peddler women!'

And so she started on those mittens, but barely had she done a couple of rows before she noticed that the edge of the table where she was sitting had a couple of stick figures carved into it with a sharp knife. Surely one of the younger boys had been at it. Those little mischief-makers knew, of course, that they were not allowed to whittle at the table's edge, but it was impossible to get them to resist hacking at anything made of wood.

She raised her head to start lecturing, but there were no flaxen-haired heads on which to take out her annoyance. There was nothing there but the whitewashed walls, staring at her, empty and expressionless.

She sat with the knitting needles in her lap for quite some time. But then she got up quickly, fetched a knife, and took out the whittled figures with a sharp slice along the table's edge. She grimaced as if she had cut her own flesh, and then resolutely picked up her knitting again.

'How foolish I am,' she thought. 'It was Karl-Artur and no one but Karl-Artur who was at it. He's the one who usually sits on this side of the table at mealtime. There have never been any children in this kitchen. How could poor people like us even dare to consider taking in strangers' children? It couldn't be done. We must be content if we have enough for food and clothing for ourselves and the little one we are expecting.'

She went on knitting, her lips tightly pursed and her eyes firmly on her work. While working, she wondered whether everything that might remind her of the children had now been removed, so that she could go on imagining that they had never been around her.

A few minutes later she heard soft noises followed by a thud. The kitten, that had been the best possible playmate for the ten children, had awoken from his nap in the corner by the hearth and jumped up onto the table to play with her ball of yarn.

Quickly, she captured it. There was nothing that could carry her thoughts to her former playmates faster than that kitten, and she wished she could toss it outside. But as soon as she felt that soft, warm body in her hands, she had no choice but to stroke it. She watched her yarn fall to the floor, and saw the kitten bound after it. The ball rolled away. The kitten tried to hold it still, but it kept on rolling. Anna, too, started trying to get hold of the yarn, so it wouldn't be ruined, and a wild game ensued. The kitten chased the ball of yarn from one end of the kitchen to the other, and the ball behaved as if it had a life of its own. Anna could not help but giggle, trying in vain to halt its progress. 'How the children must be laughing at us,' she thought, letting the game go on longer than it had to, to amuse the children.

'Children, why not come and give me a hand?' she cried.

Barely had she heard her own voice, when she remembered. She grabbed at the cat, smacked its back so roughly it let out a cry, and tossed it outside.

'How am I ever going to get the children out of my thoughts?' she said aloud, winding the ball of yarn back up. 'There's no point in going mad, after all.'

She paced the kitchen for a while, wringing her hands as if in anguish, but after a few minutes she was back at her knitting. And she was pleased of it when, not two minutes later, the door opened and old Karin from Risgården farm in Medstubyn appeared.

Karin from Risgården was just stopping by with greetings from Medstubyn as she had done both last year and the year before. But the other times the kitchen had been full of children and paraphernalia and abuzz with work. Karin's eyes grew wide at the present tidiness.

'What on earth has happened here?' she cried, looking around the room.

Anna's questions began to hail down on Karin from Risgården. She wanted to know all about how her mother was, and Erik from Job's farm, and the sheriff and his wife, and the pastor's family, as well as Ingborg from Risgården and Cantor Medberg. There wasn't a soul in all of Medstubyn Anna didn't want to hear about.

Once her initial curiosity was satisfied, Anna rushed to prepare the coffee. She hurried to the woodshed for firewood and to the well for water. She blew at the fire to make it catch. She ground the coffee beans, sliced some bread and laid the table with cups and saucers. She was quick on her feet, and clattered noisily with the cups and saucers. Karin from Risgården realized there was no point in trying to ask about the ten children until Anna was settled at the table with her coffee.

When they finally sat there with a cube of sugar in their mouths and the scalding hot coffee poured into the saucers to cool, Anna had another barrage of questions for Karin to answer. How were things going for all of the men and women of Medstubyn? Was Annstu Lisa still peddling her wares, at her age, and was she just as mad for a game of cards as always?

As Annstu Lisa was Karin's especially good friend and fellow peddler, all her misdeeds and little tricks provided conversation enough for a first cup of coffee and a second. According to Karin, a woman like her ought not to be allowed to travel the roads. Being associated with her brought shame upon her honest fellow peddlers.

Once the coffee pot was empty, it was time for Karin from

Risgården to be on her way. She was no fool, and understood that Anna had no desire to tell her what had happened to the children, but since she also knew that she could easily find it out from the neighbors, she did not bother her with any questions.

However, when Karin from Risgården had her pack lifted onto her old, bent back and had said goodbye, standing there with her hand on the doorknob, she turned once again toward the room.

'Heavens, I nearly forgot what I actually came for,' she said, and began digging around in her skirt pockets for her moneybag.

'You didn't even ask if I'd made any profit for you,' she went on, extending a fifty daler note to Anna.

The previous spring, when Karin had visited Korskyrka, Anna had given her a pack of ribbons and some lengths of lace the children had made, and asked her to sell them. Although Anna hadn't forgotten about this, she had been trying her best not to bring up any subject that had to do with the children.

Fifty dalers was also too much money by far, so Anna asked Karin if she had anything smaller, because she was unable to give her change.

'No change needed,' Karin assured her. 'It's all yours. You see, once I had sold the things you gave me, I invested your money in other goods, which led to other goods, and now you're up to fifty. So there you are. You need the money, too, having so many mouths to feed.'

Karin from Risgården was quick-witted, in spite of her age. She hurried to shut the door behind her, and hastened down the hill so as to be spared any expressions of gratitude. Just a few minutes later, Anna came hurrying after her. This time she was more like her old self, thanking Karin volubly and accompanying her all the way to the doctor's, where Karin hoped for some good trade, since the doctor's wife must have plenty of money now, thanks to her wealthy sister-in-law, and surely didn't have to pinch pennies as she always had in the past.

Anna sat in the kitchen with the fifty daler bill in her hand for quite a while, looking down at it, a smile of pleasure on her face. She cared about money, always had, but this time it was not the unexpected profit she was celebrating. This was something far greater; it was a sign and a miracle. She had been anticipating punishment for having let the children go and now, instead, she had been given this huge gift from them. Never had she imagined such happiness. All her fright and anxiety evaporated. Her soul was filled with the very opposite of what she had been imagining and fearing.

She could not possibly keep this happiness to herself, so she went in to see her husband, who was at the desk in his well-appointed room. She displayed the money and asked him to look after it for her. Out there in the kitchen, there was no safe place for her to keep it.

Karl-Artur looked up somewhat distractedly from his work when she came in. He did not really follow what she was saying, as she explained that the money was payment for little pieces the children had produced all by themselves and that they had sent her the money to thank her for taking care of them, and as a sign that neither she nor he was to be punished for having let them go.

Karl-Artur did not contradict her, although her reasoning seemed a bit blurry to him. He could see that his wife's sense of security and her good humor had returned, and that was quite sufficient for him. He even proposed that she might spend this unexpected windfall on something she would really be pleased to have.

Anna liked that idea, and went straight back to the kitchen to consider how she could best put this great unexpected wealth to use. And it did not take long for her to know what she wanted. Ever since she walked into her kitchen for the first time, she had wished it had a large cupboard with drawers in the bottom half and shelves and doors on top. A big floor-to-ceiling cupboard was not merely a useful possession. It also endowed the whole room with a certain status.

Anna could not imagine anything they could make better use of, and since her husband agreed and the money was at hand in his desk drawer, she saw no impediment to going right to see the village carpenter, a skilled craftsman, to order the cupboard from him.

The carpenter lived along the main road in the village, a couple of houses past the organist's, and as Anna was walking down the street she bumped into Mrs. Sundler, who must have been out for a walk to see whether any spring wildflowers were yet in bloom. At least it looked that way, as she had a few blue wood blue anemones in her hand.

It struck Anna that Mrs. Sundler was not wearing a coat. She had failed to notice how warm it had grown. Since the departure of the children, she had thought about nothing else, paying no attention to things like the weather. Suddenly she became aware that the sun was shining, and that the sky above was blue with little woolly white clouds. All this seemed to her to be part of the joy she was feeling that very day, and when Mrs. Sundler greeted her and extended a hand, she did not press on, as she might have done any other day, but stopped. She said to herself that there could be nothing wrong with exchanging a word. She certainly couldn't go on forever being on bad terms with a person who lived in the same village.

Mrs. Sundler told Anna that she felt like a prisoner who had been released, since her husband was so much improved that he could go out on his own again. She had been for a long walk in the woods, and could hardly find words to tell Anna what a pleasure it had been. She felt herself thawing and taking on new life, reflecting what she saw nature doing.

For the first time since her arrival at Korskyrka, Anna Svärd felt some kind of sympathy with Mrs. Sundler. She said a few words to indicate that she had heard it had been been a difficult winter for her, and started to move on.

But Mrs. Sundler kept her. Having been cooped up all winter, she found it so nice to have an old friend to talk to, and she certainly considered whoever was married to Karl-Artur an old friend. Would Mrs. Ekenstedt not come in for a few minutes of conversation? They were almost on her doorstep.

Anna had no desire to be thwarted in her errand of

ordering the cupboard, so she brusquely declined. But since she always felt uncomfortable around people of a better class, she was afraid she had offended Mrs. Sundler, and felt it necessary to explain. So she told her that she had come into some unexpected money and was on her way to the carpenter's to order a cupboard. Mrs. Sundler brightened up at the story, saying that she completely understood Anna's hurry, and congratulated her on being able to buy something as pretty and useful as a cupboard.

After that, she really did let her go, and Anna soon found herself in the carpenter's workshop. She did not rush, but took her time in there. She and the carpenter spent more than an hour discussing all the details of shape and height, drawers and handles, color and decoration. Nor was it an easy matter to settle on a price, but in the end they reached an agreement on that as well.

When Anna headed home with a promise from the carpenter that the cupboard would be ready in a month and at a price of no more than forty dalers, she was so pleased with herself she just had to go in to Karl-Artur and tell him about the agreement.

But Karl-Artur appeared anything but overjoyed.

'I would never have thought you were going to take the matter in hand so hastily. I would have liked to come along and talk with the carpenter.'

'And I'd never have thought you'd make time for such a thing.'

'No, not normally, but in this case…'

He had begun quite eagerly, but stopped in mid-sentence and bit his lip.

His wife looked at him searchingly. She could see him blushing, embarrassed as a schoolgirl.

'What is it you're getting at?' she asked.

'What I'm getting at?' Karl-Artur repeated. 'Well, in my view, since you feel the money has come to us in such a remarkable way, we ought not to use it for our own purposes, but put it to some truly admirable use instead.'

'Don't tell me you've gone and given my money away?'

his wife asked him, but without the slightest suspicion that it might be true.

Karl-Artur coughed and cleared his throat a couple of times, and then it all came out. Sundler, the organist, had been to see him. He had been terribly pleased to finally be up and about again after being ill all winter. Karl-Artur had said that he should take especially good care of himself during the coming summer, and build up his strength so he wouldn't be struck down again next winter, and the organist had said that if only he could take the waters at Loka spa, his gout would surely improve, but he could not afford the luxury.

'I cannot believe you would go and give him the money the children sent us!' cried Anna accusingly.

'My dear friend,' said Karl-Artur, going all formal and supercilious, 'can you think of a nobler use of a gift from the Lord than using it for an act of charity?'

Anna moved very close to him. She was pale, and her dark eyes gleamed like trembling sparks. She almost looked as if she were about to wrench back her money by brute force.

'But did you not realize, my husband, that the money was a sign and a greeting from the children to us? Do you not remember how that man behaved toward me the last time he was here?'

'Perhaps that is precisely what I was thinking about,' Karl-Artur told her.

Anna laughed out loud, but with no sign of mirth. Karl-Artur turned toward her impatiently.

'Do you find that so incredible?'

'Oh no, not that. But something else came into my mind. I was just wondering exactly when the organist stopped by.'

'The organist? Well, it must have been about half an hour ago. He didn't stay long. I'm surprised you didn't meet him on your way home.'

'I expect he went out of his way to avoid it.'

She laughed again, an awful, appalling laugh. Karl-Artur drew himself up, assuming as much dignity as he could muster.

'Will you please be so kind as to explain why you are

laughing?'

'I'm laughing not at you but just at myself. How could I have been such a fool as to tell that Thea about the fifty dalers? I should have known she would find a way to get it off you.'

He was a bit intimidated. His wife's eyes gleamed with such malicious delight that he knew there must be some underlying explanation to which he was not party, but he pounded the table with his fist to inspire a bit of respect.

'Now you tell me once and for all what you are laughing about!'

At last she told him the whole story, but he found himself utterly incapable of believing that Mrs. Sundler had sent her husband to see him with the express purpose of wheedling the fifty dalers out of him. It just had to have been a coincidence.

'It can't be true,' he said. 'That would almost have been dishonest. Are you trying to tell me that Thea rushed home and sent her husband over here because you told her that we were in possession of that money? Thea, who is such a generous, noble, conscientious soul?'

'Well, I sure can't tell you how it all hangs together, but you must admit there's something odd about his coming here to borrow money just today.'

Karl-Artur defended Mrs. Sundler, but at the same time he looked as distraught as if the tower of Babel had come crashing down before his eyes. Anna remembered that Sunday evening two years earlier when Thea and the organist had come to their cottage to call her to account about Thea's Sunday hat. Perhaps it was worth the fifty dalers to see the disappointment on her husband's face now.

But her restitution was short-lived. Steps were heard in the passageway, and a few minutes later there was a delicate knock at Karl-Artur's study door, and Thea stepped inside.

Karl-Artur turned toward his desk and poked through his papers, without looking at her. Mrs. Sundler, ignoring his presence, turned directly to his wife.

'My dear Mrs. Ekenstedt, ' she said, 'please accept my apology. I heard from my husband that Karl-Artur had been so extraordinarily kind as to lend him fifty dalers. I told him right off that it was probably the same fifty daler note that you, Mrs. Ekenstedt, had earned, and that we could not accept it. Mrs. Ekenstedt is buying a cupboard with it, I told him, which she needs very badly as things look so bad there now, with all her kitchenware on open shelves, gathering dust. So I asked Mr. Sundler to give me the money, so I could come over and see what the situation was. I told him that if it was Mrs. Ekenstedt's money he would just have to put up with his gout, because in that case we would have to return it. And I assure you, Mrs. Ekenstedt, that I felt terribly sorry for him because he was so thrilled to be able to make the journey to Loka spa, and take the waters for his gout. But he did realize immediately that I was right. '

As she finished her harangue she pulled out the fifty daler note from her pocket and extended it to Anna in the same way Karin from Risgården had done just a few hours earlier.

But Anna barely noticed. She was looking not at Mrs. Sundler but at her husband. He was standing by his desk not speaking, but with every word Thea said his posture grew more erect. He seemed to grow taller, and he turned further and further in Thea's direction. When she finished speaking he was standing there, his brow clear and eyes wide open, and the look on the face of that little fish-eyed woman was one which Anna might have envied her. Then he turned toward his wife, Anna, who had just reached out to take the money. His brow furrowed, his eye darkened, his arms crossed his chest.

There was no choice. She would have to sacrifice her fifty dalers, to keep the other woman from appearing to him to be a wonder of righteousness.

'You just keep that money!' she said to Mrs. Sundler. 'It's not the same money I told you about earlier today. Your money belongs to Karl-Artur.'

'Can it be true? Can it really be true?' Thea cried, over-whelmed with joy and gratitude. Then without many words she departed almost immediately, as if she were afraid something would happen after all to force her to return the money.

Karl-Artur's wife wondered about her husband, who was usually so strict when it came to the truth, wondering why he failed to tell Thea that Anna had lied. Instead, on this occasion he seemed to be more than satisfied with Anna's not having told the truth.

He accompanied Thea through the passageway and out to the door. When he came back in, he moved to embrace Anna.

'Oh, my love,' he said, 'that was one of the most generous moments I have ever beheld. Both you and Thea! I don't know which of you I admire more.'

His wife shoved him away and stood there with her fists clenched and her face distorted with rage.

'I would have forgiven you anything but that – your letting her take the money away from me,' she said, and left the room.

THE DECK OF CARDS

I

She had not created herself, she could not help being what she was. She could not do anything about the fact that she was the kind of person who went around not speaking when she was furious with someone. Even the worst people of that kind usually recovered their power of speech after a day or two, but she had been so unjustly treated that she simply clenched her jaws around it and said not a word for over a week.

Nor *could* she get down to any work. She just had to sit in the corner by the hearth, as close to the fire as possible, rocking back and forth, her hands over her face. The only thing she could do was to drink her coffee. She had a little three-legged pot that had followed her everywhere over the years, at the bottom of her peddler's sack. It was now constantly on the boil, and she drank cup after cup.

She did a bit of cleaning and made her husband's meals, but that was really all. She simply could no longer sit at the table with him, so as soon as she had put his food on the table she crept back into her corner by the hearth, and sat there rocking, without looking his way.

Her husband, oh that husband of hers! If only she had been married to a farmhand from Medstubyn, who would have understood at what a loss she was as she sat there, and that she needed his help! A man like that would at the very least have taken her coffee pot and tossed it out the door, and forced her to sit down with some darning, and that would have done her good.

But this one, he'd come over to her now and then and inquire how she was feeling and ask her nicely if she wouldn't speak just a word to him. When she remained silent, he would pat her gently on the back, reassure her that she would be feeling better soon, and walk away.

That was all the help she got from him.

She knew what he was imagining. He had surely heard it said that women often do strange things when they are in the family way. So now he likely thought that she was suffering from some such ailment.

But that was not what was going on and he, a learned man, should have known better. She was also firmly convinced that he knew what she needed but was pretending he didn't understand. He had never liked the ten children. He did not want them back. If he had to choose, he would prefer to let her sit there and suffer.

No, she had not created herself, she *could* not help being what she was. Her worries about the children ached and chafed inside her constantly. There, up north where the children were, there were so many shifty women who walked from parish to parish begging for alms. They always had swarms of children in their wake, and if they had too few of their own they would borrow others. She was now absolutely convinced that the six youngest ones had been lent out to a woman of that kind. They were dressed in rags and sackcloth, to look like indigents. They were forced to remain barefoot, although the snow had barely melted up there, and they were beaten and abused in every possible way. Beggar children were not supposed to look well-fed or content.

Not until the moment when she saw the children safe and sound would she be herself again. But how could she tell Karl-Artur that? She could not. She had to work it out on her own.

Any man back in Medstubyn would have seen what it was that was plaguing her, and he would have readied his horse and made his way to Ekshärad to collect the children the very next day. Or if he had been unable to help her in that way, he would have seized her by the hair and pulled her out of her corner by the hearth and into the middle of the floor, and that message would also have been effective. But this husband, he spoke to her gently and patted her on the back, and left it at that.

She was sick and tired of him. Not long ago he had been the person it made her happiest to see, but now she could hardly bear it when he came into the same room with her.

One dinnertime when he came in to eat, she was sitting with a little iron pipe between her lips, exhaling huge clouds of tobacco smoke. She knew this was not appropriate for a pastor's wife, but she *had* to do it. She had been commanded to do it. And now she was ever so curious as to how he would react to his wife sitting and smoking like the best of the peasants.

He looked horrified. 'Well, maybe now he'll finally see that he has to help me,' she thought.

'I must warn you that if you fill this room with tobacco smoke, I will be unable to eat in here,' her husband said. 'If you intend to carry on this way you'll have to bring my meals in to me.'

He wasn't even angry. He was kind and patient as before. She began to see that she would never receive any help from him.

After that, he took his meals in his study, but he never failed to come in and see how she was. As usual, he patted her on the back and said a few kind words. And that was how things went on, day after day.

Throughout, she heard the hall door opening many times a day, and she also heard loud, eager voices in his study. As he served a large parish, lots of people came to see him on official business, but she also knew that others came to see him concerning the state of their souls. Well, wasn't he just the person to advise others! How could he possibly counsel them? A man who was not even able to help his own poor wife!

A full week passed this way, when one day she found herself by the hearth with a knife concealed beneath her apron. She had been *commanded* to get that knife out. She was not particularly surprised about it, but she was puzzled about why it was nothing but a table knife. She could not do the least bit of harm either to herself or anyone else with it.

Later that morning her husband came into the kitchen to tell her he had been called out on parish affairs. He was off to see a crofter in the most distant part of the parish, at least twenty kilometers away. She would not need to bother about his midday meal, but he would be grateful if she had something ready for him when he returned around six that evening.

As usual she did not speak, but when he then added that she was looking a bit brighter than she had the day before, and would soon be herself again, she tugged at her apron. And when he reached out to give her one of those encouraging pats on the back, she pulled the apron roughly aside and he caught sight of the knife blade.

He drew back, as if she had been sitting with a rattlesnake in her lap. For a long time he was unable to speak. He just stood there shaking his head, at a complete loss for words.

'Anna, Anna,' he said at last, 'I think you must be very ill. We will have to do something about it. As soon as I get back tonight I will ask the doctor to come and examine you.'

And so he left. But now she knew what she needed to know. Now she knew that that man would never be able to help her out of her misery.

II

How good to leave home, even if you only have a rough farm trap to ride in, to take you away from your everyday worries! You become aware that whatever is plaguing you is transient, and that everything will be all right as soon as the little one you are expecting comes into the world, but your patience has been sorely tested of late, and it feels so indescribably good to get out into the world for a bit and see that life has more to offer than surliness and spite.

As soon as Karl-Artur had passed the doctor's garden and turned onto the village street he was met with pleasantness and good cheer. He saw red, white and yellow bunting fluttering in the air, and on both sides of the street there were market stands full of goods, while the street itself was so full of people that the horse made very slow progress.

In other words, it was market day in Korskyrka, and although it was nothing so grand as the autumn market, when people stocked up for the winter ahead, any itinerant market was a welcome sight and an excuse to have some fun. This market featured peddlers from Västergötland, selling cotton cloth, well suited to the coming warmer season, men from Dalarna selling plowshares and scythes that would be needed to plant and harvest, basket weavers wandering between the stands festooned with baskets that would be good to have for berry picking in summer. There were also weaver's reed makers with huge loads of reeds on their backs, which were selling best of all, as the long, light early summer days are precisely the right time to set up one's loom.

All in all it was a lovely sight, and what appealed most to Karl-Artur was the joy on people's faces. Wealthy merchants from Kristinehamn, Karlstad and Örebro who did not think too highly of themselves to travel around and peddle their wares were gathered there, dressed in handsome furs and sealskin hats, greeting their customers with gracious smiles. The peddler women from Dalarna were dressed in bright colors and stood cheerfully behind the simple counters on which they had set up their wares, and the villagers greeted one another, friends and acquaintances, with the natural gaiety spring brings out in us, when the cold, foul weather comes to an end and one no longer has to be shut indoors. It cannot be denied that schnapps surely also played a part in the general good humor, but so early in the day there were no reeling drunkards to be seen; there was no more than a slight edge of recklessness in the air, and a tendency toward gaiety.

In a couple of spots the road was so crowded that no vehicles could get through, they had to stop and wait. Karl-Artur did not mind, he was enjoying watching the amusing little scenes being played out in the throng. At one stall selling handsome, home-woven cotton fabric, there was a poor, threadbare old crofter holding a lovely young woman by the hand. The old man must have had a drink or two, and with the additional effects of the spring sunshine, he had been seized by a joyous abandon and shouted loudly to the stallholder:

'Bonander, Bonander, how much is that red cap? How much is that red cap, Bonander, Bonander?' However, the red cap he wanted to buy for his daughter was a grand straw hat lined with satin and sporting long, pink satin ribbons. The merchant had hung it from the front of his stall to entice the finer gentlewomen, and it embarrassed him that the crofter would want to buy it from him, so he pretended not to hear. But this only made his customer keep shouting, louder and louder, his:

'Bonander, Bonander, how much is that red cap?'

The crowd roared with laughter, the lads began imitating the poor old man, while Karl-Artur found it moving that he was so convinced the very loveliest hat at the entire market was completely appropriate attire for his daughter.

The trap moved forward a slight distance, but was then stopped anew. This time there was a foundryman, very well dressed and with a face both intelligent and handsome, who was drawing a large crowd. He stood in their midst, solemn and dignified, until he suddenly kicked up his heels in a leap and snapped his fingers.

'I'm drunk as a lord,' he said. 'And what great fun it is!'

A moment later he was serious again, standing erectly and silently for a bit until, completely unexpectedly, he repeated his leap and his finger snapping.

'I'm drunk as a lord,' he repeated. 'And what great fun it is!'

The crowd displayed its amusement, while Karl-Artur, who abhorred all kinds of intoxication, found this behavior distasteful and turned his gaze elsewhere, until his driver informed him that the whole scene was nothing but a joke.

'He's no more drunk than I am,' he said. 'He puts on a scene like that at every market he comes to, just to make people laugh.'

Karl-Artur came to think with sadness of his wife, crouching by the hearth with no idea of the merriment taking place nearby. 'What a shame that she's not here,' he thought. 'She might have met up with one or two of the old friends she holds so dear. That would bring her out of the gloom that is weighing her down.'

Soon, though, his thoughts took a different turn. As usual at markets, there were quite a few vagrants, rogues and other itinerants gathered, who made what they could from trading horses and selling clocks. One of these characters now came galloping down the road at full tilt, probably to show off his horses to some presumptive buyer. Karl-Artur saw him from a long way off, a slim, dark-complexioned man standing in his trap in order to better wield the whip over the head of a pathetic little brown nag. The man was yelling and cursing, the horse was running headlong, wild with fear, the crowd was rushing to the sides of the road so as not to be run over. Karl-Artur's driver, too, tried to move aside, but there was no room, and for a moment it looked as if the two traps would collide.

At the very last moment the tramp called out a calming word to his horse and pulled on the reins. Then, as he calmly passed the young pastor, he politely lifted his cap, which was missing half its brim.

'Greetings, cousin,' he shouted. 'Damn, you do look much the worse for wear. Toss off that black coat and join me! This is the life, you know!' He cracked the whip at his horse, which took off at a trot and Karl-Artur, embarrassed over the encounter, urged his driver to do his best now to escape the market throng.

When they eventually left the village for the main road, the young pastor sat thinking about his cousin, Göran Löwensköld of Hedeby, who had fled from the paternal home as a youth, joined a band of tinkers and other itinerants, and never shown the slightest interest in returning to a civilized life.

To date, Karl-Artur had always considered his cousin a down-and out, a failure and a disgrace to the family, but that day he was less inclined to subject him to his usual severe verdict. Perhaps the life of a tramp had a charm of its own. It allowed for freedom, it allowed for the unexpected. There was an adventure waiting around every bend. For a man like that there were no sermons to be written by a certain time, no dusty ledgers to enter things in, no endlessly dull parish meetings. Perhaps his cousin had not made such an unworthy choice after all, in exchanging the drawing-rooms of manor houses for life on the road.

Karl-Artur, too, had quite a lot of experience of being on the road. During his years at university he had made the long journey between Karlstad and Uppsala four times a year, and become quite well acquainted with the traveling life. These journeys had been quite carefree. He recalled with great pleasure colorful wildflowers growing on the roadside, lovely views from hilltops, and packed meals eaten in the courtyards of pleasant inns, conversations with the jovial drivers with whom he became acquainted over the years and who asked him with puzzled voices whether he intended to keep at it there in Uppsala until he was as wise as King Solomon.

He, who had always loved the outdoor life, had enjoyed the journeys for their own sake. While others complained he thought to himself: 'What on earth are they grumbling about? The road has always been my friend. I like the steep hills that make travel so varied. The deep, monotonous forests have their own ability to trigger the imagination. Nor do I despise a bumpy road. And once a broken axle made a whole village my friends. A snowstorm once gave me the opportunity to be a guest at the manor of a Count. '

As he sat contemplating all this, triggered by the glimpse he had just had of his relative, something unexpected happened. He had a completely new insight. It came to him like a bolt out of the blue. It astonished him so greatly that he stood up in the trap with a shout.

The driver pulled the reins, staring at him.

'Don't tell me you've forgotten your cassock, Sir?'

Karl-Artur sat back down, reassuring his driver. No, he hadn't forgotten anything. All was well. On the contrary, he had found something he had lost.

He sat for the remainder of the journey, hands clasped, eyes radiant with the delight of his new thought.

As he had said to the driver, the conclusion he had come to was nothing new. Hundreds, even thousands of times, he had read those words in the Gospel According to Matthew, the words of Jesus when he sent his disciples to preach the message of the coming of the kingdom of heaven. But never before had he taken in their full significance. Not until now had he realized that Jesus had really commanded the apostles to head out as impoverished wanderers, bearing neither sack nor stick, bearing nothing but their wondrous message to the farms along their way, to peasant cottages and noble mansions. They were to make themselves seen at markets, gathering crowds around them, they were to approach other pilgrims as they rested at inns, they were to converse with other wanderers, and everywhere they were to tell of the miracle of heaven.

How could he not previously have realized that he was meant to obey this commandment, given in no uncertain terms? He had merely stood at his pulpit like other pastors, waiting for the people to come unto him. But that was not what Jesus had meant. His intention had been for the disciples to go out onto the roads and paths themselves, to reach out to the people.

He, Karl-Artur, had had a plan of his own, a self-promoting plan. He had wanted to create a paradise on earth, which would stand as an example to the people. At that moment he realized why he had failed. He realized why he had met with so much resistance, why he had been deprived of his eloquence, why he had brought down such great suffering. God had wanted to show him that he had made the wrong decisions. Christ did not want his servant to be a man with a fixed dwelling within four walls. His rightful servant was to be a bird on the wing, a free wanderer, a poor man who lived in the bosom of nature. He was to accept food and drink offered by the mercy of God, starve and freeze according to His will. He would sleep in a bed when God saw fit, and if one morning he was found dead in a snowdrift, all that meant was that God had called his fatigued wanderer home to his glory.

'That is the path to true freedom,' he thought ecstatically. 'I thank Thee, Lord, for having allowed me to see it before it is too late.'

'When I am back at home,' he mumbled to himself, 'I shall write to the bishop. I will request to be released from my position in Korskyrka and will resign from the Swedish state church. Of course I want to go on as a preacher, and I do not wish to preach some new dogma. But I can no longer be subject to canon law, to a bishop or a consistory. I wish to preach the word of Christ as he himself decreed, to become an itinerant of the Lord, a beggar-preacher, a traveler of God.'

Utterly overcome, he allowed himself to be engrossed by these fantasies. Life seemed to him to have taken on new meaning. Once again it was full and fascinating.

'My wife may live on in my cottage,' he thought. 'She will be happy there when she does not have to see me. She will call home the ten children. There is no need for me to worry about her. She will be able to supply all her needs through her own work.'

At once he felt freed from all his difficulties. His heart throbbed gently, as if to a dance rhythm, which filled him with infinite delight.

III

Karl-Artur was not home by six, it was nearly eight before he stepped down from the trap at his own home.

A moment later when he opened the kitchen door – ah, he had not opened that door in such a fine frame of mind for a very long time – he halted on the threshold in astonishment at the sight that met his eyes.

His wife had left her place by the hearth. She had moved to the table under the window, where she sat playing cards with two men he did not recognize. At the very moment he entered she pulled a card from her hand and played it with a cheerful shout:

'Spades, and I've got 'em covered.'

'Not quite, Anna, my king takes home that trick,' said one of the others, playing his card.

The game was interrupted. They had seen Karl-Artur, standing in the doorway with a look of horror on his face.

'These are two old friends from my peddlin' days who've come to visit,' said his wife without rising. 'We're havin' a bit o' fun, like in old times, when we'd meet up at one o' the inns after a market day.'

As Karl-Artur approached, the two men stood up. One was wearing a black velvet vest buttoned all the way up, with a long black coat of duffel cloth on top of it. He was ruddy faced and bald, and looked jovial and prosperous. Karl-Artur recognized him as the vendor, Bonander, who had that lovely pink hat hanging on the post at his market stall. The other fellow was dressed in a traditional long sheepskin coat from Dalarna. He was a handsome man with fine features. His hair was cut short at the front but quite long at the sides.

'This here's August Bonander from Mark,' said Anna, 'a fine fellow with a covered stand who travels from market to market by horse and cart, selling his wares along the roads in between. It's amazing he'd even look at a poor lass like me from Dalarna or at Lars the Raven here, who have always made our way on foot, with our sacks on our backs.'

The stallholder waved politely, as if haggling with a customer and dismissing too low an offer, and began saying what an honor it always was for him to spend time with the gem of all the peddler women, Anna Svärd. But Karl-Artur interrupted.

'My wife's friends are always welcome,' he said, 'but I must inform you at once that card playing is not allowed in my home.'

He said this in a kind tone, but with great dignity. The strangers found themselves flushing and gazing around awkwardly, but Anna had a reply ready at once.

'You´re mad!' she exclaimed. 'I won't have you coming in and spreading a vile atmosphere. You go right to your room!

I've put out some supper there for you. Now you let us be!'

Karl-Artur, who had never before heard his wife address him in that tone, found it terribly painful, but he kept himself under control and said, as calmly and politely as before:

'Could you not just sit here and talk? Good friends must have plenty of old times to recollect.'

'Go on, August!' said Anna. 'Just play your card. The man's mad and won't give up until he's taken everything I care about away.'

'Anna!' Karl-Artur cried sharply.

'Well, you can't deny that you took away my three-day wedding, can you? And what about the parsonage I was expecting? Didn't you take away the children, too, and my fifty daler note? And now you want to take my card game away! Go on, August! '

The stallholder did not obey her command. Both he and the peddler from Dalarna sat still, waiting for the argument between husband and wife to end. Neither of them was intoxicated, and it is likely enough that Karl-Artur might very well have managed to persuade them to give up playing cards if he had been able to stay calm. But he had no patience with his wife's daring to contradict him, and moreover in the presence of strangers. He put out his hand to grab her cards.

At the same moment Lars the Raven, who spent his days wandering the roads with a huge sack full of cast iron goods on his back, made a movement with his arm. It was a small, almost imperceptible movement but it sent Karl-Artur flying across the floor like a swatted fly, and had there not been a chair in the way he would have fallen. For a moment he sat gasping for breath after this sudden attack, but as he had now been chopping wood for a couple of hours a day for several weeks, he, too, was a powerful man. As he began to rush at his opponent, a pair of hands pressed his arms firmly against his body, and he found himself lifted into the air and carried into his study. All this happened slowly and cautiously, and could hardly be called violence. The doors were kicked open; he was deposited carefully on the bed and left there without a word.

And there he lay, gnashing his teeth with anger and

humiliation. But from the very first, he had known there was nothing he could do. The other man's power was completely overwhelming. Unless he wanted to run for the sheriff and get him to drive the two strangers from his home, there was nothing he could do.

He lay waiting for hours. Through the thin walls he listened to the laughter and chatter, the slapping of the table when a good card was played. A terrible hatred of his wife was awakened in him, and he made wild plans for the revenge he would exact when the two men had gone.

Finally they left, and his wife went into the bedroom. There was total silence.

He got up, crept down the passageway to his wife's door, but found that she had locked it and removed the key.

He pounded on the door several times, but there was no reply. So he went back to his study to get a candle, and then hurried out into the kitchen in the hope of finding a tool to force open the door to the bedroom.

The first thing he saw in the kitchen was the deck of cards, which was still in the middle of the table. It struck him that he ought to take the opportunity to destroy it, his enemy.

'Anna is in safe keeping,' he thought to himself. 'She can't get away.'

In the drawer under the table he found a pair of scissors and started cutting up the cards. He cut each one individually into tiny triangular pieces, cutting steadily and methodically, but also with furious fervor. The fifty-two cards were quite a project for him and by the time he finished the first rays of sun were peeking in through the window.

In the meantime, the worst of his fury had worn off. He was now feeling raw and chilly, and extremely sleepy.

'I'll leave off now until morning,' he thought, 'but I shall send her a little greeting.'

Taking the whole pile of tiny pieces from the table in front of him, he began to strew them around the room, laughing all the time. He tossed them by the handful, like a farmer sowing seed, meticulously covering every inch of the room. By the time he was done the floor looked like the ground after a light snowfall.

It was an old, roughly hewn floor with big cracks between the boards. It was going to take the woman of the house quite some time to sweep up all the sharp-edged flakes that were now firmly attached to each and every knot in the wood.

THE ENCOUNTER

I

At last the day had come when they were to meet and talk, these two people who, until three years earlier, had lived at the old Korskyrka parsonage and been in love: she now an elegant lady, charming and yet practical, spreading good cheer wherever she went and he, the poor clergyman who was always seeking uncharted paths and who seemed fated to be the undoing of everyone who loved him.

And where should they meet if not in the very same parsonage garden that had witnessed not only their love but also the awful argument that had separated them? It was not yet in full summer bloom, in fact it was such a shady spot that spring arrived there a month later than elsewhere, so the hedges were not yet green, the brown autumn leaves had not been removed from the paths, and there was even a patch or two of dirt-gray snow on the tops of some of the turf benches. But this was still the place to which the two of them were drawn by the force of things they had experienced there and never forgotten.

Charlotte had arrived at the parsonage in the company of Mrs. Forsius, the wife of the old pastor, the same day the spring market took place in the village and Karl-Artur had left home on church affairs. She would have been happy to have her old mistress with her at Stora Sjötorp for the summer as well, but it would have been akin to cruelty to prevent that hardworking woman from going back to the parsonage now that the fine weather was approaching, with all the cleaning and preparations it brought with it. Mrs. Forsius spoke endlessly of her desire to walk into Forsius' study once again, to sit on the divan there and contemplate his piles of flower-pressing paper, his desk chair, his pipe rack and everything else that brought back such fond memories of her dear departed husband. Charlotte had not, however, allowed herself to be fooled. She knew this was not the only reason Mrs. Forsius wanted to get back home. Since no new parish priest had yet been appointed, she had been granted the right to go on living at the parsonage, and now it was her responsibility to uphold the reputation of the place, ensuring that the flower beds in the middle of the front courtyard were as impeccable, the creepers as well trimmed, the gravel paths as neatly raked and the lawns as evenly green as they had been in her husband's day.

Charlotte, who planned to stay a few days at the parsonage to give Mrs. Forsius a little time to become accustomed to being on her own there, found pleasure in sleeping in the bedroom of her youth. It was almost as if she would have liked to exclaim to the old walls: 'Here I am, you know, it's me, Charlotte. Of course you don't recognize me. Look at my dress, my hat, my shoes and above all my face! You see a happy woman.'

She walked over to a mirror that had been there since she was young, and studied her reflection.

'All the world calls me at least three times as beautiful as before, and I do believe the world is right.'

At once she saw, behind her own radiant image, the pale face of a young woman, illuminated by a pair of bright, melancholy eyes. She became extremely solemn.

'Of course,' she said, 'I was quite certain we two would meet again here. Poor girl, how miserable you were in those days! Just think what love did to you!'

She turned quickly away from the mirror. She had definitely not come here to become absorbed in memories of the terrible time when her engagement to Karl-Artur was broken off.

Beside which, there was no way of being certain she

considered everything that had happened to her that summer as pure misfortune. Wealthy Mrs. Charlotte Schagerström knew very well that the trait that was her most charming, a touch of unsatisfied desire, as if the bounties of life had passed her by, a poetic melancholy that made every man she met wonder whether he was not the one appointed to give to her the happiness she had never achieved, was a trait she had inherited from that poor, rejected Charlotte Löwensköld.

But that yearning, the melancholy that took possession of her face the moment it was at rest, did it have any significance? Was this radiant, always cheerful, always venturesome, always pleasure-seeking Charlotte Schagerström not happy? Did she still bear with her some yearning for the love of her youth? Ah, to tell the truth, not even she would have been able to answer those questions. She was happy with her husband, but even after three years of marriage she had to admit to herself that she had never experienced that powerful, all-encompassing passion for him that had made her soul burn for Karl-Artur Ekenstedt.

Since she had moved out into the world, she had often noted how her demands had risen in terms of people and of many other things. She had lost her high esteem of both the parsonage itself and Mrs. Forsius' formal drawing room. She might also have lost her taste for that impoverished country pastor who had married a peddler woman and lived in a cottage with only two rooms.

In fact she had not made more than one single attempt to see him again since he returned to Korskyrka, and when that failed she had been quite content. She would not have wanted their meeting to be a disappointment, and had it not been a disappointment she would have wanted it even less.

But although she was reluctant to see Karl-Artur, she could not refrain from keeping watch over him with a sort of maternal solicitude. The pastor's wife had kept her abreast of the external events of his life, his marriage and his home, Thea's dangerous influence and his wife's competence. No one had been more pleased than she to hear that this past winter he seemed to have regained the respect and affection of the parishioners, to the extent that many of them even wished he had sufficiently good qualifications and enough years of service to be able to succeed the venerable Pastor Forsius in Korskyrka.

Charlotte, who, after her marriage, had taken to rising late, did not appear the next morning until breakfast time. Mrs. Forsius had already been up and about for a couple of hours by then. She had inspected the property, stood by the gate and gazed at her favorite view of the lake and the church, and even conversed with passersby to gather the news.

'Can you imagine, Charlotte? That Karl-Artur!' she exclaimed. 'I cannot help being fond of him, but he is behaving entirely true to form.'

She went on to tell Charlotte that Karl-Artur had committed the horrendously foolish mistake of letting the ten children move out on him.

Charlotte sat there at a loss. As so often before, she felt it was pointless doing anything for Karl-Artur. There was some power that was inevitably leading him to his ruin.

'Oh, isn't it the most awful misfortune?' Mrs. Forsius went on. 'You know, I have no educational degree nor so much as a clerical collar, but even I know that I would rather have ended up in prison than let anyone take those children from me.'

'I suppose they were too much for him,' said Charlotte, who suddenly remembered having visited Karl-Artur's kitchen, the heavy air, the noise, the dust, how overcrowded it had been with paraphernalia, beds and people.

'Too much for him!' said Mrs. Forsius with a contemptuous frown. 'As if people had not grown accustomed to far worse! In spite of the predicament he'd got himself into, it finally looked as if the Good Lord was going to help him. Mark my words, had he kept those children there, he would have ended his days as parish priest here in Korskyrka.'

'What about his wife?' Charlotte asked attentively. 'Did she agree to letting the children go?'

'Certainly not,' Mrs. Forsius said. 'She wanted nothing more than to keep them. I had a word with Per-Erik's old mother by the gate a while ago. She's quite convinced that the whole thing was Thea's doing.'

'Thea! But you had forbidden…'

'Ah, I did forbid … Well, though they may not have seen each other either in his home or in hers, in a little hamlet like this they could hardly not see each other at all. Once, when Per-Erik's mother was sitting with Thea in the waiting room at the doctor's, Karl-Artur turned up there too, not five minutes later. And she started talking to him at once about sending the children away.'

The two women just looked at each other, upset and bewildered. Their best-laid plans were about to fall to pieces.

For in fact it had been arranged that a few of the most prominent men in the parish would be meeting at the inn that very morning. There were important decisions to be made. Discussions had begun in Korskyrka, where people always tried to keep up with the times, about setting up an elementary school. And that was not all. The population of the parish had grown so rapidly that it no longer seemed realistic just to have one single individual charged with the curing of all the souls. They were considering employing an assistant to the parish minister, who would be given both accommodation and a salary. In order for the parish not to be overwhelmed with expenses, the idea was that the same individual could serve both as the pastor's assistant and the schoolteacher. And that person was to be none other than Karl-Artur.

The final decision on these matters would, naturally, be made at a parish meeting, but as the plan would involve a great deal of expense, a preparatory meeting had been called to ascertain whether those members of the community who had the most to say were willing to contribute.

Surely no one suspected that this entire plan had taken shape in Charlotte's clever mind. She had been very skilled at exploiting the fact that most of the village thought highly of Karl-Artur, and so had made the whole thing fall into place without making herself visible. It was, of course, clear to all that he was far too young to be appointed head minister of such a large parish, and there was general agreement as to the suitability of setting up these new positions so as to be able to keep him close at hand.

Thus it was not surprising that Charlotte was quite beside herself upon hearing Mrs. Forsius' news. Here she was, about to arrange a permanent position for Karl-Artur, with a decent salary, and Thea had to interfere. She loved him, so surely she ought to have realized that it was the miracle of seeing an impoverished clergyman shoulder the burden of caring for that large brood of children that had won him his present status?

She looked at the grandfather clock in the dining room and sighed.

'It's just ten minutes to ten,' she said. 'The meeting is about to begin.'

She knew more than anyone what effort and what ingenuity it had taken her to see to it that the meeting took place. One of the most difficult parts had been making Schagerström promise to be there and to support these extensive plans.

'Oh yes, the meeting!' replied Mrs. Forsius. 'I wouldn't be surprised if the entire project fell flat as a pancake. People who have been to see Karl-Artur claim that his wife just sits in the corner by the hearth all day, not saying a word. She is jealous of Thea, you see. People like her never know how to keep themselves in check. And oh, I also heard that they have been meeting here, in my garden. Well, I will most certainly put a stop to that.'

'Per-Erik's old mother has always been a terrible gossip,' Charlotte said indignantly.

Yet at the same time she was surprised at how all her old feelings resurfaced. Her hatred of Thea was just as powerful a force in her heart as it had been the day she had cut off the other woman's beautiful curls with a pair of scissors.

And so breakfast passed with this discussion and Charlotte, both upset and unhappy, tossed a shawl across her shoulders to go out into the garden.

She walked with downcast eyes, as if hunting for traces of the two people whose loving trysts were said to have taken place there. They had certain chosen the right location. Karl-Artur knew from experience what excellent places for privacy the garden offered, with its hedges and bowers.

'He was not in love with her before,' she said to herself, 'but I suppose it has come to that now. He grew bored of that peddler girl from Dalarna and sought solace from Thea. What with the organist also being a jealous man, their only option was to meet out of doors.'

In spite of the fact that it all seemed a perfectly natural course of events to her, she still found it extremely offensive that the lovers had chosen this particular place to meet unobserved.

'It amazes me,' she thought, 'that they dared. There are no leaves on the hedges yet. Any passerby on the road could have seen them.'

She stopped to consider. Through the brown leaves on the hedges she glimpsed the little gazebo.

'Ah, so that is where they hid away, there, of course,' and with that thought she hurried quickly over to the simple building, which had seen far better days, so fast that one might have thought she expected to catch the two miscreants in there.

The gazebo was shut, but Charlotte easily pulled open the rusty latch. Once she was inside, she could feel that it was unpleasant in there, like a summer house that has been standing untended throughout the long winter: stale air, broken panes, peeling wallpaper. In a pile of dry leaves that must have blown in during an autumn storm she glimpsed something dark gray and shiny. It was the guardian of the garden, an enormous grass snake hibernating there for the winter.

'No, they have surely not been meeting here,' Charlotte thought, 'Our old Mr. Serpent would have made Thea tremble.'

Personally, she paid the powerless reptile no heed. Walking over to one of the windows with a cracked pane, she opened it and sat down on the bench beneath.

From there she had a fine view of the rows of hedges, their branches swelling with sap, that were shifting in all the softest spring shades now. On the ground between the rows there were patches of greening lawn, with little stands of cowslips, daisies and daffodils peeking up here and there.

Charlotte, who liked the spot, muttered to herself:

'Well, this is certainly not the first time I have found myself sitting here waiting for someone who never comes.'

Hardly had she spoken these words when she caught sight of a man walking toward her between the hedges. He was moving in the direction of the gazebo, and soon he was so close that she recognized him. It was Karl-Artur.

Charlotte sat there without moving. 'Of course he will not be alone,' she thought. 'I'm sure Thea will appear shortly.'

A moment later Karl-Artur drew to a halt. He had spotted Charlotte, and was rubbing his eyes in surprise, as people do when they suspect they are seeing a mirage.

Charlotte, now only a couple of steps from him, saw him standing there, very pale, and yet she recognized his boyish complexion. He might have aged a little, his features were sharper, but the refinement that had always characterized the son of Beate Ekenstedt, the colonel's wife, had not left him. Charlotte thought he resembled a modern-day fairytale shepherd, a prince in disguise, standing there in his gray homespun suit.

In less than one second Karl-Artur had understood that it really was Charlotte sitting at the window. He dashed up the little slope on which the gazebo stood, arms wide open.

'Charlotte,' he shouted with joy, 'Charlotte, Charlotte!'

He snatched at her hands, pulling them toward him and kissing them, tears streaming down his cheeks.

It was evident that this unexpected meeting had utterly startled him, though whether he was weeping with pleasure or with pain she was unable to tell. He went on crying so hard it was as if years of accumulated tears had broken down the floodgates.

But from the way he continued to hold her hands, to kiss and to stroke them, she was convinced that all the gossip about his love affair with Thea had been nothing but lies. It was not Thea who ruled his heart, but another.

And who was that other? It could be no one but herself, the one so disdainfully rejected, whom he had begun to love once again. No other declaration of love could have spoken more clearly than those impassioned tears.

As she realized all this, Charlotte felt a taste on her lips, as if a long-postponed hunger had been sated, or as if a constant, uncomfortable feeling somewhere in the region of the heart was now at peace, or as if she had long been carrying a heavy burden and had been relieved of it now. She closed her eyes, overwhelmed by feelings of happiness.

This, however, only lasted a moment. One second later she was wise and sensible again.

'Where could this take us?' she thought to herself. 'He is a married man as I am a married woman, in addition to which he is a clergyman. I must try to calm him. That is the main thing.'

'Now, now, Karl-Artur, you really must not carry on like this,' she told him. 'It's only me, Charlotte. Mrs. Forsius insisted on moving back for the summer, so I am staying for a few days to help her settle in.'

She spoke in her most domestic tone of voice, hoping to stop his tears, but Karl-Artur just went on weeping harder than before.

'The poor man,' Charlotte thought, and went on to say: 'I'm quite sure that you are crying for more reasons than merely the sight of me. Yes, of course, you are weeping out of yearning for all the fine, cultivated exchanges you have known here, for all the beauty, for your mother and your home. But it's no use thinking of all that now, or of anything that cannot be altered. Now we must be reasonable.'

She gave them both a moment to look out at the garden. Then she continued:

'You know me well enough to imagine what pleasure I take in seeing the dear old parsonage again. This morning my mind went to all the lovely things to be seen out here among the hedges now, before the lindens are fully in leaf to prevent the sun from reaching the ground. It's such a joy to see the grass and herbs eagerly soaking up the sunlight.'

Karl-Artur put up a hand as if to quiet her, but as he was still weeping Charlotte decided to go on speaking of such things, thinking her words would have a calming effect on him.

'There is something special about this early summer sunshine,' she went on, 'because it has to find its way to the ground through all the branches. It is so gentle and unassuming. And the flowers it encourages are therefore never very showy. They are always white, pale yellow or pale blue. If it weren't for their coming so early and in such vast quantities, no one would even notice them.'

Karl-Artur raised his eyes, swollen with weeping. It was a great effort, but he managed to press out a few words:

'Oh, how I have been longing... longing... this entire endless winter.'

Clearly, in his agitated state, he did not want her to speak so mildly of flowers and sunshine. He wanted her to take in the force of the tempest raging within him.

But Charlotte, well aware of all the words that had to remain unspoken, took up her monologue again, like a persistent nursemaid rocking a howling baby to sleep.

'I do believe the spring sunshine has unique powers. Just look – wherever it sends its light, it arouses new life. It works its magic spell. In spite of the gentleness of its rays, its effects are more powerful than those of the summer sun, which tends to burn too easily, or those of the autumn sun, that only end in withering and death. Have you ever considered the fact that the pale sunshine of spring has more or less the same impact as first love?'

Karl-Artur seemed to be listening more attentively now, as she said this. She hurried to continue:

'You will not, of course, recall such a bagatelle, but personally I often find myself back on that spring evening here in Korskyrka just after you had arrived for the first time. You and I had been out visiting some of the parish poor, some crofters who lived deep in the woods. We had ended up staying a little too long, so that the sun set before we could get home and mist began gathering in the dales.'

Karl-Artur raised his head. His tears seemed to be drying

up. He had stopped kissing her hands and hung on every word that crossed her lovely lips.

'Oh, do you remember that walk? We made our way from one hilltop to the next. As soon as we reached one, the sun broke through, but down in each valley the fog surrounded us. The rest of the world disappeared.'

What was she getting at? The man who loved her had ceased to resist. Without objecting, he allowed her to carry him along on this journey between the sunlit hills.

'Ah, what a walk it was!' Charlotte went on. 'The mild, pale red sun and the gentle, bright mist transformed everything around us. To my astonishment, I saw the nearby woods turning pale, pale blue, while the more distant forests went a deep purple. We walked through a supernatural landscape. So as not to break the spell, neither of us even dared to mention the beauty of it all.'

Charlotte reined in her words. She anticipated Karl-Artur speaking, but it was clear that he did not wish to interrupt.

'On each hilltop, we walked slowly and decorously. But each time we descended to a misty dale, we began to dance. Well, perhaps not you, but I. I danced my way along, in ecstasy at the glory of that evening. At least I thought it was the beauty that was making me unable to walk normally.'

At those words, Karl-Artur broke into a smile. Charlotte smiled softly back at him. She could see that the peak of his grief had passed. He was again master of his feelings.

'By the time we came to the next hilltop,' said Charlotte, 'you had stopped speaking altogether. I wondered whether, as a clergyman, you found it unsuitable for me to be dancing along the road, and I was so embarrassed I could barely continue by your side. However, when we descended into the next valley and the mist surrounded us… well, that time I did not dare to start dancing, but then…'

'But then,' Karl-Artur interrupted her, 'but then I kissed you.'

At the very moment Karl-Artur pronounced those words, he saw a man standing outside the window opposite him. He could not tell who it was. The figure vanished just as his gaze began to focus on him. He was not even completely certain he had really seen anyone there.

In any case, he decided not to worry Charlotte about it. All they had been doing was standing by the window talking. What difference did it make if one of the tenant farmers or gardeners had seen them? It could not mean a thing. Why disturb this moment of happiness?

'Yes,' said Charlotte. 'You kissed me, and suddenly I understood why the woods had turned blue and what had been making me dance through the mists. Ah, Karl-Artur, my entire life changed at that moment. You know, I even had a strange feeling. I felt as if I could gaze down into my own soul, and that spring flowers were pushing up through the soil of that endless plain. Everywhere, everywhere. Pale white, light blue and pale yellow spring flowers. I saw them there by the thousands; the earth was alive with them. I do not believe I have ever seen anything more beautiful.'

She was touched by her own words. Now a tear glistened at the corner of her eye, and her voice trembled for just an instant before she pulled herself together again.

'My friend, do you see now why these spring flowers remind me of first love?' she asked.

He seized her hand in a tight grip.

'Oh, Charlotte,' he began.

But at that she stood up.

'Well,' she said, 'it also explains why we women can never entirely forget the one who first made the sunshine of love radiate down on us. No, we can never forget him. And yet only a few, only a very few among us, remain in the country of spring flowers. We are transported to something more powerful, something greater.'

She nodded, amused and melancholy at once, indicated to him that he was not to leave with her, and vanished.

II

That morning when Karl-Artur woke up, the sun was streaming straight in through his window, indicating to him that he had slept away a good bit of the morning. He rose at once. Still a bit sleepy, he wondered to himself what had made him sleep so late, and then he remembered that he had been up until dawn cutting a deck of cards to shreds.

This brought all the other events of the previous evening back to him, and he was overwhelmed with disgust and loathing, not only for his wife but possibly even more so for himself. Who did he think he was, to allow himself to be so offended by an insult that he felt like taking the life of his wife? Was he really the one who had done that, he, who had been so vile as to cut up a deck of cards and toss the pieces all over the floor? What kind of evil forces did he harbor inside? Was he a monster?

Because he had not eaten the previous evening, the meal his wife had brought in to him still stood there, untouched. He hurried to eat his fill of cold porridge and milk, after which he took his hat and went out for a long walk. He was pleased to be able, in this way, to postpone the necessary discussion with his wife for a few more hours.

He followed the main road to the parsonage and, finding himself there, he opened the gate and turned into the old-fashioned garden, a place of refuge he had sought out many times during the past winter to get away from all the noise and crowding in the overfull cottage.

And there he found Charlotte, more beautiful and enchanting than ever. Why would he not be overwhelmed by his feelings? Initially, his only thought had been to cry out to her that his love for her had returned, and to take the woman he was so longing for to his heart.

But his tears had muted him and Charlotte, wise and good human being that she was, had thus gained the necessary time to bring him back to his senses. He understood perfectly what she was trying to tell him with her memories of the days of their early love. She wanted him to know that she still cherished those memories, but that her heart was now committed to another.

When Charlotte left, he had a moment of feeling that his soul was dark and empty. But he did not experience the incapacitating hatred that can possess a rejected lover. He knew far too well it was his own fault that he had lost her.

In that great darkness, a little gleam of light soon appeared. The thoughts he had been having the day before, those wondrous visions of a future, that had been pushed aside by his domestic quarrel, returned to him, forceful and irresistible. Far more wonderful than any earthly love was the enticing task of finally serving his Redeemer in the only proper fashion, devoting the rest of his life to the nomadic existence of an apostle of the roads, a free flying bird who would deliver the words of life to the starving masses, a beggar of Our Lord who, in his own destitution, distributed riches of the kind that neither moth nor rust can despoil.

He began to walk back toward the village, slowly and contemplatively. First and foremost, he would make peace with his wife. What would happen after that was unclear to him, but his soul was fortified with a singular confidence. God had taken him under his wing. He no longer had to make his decisions by himself.

As he was passing the first little home in the village, the same little cottage with a front garden out of which Anna Svärd had been coming the first time he met her, the door opened and the owner walked out to him. She was originally from Dalarna, and was the person who used to lodge Anna Svärd when she passed that way with her peddler's sack.

'You mustn't be riled with me now, Mister Minister, for being the bearer of ill tidings,' she said, 'but our Anna passed by here this morning and asked me to tell you that she was taking off.'

Karl-Artur stared at the woman, uncomprehendingly.

'That's right,' the woman went on, 'she's gone home to Medstubyn. I told her she ought not to leave right now.

"There's not more than a few weeks left till you'll be in childbed," says I to her. But she answered that she just had to go anyway. And it was very important to her that I tell you where she was headed. "He needn't think I'm planning to do myself in," she said. ''I'm just goin' home.'''

Karl-Artur was gripping the fence. Although he no longer loved his wife, they had shared the same life for a long time, and he felt as if something in his soul had been torn in two. Moreover, it marked a terrible failure. The entire world would now know that his wife had been so unhappy that she had left him of her own accord.

And yet, at the same time as this new suffering came over him, so did the comforting thought of vast, enticing freedom. A wife, a home, a reputation among others, none of these had any importance to him in relation to the path on which he was about to embark. His heart was beating, in spite of all he had been through, easily and regularly. God had released him from the cares of the common man and his heavy burden.

A few minutes later, when he returned home and entered his study, he was astonished to find it neat and tidy. The bed had been made and the tray of food removed. In great surprise, he hurried into the kitchen, where he also found everything in perfect order. There was a woman on her knees on the floor picking up those stubborn little shreds of the deck of cards that had been impossible to get at with the broom and dustpan, where they had caught in the uneven floorboards. She was humming and singing and appeared to be in the best possible state of mind. When he came into the room she raised her head and he saw that it was Thea.

'Ah, Karl-Artur!' she said. 'I hurried right over the moment I heard that your wife had left you. I knew you would be needing help. I hope you do not mind.'

'Certainly not, Thea! In fact it was very kind of you. But do not bother yourself, please, with those ridiculous scraps of playing cards! Just leave them where they are.'

Thea did not allow her work to be interrupted. She went on humming and collecting the bits and pieces.

'I am gathering them up as a memento,' she replied. 'When

I came in a while ago, I could see that she – you know who I mean – had made a vain effort to sweep them up with the broom. But when she saw how so many were stuck, she tossed the broom aside. Abandoned the entire enterprise and went on her way.'

She laughed and hummed. Karl-Artur considered her with something resembling distaste.

Thea extended a bowl up to him, containing a whole pile of little cut-up bits of card she had gathered.

'She is gone, and these are what chased her away,' she said. 'Isn't it only right and fitting that I gather them up and hide them?'

'Thea, have you lost your mind?'

His voice was full of contempt and verging on hatred. Thea looked up and saw him standing there, his brow furrowed, but all she could do was laugh.

'Oh yes,' she said, 'you can use that on the others and it will work, but not on me. Strike me! Kick me! I will still come back. You will never be able to get rid of me. The things that frighten off the others are the things that keep me here.'

She took up her humming again, the melody growing louder and louder. It sounded like a triumphal march.

Karl-Artur, who was thoroughly horrified by this hysterical outburst, went back into his study. As soon as he was alone there his joy returned, and his sense of freedom. He set about drafting a letter to the bishop, tendering his resignation.

THE ACCIDENT

I

Schagerström left home in good time that morning in order to attend the important meeting at the inn. It began on time at ten, but as it had turned out to be unexpectedly brief, he was able to continue his journey on to the parsonage as early as eleven o'clock to pay a little visit to Mrs. Forsius and Charlotte. He was missing his wife, although they had only been apart for a single day, and he harbored some slight hope that he might persuade her to return home with him.

'I actually ought to get right back and check on the sawmill problems,' he thought to himself. 'But that would mean a very quick visit indeed. Perhaps I could stay on until evening? By about five or six Charlotte ought to be ready to accompany me home with no pangs of conscience.'

Upon his arrival at the parsonage he was welcomed by Mrs. Forsius, who immediately began to ask him about the meeting. Of course she had no doubt that the plan would have failed. She had heard about Karl-Artur's allowing the ten children to move away, and she knew what a terribly foolish mistake that had been.

Schagerström hastened to assure her that it had made no difference. No, they had been about to approve Karl-Artur's taking over both the schoolhouse and the smaller parsonage, when foundryman Aron Månsson had risen to ask whether it really was worth the while of the congregation to go to such expense to retain a clergyman whose conduct was such that his wife had felt compelled to leave him.

'What am I hearing!' cried Mrs. Forsius. 'His wife! Gone away? Oh, who will keep him in check now?'

In fact, everyone at the meeting appeared to have asked himself the same question. They had all placed their confidence in his wife. One might have thought that the person about to be appointed assistant minister and schoolteacher was Anna Svärd, because the moment the men heard that she was no longer part of the plan, they decided to postpone the whole matter indefinitely.

Mrs. Forsius, who was both angry and upset at this result, then chanced to say a few improvident words.

'Oh, it's exactly as I always said to Charlotte – it's no use trying to help Karl-Artur.'

Schagerström was never pleased to hear of Charlotte's interest in the wellbeing of her former fiancé, and began to frown, but then Mrs. Forsius, aware of her lack of tact, tried to distract him by saying that Charlotte could be found out in the garden.

She didn't have to say it twice. He headed right out into the maze of hedges to find Charlotte, and when he thought he heard her voice coming from the old gazebo he glanced in through a window. Yes, indeed, there was Charlotte, sitting talking with Karl-Artur, and so, moving so fast that he did not hear a single word of their conversation, Schagerström fled.

He did not even remain in the garden, but just went and stood to wait for his wife on the front porch steps of the parsonage. What he had seen had put him into a state of mind akin to stupefaction, when one does not seem to be thinking one's own thoughts, but rather thoughts that are coming at one from outside. Someone, he had no idea who, was reminding him of a conversation he had once overheard. People were talking about Mrs. Romelius, the doctor's wife, and saying how astonishing it was that she went on loving her husband, even though he had become such a terrible drunkard.

'Well, there's nothing surprising about it,' the other person had responded. 'After all, she is a Löwensköld, and Löwenskölds never give up their first love.'

He did not know when or where he had heard it. In fact, he thought it was probably before he had ever met Charlotte, but now the words came back from the depths of his soul, and nearly frightened the life out of him.

A few minutes later he noted that he was standing there holding his head in both hands, as if trying to prevent his mind and reason from escaping.

A little while later, he saw her approaching. She was dawdling along, frowning, as if thinking through a very difficult and highly complex problem. But the moment she saw her husband, her expression cleared and she hurried toward him.

'Oh, here you are already!' she cried, beaming, as she threw her arms around him and gave him a kiss. He could not have wished for a warmer welcome.

'What a good show she puts on!' he thought. 'It isn't a bit surprising that I led myself to believe that she truly cared for me.'

He expected Charlotte, always so open, to tell him that she had bumped into young Ekenstedt, but she refrained. Neither did she ask him how the meeting had been. One might have thought that she had forgotten the matter entirely.

Schagerström, of course, drew his own conclusions from this silence. The sense of having been deceived and defeated grew in him.

All he wanted to do was to leave as soon as possible, so as to consider the implications of his discovery in peace and quiet. Trying to persuade Charlotte to return home with him was now the farthest thing from his mind.

What helped him to get away from the parsonage without having to reveal his ill feelings was the old sawmill at Stora Sjötorp. He hastened to explain to Charlotte that it had come to a standstill the previous afternoon, just after she and Mrs. Forsius had departed, and that the mill foreman and various inspectors and managers had tried in vain to determine the cause. And so they had had no choice but to consult Schagerström himself but he, too, had failed.

Charlotte, who knew that her husband considered himself

a mechanical genius, and that nothing gave him greater pleasure than having an opportunity to prove it, took the matter calmly.

'Ah, I know that old sawmill well,' she said. 'Sometimes it just wants a couple days' rest and then, as if nothing had ever happened, it starts up again all on its own.'

As they were talking, Mrs. Forsius came out onto the porch, curtsied deeply, and inquired as to whether she might have the great pleasure of inviting Mr. Schagerström to dinner. But, using the sawmill as his excuse, Schagerström refused her invitation. He explained to Mrs. Forsius that this particular sawmill had its own unique mechanical peculiarities and complexities. The workmen who had been at Stora Sjötorp longest claimed that it was a full hundred years old, and had been designed by none less than the great engineer and inventor, Christopher Polhem. And he was inclined to believe them, because only a mechanical wizard could have built something so intricate. Yesterday he had truly despaired of ever finding a solution, but today when he was away for the meeting he had had a new idea. He thought he knew what needed to be done. And so, of course, he would have to be getting home immediately.

And having heard that, both his wife and Mrs. Forsius understood that since he was completely preoccupied with the old sawmill and its puzzling mechanics, it was best to let him be off.

Practically the moment he sat down in the trap a dark, despairing process began, an attempt to find excuses for, or even better, to drive out of his mind, the memory of what he thought he had seen through the gazebo window. But, alas, our eyes have a tiresome ability to take in certain sights with relentlessly perfect focus and to replay them endlessly.

He had to admit to himself that there had been no kissing between Charlotte and Karl-Artur, or even any exchange of embraces. He might very well have imagined that they were deep in ordinary conversation, had he not seen the eyes of the young clergyman, red from weeping, and the romantic admiration in his gaze when he looked up at Charlotte, not to mention the look of compassionate kindness she had bestowed upon him.

In addition, there had been Mrs. Forsius' words and her reservations about the situation, which led him to see that Charlotte was still trying to help Karl-Artur, as well as her own guardedness. Was not all this sufficient evidence?

He did try to tell himself that he and Charlotte had been extremely happy, and that she had never so much as implied by a single look that she was still pining for another, but none of that seemed to count in comparison with the looks that had passed between Charlotte and Karl-Artur that morning.

'Perhaps she had led herself to believe that her old love was dead,' he muttered, 'but then as soon as she encountered him, it flared up anew.'

After some time he had managed to persuade himself utterly and completely that Charlotte's heart belonged to Karl-Artur, and he had begun to consider what measures he would now have to take.

Charlotte would never allow herself to be enticed into infidelity, which was some consolation. But did it suffice? Can a real man be content with knowing that his wife is going about longing for another? No, divorce was a thousand times preferable.

But at that thought, his whole world was eclipsed. What? Separate from Charlotte? Never again hear her laughter, her repartee, never again see her enchanting face? His whole body was gripped by a fit of shivering. He felt as if he were wading through icy water.

On his arrival at Stora Sjötorp, he refused any dinner. Instead, he called the manager to him at once, to accompany him down to the sawmill.

'I must tell you,' he said, 'that while I was away I had an idea. I believe I know where the fault lies.'

At the sawmill, they went straight in to the big machine room, where the brilliant old inventor seemed almost to have taken perverse pleasure in building up an indescribable maze of wheels, cranks and levers. Schagerström seized one of the controls firmly, and pulled.

However, he had probably not expected this action to have an immediate effect, or perhaps his mind was elsewhere. What happened was that the powerful equipment was instantly set in motion, and he did not manage to move away fast enough. He was pulled into the sawmill.

II

Schagerström came to with a sensation of being shaken back and forth in a horribly painful manner. He found himself being carried on a stretcher. His bearers were treading slowly and carefully, but every step shook him intolerably, and with each step he moaned.

One of the bearers saw that he had come to, and indicated to the other to halt.

'Is this too painful for you, Sir?' he asked, addressing Schagerström as he would a little child. 'Shall we stop where we are?'

'We're nearly there,' said another persuasive voice. 'You'll be better off, Sir, once you're comfortable in your own bed.'

With those words they started off again, and the unbearable agony was renewed.

'Still and all, it could have been much worse,' one of the men said. 'I thought he'd be sawn in half like a log.'

'Sure and it was an awfully close call,' said yet another voice. 'But your arms and legs are all intact, Sir.'

'It's possible you've got a broken rib or two,' came from yet a third man, 'but that would be no great surprise.'

Schagerström realized these simple workmen were trying to console him, and he was indescribably touched and grateful to them for their kindness. He tried, too, to keep his courage up and not to moan and groan. But he was still a bit confounded by the fact that no one had mentioned the remarkable fact that he had succeeded in starting up the sawmill again. He was eager for that praise.

When the men had been carrying him a little while longer,

he was overwhelmed with exhaustion. He could bear it no more. If they went on rattling him, he would simply die.

Had he had the strength, he would have instructed them to stop, but he was unable to do so. What he did feel was that his body, bit by bit, was losing sensation, felt as if it were dying away. It all happened very fast, from his feet up to his head.

—— —— ——

The next time he came to, he smelled a soft scent of dried rose petals, and figured that he must be in the guest room at Stora Sjötorp. Indeed, they must have brought him in there so as not to have to carry him upstairs to his own bedroom.

Someone was removing his footwear, but it was more than he could bear. He groaned so loudly and was in such pain that they had to stop.

'We'll have to leave him be until the doctor arrives,' he heard the manager say.

'Well,' said another voice he thought he recognized as that of Johansson, his man, although it was so hoarse with weeping that he could barely tell. 'Yes, it's possible he's got a broken ankle.'

Schagerström opened his eyes to show them he was conscious. He was on the large divan in the guest room, and he could see his housekeeper and two serving maids preparing the bed while the manager and his servant attempted to undress him.

He said a few words, trying to ask them to leave him alone. The sounds that uttered forth from his throat, however, bore no resemblance to the human voice. Even he thought it sounded like the wheezing of an animal that had been mortally injured in the hunt, and yet they seemed to know what he meant. They let him be, fully clothed, and stopped making the bed as well. His housekeeper approached carrying a cover to put over him. It seemed to him much too heavy for him to be able to stand. He hissed something in her direction, and she abandoned the idea. Then she tried to put a pillow under his head. That, too, proved intolerable.

The entire time, he was annoyed by the fact that the manager, who knew very well how complex Polhem's old machinery was, gave him no praise. The sawmill might not have been working again for ages, had it not been for his idea.

He blinked once or twice in the direction of his manager, who approached to hear what he was wanting. But not even then did he comment. Schagerström whispered his instructions, that the kind workmen who had carried him home should be duly recompensed for their efforts, and the manager nodded, seeming to understand. He asked whether his employer had any further requests.

Schagerström would have liked not to have to say it himself. He was also aware that the other man must think him very childish, but the words were burning his tongue and must out.

'Well, at least I got the mill up and running.'

'Dear God,' said his manager. 'That you did, Sir, that you did.'

Schagerström found it annoying that this made his manager so emotional he began to cry. He had been expecting some long-winded recognition.

He was not at all comfortable with hearing sniffling and crying around him, so he sputtered a few words about wanting to be alone, and his housekeeper, manager and serving girls left the room at once. Only Johansson remained sitting by his bedside.

Schagerström felt better once things quieted down. He was calmer, less readily irritated and less assertive. 'I'm not a helpless child,' he thought. 'People do as I tell them. Now that they have left me here lying still, quite still, I am not in pain. And I still wield enough power to ensure I have quiet.'

He understood that he was going to die, and was far from displeased at the prospect. All he wanted was for death to come gently, so softly that he would be able to accept it in peace, without a great deal of fuss being made about its arrival.

He began to blink very hard in the direction of Johansson. He had realized how fortunate it was that Charlotte was not at home. She would surely not have allowed him to die like this, on a divan and fully dressed. He whispered a command to Johansson; no one was to notify the lady of the manor. He did not want her frightened. They must send for the doctor and the local justice, but no one was to notify his wife.

Johansson looked distressed, but Schagerström was very pleased. It probably wasn't visible, but he was smiling softly to himself. Did it not sound lovely, not wanting to frighten the lady of the manor? He was proud of himself for coming up with it. Imagine if he really managed to fool Charlotte! Imagine if he managed to die before she knew anything about it!

He heard when the traps left to collect the doctor and the judge, and looked at the wall clock opposite where he was lying. It was three thirty, and, thank goodness, the village was a full 20 kilometers away. Lundman would, of course, drive like mad, but even so it would be four hours before the doctor could possibly arrive. Quiet, uninterrupted quiet straight through until seven-thirty!

Something boyish had come over him, he felt. It was as if he were pulling some kind of prank. It wasn't really right of him to sneak off toward death without being nursed. But he didn't care. Really he didn't. Wealthy Schagerström would soon be out of the picture. So now, at last, he ought to be able to do as he pleased.

Charlotte would, of course, be upset and angry, but he didn't care about that, either. Moreover, he'd had a bright idea. He would leave all his property to her. That would be her compensation for not having been able to fuss and bother and boss him around as he lay on his deathbed.

It did cross his mind and seem odd to him that now, with death only hours away, he was not thinking great and solemn thoughts. But he wasn't. All he wanted was an end to his suffering and worries and miseries and all his other troubles. He just wanted some peace. He was like a child about to get a thrashing at school who wanted only to creep off into a deep, dark forest and hide.

He recalled the events of that morning, but they no longer

concerned him. Mental torment of that kind now seemed absurdly banal. Her having stood there looking lovingly at Karl-Artur had nothing to do with why he did not want to see her now. No, it was because she was the only person who would not obey him. He could cope with his manager, his housekeeper and Johansson, but not with Charlotte. He even thought he would be able to talk sense with the doctor. But Charlotte – never! She would show him neither pity nor respect.

Yes, it was cowardly to be so afraid of pain. But since he knew he was going to die anyway, he could not imagine what the point of arguing with him would be.

A little before seven thirty he heard a trap approaching. No, he did not feel the hours had dragged by, instead he sighed over the fact that the doctor had arrived already. He had been lying there hoping the man was away on other urgent business and that it might be nearly nine o'clock before he arrived. But of course Lundman had driven at top speed to fetch help for his employer. It would have been impossible to make anyone understand that he really didn't want to be bothered at all.

Johansson sneaked out of the room to meet the doctor. Now there would be a fuss. The doctor would poke and pull and set his joints right. He could see as he was lying there that one of his feet was twisted round: his toes were pointing down toward the divan and his heel up toward the ceiling. But that was not important to a man who was dying, he only hoped the doctor would not feel obliged to set it right while he was still alive.

Romelius entered the room, tall and confident. Schagerström, who had anticipated his arriving drunk as usual, felt a bit let down.

'Oh, no. If he's sober he may feel it is his duty to do something,' he thought.

But he made a valiant effort to persuade the physician to leave him alone.

'You do see, my good fellow, that there is no point? I'll be done for in a few hours' time in any case.'

The doctor leaned over him. Schagerström saw his bloodshot eyes and his totally vacant expression, and could smell the spirits on him. 'I suppose he's as drunk as ever,' he thought, 'but realizes that the solemnity of the occasion requires him to stand upright. There's nothing for me to worry about.'

'Indeed, my dear Schagerström, you appear to have assessed the situation correctly. I don't think I can do much for you.'

But, not being completely under the table, Romelius attempted to gather his dignity and look as if he were accomplishing something. He felt Schagerström's pulse, sent his servant to fetch ice water and gauze to make a cold compress for his forehead, and then very softly touched his twisted leg, after which he shrugged.

'I understand, my friend, that you would like to be left in peace,' he said. 'And that would be the best thing for you. But shall we not try to get you into the bed, at least? Oh no, not even that? All right then, never mind.'

He sank down to a chair and sat there for a few minutes, deep in thought. Soon he went back to Schagerström's side, and delivered a solemn message.

'I'll spend the night,' he said, 'to be at hand if you have second thoughts, my dear Schagerström.'

He sat back down, clearly trying to decide whether anything was expected of him.

Just a few minutes later he was standing at the injured man's side again.

'It has always been my personal rule, Schagerström, and it has served me well, that when there might need to be an amputation, I refuse to carry it out without the permission of the patient. Are you certain, my dear Sir, that you do not wish to have medical treatment?'

'No, no, no, please feel completely confident of my wishes,' said Schagerström.

The poor physician returned to his armchair with the same stiff dignity and sank back down.

Schagerström blinked in Johansson's direction, and

Johansson was receptive as ever. A moment later the doctor was gently but firmly accompanied out of the room. When the servant returned, he explained that Romelius was now in Schagerström's study, already in a corner of the sofa, sound asleep.

Johansson was looking more dejected than ever. He had undoubtedly been expecting the doctor to work wonders. Schagerström, who felt it a blessing to have peace and quiet again in his infirmary, had a little twinge of compassion for the man's disappointment.

'What pleasure it would give this kind man if I let that carouser operate on me,' he thought.

A couple of minutes later Mrs. Sällberg, the housekeeper, snuck in. She whispered a question to Johansson, who went over to his master.

'Mrs. Sällberg would like to know what she should tell your estate workers. They've been waiting outside all afternoon and refuse to leave until they hear what the doctor had to say.'

It was clear to Schagerström that all those who were dependent upon him for their livelihoods were very much afraid that he was dying. They, too, would have liked nothing better than for him to subject himself to the torture of surgery.

'Tell Mrs. Sällberg it is the doctor she must ask!' he replied.

Now all these disturbances seemed to have had an unfortunate effect on his contorted body. The pain resurfaced. His blood pulsed and throbbed mercilessly. His breathing grew more labored, and his head had also become dreadfully hot.

'The end cannot be far away,' he thought.

He heard the sound of an approaching trap, and knew it must be the district judge arriving, with his secretary.

Shortly afterwards, his servant showed the two men in. Paper and pen were set out on a table, and Schagerström began to dictate his last will and testament.

The judge stood close to him, leaning in to be able to catch the slowly whispered words, and to repeat them to his secretary. His wife was to be his principal heir, so much was clear. But there were a great many workers at the various mills and foundries, innumerable poverty-stricken people, widows and orphans who were to be remembered.

This required a terrible effort. He felt the sweat run down his cheeks. He clenched his teeth so as not to give in to pain and exhaustion.

'Shall we not leave it to Mrs. Schagerström to determine suitable donations?' asked the judge, aware of the man's suffering.

Well, of course that would be all right, but there was another matter. His parents and siblings. Surely they, too, ought to see that he had not forgotten them in his final hour.

He was straining in vain to make himself understood, but had to abandon his effort so as not to lose consciousness again.

The man of the law began editing the text, after which the will would have to be read aloud to him, and he would have to declare, before witnesses called in for that purpose, that this was his last will and testament. How was he going to manage all that?

It was now so late that dark had fallen, and candles had been carried in. To him, however, the room was as dark as ever. The candles seemed to have no effect. He was lying there, in the shadow of death.

Well, this would be the last effort required of him, and then all his obligations would have been fulfilled and he would be left to die. The worst thing had not transpired. Charlotte had not arrived.

But was not that the sound of another trap? Was it not drawing up to the door? Was the door not thrown open, as only one person ever opened it? Did not a bolt of life, of hope, infuse the entire estate? Was there not a lively, commandeering voice asking the servants out there in the hall what on earth was going on?

Johansson, Schagerström's man, raised his head, his eyes began to gleam, he hurried toward the door. The housekeeper had opened it a crack to announce what the entire household already knew.

'My lady!' she whispered. 'My lady!'

So now he was unable to just let go. Now he would have to fight the worst battle yet.

When Charlotte entered the room, the first thing she should have wanted to do was to go to him, to Schagerström, and inquire as to his state. But nothing like that happened at all. Instead, she turned to the judge and requested, firmly and yet perfectly civilly, that he and his secretary kindly leave the room.

'My husband has been lying here for hours without receiving any medical attention at all,' said Charlotte. 'His clothing must be removed immediately. I am sure you will understand, Sir, that this is the highest priority at the moment.'

The man of law said something, very softly. He was informing Charlotte that Doctor Romelius had determined that there was nothing to be done.

Charlotte continued to control herself. But Schagerström could see that she was fiercely furious, and he hoped that the judge would watch his words.

'Need I repeat my request that you, Sir, allow me to see to my husband?'

'But, Mrs. Schagerström, it was your husband himself who asked me to be here.' To which he added, under his breath, 'It will not be to your detriment, Mrs. Schagerström, to see this will-writing completed.'

Schagerström heard a huge noise. Oh my, it was Charlotte, tearing the will in two. Well, she was certainly true to form.

'But Mrs. Schagerström, this is – to say the least – extremely…'

'If that will was to my advantage, there was no need to write it. I would not have accepted a shilling.'

'Well, if that is how you feel …'

Schagerström understood that the judge was so offended that he felt Charlotte deserved to lose her fortune. Leaving her to her fate, he walked out of the room.

But not even then did Charlotte approach Schagerström on his divan. Instead, she gave yet another a curt order.

'Johansson, go and fetch the doctor at once!'

Schagerström's servant left, and while he was gone

Charlotte carried on a whispered conversation with Mrs. Sällberg, who explained how distressed she and all the others had been about not being allowed to notify their mistress.

'Well, it was my sister Marie-Louise who came running to the parsonage,' Charlotte told her. 'I came home in the old pastor's rickety trap, pulled by one of his workhorses.'

Schagerström just lay there, silent and immobile. He did not want to admit that the pain was somewhat less acute since the arrival of Charlotte; or, no, it was raging just as ruthlessly as before, but he was somewhat less attentive to it. That is how things always were in Charlotte's presence. If she was in the room, it was impossible to think about anything except what she was doing.

The doctor entered, and the moment he stepped in Charlotte cried:

'How dare you sit down and sleep, brother-in-law, when my husband is dying?'

'How dare he!' Schagerström could have laughed. That was the turn of phrase she used to him the first time he proposed. He could not see her from where he was lying, but he could imagine the look on her face perfectly.

The doctor responded with the same sense of dignity he had maintained throughout.

'I assure you, madam, that it is against my principles to perform surgery, which might even require amputation, against the will of the patient.'

'Well, to begin with you could at least help us to get him undressed, don't you think?'

But no, Romelius was not willing.

'Mr. Schagerström and I have already discussed the matter. He does not wish to be disturbed. And I find this appropriate. In line with my principles, my dear sister-in-law… '

Schagerström followed this discussion with great interest. What would be Charlotte's next move? Would she hit her brother-in-law on the side of his head or throw him into a tub of ice-cold water?

'Johansson, bring us a bottle of champagne and two glasses!!'

While the servant was getting them, Charlotte said no more to her brother-in-law, but Schagerström heard her whispering to Mrs. Sällberg.

Johansson returned, there was the sound of a champagne cork popping, and the liquid being poured, fizzing, into the glasses.

'Mrs. Sällberg, take Johansson and prepare things as we agreed,' said Charlotte.

'And now, Doctor brother-in-law,' said Charlotte when the two employees had left the room, 'now I propose that we raise our glasses to Gustaf Henrik Schagerström, the foundry and mill owner. I assure you that he is a true Polhem himself. Not only did he get the old sawmill here at Stora Sjötorp going again, he also arranged things so that he would be pulled into it personally. And no one will ever imagine that it was anything but an accident. *Skål*, brother-in-law, for Gustaf Henrik!'

Schagerström allowed these words to pass without even the slightest sign of life. 'She couldn't possibly believe it,' he thought. 'All she's trying to do is to frighten that idiotic doctor.'

'Oh, my honored sister-in-law, whatever are you saying? Why on earth?'

Schagerström heard the soft fizzing of the champagne, and understood that Charlotte was pouring her guest another glass.

'If, brother-in-law, you will permit, I would now like to propose a toast to myself. This very morning I encountered my former fiancé in the parsonage garden, and he made it clear to me that he loved me now every bit as much as I once loved him. And I liked hearing those words. That might have been wrong of me, as I am now living happily with another man; what is your opinion, brother-in-law? Was it not quite human and natural for someone who has been despised and rejected to react in that way? And if we go on to assume, brother-in-law, that Henrik came walking through the garden and saw me with Karl-Artur, would it not have been advisable for him to hear how I responded to the man I loved in my youth, before rushing home to throw himself into the sawmill?'

'Indeed, I must admit I agree with you,' the doctor replied. 'I'll deal with him, that rogue. And to think he imagined he would be spared my surgical knife! *Skål*, Charlotte!'

The doctor was speaking with a different voice, in a different tone. Schagerström lay there breathless with excitement. Would Charlotte emerge victorious?

The doctor's glass was filled again, and Charlotte embarked on another little harangue.

'And now a toast to Doctor Richard Romelius. Two and a half years ago his wife was on the verge of death, his home in complete poverty, his children running around like wild colts. Now all that has changed, and yet today he refuses…'

Schagerström heard a glass being set firmly down on the table.

'Today,' the doctor's voice said, 'today Richard Romelius will save the life of the man who gave him back his wife and his home, and who aids his children. No more champagne, thank you, sister-in-law. I am determined to save the life of that man, with or without his consent, come what may.'

Immediately, he rose and left the room. He was probably going to collect his physician's bag. Schagerström knew that Charlotte and the champagne had won. He would undergo surgery, no matter how hard he fought it.

At that moment, Charlotte approached his divan. She stood behind the armrest, bending down over him. He shut his eyes.

'Henrik,' she said, 'you do understand what I am saying?'

A barely perceptible tremor of the eyelid was all the answer she received.

'Well, it is important for you to know that this afternoon Sundler, the organist, came to the parsonage to vent his woes. His wife intends to leave him. You see, Karl-Artur has a new idea. He no longer wants to be an ordinary minister of the church. He wishes to follow the commandments of Jesus and go off as one of His apostles, bearing neither sack nor stick. He wants to preach from village to village and market to market, at the inns and the resting places. And Thea intends to abandon her husband to accompany him. My poor friend, do you not see now that Karl-Artur, in order to go to such an extreme, must have received a reply this morning from someone he loves which has brought him to the verge of despair?'

Schagerström did not move. He had still not heard the right words.

Charlotte sighed, a little impatiently.

'How can you still be such an idiot?' she asked. 'Must I tell you that you are the one for me, that I love you, you, and none other?'

Schagerström opened his eyes. He met Charlotte's gaze eagerly, tenderly, his eyes full of tears. His irritation, his cowardice, his childishness, all of which had ruled him since his accident, vanished. His desire for life was reignited. He did not fear pain. He did not want to die. All he wanted was to be cared for, to be saved.

MADEMOISELLE JAQUETTE

One morning, Mademoiselle Jaquette Ekenstedt was sitting in her usual spot at the bay window in her mother's room, reading aloud to her from the letters her brother had sent home in the old days when he was at the university.

She was reading very clearly and carefully, emphasizing expressions like 'my beloved mother,' 'my loving parents', and 'my filial respect and gratitude,' and placing even greater stress on the parts about Karl-Artur's admiration for his mother's talents, not least her ability to write poetry. She would repeat sentences like that and then sometimes repeat them again, because her mother's cheeks took on such a sweet blush when she heard these strong expressions of her son's appreciation.

Not the least bit of distraction or fatigue could be sensed in Mademoiselle Jaquette. But occasionally she would raise her eyes and go on reciting full paragraphs without looking down at the written text, as if she knew it all by heart.

She looked out over the Klara River, wide and powerful as it flowed below her mother's window, her gaze following the steady stream of people crossing the West Bridge. Farmers from Grava and Stora Kil on their way home after successful purchases at the market. Schoolboys rushing to their lodgings on their lunch hour, books dangling from a strap slung over their shoulders, and the occasional carriage of the wealthy passing by, with fast horses and well-liveried drivers, streaming to the county seat.

Mademoiselle Jaquette was in a despondent frame of mind that day. She was thinking about how monotonous her life had become, about how she never had the opportunity to experience the joys and sorrows of truly living. This did not bother her every day, of course, but now and then she could not help being overcome by disappointment at how tedious and uneventful her life was.

Her mother, the colonel's wife, sat looking at her knitting oblivious to the fact that her daughter's eyes were glued to the flow of people crossing the bridge; everything went on very smoothly until Mademoiselle Jaquette lost her place. She was in a different letter than the one from which she had just been reading. There was a rapid leap from the autumn semester to the spring, and as the letters were very similar she went on reciting with the same choice emphases and the same patience, until her mother eventually began to weep, saying that she would rather read on her own. Jaquette had skipped again, a full seven or eight epistles. She begrudged reading them, complained her mother. She was simply a careless reader. But that was not strange, because she had never really loved her brother, nor had Eva, for that matter, nor Arcker, Eva's husband, in fact not even his own father had loved him.

The colonel's wife sighed and wept bitter tears over the want of love in the family, but Jaquette could not muster the energy to defend herself or any of the others. She rang for the serving girl to ask for some jam and pastries, which gave the colonel's wife such pleasure that she forgot her misery. Still, no sooner had she set her spoon down than she asked Jaquette if she would not be so good as to read to her a bit from Karl-Artur's letters. They were so strikingly beautiful, and it had been such a long time since she had heard them.

So, once again, Mademoiselle Jaquette picked up the pile of letters and began reading, again with fine diction and very expressively. Her mother sat listening, elegant and noble, as she had been listening now, to the same letters, for nearly three years.

She was extremely finely dressed and coiffed, and on her feet she wore little brocade pumps, as always. But now she was a pale, yellowing little old woman, bent and weak. One could barely discern the beauty that had once possessed those features, and the twinkle in those dear eyes. The colonel's wife was like a withered rose. The last petals were still there, but with the next slight breeze, they would fall.

Mademoiselle Jaquette, however, was a most unsatisfactory reader that morning. Her mother was being transported to a lecture by Professor Atterbom, who was explaining the Romantic philosophers, when she noticed Jaquette beginning to stumble and stammer over the words, and reading most distractedly. Once again, Mrs. Ekenstedt was distraught, and pleaded with her daughter to let her read for herself, since it was clear that Jaquette had no interest in following the course of her brother's studies, but far preferred sitting watching the young men loafing about on the West Bridge.

It was true that Jaquette's eyes had been on the West Bridge, but far from spying out for young men, what had captured her attention was a peddler woman from Dalarna, a tall, handsome woman with a black leather sack on her back, who had already been standing for quite a long time, leaning over the railing, staring down at the water.

'It cannot be!' thought Mademoiselle Jaquette. 'And yet I'm sure I recognize the folk costume. Oh, please let that poor woman move on and stop hanging over the river!'

In spite of her mother's eternal complaints about her inadequate reading skills, she was unable to stop herself from glancing over and over again at the woman standing staring down into the Klara river. That wide body of water just now, when all the snow had recently melted, was in its prime, and looked most impressive as it gushed under the arches of the bridge. But who had ever seen a poor peddler girl take the time to stand for hours, delighting in the play of the waves?

'Something's not right about that,' Mademoiselle Jaquette thought. 'Someone ought to go and talk to her, and find out why she is standing there.'

She began to consider asking her mother for permission to stop reading and take a walk in the lovely spring weather, but the next time she looked up the woman was gone.

Reluctantly, her eyes went to the surface of the water, looking for something red and green whirling in the white foam. Fortunately she saw nothing of the kind, and to the great satisfaction of Mrs. Ekenstedt, the next few minutes of reading were absolutely faultless.

But, alas, that peculiar stuttering and stammering returned quite soon. Jaquette was certainly being insufferable that morning.

Indeed, Mademoiselle Jaquette was once again distracted. Now she sat listening to the voices rising from the colonel's study, which was right below her mother's room.

She could hear her father's booming bass voice very clearly. Whether it was expressing astonishment or fury she was unable to determine, but she was certain it was booming even more deeply than usual. She also thought she could discern a woman's voice, rising and falling in an unusual cadence.

To the vast astonishment of the colonel's wife, Jaquette stopped reading from her brother's extraordinarily well-written and fascinating accounts without so much as an apology or an explanation. She merely rang for the serving girl, asked her to sit with her mother for a while, and left the room.

A moment later Jaquette entered the colonel's study, and found him in conversation with his daughter-in-law, former peddler Anna Svärd, a person whose name no one had dared to utter in the Ekenstedt household ever since the fateful day of the funeral of the cathedral dean's wife, Mrs. Sjöborg, God rest her soul. The colonel was behind his desk, angled away from his daughter-in-law. His posture made it eminently clear that her visit was highly unwelcome. Anna Svärd was standing behind him. She had removed her sack from her back and was in the process of untying it. Neither of then paid any heed to the arrival of Jaquette, but continued their discussion.

'At first I'd thought to go straight home to Medstubyn,' said Anna Svärd, 'but as I didn't fancy going back to Mother without a shilling in my pocket, I passed through Karlstad to ask Hoving, the merchant, to give me some goods on credit, just enough to carry in this pack of mine. I thought he ought to do it, for old times' sake, but he wouldn't hear of it.'

Mademoiselle Jaquette, whose head was full of both

what she had recently seen from her mother's window and the contents of a letter she had received that very morning from the widow of Pastor Forsius in Korskyrka, looked at her sister-in-law with great curiosity. That she was in advanced pregnancy was immediately obvious, but as she was a large woman with fine bearing, it was not particularly unbecoming. Her face was as lovely as always, although her eyebrows were so tightly knitted as to form a dark, unbroken line, under which her deep blue eyes gleamed defiantly, perhaps even maliciously.

The colonel did not answer his daughter-in-law right out, but turned instead to Jaquette.

'Your sister-in-law has come to inform us,' he said quite drily, 'that she has tired of living with your brother and wishes to resume her former profession.'

Anna Svärd was now finished undoing her knots. She raised the sack, full of nothing but straw and hay, and pushed it under the colonel's nose.

'Here's proof I've nothing at all in't,' she explained, 'but since I was ashamed to go round with an empty sack, I filled it with a sheaf of hay.'

The colonel jerked back, and pushed away the sack, showing every possible sign of aversion. The peddler woman turned to Jaquette.

'You were kind to me, you were, Jaquette, once upon a time. Do put in a good word for me now with your father, so he'll lend me two hundred dalers. He'll get them back next year at Michaelmas market time.'

Mademoiselle Jaquette, who had been sitting and sighing just a few minutes earlier over how tame and empty her life was, looked a bit taken aback by this request to intervene on behalf of her sister-in-law. She found herself speechless, and so it was the colonel who went on.

'I'd strongly advise you to refrain,' he roared. 'We know very well, of course, who really sent you here. He daren't come in person, and so we have received the pleasure of your visit in his stead.'

'But, dearest Father…'

227

Anna Svärd was not particularly ruffled by this accusation.

'You must be mad!' she replied. 'As you couldn't put up with having 'im as your son, I'd 've thought you'd understand that being his wife could drive anyone to distraction.'

'Dear Father, this very morning I had a letter from Mrs. Forsius, the old pastor's widow in Korskyrka. It is quite true that Anna and Karl-Artur have separated on unfriendly terms.'

'Be that as it may,' the colonel answered, 'it still strikes me as extremely unpleasing to have a daughter-in-law peddling her wares on the roads.'

'Oh, yes, I can see you might think it a bad thing,' said Anna Svärd. 'But if you won't lend me a helping hand as I'm askin', then make me a better offer! If you'd consider givin' me three thousand to buy a little farm so's I could keep a horse and a cow and stay at home with my child instead of having to wander on the roads, I don't s'pose I'd object. Just so's you know.'

She stood there in silence a moment, having made that proposal. She seemed to be waiting for an answer, but none was forthcoming.

'You couldn't do somethin' along those lines?' she asked.

'No,' said the colonel, 'I couldn't'.

'All right then,' said his daughter-in-law, 'since you won't, there are others who will lend me money, so I can get back to peddlin' my wares. I've heard Agust Bonander's in town. I've not wanted to do business with him in the past, him bein' a crook, but I'll go see him now.'

Again she seemed to be waiting for an answer, but when none was forthcoming she bent down over her sack to tie it back up. Her fingers were moving at breakneck speed, and Mademoiselle Jaquette realized that if she were going to say or do anything in an effort to move her father, she would have to act at once.

And certainly Mademoiselle Jaquette wanted to, but she had no idea how. There were too many obstacles.

The colonel was still a tall, strong gentleman. He was neither bent nor aged like his wife. But he had developed a large number of deep lines in his brow, and his eyes shone with a burning, piercing glow that seemed to issue from some inner fire that would not die down. Mademoiselle Jaquette often felt more sympathy with him than with her mother. Memory is an invaluable gift, but perhaps it is better to lose it than to nurture a hate that can never be placated or extinguished.

There was only one key to open the way to the colonel's mercy, and of course Mademoiselle Jaquette knew what that key was called, but she could not see how to make use of it.

Suddenly Mademoiselle Jaquette appeared to have tired of the entire scene. Leaving the hostile parties to their fate, she walked out of the room.

However, she was not gone long. At the very moment her sister-in-law had raised her sack onto her back and was about to go, Mademoiselle Jaquette reappeared, this time in coat and hat. She walked straight over to her father and extended her hand.

'Well then, farewell for now, dear father!'

The colonel looked up from his desk.

'What's wrong with you? Where are you off to?'

'I'm off with Anna, father dear.'

'Have you entirely taken leave of your senses?'

'I assure you not, father. But when I turned thirty last month, you were kind enough, dear father, to give me your country farmstead, not far from here. I realize that it is your intention, father, that I move out there once you have passed on, and indeed it is a sweet place, nice and cosy, and there is even a bit of livestock and a garden to tend. No one could wish for a nicer home. But I am sure I will manage when that time comes in any case and so, father, with your permission I intend to bestow the farmstead on my sister-in-law. I will accompany her there now, and stay until she gets settled, and at least until the baby is born.'

The colonel had sprung to his feet. He looked far from approving.

'No, I swear…'

But the colonel and his daughter had always been most intimate friends, and Mademoiselle Jaquette did not fear him in the least. She was just completely unaccustomed to intervening and making decisions and arrangements. She had never had to do anything along those lines in all her life.

'Father dear, you gave me the property with a deed of title,' she said, 'and you cannot now take it back. And Anna will take much better care of the place than I ever could. Because, dear father, since you never allow us to speak of Karl-Artur, you have no idea what a capable wife he has. Eva and I have often wished we could show her some kindness, but we have not dared, because of you, Father.'

Mademoiselle Jaquette stood there, a bit of a blush on her already slightly sunken cheeks, going on with sheer satisfaction about her plan.

'Once summer comes I expect that you and dear Mother will row down to Älvsnäs to visit your grandchild. We'll receive you there with pleasure. I think the baby will bring life back to my dear mother.'

The colonel's face twitched. He had never before considered how he would manage with his wife if Jaquette left home.

'Will you be gone all that time?' he exclaimed. 'Who will read aloud to your dear mother?'

'Father dear, you will just have to tell Eva to come around and read for a few hours every morning and every afternoon. Unless, Father dear, you think it more suitable to engage a new nurse?'

The colonel stuck his hands in his trouser pockets and gave a whistle. He was thinking about what a dismal failure it tended to be when Eva read to his wife. He also knew there was no nurse in the world who could bear to read Karl-Artur's university letters day out and day in. Jaquette was the only person who had the patience.

'Now listen, Jaquette!' said the colonel. 'What will it take to make you desist from this madness?'

'Three thousand dalers, dear Father.'

The colonel opened one of the desk drawers. Pulling out three large bundles of cash, he gave the money to Mademoiselle Jaquette. She, in turn, put it in her sister-in-law's pocket and gave her a kiss.

'Dear Anna!' she said. 'You have been most ungently treated at someone's hand, I know. But when you get back to your village and are settled there in peace and quiet, remember that at least you have had the opportunity to experience the give and take that is life!'

She then walked her sister-in-law to the garden gate. And it seemed to Mademoiselle Jaquette that the gleam in her eyes was a little less harsh and fierce when they said good-bye.

When she returned to the house, Mademoiselle Jaquette removed her coat and hat and went upstairs to sit at the window opposite her mother. Setting the bundle of letters in her lap, she began to read in a beautiful voice and with excellent diction. Her usual lapse, of skipping from one letter to another, still occurred now and then. But that day it was not the throngs crossing the West Bridge that distracted Mademoiselle Jaquette. Instead, she was sitting there daydreaming of herself and her sister-in-law having moved out to the farm, of her brother's baby having come into the world, of herself living a life in the service of something young and growing rather than just for things old and withered.

ANNSTU LISA

It really did seem as if Mademoiselle Jaquette's kindness had made an impression on her poor sister-in-law.

'You see, Anna, not all the honesty and fairness in the world has come to an end,' she must have told herself. 'You didn't have to get all the way to Medstubyn to meet a kind soul.'

Truth be told and now that she had thought about it, the idea of returning to her home parts and having to bear all the sneers she would face was not particularly appealing. 'What did I tell you? She wouldn't do as a minister's wife,' everyone from the sheriff's wife to the young men who were learning to read around the big table in Cantor Medberg's schoolhouse kitchen would say.

In addition, she had always been partial to money, and having those three thousand dalers in her pocket would make it easier to be on the road, she thought. She had plenty to ponder as she walked along.

When it came right down to it, she had always been quite at home in the little cottage on the doctor's property, above the garden, and so she began to wonder whether it might not be a mistake to abandon it. Would it not be wiser to buy a few acres of land, build a cowshed and get herself some livestock? God willing, she might have a well-to-do farmstead in a few years.

And so she did not turn north, along the Klara River valley, which would have been the shortest route to her home tracts, but instead took the main road east, along the shore of Lake Vänern, the right direction for someone heading for Korskyrka.

As far as her husband was concerned, she imagined

nothing but to find him sitting at the desk in his fine study, quite as usual. Nor did she believe that he would make it difficult for them to resume their life together.

'He'll certainly need someone to do his cleaning and cooking,' she thought. 'No reason to think I won't do for him just as well as the next person.'

Clearly, her days on the road had done her good, with the fresh air of spring and, not least, Mademoiselle Jaquette's kindness. Her riled spirits had settled. She could see things rationally, without making a whole mountain out of a grain of sand.

Mile after mile she wandered through the verdant farmlands east of Karlstad. She saw manor houses and villages scattered over the plain. The fields in those parts were large and not broken up by rocky ridges. The forests had been cleared as far as the eye could see. With the three thousand dalers in her pocket, she regarded this part of the country with renewed interest. 'Perhaps the best thing to do would be to stay on in these parts,' she thought. 'There could hardly be a place where the earth was more welcoming to the plow.'

Of course, she inspected closely every single farm she passed. At each one she found there was something to learn and to contemplate. Her eyes had opened to the world at large. No longer did her thoughts orbit in unbroken circles around the ten children, Thea, Karl-Artur and her fear of punishment.

Just after she had passed one of the little white churches in the area, she found herself in the midst of a spring market. There were more or less the same merchants and the same goods, the same stalls and flapping signs as there had been at the market in Korskyrka a week or so before. But as it was late in the day, the people in the ever-moving throng had had time to get quite a bit of aquavit under their belts. The atmosphere was wilder, rougher and coarser. Everywhere there were rowdy people trying to pick a fight. The horse traders and tinkers were particularly bellicose. It felt as if a huge brawl might break out at any moment. Anna Svärd, experienced as she was in such situations, picked up speed in an attempt to get out of the crowd before the fracas.

Suddenly, however, she heard something that made her stop and listen. In all the chatter, with all the grinding of the barrel organs, the lowing of livestock, the rattling of traps, in all the general noisy market buzz, a woman's voice rose in a hymn. It sailed upwards, lively, beautifully clear, and audible far and wide. Anyone listening had to ask whether it was not some heavenly wonder they were experiencing, with this wonderful singing rising up out of the rough, roaring din.

Everyone at the market was dumbstruck. All trading and haggling ceased, people stopped talking mid-sentence, stopped drinking with their bottles halfway to their mouths.

The woman who was singing was standing on what people generally thought of as a vagrant's trap, a very simple wagon with neither seats nor cover, in order to be higher than the heads in the crowd. She was short and fat, dressed in a simple black coat, her features were ugly, her bulging eyes were watery.

A circle of listeners had already gathered around her. It was a shame that the woman with that glorious voice was not also lovely to look at, but the beauty of her song was such that they were glued to the spot, listening attentively.

'Had it not been impossible…' thought Anna Svärd. 'No, I must be seeing wrong.'

She refused to believe what she saw. She said to herself that as the woman was singing she was transformed and became beautiful, pure and holy. She had never seen that happen to that other woman, the one who looked so similar.

The hymn drew to an end. The woman stepped down off the trap and a man rose up from the crowd to take her place.

He was dressed in gray homespun, with a wide-brimmed hat on his head. He pulled it off at once, tossing it down into the trap, then stood for a moment, hands clasped and eyes lowered, deep in prayer. The wind was playing through his hair, which blew over his brow, making the contrast with his pale, radiant face even more marked. As he stood there, a sunbeam cast its glow down on him, turning his fine face almost translucent and framing it, for a moment, with a halo.

It was as if the sunlight wanted to help draw everyone's attention to him.

Anna Svärd, who of course did not fail to recognize her husband, thought that she had never seen him so beautiful. And the whole crowd, too, who had planned to get back to their buying, selling and carousing when the singing came to an end, found themselves standing there, silent with anticipation of what that man might be going to tell them.

Nor did they have to wait long for Karl-Artur to begin to speak. He raised his dark eyes and let their gaze sweep across the throng, as he stood there, otherwise completely still. From the middle of the vast, solemn silence that had overtaken the marketplace, his voice could be heard far and wide.

It is easy to imagine how the blood rose to his wife's head. She was unable to take in a word of what her husband had to say. Instead, she was preoccupied with asking herself what all this might mean. What were Thea and Karl-Artur doing here, at the market?

After some time she was calm enough to hear a few sentences. She listened as Karl-Artur told the crowd that he wished to follow Jesus' commandment to walk the roads and byways to preach the gospel of Heaven. He no longer wanted to preach from a pulpit. He had resigned from his clerical duties.

The crowd, finding all this both appealing and astonishing, listened in almost dead silence. The silence was broken now and then by some tipsy ruffian shouting that he was tired of listening to that prattler on the gypsy trap. This was a market, wasn't it, where there were supposed to be fun and games, not standing through sermons. But such mischief-makers were soon put in their place.

Those wanting to listen to this new kind of sermonizing were in the majority.

It would be tempting to say that no one but Anna Svärd felt any anger or ill will. All that is certain is that she was extremely upset. Was her husband no longer a man of the cloth, then? Were he and Thea planning to wander the roads from north to south like other vagrants? Shouldn't she, his wife, have any say in the matter? She soon found that she could not restrain herself. She wanted to make her way to the front of the crowd and bring all this fancy talk to an end. She would proclaim the truth about Karl-Artur and Thea. Each one married to somebody else. Whoremonger and harlot. And wanting to stand there all holy and preaching the word of God!

Just as she was about to work her way forward, a hand grasped her shoulder. She looked up and not until then did she notice that the person standing next to her was old Annstu Lisa, the most elderly and most prominent of all the peddler women, a tall, bony woman with a weather-beaten face, and clouded, inscrutable eyes, altogether heavy and implacable as a block of granite.

Renowned as she was for her craftiness and for her insatiable needs for tobacco, coffee and card playing, the woman also had other talents, less often spoken of. But Anna had heard whispered that Annstu Lisa was both clairvoyant and intuitive, and somehow able to make people buy from her stall and pay what she was asking. And feeling that hand on her shoulder, Anna knew right away that the old woman had not placed it there by chance.

The old woman said not a word, and it would have been possible for Anna just to shrug off the hand, but the peculiar thing was that she did not do so. Instead, she just stood there, quite still, listening to the man who was speaking, just like all the others.

But the way Karl-Artur was speaking that evening at the market she had only heard one other time, that Sunday in Korskyrka when his sermon had been on the wonderful text about love.

She remembered very well exactly what had happened that day, how she had sat there hoping Thea would not arrive and use her tricks to frighten him, and how unhappy it had made her when she did eventually come and he lost track of his sermon.

So she could completely understand what pleasure it must give him to have his great gift returned to him. And if she, his wife, stepped forward, he would surely lose track of what he was saying, like that other time, and there was no worse hurt she could inflict upon him.

And as she was standing there thinking about the worst possible way she could hurt him, it seemed to her that it was no longer Annstu Lisa standing next to her, but the old pastor's widow, Mrs. Forsius, standing quite solemn and still to show her how a pastor's wife in Korskyrka ought to behave when her husband was at the pulpit.

So Anna Svärd began to move, but not forward to make her way to Karl-Artur. Instead, she headed out of the crowd in the opposite direction, as if to leave the market, which was easy enough to do thanks to the fact that Annstu Lisa was there, preparing the way ahead.

Almost the moment they were back out on the main road, however, Anna felt her wrath rising again, and she turned to the older woman, making no effort to mask her anger.

'Why did you have to stick your nose into my business?' she asked. 'Couldn't I have exposed them to the crowd for what they were?'

'I saw you startin' to bring misfortune down on yerself,' answered Annstu Lisa in her dry, strong voice, 'and I wanted to help you in return for three years back when you left the autumn market to me and Karin from Risgården and the other poor peddlers. By this late in the evening people are off their heads with drink, and ya never know what ya might've fired up.'

Anna Svärd looked at the old woman in surprise. Never in her entire life had she mentioned to a single soul that it was for the sake of her fellow peddlers that she had walked away from that autumn market.

'You's innocent as a lamb,' Annstu Lisa went on. 'Been married to that fellow for nearly three years, ya have, and yet ya canno' see that you two've always gone separate ways, while him an' her, they go the same way. There's no use thinking ya can evade what's ordained for yer.'

When Anna Svärd heard these words, something old and nearly forgotten awoke in her. She remembered that somewhere in God's heaven, everything she was going to experience was already written, and what is written is written and cannot be undone. No power in the world could change it, no, not even Our Lord himself. This was in accord with the beliefs of her own mother and Erik from Jobsgården farm, and in fact of everyone in Medstubyn; it was the faith they lived and died by, the source of their contentment with their lot, and of their courage.

After a few moments she turned to the old woman, who still walked beside her, silent and forbearing.

'Ah, I thank you, Lisa. I would never be such a fool as to struggle against whatever's intended for me.'

Immediately, Annstu Lisa stopped and extended one of those enormous hands of hers which, in spite of their size, never applied more than the slightest pressure.

'And now I'll get on back to my own business,' she replied.

But Anna Svärd had a question for her before they parted.

'As you know so much about me, Lisa, won't you advise me as to where to turn my steps now?'

The answer came without an instant's reflection:

'You must just walk on straight ahead, and what's intended for you will come to meet you tonight.'

Annstu Lisa turned right around, heading back to the market, and Anna Svärd stood there for a long time and watched her go. She had been of great help, as had Mademoiselle Jaquette.

So she walked on in the lovely spring evening, now waiting confidently for whatever was to come, knowing it would be something good and favorable.

She had to walk for a long time, however, before anything happened. In the end she was both hungry and tired, and so she sat down on the verge to take out the food in her pack.

But alas, just as she raised a sandwich to her lips, who should come along the road but two beggar women, gray and dirty and with an incredibly long trail of gray, dirty children tagging along behind.

'I s'pose they'll be taking the food right out of my mouth,' she thought, moving quietly behind a rock in the hopes that the pack of mendicants would pass without catching sight of her.

The way those old women and the ragamuffins who were with them were dressed was indescribable. They had dishrags for headscarves, and, instead of skirts and blouses, sacking that had spent the whole summer on scarecrows, while what passed for shoes were patched with old bits and pieces of birch bark.

But the two beggar women did not seem unhappy about their dirt or their rags. They were laughing and talking so loud they could be heard from afar.

'Never did I imagine it could be so much fun to go about begging,' one said to the other.

'And never would I have thought you'd be so lucky,' said the other. 'Given ten kids, scott free!'

Anna Svärd began to suspect that all was not as it should be. She had heard that it sometimes happened that well-to-do farmers' wives from the parishes in the north of Värmland would go out begging in springtime, when their larders had emptied out, to beg for grain to use for baking and sowing. This pair had not headed out in vain. Both of them and the children were carrying full sacks on their backs.

'If only it weren't such a long way home now,' laughed the first one. 'I wish we could hire a wagon at the inn to take us back to Ekshärad.'

No sooner had she heard that word than Anna Svärd rushed up onto the road, staring at the beggar women. Under their dirt and the scraggly hair hanging down into their eyes, she recognized their features. One of them lived in a forest cottage – she might actually have been poor enough to need to beg – while the other was a wealthy widow the last time Anna saw her. On that occasion she had invited her in for coffee made from real beans, and bought both a comb to hold up her hair with and a length of silk.

The instant the women set eyes on Anna Svärd they set to with their begging.

'Ya wouldn't have some old scrap in your sack that we could give to the young'uns?'

'Aren't you the mistress of Norviken farm?' Anna asked, in

a facetious tone. 'How can things have gone so badly for you that you now have to go about with a beggar's sack?'

'Me farm's burnt down,' said the woman, 'and the cows've died, and the crops've froz…'

That was all she managed to say before a sharp cry was heard from the children. Ten of the beggar children came rushing at Anna Svärd, embracing her, nearly bowling her over.

To begin with, Anna Svärd did not direct her attention toward them. She lay a heavy hand on the woman's shoulder.

'I see, you're the wife of these children's uncle,' she said. 'Well, now you and I are going to see the sheriff. And you'll get that wagon, you and the children, but to jail, not home.'

When the beggar woman heard this, she gave a cry. Throwing the bag aside, she began to run down the road as fast as her legs could carry her, and the same applied to the other woman and the children who were hers.

But Anna Svärd just stood still on the road with her own ten children surrounding her and with joy and peace in her heart.

And before she began to talk to them and to ask them about what things had been like at their uncle's, she felt it fitting to thank God for having brought them together again. So she raised her voice in an evening hymn, the first one she had taught them:

Now the day is over,
night is drawing nigh
shadows of the evening
steal across the sky.

PART THREE

Selma Lagerlöf

THE ROGUE BARON

Oh, how it must have upset the men who had inherited the venerable manor houses, mills and foundries along the long shores of Lake Löven, those men who could still tell traditional tales of proud cavaliers, who ruled their estates with absolute authority, who held the casting vote on every matter at parish meetings and whose birthdays were celebrated as if they were royalty, oh, how it must have distressed them that their marriages were not blessed with sons, and that their wives, who in all other ways obeyed and acquiesced to them, seemed to have entered into a malicious conspiracy to bring into the world nothing but daughters.

During those years when daughter after daughter was born, these men must have brooded time and again over the mysteries of existence and the dispensations of destiny. They asked themselves whether this might be a new means by which the ancient powers were indicating their displeasure with the mortals, and whether they might be intending to send out over the world a flood of women, a flood that would actually destroy the multitude of sinners more effectively than had been possible in Noah's day.

And they certainly had good reason to be worried. Because although it was still far from a question of extinction or the end of the entire human race, the continued existence of a number of ancient families was certainly in jeopardy. The Sinclaires, powerful mill owners, and the Hedenfelts, majors and colonels for generations, were under threat. The noble, revered family of clergymen who had ruled the parsonage at Bro for more than a century were threatened, and there was a risk that there might be no more offspring of the old German organist Faber to run their fingers skillfully over the keyboards of the bellowing, trumpeting organs of the churches of Värmland.

But although there was cause for alarm, it penetrated no more deeply than that most of the gentlemen of the parish of Bro were able to go on enjoying life to the hilt. There was only one among them who was of such a nature that he was unable, day and night, to forget his longing for sons; he would far rather have been a menial day worker than a Baron Löwensköld living in the knowledge that his lineage would not continue.

Never could Adrian Löwensköld, that fine gentleman, owner of Hedeby manor, who was always improving and beautifying his home and his property, that just master who did his best to make all those who worked for him happy, never could he rid himself of the feeling that he had offended his country, his forefathers and all of humanity by having given the world nothing but five daughters and no son, not a single diligent worker of the kind who, in times past, had aided Sweden's struggle for greatness and power. In spite of his efforts to be fair and not to put the blame on anyone innocent, he could not help feeling that life was repugnant now that he had nothing but female company to spend it with. He did know that neither his wife nor his old aunt nor his five daughters nor their nursery maid was the cause of his unhappiness. And yet every day he joined their company only to spoil their pleasure, unable to forgive them for not surrounding him, rather than with quiet, modest women, with a band of mischievous, noisy, ravenous young scamps.

This constant disgruntlement made him old before his time. There was really very little left in him of the merry young gentleman who had once upon a time married that renowned beauty, Marianne Sinclaire. It was said that he lost a sizeable portion of the happiness of his youth when Marianne died after a single year of marriage. His second, to the wealthy Miss Wachthausen from Kymmelsta, had been a marriage of convenience, and as his wife she was unable to rein in his all-consuming yearning. But his old, powerful *joie de vivre* would undoubtedly have returned if only he had had a son. The two of them would have gone hunting or taken long fishing expeditions. As in his lighthearted youth, he would once again have traveled all day for the pleasure of dancing all night. Instead, however, he tramped his property, bored to death with all the delicate, small-minded femininity he encountered everywhere he turned.

One day, however, just when Baron Adrian's heart was hardening irrevocably, his brother Göran, a pathetic, scorned vagrant who had made himself the object of the animosity of the entire family, drove his sledge up to the main entrance of Hedeby manor.

This was unheard of. This peculiar, disreputable man, who lived amongst tinkers and horse traders and was married to a gypsy woman, often appeared at other manors in the area with his filthy trap full of rags, children, and all kinds of foul bundles, to trade horses or buy junk. But never before had he dared to darken his brother's doorstep.

It is not easy to determine the extent to which the life Göran Löwensköld had been living had wiped the past out of his memory.

For several days there had been terrible snowstorms, and as his sad little dun nag slowly made its way through the drifts in the lane leading up to Hedeby, the poor rogue baron may have been dreaming his way back to younger days. Perhaps he was imagining that he was once again a lad on his way home from school in Karlstad, and perhaps he was even expecting his two handsome parents to be waiting at the door to welcome him. He was thinking about how the servants would come rushing out to the sledge to free him from foot furs and animal hides. Eager hands would remove his fur coat and the cap from his head, and unbuckle his tall boots. His mother would be waiting impatiently for his outer garments to come off so she could embrace him, lead him to the hearth, pour him some scalding hot coffee and finally sit next to him, quite still, just taking him in.

Everyone knows that during the winter, when the snowstorms follow one another day after day after day, when all the roads are blocked and no one dares undertake a journey, the windows of the isolated manor houses in the countryside are seldom void of curious lookouts who never tire of gazing down the lane, waiting for something new, something impossible, something – who knew what?

On such days the arrival of even a sledge carrying vagrants is a great event, reported from room to room, and so while the little dun nag was struggling up the lane Baron Adrian had already been informed of the name of the approaching visitor.

And still – as he stepped into the doorway with his most dismissive frown and was about to greet his brother in such a way that he would neither dare to make a joke nor to contradict him, he saw that Göran, the idler he held in such contempt, the prodigal son, who had brought down disgrace and damage upon him all his life, had not arrived this time in the company of black-eyed vagrant children or shameless beggar women, but with the very thing he wished for more than anything, and that had been denied to the faithful and just man he was.

And the child this careworn vagrant with the haggard jailbird face had with him amongst the bundles and sacks in his trap was no bogus child. In fact he bore a very close resemblance to the portrait of Baron Adrian's father that hung in state over the sofa in the drawing room at Hedeby. He recognized the soft, fine-featured face with its large dreamy eyes he had so often admired. So not only did his brother have a son, he was a beggar child blessed with the beauty inherited from his maternal ancestors, of which his own daughters had not inherited a drop.

But at that very moment the last of the Löwenskölds was not up to much. When he was lifted out of the sledge, he lay in his father's arms semi-conscious, his eyes sunken and his hands and cheeks frostbitten.

And so Baron Adrian did not follow his intention to send his brother packing with a few rough words. No, when his brother approached with the child in his arms and a tentative question lingering in his eyes, Baron Adrian forgot all the suffering he had been put through on his brother's account as well as all the worry his brother had caused their parents, and he opened the door wide to him.

Göran Löwensköld, however, refused to go any further in than the vestibule, and when his brother went on to open the drawing room door and he saw the bright fire in the fireplace and the furniture and the wallpaper, all of which he recognized from childhood, he stood still, shaking his head.

'No,' he said, 'that is not for me. I will go no further. But if you would consider taking in the child?'

Baron Adrian accepted the child as the most precious of treasures and began at once to rub and massage the little body to warm it. He did not call out to any of the womenfolk for help. He was of course aware that he would eventually have to do so, but for these first few minutes he wanted the child to be his and his alone. And suddenly he put his whiskered cheek up against the cold, dirty one of the little beggar child in a bashful caress.

'He looks so much like Father,' he said, a note of hesitation in his voice. 'You are fortunate, Göran, in having a son.'

When Baron Göran saw how his brother pressed the child to his chest, he ought to have known that the owner of Hedeby manor would have been prepared to give his brother room and board until his last breath simply because he was fortunate enough to have a son. He ought to have known that from that moment on his brother would tolerate his mockery, his sloth, his card playing, his drinking without ever again raising his voice in criticism.

And yet he did not seem to have the slightest desire to stay, but rather moved back toward the front door.

'I'm sure you'll understand that I would not have come here if I had had a choice,' he said. 'We've been traveling through the snowstorm for so long I was afraid he might freeze to death on me. I had to bring him here or it would have been the end of him. I have work awaiting me at the parsonage, so I'll be off. I'll come and collect him once the storm is over.'

He stood there with his hand on the doorknob as he said these words. Baron Adrian gave him no direct reply. Perhaps he had not even heard his brother's words. He was completely preoccupied with the child.

'Listen, Göran, his hands are frostbitten. We need to rub them with snow. Could you bring some in please?'

Göran Löwensköld mumbled something indistinct that might have been thank you and goodbye, and opened the door. Baron Adrian thought he was going out to get snow as he had requested. But a moment later he heard a sleigh bell, and when he looked out he saw his brother departing. He was striking the poor dun creature with his whip, making it set off at full speed, the light, powdery snow blowing around the sledge like a cloud of dust.

It was understandable to Baron Adrian that there were many aspects of their home that were painful for his brother to reencounter, and he was not surprised to see him take flight. Aside from that, his head was full of nothing but the child. He went outside himself and brought in snow to rub some life back into the frostbitten little face and hands, and while he was completing this task he began shaping plans for the future. There was no chance that he would allow the last of the Löwenskölds to be returned to his brother and grow up among wild companions.

It is not easy to say what Göran Löwensköld had in mind as he departed from Hedeby. Possibly he intended to return in a few hours to collect the child and at the same time take the opportunity to bask in his brother's rage at once again having allowed himself to be deceived and deluded. Even as he drove away from the estate he was laughing loudly at the thought of his brother laying his cheek against that of the beggar child, and of the pride with which he lifted this new bearer of their name and their lineage in his arms.

But somehow the laughter stuck in his throat. He sat there with his threadbare fur cap pulled down nearly to his eyes, traveling the road without a thought of where he was going. Deep, remarkable thoughts possessed him, thoughts demanding to be put immediately into action.

He did not travel to the parsonage at Bro as he had said he would, and the next morning when a messenger from

Hedeby arrived there to ask for him, no one at Bro had any information. Later that morning, however, two farmers who had been out clearing the road of snowdrifts arrived at Hedeby and informed the baron that his brother, the tramp, had been found dead in a roadside ditch. He had driven into the ditch in the dark, and his sledge had overturned. It seemed he had not been able to right it himself, and so had lain at the bottom of the ditch and frozen to death.

Nowhere was it easier, in the dark and in a snowstorm, to lose track of the road than on the flat plains around Bro church. It did not at all seem impossible that Göran Löwensköld, the rogue baron, had fallen victim to an accident.

There was absolutely no reason to believe that he had voluntarily sought death in order for his child to be kept on in the fine refuge he had arranged for him at a moment when his usual, cruel sense of humor had taken the upper hand.

The man, Göran Löwensköld, was nearly out of his mind, and it is certainly not easy to explain his behavior. But everyone knew that this child, his youngest, had been the object of his special affection. He had noted the Löwensköld features in the child's face, and he must have experienced the child as his in a way he had not the other black-eyed vagrant children who had grown up around him. It is not utterly inconceivable that he had sacrificed his life to protect this child from poverty and misery.

When he drove up to Hedeby he may not have had anything in mind beyond playing a joke on his fine gentleman of a brother, who was pining for sons. But the moment he entered his old home, he had felt integrity, security and good will rushing at him, and said to himself that what he wanted was for his youngest child, this child who was the only one who was completely his own, to be able to stay there, and so he had to arrange his journey so that he would never have to return to collect the child.

But no one knows how things really were. Life was probably not dear enough to him that he hesitated to reject it. Perhaps he had long cherished a wish that could now be fulfilled. Perhaps he was pleased to have ultimately found a reason to do what he had been postponing out of indifference or apathy.

And who knows? Perhaps at the very moment of his death he was still pleased to be playing a trick on his only brother, who had always been so good at staying on the right side of life, a final trick. Perhaps it gave him satisfaction to deceive him one last time. Perhaps his lips sneered wryly one final time at the thought that the child he had put into his brother's arms was nothing but a girl, and that a disguise was all that had been needed to open the doors of his patrimonial home to the wretched little lass.

THE BARONESS

The day the rogue baron left his child at Hedeby, Baron Adrian Löwensköld came to the dinner table in high spirits.

Finally he would not have to sit with only women. Today there was a boy at the table, too. He felt that the air in the room was different. He felt young, cheerful, invigorated. Indeed, he even planned to suggest to his wife that they have some wine brought in so they could raise their glasses to the new arrival.

He went straight to his own seat at the round dining table, clasped his hands and listened, head raised, to grace being said by the youngest of his little daughters.

Once seated, he grinned, looking around the table, searching for his nephew. But however hard he tried, he could not see a single child in a jacket and trousers. There was nothing but skirts and tight bodices at the table, as always.

He drew in his compelling eyebrows and snorted. Of course it had been necessary to send his nephew to the nursery for a wash and some clean clothing, but was his wife really foolish enough not to allow him to join them for dinner? Needless to say, he was the child of vagrants, and he would behave accordingly, but none of his five well-mannered daughters was worth so much as the little finger of that child.

Before he could express his disappointment, the baroness made a slight movement with one hand, pointing at a little girl on the chair next to him, her hair neatly plaited.

After a quick head count, he realized that that day there were six little girls at the table. He understood that they had dressed the lad in girl's clothing. Perfectly natural, since the rags he had been wearing upon arrival would not do for the dinner table, and there were only girls' clothes to be had at Hedeby. Still, surely there had been no need to braid that hair, those curly golden locks, into two braids that dangled alongside his ears, just as on his daughters.

'Couldn't you have borrowed a pair of trousers from the foreman,' the baron inquired, 'so you wouldn't have had to dress the boy up so foolishly?'

'Certainly,' his wife responded, her voice just as controlled as usual, with no trace of ridicule or malicious pleasure, 'certainly we could have done that, I imagine. But now she is dressed as rightly becomes her.'

Baron Adrian looked at his wife, at the child, and then back at his wife again.

'I'm afraid Göran has deceived you once more,' said the baroness.

And there was not a tone to her voice, not a glimmer in her eye, to let on that she felt any differently about the whole matter than her husband.

And indeed she did not. She absolutely thought that Göran had behaved shamefully, and exposed his usual spiteful nature. If, deep down, something else was shifting in her soul, it was quite involuntary.

But, well, if a person has been made into a doormat, stepped on every day, it cannot be helped, can it, that the mat would feel a little jolt of satisfaction if the man who has stamped hardest and with the sharpest iron spikes on his heels took a tiny, harmless plummet.

And when the baroness saw her husband's brow furrowed, saw him reject the platter of meat offered by the serving maid, quite as if this little mishap had deprived him of his appetite, her body began to tremble, although her face remained frozen.

Later she had pause to wonder, often, what would have happened to her, to his old aunt, the nursery maid and the six girls, had her husband not risen from his chair with an ugly expletive and rushed from the room. She, personally, would not have been able to stay solemn for a single second longer. She just had to burst out laughing, and so did all the others.

Each and every one just had to lean back in her chair and dissolve into laughter.

They laughed loud and long, each one louder than the next, though at the same time they were embarrassed. It was, of course, not proper to laugh when the head of the family and household had been duped. They were decent, well-bred women and they definitely disapproved of themselves. But their laughter quite simply came from natural human depths, and could not be restrained without risk of suffocation.

The room was in an uproar. For a few minutes they cast aside anything that might otherwise be weighing them down or smothering them, and felt free and superior. They thought they would never again be as suppressed and intimidated as in the past, because they had found themselves able to laugh at their oppressor. As they laughed at him he lost his terrifying power and became an ordinary little human being just like them.

And the baroness, who always spoke of Baron Adrian as the best of all possible husbands, and of herself as the happiest of wives, who never let any stranger, in fact not even his aunt or the nursery maid, make the slightest comment on her husband's behavior, the baroness swore to herself that if she should ever encounter Göran Löwensköld she would try to do something to thank him for this wonderful joke.

But the next day, when the rogue baron was found frozen to death in a wayside ditch near the parsonage and had been transported back to Hedeby, stiff and cold, she did not actually lift a finger to show him the sympathy she had felt for him for a few transient moments. She left all the funeral and burial arrangements to her husband and never protested about a thing.

Baron Adrian went to the expense of having him shrouded, ordered a coffin, and had the family grave opened. He arranged a date for the removal of the body to the chapel with the clergyman from Bro, and took a number of members of the household staff along to the funeral.

But he did nothing more.

He did not allow the windows at Hedeby to be covered

with white sheets, had no evergreen branches spread along the lane, did not let the baroness and her daughters dress in mourning. He did not invite any of the gentlemen of the parish to accompany the coffin to the cemetery, ordered no funeral sweetmeats, and had no funeral reception at home.

In the whole parish of Bro there was not a soul who was anything but glad that Göran Löwensköld was dead. Never again would he assault the gentlemen at the Broby market, pat them on the back and refer to them informally as his brothers just because they had once been classmates at school in Karlstad. It was a relief to almost everyone to know that it would never again occur to him to ask for a fine old gold watch in exchange for a cheap, battered silver one, or a handsome four-year-old mare for an old nag of a horse that was nothing but skin and bones. Indeed it was good to know that he had passed on. While he was alive no one could ever be sure what he might ask for or what revenge he might exact if his request was refused.

Still though, the whole parish of Bro felt that Baron Adrian's behavior seemed overly vindictive. They said that since Baron Göran had lost his life, his brother ought to have been prepared to let bygones be bygones and see him to the grave in dignity and honor.

Moreover, they were almost more critical of the baroness than of her husband, because they would have expected a woman to show greater compassion. Just imagine, she had not so much as put a flower on his coffin! Everyone knew that the enormous calla lily in the dining room at Hedeby was in bloom at the time, and there is nothing as appropriate to see a person who has passed on through his final journey as a calla lily, but none had been given. What could they say about that? Was it not almost inhuman to be unwilling to sacrifice as much as a single calla blossom for her brother-in-law?

Many people probably also thought that Baron Göran's wife ought to have been informed of her husband's death, and were surprised that the baroness did not remind her husband of it. And at least the little girl, Göran Löwensköld's most beloved daughter, ought to have had a mourning dress made up for her. Surely the baroness could not be so subordinate to, and intimidated by, her husband that she did not dare bring a seamstress to the house to arrange suitable clothing for a fatherless child.

As everyone knew, the baroness at Hedeby was a perceptive woman who knew very well how things should be done. And of course she ought to have felt it her duty to bring her husband around when he erred. But on that occasion, she did no such thing.

The dirty sledge with its bundles and rags, its tinplating tools, aquavit keg and greasy decks of cards, and the tramp's little horse, who had not left the side of the his master until people found him dead and dug him out of the snowdrifts had, of course, also been brought to Hedeby. The sledge was standing in an outbuilding and the horse was stabled, but except for giving the horse fodder and water no one had paid any attention to that aspect of the rogue baron's remaining property. The day after the funeral, however, the baron gave orders for the horse to be shod and given an extra ration of fodder, and thus it was clear that he intended to send it off on a long journey.

The foreman at Hedeby at the time was a man born and raised in northern Värmland, where the itinerant vagrants had their winter quarters. He was acquainted with the vagrant family into which Göran had married, and knew where they were to be found. Baron Adrian instructed him to take the pathetic little horse back home, with the sledge and its entire contents, and to inform Baron Göran's wife that he was dead.

However, the baron intended not only for him to return the sledge and the tinplating things, the card games and all the other tattered bits and pieces. He was also to take his niece. She had no right to be staying at Hedeby. She should be returned to the people from whom she came.

And so the day after the funeral Baron Adrian informed his wife that the girl would be sent home the next morning, that she was to be returned in the same rags she had been wearing when she arrived, adding a few words to the effect that he assumed that she, his wife, would be pleased not to have to have the vagrant child in her household any longer.

The baroness did not say a word in reply. She did not protest against the child being taken from Hedeby. She just stood up to go to the nursery and inform the child.

That whole day, it was clear that the baroness was unusually restless; she was unable to sit still. She went from task to task, all the time moving her lips, although not a single word crossed them.

She was to be found in the nursery more often than usual that day, silently watching the one child who was not a daughter of the house. The little girl stood at the window gazing down the lane until there was not a shred of daylight left. She had spent her days that way ever since her arrival at Hedeby. She was standing there waiting for her father to come and collect her. She was bashful and withdrawn, and played very little with the other children. She would probably not be unhappy to be sent home.

When night arrived and the baroness was at her husband's side in their wide bed, she was still very unsettled, and unable to sleep. She told herself that a limit had been reached, that the time had come, that she was now going to have to stand up to her husband. What he was intending must not come to pass.

It was clear to the baroness that Baron Göran had brought about his own death, intending for his daughter to be kept on at Hedeby. He had loved her, and had been possessed by a desire for her to grow up in a good home and become a decent human being. His idea was for her to be raised in accordance with her social standing, and to marry a gentleman. She was not meant to become a vagrant woman driving a vagabond trap, cursing and calling out, surrounded by shrieking, crying beggar children.

In order for that to happen, he had given up his life. He realized that it was a high price to pay, but he had thought nothing of it, simply paid up.

Did her husband realize what his brother had intended? Well, even if he did, he was now taking pleasure in denying his brother that for which he had been prepared to pay with his life. And she, his wife, was going to have to forbid him from doing it.

She would have to put it in a way that would make him do her bidding. She would have to speak with authority and force. He must not be allowed to send his niece away. It was wrong. She knew that this was an action for which retribution would otherwise be exacted. She had swallowed everything thus far. She had let him arrange the funeral just as he chose. She had been saving her ammunition. Nothing was as important as this.

She lay there thinking about how she had seen her brother-in-law huddled down in the sledge as he left the estate. She tried to imagine his dark, morbid thoughts as he drove aimlessly in the snowstorm. Was it possible for a man like that to find peace in his grave if he were denied that which had been the aim of his self-sacrifice? Here at Hedeby, if nowhere else, they knew very well that a dead man had the power to call for revenge.

She had to speak out. Her husband must not be allowed to refuse to obey a dead man. No matter what he had been like in life, he now had the right to be obeyed.

She clenched her fists and beat at her own body, as if to punish herself for her cowardice. Why did she not wake her husband? Why was she not having that conversation?

She had suspected what her husband was planning, and had taken a small countermeasure of her own. The very day Baron Göran was found dead, she had taken his daughter with her when she went to visit a poor crofter where three children were laid up with the measles. Her own daughters had already had measles, and although she could not know whether this child who was not theirs had, she hoped that she had not. Every day since, she had kept an eye out for symptoms of illness in the girl. But so far, nothing. Actually, she knew very well that it would not be until the eleventh day that the illness appeared, and only eight days had passed.

Minute by minute, hour by hour she procrastinated. She was beginning to fear that she would never have the courage to speak up.

But if she did not, what kind of a woman was she? How could she be such a pitiful cur? After all, what could possibly happen to her if she did speak out? Her husband would not strike her. There was no question of that.

But he had a way of looking right past her, paying no attention to what she said. Speaking to him was, to her mind, like talking to a block of ice.

The baroness had another problem as well, which troubled her greatly. A year earlier, at a dinner party in Karlstad, her husband had bumped into a distant relation, Charlotte Löwensköld, now married to the eminent man of affairs, Mr. Schagerström. Charlotte and Baron Adrian had known each other in the day when she was betrothed to his cousin Karl-Artur Ekenstedt; in fact she had once visited Hedeby in the company of her fiancé. The two of them had quite an intimate conversation during which the Baron had expressed his regret over having no son and a whole slew of daughters, and Charlotte had asked whether she might not be allowed to take on one of the daughters, since there were no children at all in her home. She had had one single child, a daughter who had died.

Naturally, the baron exclaimed that he was more than willing, and Charlotte had said that she would have a word with her husband and see what he thought of the idea. Shortly thereafter, the baron and his wife had received a letter asking whether the two of them might really be willing to turn one of their daughters over to the Schagerströms, to raise as their own. The baron had immediately replied in the affirmative. He had not even taken the trouble to inquire whether his wife might be of a different opinion. There was no question about it, such an offer from the wealthiest family in all of Värmland could not be refused. The child would grow up being treated like a princess, not to mention all the innumerable advantages that might be gained from a familial bond with a powerful man.

Although the baroness had not explicitly objected, she tried to win time. Charlotte wanted to come to Hedeby personally and choose the little girl who suited her best, but her visit had been put off now for more than six months. This was mainly the baroness's doing. She had written that she was in the process of having some dress fabric woven and preferred not to have a visitor until the cloth was ready and the dresses made, so her daughters would be nicely dressed when Charlotte came to inspect them. Another time Charlotte had wanted to come, the children had the measles, so that visit, too, had to be postponed. Now it had been ages since she had heard anything from Charlotte, and she had been hoping, deep down, that that wealthy woman, who had such a large household to run, had forgotten the matter entirely.

But after the business of Baron Göran, the baroness had written to Charlotte, asking her to come. Now she was really ready to give one of her daughters up to her. It would be a sacrifice she would make to placate her husband. She was thinking that if she acquiesced to him on that matter, she could demand, in return, that he allowed her to keep the vagrant child under their roof.

Now, however, she knew that it had been to no avail. Her husband was one step ahead of her. The measles had not broken out. Charlotte had not arrived. In a few hours the little girl would be sent away.

She lay there calculating the distance from Hedeby to Stora Sjötorp. Her letter had probably only just arrived there. And the weather had turned so terribly cold after the snowstorm! Charlotte could hardly be expected to venture out in such weather. All night she heard the shutters blowing, as if someone had been standing outside banging a huge mallet against the wall.

She heard the kitchen coming to life. The kitchen maid was feeding the fire and banging pots and pans. There were also sounds from the nursery; the children's nursemaid getting up to dress the vagrant child in her old rags.

The baroness said her husband's name a couple of times, not very loud but quite distinctly. He shifted a bit in his sleep. Had he woken up, she might have spoken, but trying any further to awaken him was beyond her.

She heard the kitchen door open. It must be dreadfully cold

outside. The creaking of that door on its hinges was audible throughout the manor. She could tell that the foreman, who was to take the child away, had come in to collect her.

A moment later the housemaid peeped in through their bedroom door, asking whether the baron or baroness was awake.

Baron Adrian sat right up in bed and asked what on earth was going on.

'It's the foreman,' the girl said. 'He asked me to come up and tell you, Sir, that it is so cold outside he daren't make the journey today. He says when he turned the iron key in the lock it stripped the skin off his hand. At his cottage the bread and butter both froze overnight, and the layer of ice on the water tub was so thick he had to use the hatchet to break it. And he says if it's that cold here you can only imagine how cold it is further north, where he is headed.'

'Bring your candle over here and light mine!' Baron Adrian ordered.

The girl entered the room and lit the tallow candle on his nightstand. The Baron got out of bed, pulled on his dressing gown and walked over to the window to read the thermometer. The whole window was blanketed with a thick layer of hoarfrost, but there was still a little bit of clear glass right where the thermometer was. The baron looked for the line of mercury, but it had vanished entirely, crept right back into its orb.

He moved the candle up and down the thermometer.

'It must be more than forty below,' he muttered.

'The foreman says he would probably be all right on his own, Sir, if you are intent on getting the sledge off,' said the housemaid, 'but he daren't take a child along with him, this winter being what it is.'

'Tell him to go to hell!' cried the Baron, dropping back into bed and pulling the quilt up over his ears.

The maid just stood there, not sure what this answer was supposed to mean, until the baroness explained:

'What the baron means is that you should please inform the foreman there will be no need for him to make his journey until the cold weather breaks. You may also go up to the nursery and tell Marta the child will not be leaving.'

The baroness' voice was just as controlled as usual. Nothing in it gave away the enormous sense of relief she was experiencing.

The cold spell continued. The child could not be sent off that day, or the next. But toward evening on the second day the weather changed. And the baron at once gave instructions for the little girl to be removed from his house the next morning.

Although the baroness did not contradict him outright, she did imply now and then that the child had not been looking quite well for the last couple of days. She was afraid she might be falling ill.

Baron Adrian looked coldly at his wife.

'There's no point,' he told her. 'That child will not remain under my roof. Do you think I have such a weakness for little girls that I want another one to support?'

But that evening after supper when the baroness went to the nursery to look in on the children, the child of the wanderer was in bed, red-faced, feverish and coughing endlessly.

'I'm quite sure, Ma'am, that she's coming down with measles,' said the nursemaid.

And the baroness could not deny that this was roughly how the illness had begun when her own daughters had measles the previous autumn.

'Isn't that awful?' the baroness replied. 'What with the baron having determined that she is to be sent home in the morning.'

After a minute's thought she asked the nursemaid to tell her husband he was wanted for a moment in the nursery, to see what he thought might be wrong with the child who was not theirs.

The baron arrived, and although he was not very familiar with illness, even he had to admit that all was not well with his niece. He had no doubt that she was coming down with measles, for it seemed to be impossible to get rid of the child of his vagrant brother.

Measles it was, and whether or not the baron had any reason to suspect that his wife had anything to do with the child's developing an illness, he had no choice but to keep her in his home for another week, which put him into a terrible humor. Fortunately for the peace of mind of the household, however, a letter soon arrived that helped lift his mood. Charlotte Schagerström wrote that as long as the roads were not icy she would begin her journey to Hedeby in mid-March, and could be expected to arrive on the sixteenth or seventeenth.

Every day, the baron went to the nursery to check whether the little girl who was not theirs was still in bed, which was his standard for decision-making. And the baroness, who could tell that the child had only a light case of measles, and that her spots were already gone, had her hands full with keeping her there. The nursemaid began saying she could very well get dressed and be up and about. It was very difficult for the baroness to persuade her that the child ought to spend a few more days in bed.

It was with indescribable relief that she saw Charlotte's sleigh arrive on the afternoon of the sixteenth of March. Their visitor was so well received, so warmly kissed and hugged by her hostess that it seemed to astonish her. Perhaps the many postponements had made her wonder whether the baroness thought of her as a thief who was coming to appropriate the household's most precious property.

The five little Löwensköld girls were washed with soap until their chubby, rosy faces shone and combed until every strand of their hair lay right up against their heads, with their tight little braids ringed around their ears. They were dressed in their homespun, home-sewn woolen frocks and their thick-soled home-cobbled shoes. The baroness regarded them with great maternal pride as she ushered them into the drawing room. She thought they were the sweetest little girls to be found on this side of the earth.

She knew they were fine, healthy and well brought up, and she felt a sense of expectation when she entered the drawing room, where Charlotte was waiting, with this whole long line behind her.

Charlotte took a cursory look at one after the next, holding her emotions completely in check. She was as kind and pleasant as could be as she shook the hand of each little Löwensköld girl, asking her name and age.

But they did not seem to evoke in Charlotte quite the pleasure the baroness had anticipated.

Perhaps she was calling to mind the fine features and noble beauty of Beate Ekenstedt, perhaps she was thinking of her sister Marie-Louise or perhaps even of her own little baby, all of which made it a bit difficult for her to believe that these little girls bore the name of Löwensköld.

She could see right away that they were good and healthy and cheerful and that they were all going to be splendid people and keep fine houses, like their mother, because they resembled her in every possible way. Like her they were redheaded and short of stature and somewhat stout, and they had short hands with stubby fingers. All five of them were as alike as peas in a pod, with round cheeks and upturned noses and clear blue eyes, and when they were fully grown and not, as now, of varying heights, it was going to be impossible to tell them apart.

Charlotte, who was thirty years old at the time, was still in her best bloom. The baroness found her far more beautiful than when, in her youth, she had last paid a visit to Hedeby. Now she was also elegant and wise in the ways of the world, and the thought may have passed through the baroness' mind that her daughters would not really fit into Charlotte's present environment. But she banished it. She knew that no matter what situation in life her daughters were placed in, they would fill it simply and well.

Charlotte, in turn, was having roughly the same thoughts. She sat there wondering how she could possibly become accustomed to having a farm lass, a little, homely, graceless farm lass at her side in her home, no matter what a paragon of virtue she was.

Not that she was the least bit patronizing or conceited.

Good heavens, no one would ever say such a thing about her. And she definitely knew how to appreciate solid citizens. She told herself that if she took in one of those nice little redheads and taught the little girl to be fond of her, then she would have a friend who would never fail her. Never would she put herself first, and she would stay with her in her old age since she would never have any prospects of marrying, ugly as she was.

Quickly she came to her senses once again and began to consider herself fortunate to be gaining a homely little foster daughter. Surely it was an act of Providence. Given free choice, she would probably have picked a pretty little thing who would have turned spoiled and tetchy and thought of nothing but what was best for herself.

Charlotte was not a person who had difficulty relating to other adults or to children, and in an instant she had all five little Löwensköld girls under her thumb. All ten pale blue eyes hung on her every word, all those little hands crept toward hers whenever the occasion allowed. She realized that no matter which of them she decided on as her foster child, that child would follow her with nary a complaint or a second thought.

She liked the innocent way in which they answered questions; indeed, they made the best possible impression on her. They were really very sweet and amusing.

It all went off exactly as intended. Baron Adrian spent the entire evening in the drawing room with them all, as pleasant as could be with their visitor, and the baroness did her best to be happy as well, since it appeared that her sacrifice would be accepted.

The five little misses were not the least bit forward, and yet they stayed close to Charlotte throughout, devouring her with their eyes and waiting patiently for her to grace them with a nod or a smile.

She enjoyed being admired by them, but she found it peculiar that she had no sense at all of being related to them.

As they sat having their evening meal, with all five red heads opposite her still, five pairs of pale blue eyes staring at her, she was seized by a secret fear. Just think if she was taking on something that would prove to be too heavy a burden, just think if she could not bear it! Just think if she found herself having to send the child back to her parents because she was too homely! She immediately thought to herself that she was worrying too much, but still she decided to err on the side of caution. She would make no choice that very first night. She would wait until the next day.

Just as the baron's family was finishing dinner, loud peals of laughter were heard from an adjacent room. Charlotte looked a bit taken aback, and the baroness hurried to explain that her husband had had the kitchen moved from the side building where it had been at the time of Charlotte's previous visit, into the main building, which was of course highly advantageous, and yet it could not be helped that voices from out there were sometimes heard in the dining room.

They went on to speak of this change at length, and when the meal was over, Baron Adrian offered Charlotte his arm to show her how he had arranged things.

They passed through a little parlor, where the baron explained that they had pulled down a wall here and raised another there, and Charlotte listened attentively, because she was quite good at that kind of thing herself.

But while they stood discussing all this, that laughter came from the kitchen again even louder than before, and of course they all began to wonder. The little misses ran over and opened the kitchen doors wide, and no one even tried to stop them.

Up on the large kitchen table stood a four-year-old girl, dressed in a camisole and bodice, but wearing neither skirts nor stockings. She held a whip in one hand, made of a porridge stirrer and an end of yarn from the spinning wheel, and on the floor in front of her were two spinning wheels, over which she was clicking her tongue and cracking her whip; it was clear that she was pretending they were a pair of horses.

It was also clear that she was pretending to be racing her horses through the crowd at a market. They were making their way at great speed, urged on by shouts and the cracking whip; the crowd had to part in haste.

'Gid out the way, Per Olsa! You move along now, farm louts!'

'An' here comes somebody who's not afeared of the sheriff or the coppers!'

'An' here comes the rogue baron!'

'An' hip hurray it's market day in Bro!'

'An' hip hurray, life's fun and laughs today!'

The entire kitchen was alive with high spirits. Everyone's gazes were fixed on the child with her bright eyes and rosy cheeks.

They were all so caught up in the game that, to them, the child's blonde hair really seemed to be flying in the wind. The whole kitchen table seemed to be rushing through the crowd at the market, as if it were the rocking, rounded trap of the vagrants.

The child stood there, nimble and wild, full of jest and mischief. Every person in the kitchen, from the housekeeper to the stable hand, was completely giddy with it. Each of them had let their chores drop to follow the perilous journey of the child.

The same was true of the people standing at the door between the parlor and the kitchen. They were dumbfounded. They, too, saw the child standing not on a table but high on a trap; they, too, saw the crowds as they threw themselves out of the way, and the horses with their manes flying, rushing at full tilt, weaving between the market stands and the other vehicles.

The person to break the spell was Baron Adrian. He had pleaded with his wife that the little adventure with his brother was not to be mentioned to Charlotte, and that she should not see the vagrant child. And, as usual, the baroness had agreed to his request, adding that because the little girl was still not fully recovered from the measles, she would of necessity be kept in the nursery. So the baron stepped firmly up to the kitchen door and closed it, after which he offered Charlotte his arm again, to lead her back into the finer rooms.

But Charlotte stood transfixed, as if she had not even noticed the proffered arm.

'Who is that child?' she asked. 'With that face, she must surely be family.'

She grasped the baron's arm tightly, the tears seeming to well up in her voice as she went on.

'Please, my good cousin, tell me that she is family! I can feel that we are related.'

Baron Adrian turned away without answering. It was his wife who informed Charlotte:

'She is the daughter of Göran Löwensköld. She has had measles. The nursery maid allowed her to come down to the kitchen without our permission.'

'You must have heard of my brother, the rogue baron, Charlotte?' the baron asked in a rough voice. 'The girl's mother is a gypsy wench.'

But Charlotte just walked back to the kitchen door, as if walking in her sleep, opened it, and approached the table, arms open wide.

The little vagrant girl, standing up there playing at horse trader, looked her way, and her wild little brain must have noted something in Charlotte that appealed to her. She tossed down her whip and flew into Charlotte's open arms.

Charlotte embraced her, kissing her.

'You're the one I want,' she said. 'You, you, you.'

This was her rescue. She breathed a sigh of relief.

The homeliness, that awful homeliness she had been resisting all evening, the homeliness she had done her best to find creditable and positive, she now abandoned to its fate. What the baron would say and what the baroness would say she had no idea, but this was the child she had journeyed there to find.

Suddenly she recoiled a step or two. Baron Adrian had come up very close to her, his eyes bloodshot and his hands made into fists. 'He looks like a bull who wants to gore me,' she thought.

In a flash the baroness stepped between her and the baron, her voice as calm and restrained as ever, but she was also extremely emphatic.

'If you take that child as your own, Charlotte, both my

husband and I will be tremendously grateful to you. '

'Oh, will I indeed?' the baron burst out with a scornful laugh.

The baroness went on, in a very warm tone of voice.

'I shall be grateful to you, because I will not have to give up one of my beloved little daughters, while Adrian will owe you an even greater debt of gratitude for preventing him from committing an act he would have regretted for the rest of his life.'

Perhaps it was the truth of his wife's words, or perhaps it was pure astonishment at her daring to stand up to him, that struck Baron Adrian silent. He turned away and left the room without another word.

THE MARKET PREACHER

Is there a lovelier awakening imaginable than hearing that the serving girl, who comes in in the morning to light the fire in the tiled stove, is accompanied by a pair of tripping footsteps? Or can there be anything more pleasant than lying stock still, eyes shut, and noting that a little creature, paying no attention to the soft words of warning not to disturb the sleeper, insists on tugging at the quilt in order to climb up into the bed? And what a grand shout of jubilation when you extend your arms to help the little climber and she lands right on top of you, slapping your cheeks with her palms, still cold from her morning wash, punching and kicking and kissing! There is nothing to do but join in the jubilation, and you start talking some kind of baby talk, suddenly awash with silly nicknames. The serving girl certainly need not apologize for having let the child come along in. The little one had been doing nothing all morning but pester and beg her to let her see the beautiful lady from the night before, and she had promised to be good and quiet and not disturb her at all.

The serving girl tries to take the child out again with her when she leaves the guest room, but it is inconceivable. The little girl, who may have feared something of the kind, has crawled down under the quilt and is pretending to sleep. The moment the door closes she is wide awake and chatty. She talks a little about her father, but her speech is rapid and indistinct, and Charlotte doesn't really follow. She doesn't mind, though, charmed as she is by the sweet delight in the child's voice.

Once the fire has picked up, the door opens and the serving girl comes back in with a breakfast tray. On her heels follows the woman of the house, the portly little baroness, wondering whether her visitor slept well. She pours Charlotte some coffee, and some for herself, sits down by the tiled stove and begins to speak.

The child is silent now, but holding tightly to her bedmate's hand so as not to be taken away. In a few minutes she is truly asleep, and Charlotte lies there entranced, gazing at her rosy cheeks. She laughs to herself. She is completely under the spell of this vagrant child, who has decided to love her.

What the baroness has on her mind is to ask Charlotte not even to consider leaving Hedeby for the next few days. Not only did she and everyone else in the house dearly wish that she might stay and liven up their solitude, but Charlotte also must allow her to see to it that the child is provided with suitable clothing before she departs. After all, she is a Miss Löwensköld, and must have a couple of morning gowns and a few sets of underwear with her when she arrives at Stora Sjötorp, so she is not all too shabbily equipped.

And is it not both new and amusing to be called to the nursery, time after time throughout the day, by a tyrannical little despot who is longing to see you? Children must have a wonderful sense of inference. This little girl has immediately realized that you are a horse lover like her. She has discovered that you are better than anyone else at trotting in front of the upside down stool in the nursery, better than anyone else at holding the reins with such a realistic sense of horsemanship; no one is equally attentive to her geeing up and her whoaing. And is it not tragicomic to be introduced, through the little one, into the mysteries of the life of a vagrant, to pretend that one of the chairs is Ekeby and the other Björne, to travel back and forth between them inquiring about work, receiving curt and dismissive responses, having to put all your experience to work in discussing your prospects at each of these places?

But perhaps most enchanting of all is just to watch the little girl, now and then, toss down the reins, abandoning her game to stand at the window and wait for him, the man who has left his child forever. She stands there for hours, deaf to every temptation and persuasion, engrossed in her yearning.

It nearly brings tears to your eyes, watching her there, her little face pressed to the windowpane, her hands blocking all other sights out. You think to yourself that no matter what shortcomings the child might have, she certainly knows how to love. And what knowledge could be more important than that?

But to judge by the wealth of games and high jinks she devises, she must also be a very gifted child in terms of the mind. It is truly thanks to her that the days at Hedeby do not feel far too long and monotonous, since there is definitely an air of gloom about the old manor.

The fault is entirely Baron Adrian's. He is surly and sulky, and seems to have an oppressive effect on the rest of the family, who would otherwise not have been so bleak.

The day after Charlotte's arrival at Hedeby the Baron sends that foreman, the one who is so familiar with the villages in the northern Värmland parishes where the tinkers congregate, up north with Göran Löwensköld's little dun nag, the filthy vagrant sledge and its entire content. His primary task was to hand over this pitiful legacy to his brother's widow, after which he was to inform her that her husband, the rogue baron, had frozen to death in a roadside ditch and, finally, that their little daughter was in the care of relations.

A couple of days later, when the emissary returns, Baron Adrian tells Charlotte that as far as the foreman could tell, the child's mother was pleased to be rid of the girl, and so he was of the opinion that Charlotte could consider the child her personal property now. He warns her against taking any further steps toward legal adoption for some time. After all, he tells her, she is a vagrant child, without much goodness to take after, and it was not impossible that in a month or two Charlotte might feel compelled to return her to her mother.

In this respect, then, the baron behaved quite properly, but beyond that he made no visible effort to restrain his displeasure. Fortunately, he very seldom appeared except at meals. But at those times it became increasingly difficult to find a subject of conversation he did not interrupt with a scornful laugh or a caustic comment.

To a person who is utterly, indescribably happily married, and who also has a natural inclination to be helpful and make things right, it feels difficult to let this go on without intervening. But she has to admit her inadequacy. The trick Göran Löwensköld had played on his brother at their final encounter was far too merciless. Baron Adrian was unable to forgive him for having torn out of his hands the revenge he wanted so badly to exact.

But if Charlotte feels helpless in relation to Baron Adrian, she merely devotes all the more energy to relieving the pressure on his wife and little daughters. The poor baroness seems to gain courage and tranquility merely from knowing that Charlotte is in the house. And after some time Charlotte manages to have them bantering and laughing at meals, and telling folk tales and reading stories around the fire at dusk. She arranges sledding parties, takes the ladies of Hedeby for long outings in the sledge, drawn by her own horses, who are otherwise at repose in the stables. She entices the baroness into playing lovely little pieces by Händel and Bach on her small pianoforte, and once she sees what nice voices the five redheads have, she breathes enough bravery into them that they form a semicircle around the piano and sing, to their mother's accompaniment, *Spring, the sweet spring, is the year's pleasant king* --

Eventually, however, the baroness seems to think the little vagrant girl has had a sufficient number of dresses, undergarments and skirts made for her, and no longer objects to Charlotte's departure. It is now necessary for another reason as well. Every day since Charlotte's arrival at Hedeby, there has been glorious sunshine. The huge snowdrifts have sunk down, and the road to the church at Bro already sports some bare patches. The ice down on Lake Löven is still thick and strong, but there are puddles on the surface, and the long furrows made by various sledges, which have been visible in all directions, are gone. Charlotte must not stay much longer. She has to leave before the road becomes impassible.

The day before their departure, the baroness proposes to Charlotte a walk to the churchyard at Bro, for a look at the infamous family tomb. Charlotte readily accepts the suggestion and shortly after dinner, always served at half past twelve at Hedeby, they depart. It is not far, but the walk is slippery and difficult because of the snowmelt. This complication, however, is more than offset by the pleasures of having a walk in the lovely sunshine, of feeling the gentle, warm air on their cheeks, by the joy of hearing the trilling of the first lark over the still snowy fields.

As they walk, the baroness tries, very tactfully, to touch on a sensitive subject. She brings up Karl-Artur Ekenstedt and although she notes how Charlotte virtually starts at his name, she persists. She hopes to spark Charlotte's compassion. Charlotte, who is such a wealthy woman, with a husband who gives her anything her heart desires!

Charlotte shrugs. Yes, it is true that no one could have a finer husband than she, but for that very reason… That old Polhem sawmill is still standing at Stora Sjötorp. She would not take a risk. Throughout these four years she has not permitted Karl-Artur Ekenstedt a moment's thought, and she has certainly never considered helping him. Immediately, she tries to change the subject.

So the baroness gives in, as always, and by then they have arrived at the raised tomb, so she shows Charlotte the spot where, once upon a time, Malvina Spaak managed to return the fearful ring to the grave, asking:

'Is it true, as I have heard, that the woman who is now traveling with Karl-Artur is Malvina Spaak's daughter?'

'Indeed she is,' replies Charlotte. 'In fact that was what gave him such boundless confidence in her. But, please, let us speak no more of the two of them! I have had woes enough on their account.'

The little baroness obeys this command, but now suddenly Charlotte is moved. 'Good grief,' she thinks. 'I'm beginning to behave like her husband, not letting her get to the point.'

'I can tell you have something troubling you, something you think I ought to know,' she says out loud.

The baroness begins at once to tell her how, the previous autumn, she had been at the big market at Broby, which lasts over a week, and is attended by thousands. While strolling among the stands, buying the things she needed, she heard a woman's voice rise in a hymn. This was quite a remarkable sound in the midst of the market hubbub, so she stopped to listen. It was not an attractive voice, and the hymn was sung so forcefully it blocked the baroness' ears. With no idea who was singing, she had soon had more than enough of the cacophony, and turned in a different direction, but it was difficult to walk against the crowd.

You see, that woman's awful singing drew people to her from all directions. People were excited and laughing, as if the hymn were the prelude to some especially amusing market entertainment. The baroness, caught up in the crowd, could see no escape. On the contrary, she was pressed forward, and soon found herself up close to the singer, who was standing on a simple itinerant's trap full of ragged, gray bundles. The woman herself was homely and thickset. It was impossible to say whether she was young or old. She was dressed in a long, quilted coat, mended both here and there, but surely quite warm. She wore a big, thick shawl over her head, pulled under her arms and tied at the back. She looked just like a woman with a barrow of vegetables for sale. It was clear that she had not the least desire to make herself pleasing or attractive to the eye.

The crowd did not let her finish the hymn. People shouted for her to stop that yowling, and when she did not do as they said right away, some of the young high-spirited young men began to mimic her song. That shut her up, and she sat down among the sacks in the trap, huddling herself up with her back to the crowd. There she sat, rocking slowly back and forth, and intermittently the baroness seemed to hear her teeth chattering, as if with the cold, or with anxiety.

However, as soon as the woman stopped singing, a man jumped up onto the trap and began to speak, and from that moment on the baroness forgot all about the singer. He had a bushy, graying beard, and when he threw down his wide-brimmed, black hat, she noticed that his head was nearly bald. In any case, she knew right away that the man was Karl-

Artur Ekenstedt. He could be no other. He was dreadfully thin and not at all his old self; not a trace remained of his former good looks, but the baroness would have recognized his voice anywhere, as well as the way he kept his heavy eyelids lowered. She had also heard that he was an itinerant preacher now, frequenting the markets and other such places where people congregated.

But Charlotte must not imagine that Karl-Artur gave an edifying or solemn address. He began with quotations from the Bible, but after that all he did was to reproach the crowd. He seemed to have been upset even before he began speaking. He shouted accusations. He was enraged with the crowd for having gathered around him for no other reason than a laugh. He turned to one farmer's wife, insulting her for being too finely dressed, then he pointed out a young man he thought too stout and rosy-cheeked. There was no rational explanation for his choice of victim, except that he seemed to have some inextinguishable indignation coming from inside and aimed at everyone and everything.

His hands were clenched, and he hurled his words with such force that they battered the crowd like a hailstorm. And the baroness could not deny that he was successful in some respects. The people thronged around him, laughing at everything, absolutely everything, he said. No one seemed to consider that he might have some other point to make than simply making a laughing stock of himself.

But to the baroness, who had known him before, nothing could have been more surprising than to hear how the brunt of his anger turned on poverty, a state he had always been at pains to celebrate. That day, however, he showed the crowd how patched his clothing was, and cursed those who were the cause of his destitution. His main complaints were against his father and sisters. His mother had died; he ought to have inherited her property, and he would have been a wealthy man now, but for his father and his hypocritical, greedy thieving sisters, who denied that he was, by rights, her main heir.

When the baroness says this, Charlotte objects.

'That's impossible. It cannot have been Karl-Artur.'

'My dear, he mentioned them by name. There is no doubt about it, it was him.'

'Has he gone mad?'

'No, not mad. There was a sort of sense to what he said, but I would put it like this: he had become a different person. Nothing of the old Karl-Artur remained. Or what do you say when I tell you that he boasted that he could have become bishop, had he only wanted to? There was no one in the whole country that could preach like him. He could have become archbishop, had not vicious individuals brought him to ruin. You can imagine how the crowd laughed at the pathetic, ragged heap of skin and bones who stood there claiming that he could have been bishop. They laughed until they ached. Personally, I was unable to laugh, of course. I only wanted to get away.'

The baroness pauses a moment to glance Charlotte's way. She stands there, frowning, not looking directly at the baroness, as if she were being forced to listen to a story that actually bored her.

'There's not much more to tell,' the baroness goes on with a sigh. 'I just want you to know that when Karl-Artur claimed he could have become the bishop of all of Sweden, that woman sitting at his feet in the trap uttered a little snort. He heard her, and from that moment on, you know, his anger turned on her. He stamped on the floor of the trap, demanding to know how she could have the nerve to laugh, she who was the cause of his entire misfortune, who had separated him from his fiancée, from his mother, from his wife, she who was the reason he was no longer a clergyman able to preach in the churches, she who was the noose around his neck, his venomous serpent, who dripped poison into his wounds every day, she who would never stop exasperating him until, one day, he found himself forced to dispatch her with a dagger.'

The baroness pauses again, as if to see whether she has still made no impression. Charlotte has turned completely away from her. She displays no interest in this story with either words or gestures.

'When he began to accuse the woman,' says the baroness who, as if in desperation at this indifference, begins to speak at a furious speed, 'he used those formal phrases of his, you know. This did not seem to affect the woman, who sat perfectly still for a long time. But then he must have happened to say something that hit a nerve, as they say, and so she responded. And then the two began to quarrel. No, I cannot tell you what they said to one another. It was dreadful. They went into the most intimate detail. They looked as if they might come to blows. I was truly frightened that I might have to witness such a thing. I do not know how I managed, but I pushed my way through the crowd, where everyone was still laughing, and broke away. But since that day, Charlotte, I cannot forget those poor, unfortunate creatures. I suppose they are still traveling around like that this very day. And his father and sister are still alive, and you, Charlotte…'

'I cannot imagine it,' Charlotte interrupted in a disapproving tone of voice, as if to say she regarded this entire story as an exaggeration, even an invention. 'I saw Karl-Artur four years ago. Although he wore a suit of homespun, he looked like a prince in disguise. Are you telling me that in the short span of four years he has gone downhill so fast, changed so utterly?'

'But his suffering, dear Charlotte, imagine how he has suffered, all he has been through! Imagine his defeats, his disappointments, his humiliations! Imagine living with that woman! Imagine the despair, the self-reproaches! Imagine his having to live more or less the same life as my brother-in-law, the rogue baron. Imagine if he ends up a murderer! If ever you have loved him…'

'How can you say if,' Charlotte asks softly, 'if I have…?'

Quite suddenly she is in motion. Without turning around, she crosses the cemetery and walks out onto the road to Hedeby. She is biting her lips so as not to scream. She has believed she was completely done with that man, and now he returns this way, miserable, lost, forcing himself upon her in his degradation, with his terrible ill fate.

The two women walk apart nearly all the way back to Hedeby: Charlotte a few steps ahead, her hostess just behind.

Neither of them utters a word.

But as they enter the lane Charlotte stops and waits for the baroness. She gives a sad little smile, shakes her head, but does not mention the subject of their recent conversation.

'Do you know what?' she asks with somewhat forced joviality, 'I don't believe we were away for more than an hour, and yet I am delighted to be back. Can you imagine what power that beggar child has gained over me? I am truly yearning to see my little girl.'

And as they walk down the lane, she casts an eye up at the nursery window to see whether there might not be a little face there, pressed right up to the glass. When she enters the front yard, she expects the vestibule door to be thrown open and the child to come rushing out to run toward her through the puddles and slush.

But no such thing occurs. In contrast, the person who comes rushing toward the homecomers in great haste is none other than Baron Adrian.

The Baron has on his wolfskin coat, with a long, colorful traveling belt wrapped around his waist several times. He has on his traveling boots as well, so tall and wide that one suspects they were cut according to the model of the Carolingian cavalry boots in the portrait of his ancestor. It is obvious that he is about to undertake a journey and is approaching them to explain the reason.

The baroness immediately suspects that an accident has happened during their absence, and Charlotte hears her sigh.

'Oh me oh my! What's happened now?'

It does not appear to have been anything too worrisome, in fact one might have thought the opposite, since Baron Adrian is suddenly no longer his sullen self, but lively and cheerful.

'Well, let me bring you abreast of events,' he says. 'It must have been about half an hour after you left, when a vagrant's sledge drove right up to the front door, full of the usual bundles and with the usual kind of man and woman sitting in the middle of all the clutter. The woman remained in the sledge, while the man stepped out and came in to my study to see me. And what do you think he wanted? That's right, nothing less than a request for compensation to my honorable sister-in-law for allowing us to care for her child.'

'How do you like that?' Charlotte asked. 'Though it's not unexpected, really.'

'How true,' Baron Adrian admitted, 'but that was not the remarkable thing. The man who had come in to see me was poorly dressed, and looked like that kind of riff-raff usually looks, and to begin with I took him for an ordinary vagrant. But there was something about his voice that rang familiar, and the whole time he was talking to me I stood trying to figure out where I might have met him before. Also, he was not really behaving like that kind of man would normally have done. '

'Oh my God!'

'I see, dear Charlotte, that you have already guessed who he was. As for me, I was not so quick on the uptake. I was wracking my brains, remembering all the vagrants' faces I usually saw at Broby market. While I was thinking, I gave him a piece of my mind for putting forward such a shameless request. I did not spare my curses and expletives, as that is the only kind of language such people understand. Had the man been an ordinary vagrant he would have listened in stony silence to my abuse, because they do tend to have a bit of respect for the gentry, but this fellow, well he threw it all right back at me, telling me in no uncertain terms what he thought of me. He told me I had treated my brother lamentably, that I ought to have invited my sister-in-law to the funeral, and all manner of such things. I pounded my fist on the desk and ordered him to leave, but it did no good.'

'Did you then tell him…'

'If you are asking whether I let him know that wealthy Mrs. Schagerström was the one who intended to take the child in, the answer is no. No, my dear, I was careful not to do that. It would only have multiplied his demands. But the man was harping on at me the whole time, almost as if it were giving him great pleasure. He finally left; by that time I was so furious I was about to throw him out, but he displayed no fear. And all the time he went on about how if I were not prepared to pay for the child, I would not be able to keep her.'

Charlotte listens, her concern rising. While walking back from the cemetery she concluded that she neither could nor dared to do anything for Karl-Artur. Was her battle going to have to start over again?

'But just as he slammed the door,' the baron continues, 'I had an insight. The man with whom I had just had the honor of speaking was Karl-Artur Ekenstedt. I imagine he had spent a lot of time with my brother, they were tinkers of the same sort, and I suppose they also spent the winters up north, as all the vagrants do. It was perfectly natural for him to have agreed to try to blackmail me on behalf of the wife of that rogue baron of a brother of mine.'

'Ah, my dear Adrian, and once you had recognized him, did you just let him go?'

'No, of course I wanted to speak a bit more with him once I had realized who he was. I ran out onto the steps, but he had already taken a seat in his sledge and was on his way off. I shouted "Karl-Artur" after him at the top of my lungs, but it had no effect.'

'So now you plan to follow him, is that it?'

'Indeed. That is my intention. You'll never guess, my dear, what happened next. When Karl-Artur was about halfway down the lane he came to an abrupt halt. Our nursery maid happened to be approaching, with all the children. They had probably gone out to meet you. The woman in the sledge recognized my niece, I heard her call her name. And when the child ran toward her, that woman leaned forward, took hold of the girl, and pulled her into the sledge. Karl-Artur cracked his whip and the horse was off. So, my dear, they absconded with the child right in front of my eyes, you might say.'

'Is my little girl gone, then?'

'And there I stood, helpless. I could not possibly catch up with them. All the Hedeby horses are deep in the forest, bringing in this winter's felled trees.'

'What about my horses?'

'Naturally, my dear. I remembered that they were here, and since the matter was just as dear to your heart as mine, I took the liberty of asking your driver to harness them. I was waiting for him to get ready when I saw you and Amelie approaching. There is no cause for alarm. We'll have the child back in no time. Ah, here are the horses and the sledge.'

As he heads for the sledge, Charlotte takes him by the arm.

'Just a moment, please, Adrian! May I not accompany you?'

Baron Adrian flushes a deep red. But he turns to Charlotte with the frank honesty that characterized him in his youth.

'Charlotte, dear, you have nothing to fear. I will get your child back, even if it costs me my life. Good grief, I have spent the entire week here feeling ashamed. I would very much like to show you my gratitude, Charlotte, for saving me from returning that poor girl to her origins.'

'Indeed, Adrian, but that is not the reason I would like to come along. This is the way I am. I never want to believe the worst, but now that he has stolen my little girl, I see what a terrible state Karl-Artur is in. Do allow me to come, so that I will have the opportunity to speak to him!'

THE JOURNEY OUT

It was clearly not going to be as easy to catch up with the fugitives as Baron Adrian had imagined. This was partly because they had got quite a good head start, and partly because the road conditions proved to be worse than they had assumed. Charlotte's splendid horses worked their hardest, but where the road was free from snow they could only manage to move the heavy sledge forward at a walk. Charlotte felt as if she were tied down, as she stared furiously at the tracks from the smaller vagrants' sledge that had been able to make the most of the thin, snowy edge of the road and even sometimes to take shortcuts across snow-covered fields.

The road improved, however, the further they traveled from the wide plain around the church at Bro, and her hopes of reclaiming her little girl therefore did not vanish altogether. Another encouraging thing was that she and Baron Adrian were suddenly the world's closest friends. She could not really understand how it had happened, but each of them must have discovered separately that they were sincere and honest individuals, albeit perhaps sometimes a little unreasonable, but in any case precisely the kind of people it is a pleasure to deal with. The Baron even proclaimed how pleased he was that Charlotte had not left Hedeby without his having discovered it.

Charlotte offered no such openhearted assurance in return, but because she doubted that she would ever be able to persuade her husband to come to Karl-Artur's aid, she was thinking she could ask Baron Adrian to take him in hand. After all, they were cousins, and it could hardly be nice for him to have such a close relation roaming the roads.

She had barely broached the subject, though, when the Baron interrupted her.

'No, my dear Charlotte,' he laughed, 'there is no question of it. I wish to have nothing further to do with those people, and in truth I think you would be wise to follow my example.'

Charlotte was a bit taken aback by this abrupt reply, but thought she knew the reason for it.

'Ah, perhaps you find it upsetting to see Karl-Artur, a married man, roving about with another man's wife?'

'Ha ha! Oh dear, do you take me to be such a paragon of virtue? No, that is not what I was thinking about, although it is a crying shame. But heavens, what possessed Karl-Artur? Could he not see that traveling with a woman like that would turn all his preaching into an abomination?'

'It is also my view that the first thing that needs to be done is to separate the two of them.'

'Them!' Baron Adrian turned to Charlotte, placing one hand, in its large, furry wolfskin glove, on her shoulder. 'Charlotte, dear, nothing will be able to separate the two of them but the executioner's platform or the hangman's noose.'

Charlotte, sitting wrapped up tightly in her traveling rug, tried in vain to see the face of her traveling companion.

'Adrian, surely you jest?'

Baron Adrian did not provide a direct answer to this question. He removed his hand, straightened up in the sledge and, in the same light, jocular tone of voice in which he had been conducting the entire conversation, said:

'Charlotte, dear, dare I ask whether you are aware that there is a curse hanging over the Löwenskölds?'

'Yes, Adrian, of course I know of it. But I must admit to not being able to recall what it is all about.'

'Ah, Charlotte, you lead such a busy life in the real world that such base superstition naturally does not concern you.'

'Worse than that, Adrian, in fact I have no interest whatsoever in the supernatural. I have no feeling at all for it. My sister Marie-Louise, on the other hand…'

Baron Adrian chuckled.

'If you're not a believer, Charlotte dear, all the better. I was eager to tell you about the judgment, but afraid of frightening you.'

'No need at all for you to be worried about that.'

'Well then, my dear,' Baron Adrian began, only to cut himself short with a gesture toward the driver, who was sitting so close in front of them he could surely hear every word. 'Perhaps we ought to wait.'

Charlotte tried once again to look Baron Adrian in the eye. Although his tone of voice was still jocular, as if making fun of the old family legend, he was clearly quite serious about not wanting the driver to hear. So she hurried to assure him:

'Oh, Adrian, surely you know my husband well enough to realize that he would never engage a driver without ensuring that his hearing is sufficiently poor to permit the passengers to converse freely.'

'Excellent, my dear. A model to be emulated. What I was about to say, then, was that once upon a time we Löwenskölds had an enemy, one Marit Eriksdotter, a farm woman whose father, uncle and fiancé had been wrongfully suspected of having stolen the ring belonging to our ancestor, but who still lost their lives to the hangman. As was perfectly natural, the poor woman sought revenge, with the aid of the ring itself. My own father was close to being the first victim, but by good fortune he was rescued thanks to Malvina Spaak, who had won the confidence of Marit Eriksdotter, and with her assistance Malvina Spaak was able to dispatch the unfortunate ring back down into the family grave.'

Charlotte interrupted the speaker with an animated gesture.

'Ah, but Adrian! There is no need for you to think me such an ignorant heathen. I do believe I know every detail in the story of the Löwensköld ring.'

'Well, what you certainly won't have been told is that as soon as my father had recovered from the terrible shock, Marit Eriksdotter sought out my grandmother, Baroness Augusta Löwensköld to demand that her son, in other words my father, marry Miss Spaak. She claimed that my grandmother had made her a pledge to that effect that previous evening, and that it was for that reason and that reason alone that she had refrained from exacting her revenge. My grandmother replied that she could not possibly have made such a promise, as she knew very well that her son was already betrothed to another. She was prepared to give Malvina Spaak whatever reward she might desire. But she could not fulfill Marit's request.'

'Oh yes, Adrian, now that you mention it I vaguely recollect having heard something like that before. And it does seem perfectly natural that Marit would not have been prepared to accept this state of affairs.'

'Nor did she, Charlotte dear. And when she persisted, my grandmother had Miss Malvina called in to confirm that she had never received a promise of marriage to her son. Miss Spaak completely corroborated all that her employer said, and with that Marit Eriksdotter, probably feeling that she had refrained from her revenge for the terrible miscarriage of justice in her family for no good reason at all, was seized by a terrible wrath. She told my grandmother in no uncertain terms that the intended vengeance would be extracted after all. "Three members of my family suffered a sudden, violent death," she cried, "And so shall three of yours, equally violent and sudden, because you have failed to keep your promise."'

'But, Adrian dear…'

'I believe I suspect your objection, Charlotte. My grandmother was of precisely the same opinion, that that poor woman could have posed no threat. She was not the least bit intimidated, and responded, very coolly, that Marit was now far too old to be able to take the lives of three Baron Löwenskölds.'

'Yes, I am an old woman and my life will soon come to an end,' Marit is said to have replied, 'But whether I am on this earth or underneath it, I believe I have the power to send an avenger.'

Now Charlotte twisted in her sledge furs with such force that she was able to look the baron right in the eye.

'You don't mean to tell me, dear Adrian, that you believe that words to that effect, proclaimed by an impoverished, ignorant peasant woman, could possibly be of any significance?' she then asked, with all the equanimity in the world. 'And I have heard the entire story before. If I recall correctly, it was my dear friend Beate Ekenstedt who often told it as an example of how insignificant such predictions tend to be. She regarded it as completely meaningless.'

'I am not quite so sure that my aunt was right that time,' said Baron Adrian, rising in the sledge to have a look at the road ahead. 'It does not look as if we are going to catch up with those good friends of ours very soon,' he went on, sitting back down. 'With your permission, Charlotte, I would like to tell you of a strange little thing that occurred at Hedeby in my parents' time.'

'Please do go on, Adrian. The time goes so much faster when we converse.'

'It may have been during the summer of 1816,' the baron began, 'when a large party was being planned at Hedeby to celebrate my mother's birthday. As usual for such occasions, my parents had sent for Malvina Spaak to come a few days early and help with the party preparations. By then she was married, and her name was actually Malvina Thorbergsson, but at Hedeby we never got used to calling her by any other name than the one she was known by for the fifteen years she had been our housekeeper, and I think she preferred to keep it that way, too. I also think, my dear, that it was a source of great pleasure to Mrs. Malvina to come to Hedeby and help out with parties and other important occasions. She had married a poor tenant farmer. She therefore had no opportunities to make use of her finer culinary skills at home. Only when she came to Hedeby could she display her talent.'

'Was there not another source of attraction as well?' Charlotte asked, thinking of certain aspects of the old family legend.

'Quite right, Charlotte. I was getting to that. Mrs. Malvina's former employers, my grandfather Bengt Göran, and my grandmother Baroness Augusta, whose name I mentioned a moment ago, had both gone to meet their maker by then, but my father, who now owned Hedeby, had, as we all knew, been her youthful romance, and although they were far past first love, she still had something of a weakness for him. It always seemed to us children that my father and mother considered Malvina Spaak a true friend. They were always very pleased to see her, she had her meals at the family table, and they spoke to her in confidence of all their joys and woes. It never occurred to us to suspect that there was any guilty conscience underlying this kindness.'

'Beate Ekenstedt always spoke of Mrs. Malvina's sincere friendship with the family,' Charlotte commented.

'She was always a completely good friend to all of us; there is no reason to think otherwise. And she also transferred the devotion she felt to our parents to us boys as well, Göran and myself. She was always fixing our favorite meals, always had something sweet for us when we visited her in the kitchen, and she had an indefatigable supply of the most hair-raising ghost stories. I would, however, add that Göran clearly held a special place in her heart, probably owing to his appearance. With my rosy checks and fair hair, I looked like all the other farm children, and did not trigger tender memories in her. He was different. A handsome lad, with large, dark eyes, he was thought to resemble my father. It is very probable that Mrs. Malvina, looking up from her bowl of dough or simmering stew, often imagined that time had stood still; she saw the return of her first love, come back to ask her advice about how to prevail upon a dead man to stay at peace in his grave.'

Charlotte's face had taken on a slightly melancholy expression.

'I know those eyes very well,' she muttered, as if to herself.

'The good relationship between Mrs. Malvina and us lads continued until 1816,' the baron went on, 'but that summer Mrs. Malvina had the indiscretion to bring along her young daughter Thea when she came to Hedeby. The girl was thirteen, and with me being eighteen and Göran sixteen, we saw ourselves as far too grown up to play with her. She would have had to be extremely attractive for us to disregard the age difference, but poor Thea was short and awkward, with bulging eyes and a lisp. We found her loathsome and avoided her, and Mrs. Malvina, who regarded little Thea as an unusually gifted child, was rather offended on her behalf.'

'Goodneth me,' lisped Charlotte, 'just think that I am sitting here alongside a Baron Löwensköld, one of the thons of that very Baron Adrian Löwensköld my mother loved, and who has funded my education!'

She stopped suddenly.

'Do forgive me, Adrian! I'd forgotten her present circumstances for a moment. I should be ashamed to be making fun of the unfortunate woman.'

The baron laughed.

'Your pangs of conscience are my loss. You have a real talent, Charlotte. I thought for a moment that little Thea was next to me here in the sledge. But before I go on I must ask whether this is terribly boring for you. I do not have the privilege of spending time with a member of my extended family very often. Being with you makes me feel younger somehow. So many old memories come rushing back.'

Charlotte, who had truly been listening with the greatest interest, reassured him quickly, and Baron Adrian went on speaking.

'Well, Charlotte, perhaps you would have been more inclined to forgive our incivility to little Thea than our parents were,' he said. 'But my mother, who noticed that Mrs. Malvina was not in her usual bright mood, guessed the reason and gave us strictest orders to be polite to little Thea, and my father also had one or two things to say. We were accustomed to obedience, and took the girl along rowing once or twice, and shook astrachan apples down from the tall trees for her. Mrs. Malvina, that kind soul, perked right up, and everything went as smoothly as could be until the day of the party.'

'I'd have understood if you'd drowned her,' said Charlotte.

'Yes, Charlotte,' said the baron, 'I see you can imagine how we felt. All the local gentry arrived, we received young women and men we had known forever and liked, and we could not imagine spending such a day being attentive to little Thea. My mother had specifically said that Thea was going to attend the party, and I can remember nothing unsuitable about her clothing, but as no one knew her and her appearance was off-putting, she was probably sorely neglected. We did not include her in our outdoor games, and later in the evening when the dancing began in the drawing room, she remained a wallflower. Unfortunately, my mother was so busy conversing with the gentlemen and ladies that she forgot to see how things were going for little Thea. Not until the evening meal was to be served did she come to think of her, and by that time it was too late. She asked the housemaid where the girl had got to, and was told that she was out in the kitchen, sitting with her mother, crying. No one had spoken a word to her. She had not been included in the games or the dancing. Well, dear Mother was a bit upset about this, but could not leave her guests in order to comfort a spoiled child. Not to mention that I am quite certain she found little Thea every bit as loathsome as we boys did.'

'Thea has always had an astonishing ability to cause trouble,' remarked Charlotte.

'So true, Charlotte. Of course Malvina Spaak was offended on her daughter's behalf, and the next morning no sooner was my mother was awake than the housemaid came in to report that Mrs. Malvina was ready to leave and wondered if transport could be provided. My mother was taken aback. Their agreement had been that Mrs. Malvina would be staying on at Hedeby for a couple more days to get some rest after all the hustle and bustle of the party. My mother hastened to Mrs. Malvina, but found her implacable throughout, until she realized she ought to call in her husband. My father said a few words about having observed little Thea the previous evening and noticing how sweet and proper she looked, and Mrs. Malvina was instantly appeased. Her journey home was duly postponed, in fact it was agreed that Mrs. Malvina would stay on at Hedeby for a full week in order to give us children the opportunity to get to know one another better and become good friends.'

'Oh my, could it have been much worse, Adrian?'

'Once it was all arranged, my father had us boys called to his study. He asked how we had dared to disobey his order, and boxed each of our ears. My father was otherwise a very meek and gentle man. He never resorted to physical punishment, so you can imagine, Charlotte, how shocked we were. We could not possibly understand what gave our father such a weakness for little Thea. But now he informed us that there was no one on earth to whom we should accord more respect than her, and he also told us that she would be staying for another full week, so that we would learn to appreciate her.'

'Which, of course, you could not stand?'

'I managed to keep quiet, but Göran, who had more of a temper and had furthermore been provoked by having his ears boxed, shouted in full fury: "Father, just because you were once in love with Malvina Spaak, doesn't mean that we have to be charmed by little Thea." I thought he would be shown the door, but what happened was just the opposite. Father reined in his anger. He sat down in his large chair and asked that we come closer. He took our hands and said it was time for us to learn that he was afraid a great injustice had been done to Malvina Spaak. Once – he was sure we knew the occasion to which he was referring – his life had hung in the balance and he suspected that his mother, Baroness Augusta, had led Malvina Spaak to believe, albeit not explicitly, that she had prospects of becoming her daughter-in-law if she saved me. It had not been possible to keep this promise, you know, and Miss Malvina had behaved as tactfully as anyone could wish, but my father felt that he owed her a great debt he would never be able to repay, and he appealed to us to always be on our very best behavior in relation to Mrs. Malvina and her daughter.'

'He did put it very nicely, Adrian.'

'Sorry to say, though, we boys found the entire matter more ridiculous than touching.'

At that moment Lundman, the driver, turned toward his passengers to report that he thought he could see a conveyance at the top of one of the nearby hills.

The baron rose up in the sledge. He, too, discovered the conveyance in question but informed the others that that particular hill was at least a mile away. It was impossible to know if it was the right sledge. Still, he requested that

Lundman drive at the greatest possible speed, and he rapidly began to draw up a plan of attack.

'When we come up alongside that sledge, Charlotte, you take over the reins,' he said. 'Lundman will hop out and stop the rogues' horse, while I move the child over to our sledge.'

'We'll fall upon them like true highway robbers.'

'We'll give them a dose of their very own medicine.'

Baron Adrian was hanging over the side of the sledge to be able to see past the horses and look down the road. He was now closing in for the chase, and every thought of the old story he had been so eager to relate a few moments ago was gone from his mind.

'Dear Adrian, it will be a good half hour before we catch up with them. Might I hear the end of your adventure?'

'Gladly, gladly, Charlotte. The end was that Göran, who could not bear the idea of another week in little Thea's company, came up with the idea of making a large signet ring out of wax, gold paper and a bit of red sealing wax. He showed it to the girl, persuading her that it was the real, infamous Löwensköld ring, and that he had found it in the churchyard. Thus we ought to expect the old general to start haunting Hedeby again at any moment to demand back his dearest possession. Little Thea was frightened, Mrs. Malvina once again wanted to depart, and the matter was investigated by the adults. Göran was forced to display the wax ring and tell the whole story, and Father gave him a beating. It was after that unpleasant experience that Göran ran off, headed for the woods, Charlotte, never to return. In twenty-six long years he never reappeared at Hedeby again until this past winter. Instead, he has lived the life of a vagrant, on the road, to the vast grief of my parents and the shame and dishonor of the entire family.'

'Heavens, Adrian, I had no idea his misfortune began that way.'

'Yes, Charlotte, so it did, and if you consider the details you might say that little Thea was thus the cause of his death in the wayside ditch. And hence she has done away with one of us. Ah, look, there they are again.'

291

Once again the baron was hanging out over the road, but as the sledge on which he was keeping an eye soon vanished from sight, he turned back to Charlotte.

'Whatever will you think of me, Charlotte? Oh, I'd nearly forgotten why I forced this entire story upon you. I wished to warn you against trying to separate Thea from Karl-Artur. You see, I believe, I do believe, that Mrs. Malvina's daughter has an assigned task, about which she knows nothing. Remember how Marit Eriksdotter spoke of sending an avenger?'

With this Baron Adrian turned to Charlotte and looked into her eyes, an expression of horror-filled anticipation on his face.

And in a moment of inspiration Charlotte realized that this melancholy dreamer, this man who had not a soul among those around him in whom he could confide, must often sit, unhappy and alone, imagining the ancient curse, so that he had gradually come to imagine that Thea Sundler had been called to bring it to fruition.

And although she also reminded herself how, during the unhappy time when her engagement to Karl-Artur was broken off, she had had a feeling that there was something threatening and implacable on Thea's side that was causing all her own efforts to rescue her beloved to fail, she was not at all inclined to agree with his conjecture. Instead, she met his questioning gaze with a good imitation of astonishment.

'I do not understand,' she said, 'why you are bringing up Karl-Artur in this context. He is not, of course, a Löwensköld.'

'But the prophecy does not explicitly state that all three victims shall bear the name of Löwensköld. It only says that they will be descendants of my grandmother.'

'And so you mean to say, Adrian, that just because of that wretched old legend I ought to refrain from trying to speak with Karl-Artur if I encounter him this evening? I must not separate him from Thea, I may do nothing at all to restore him to a way of life with greater dignity?'

Baron Adrian's gaze rested on Charlotte with the same uneasy question, and even his voice now revealed his deep despair.

'I would not prohibit you from trying, Charlotte. I am merely saying that it will do no good. I saw Karl-Artur a few hours ago, and I can assure you that he will soon be ripe for death in a wayside ditch, just like my brother. A violent, sudden death, Charlotte, at the prime of his life.'

'I simply cannot understand, Adrian, how you can imagine anything so absurd.'

Baron Adrian stared out across the landscape.

'What do we know, Charlotte, of all that occurs around us? Why do things go badly for one man and well for another? How large a debt must there not be, to be paid?'

In spite of the compassion she felt, Charlotte's patience was growing thin.

'And I suppose once Thea has done away with Karl-Artur, it will be your turn, Adrian?'

'Yes, then it will be my turn, but that is insignificant. I assure you, Charlotte, that had I had a son I would gladly have given up my own life so that the debt of the Löwenskölds could be repaid. My son, you see, would then have been able to live a happy life, he would have restored honor to our lineage. Nothing would have kept him from becoming a useful, respected man. We three, my brother, Karl-Artur and myself, we have been incapable of accomplishing anything, with the curse resting upon us, but he, Charlotte, he, my son, would not have been burdened with it.'

Lundman turned to his passengers, saluted with his whip and pointed ahead.

Baron Adrian did not move a muscle. He had slumped back into his corner, where he sat totally indifferent to the chase. Charlotte could only see his profile, but it seemed to her that his expression was again the way it had been for the past week, sullen, surly and stern.

'What am I to do?' she wondered to herself. 'His melancholia has returned.'

They continued in this way for a while. The road they were traveling was particularly hilly and winding. Sometimes it ran along Lake Löven, sometimes through deep woods, and at other times it made its way between closely built houses in a farming village. Thus there was never a long view ahead. Now and then they caught a glimpse of the sledge they were following, only to have it vanish again a moment later.

Although Charlotte could hardly believe the figments of Baron Adrian's imagination, she was still seized by a growing sense of compassion, and quickly decided to grasp at the only possible source of comfort she could think of. Not that she had any hope of success, but she simply felt an irresistible urge to do something.

'Adrian?'

'What is it, Charlotte?'

'There is something I need to tell you.'

'I am all ears. You were incredibly patient with my silly story.'

His tone of voice was unpleasant and sarcastic, but Charlotte was grateful he had answered her at all.

'God forgive me if I am doing something wrong, but I must tell you, Adrian, that the fellow you sent northwards to the village where the vagrants live, he returned to Hedeby and asked to speak privately with the baroness. He wanted her to know that Göran Löwensköld, your brother, had left a son behind.'

Baron Adrian's hand in its large wolfskin glove once again lay heavily on Charlotte's shoulder.

'Are you making this up, Charlotte?'

'What kind of monster would that make me, to lie in this case? No, Adrian, there is a lad up there. He is six years old, well-grown and hardy. Not as great a beauty as his sister, more like Bengt in the portrait. What the manager wished to ask the baroness was whether he even ought to mention the boy's existence to you. There is something wrong with him.'

'Is he an idiot?'

'No, Adrian, he is as intelligent as you and me, he is cheerful and kind, but he is…'

Her voice, tense with excitement, failed her. She was unable to utter the word.

'Adrian, he is blind,' she whispered.

'Pardon me?'

'He is blind,' Charlotte nearly shouted this time. 'That is why the manager did not dare mention the matter to you, Adrian, and Amelie asked him to continue his silence. She did not think the time was ripe for such a piece of information. She wanted you to find out later, when you were less sensitive.'

'Amelie always has been and always will be an overcautious fool.'

'He has been blind since birth. It is not something that can be cured.'

Baron Adrian grabbed hold of Charlotte, and shook her, as if to shake the truth out of her.

'And this is true? You can swear, Charlotte, that there is a lad up there?'

'There most certainly is. His name is Bengt Adrian. The little girl often speaks of her brother. Surely he is the one she means. What is it, Adrian?'

Carried away by his delight, Baron Adrian was embracing her and kissing her on both the lips and cheeks. Then, laughing loudly, he released her.

'Well, excuse me, Charlotte, but you are the best. Nothing namby pamby about you, you are courageous as a man. You are quite simply a woman of my lineage. And now you'll see. The next time you come to Hedeby, Charlotte, it will be a different place altogether. '

'I am thrilled, thrilled beyond description, but do not forget that he is blind!'

'Blind! You know I have five daughters with nothing better to do than to guide and feed him if need be. I will continue north this very evening. Let's just get that little girl back first. Hey, Lundman, can you see them?'

'They're not far away, Baron.'

'Hurry it up then, Lundman! We've got to catch them now. Oh, merciful heavens! What did you say his name was?'

'Bengt Adrian.'

'So Göran still had a sense of tradition. And what were you saying, Charlotte, that you would like me to do for Karl-Artur?'

'But he is a doomed man.'

'In whose opinion? You mustn't sit around, Charlotte,

pondering on things some melancholy old baron put into your head. Who cares about that old curse, if you don't mind my asking? So you want me to take Karl-Artur under my wing and I shall. But what do we do about Thea?'

'She's still got a husband who wants her back.'

'And he shall have her, Charlotte. Then, first off, I'll bring Karl-Artur to Hedeby and put some meat on his bones. I'll put Amelie in charge of him; she likes that kind of thing. Oh, look, here we are. We'll get them on the next rise.'

They were both hanging over the sides of the sledge for a better view. They were traveling downhill now, and the road was steep, running down to the lakeside. After that there was a brief straight stretch, followed by another hill. That was where the baron expected them to catch up with the fugitives.

So Karl-Artur was still a bit ahead. He was on the straight road by the lake, with Charlotte and company rushing downhill behind them.

Now, however, the fugitives seemed to have realized that they were going to be overtaken on the hill in front of them. Karl-Artur made his horse take a sharp turn, and they headed off the road and out across the lake.

'Aha,' said Baron Adrian with satisfaction, 'that will make it all the easier for us.'

Lundman, who had finished navigating down the hill, also turned off the road and onto the ice without a second thought. It was covered with a mixture of water and snow, but still thick enough to hold.

However, they had not driven far onto the lake before the Baron gave a shout:

'Stop, Lundman! Rein in the horses. What are they thinking of, to turn their sledge out onto the ice right here? This is where the river runs through.'

From Charlotte's sledge, which was quite high, it was clear that the ice not at all far ahead of them was a much darker color, indicating that it had been thinned by a lively little stream that ran out of the deep forest.

They came to a halt. The baron stepped out of their sledge,

put his hands to his mouth like a cattle-caller, and cried out a warning. Charlotte pulled and tugged at the drawstrings of her sledge rug, and was eventually able to move about.

A couple of seconds later it was all over. There was a crashing sound from the ice. Karl-Artur's horse vanished into the deep water, pulling its sledge behind it.

But at the very moment the ice broke, Karl-Artur managed to jump out of the sledge, and the woman alongside him followed his example. The spectators from Charlotte's sledge saw them standing, saved, at the edge of the ice.

But suddenly Baron Adrian, large and heavy as he was in his huge furs and enormous traveling boots, ran toward the hole in the ice.

'The child!' he shouted. 'The child, the child!'

Charlotte ran after him, and Lundman the driver tossed the reins aside and ran as well. The baron had a head start. He was almost at the hole, and Charlotte thought she heard him cry that he saw the little girl. Then the ice broke under him

Charlotte was so close by that the cracks in the surface of the ice reached her feet. Still, there was no thought in her mind but to rush forward and be of assistance, until Lundman grabbed her from behind.

'Do not run, ma'am! Crawl, for God's sake, crawl!'

Both of them lay right down on the ice and crept up to the hole. But there was nothing to be seen.

'The current's so strong here,' said Lundman. 'They're already under the edge of the ice.'

THE JOURNEY HOME

Charlotte is traveling the road in the deepest darkness. She sits there crying and sobbing softly, all the way. The handkerchief she has been using to dry her tears has become wet, and as the night is cold, it is starting to freeze stiff. She hurries to tuck it back under her fur, to thaw it out again.

But no matter what she is doing, whether it be wiping her tears or shifting her handkerchief, she does it mechanically and without thinking. All her concentration is focused on listening for the answer to a prayer she is repeating over and over again.

She no longer has Baron Adrian alongside her in the sledge, as she had on the journey out. There is no one there to help and comfort her except the driver. And she and Lundman are very comfortable with each other, in fact he considers it his duty to turn around in his seat every now and then and say a compassionate word or two.

'Yes, ma'am, I think I can safely say this is the very worst day of my life.'

Although that is very probably true, Charlotte does not take the time to reply. She goes on repeating the same prayer and listening for an answer.

The sledge glides ahead very quietly. Lundman has removed the bells from the horses and put them in the box under the seat. They make a ringing sound at every bump in the road, but it is muffled and sad sounding, and very well suited to this particular journey. They do not at all ring out the kind of cheerful melodies one hears when they are hanging from the horses' harnesses.

The horses seem to know that they are on their way home,

and try to pick up speed, but Lundman does not think it is appropriate, and reins them in. Although no one is there to see them, he drives almost as if it were a funeral procession.

'He was a fine man, that he was, Baron Adrian,' says Lundman, 'and he died for a worthy purpose.'

But Charlotte does not react to these words, either. Her mind is otherwise occupied, she is praying, praying non-stop, and listening for an answer.

Lundman and Charlotte are not alone in the sledge. When Charlotte turns her head, she can make out a huge bundle alongside her on the seat, apparently containing a person. But definitely not either of the two people who drowned, neither Baron Adrian nor the child, no, not a dead person at all. Not a word comes from that direction, and not a movement can be seen, but they are traveling so silently, and it is so silent all around them, that Charlotte can discern the faint sniveling sound that sometimes accompanies the breathing.

She tries turning her thoughts to Baron Adrian and the little child. That would be a relief. They are dead and gone, but there is no horror associated with their memory, only grief. No, she must continue her prayers. She must press forward all the way to the throne of God. She must pray that the terrible things that happened that evening will bring some blessing in their wake.

When she and Lundman had crawled forward to the edge of the crack in the ice and searched in vain for even a trace of the two who had drowned, Karl-Artur had shouted to them that he was going to run to the shore and fetch help. He ran, and Thea ran with him. Nearby there was a little iron foundry, powered by the same stream that caused the accident, and people from there came rushing down to the ice. They were carrying poles, which they drove far under the edge of the ice, but there had been no point. A powerful current had carried the bodies off. In order to find them, it would have been necessary to break up all the ice on the lake.

Charlotte did not see Thea Sundler again, but Karl-Artur returned and was one of the most devoted helpers, in fact he jeopardized his own life more than once. Throughout, he avoided coming near her. Not until it was all over and the many zealous helpers had begun to turn back, distressed and dispirited, did he approach.

He walked toward her slowly and hesitantly, eyes lowered, as was his wont. Once he was close by her, he raised his eyes slightly, so he was able to see her dress and her fur, but not her face. Standing thus, he said a few words, perhaps meant as comfort, perhaps as an apology:

'Well, Göran must have wanted his child back. And maybe also to thank his wealthy brother for the fine funeral.'

'Karl-Artur!'

He had looked up, his face reflecting the greatest amazement. He had clearly not expected it to be Charlotte who had been accompanying Baron Adrian, but rather the baron's wife.

He did not say another word, just stood silently staring at Charlotte, just as she stood staring at him. All the pain and horror she felt over his decline and his vicious words was visible in her face, and there was no way he could fail to read her expression.

At that moment he experienced a change Charlotte remembered very well from long ago, when he had heart seizures. His eyes grew wild and bulging, his lips opened as if to scream, and he pressed both his hands hard to his chest. For just an instant he stood there like that, after which he began to stagger and would have fallen if Charlotte had not put her arms around him.

He tottered around for a moment, but Charlotte quickly called for help, and a couple of men hurried over and carried him to her sledge. By the time they laid him there, he had lost consciousness.

Charlotte had the sledge driven to the little foundry, where she spent several hours. Karl-Artur needed a doctor. She and Lundman were soaking wet, having crawled through the slush on the ice, and needed to dry their clothes. The horses needed to rest and eat. But Charlotte had no memory of anything that had happened in the last few hours. She had just been praying and praying to God that she would be able to save Karl-Artur, to get him away from that woman, who was destroying him.

No one was able to bring him round before they departed, but as it was clear that he was still alive, Charlotte wrapped him in her furs and took him along in the sledge.

It is a cloudy, calm night, no stars in sight. Charlotte sighs over the endless silence in which the Almighty has enveloped himself. Never before in her life has she longed for the answer to a prayer as much as now.

Suddenly she notices that the unconscious man has begun to move.

'Karl-Artur,' she whispers, 'how are you?'

At first there is no reply, but now that she notes that he is likely to recover, she is seized by increasing anxiety. What will he be like? Will he speak crudely and viciously, as he had earlier that day, on the ice? She must not forget that he is a different person now.

Soon she hears him ask a question, very softly:

'Who is that next to me in this sledge? Is it Charlotte?'

'Yes,' she says. 'Yes, Karl-Artur, it is Charlotte.'

She can hear that he is speaking in his old voice. It is very weak, but not crude. It is as beautiful as before but, oddly, he sounds affected and ingratiating, well, even a little childish.

'I suspected it was you, Charlotte. There is no one who radiates good health and energy like you. I am recovering thanks to sitting beside you, Charlotte.'

'So you are feeling better?'

'Quite well, Charlotte. There is nothing at all wrong with my heart at present. I am not in pain, in fact I have not felt this well for years.'

'I think you have been extremely ill, Karl-Artur.'

'Yes, Charlotte, very ill indeed.'

He says nothing more for a while, and Charlotte sits still, waiting.

'Do you know what, Charlotte?' she soon hears him begin, still in the same weak, silly voice. 'I am passing the time by holding my own funeral sermon.'

'What do you mean? A funeral sermon?'

'Exactly, Charlotte. Have you never wondered, yourself, what the minister will say at the graveside, when you are dead?'

'Never, Karl-Artur. I don't go around thinking about my death.'

'Charlotte, would you be so kind as to ask the minister who will speak at my graveside, to say to those gathered there that it is the final resting place of the wealthy young man who followed the word of Jesus Christ, sold his possessions and became a poor man.'

'All right, Karl-Artur, but you are not going to die at present.'

'Perhaps not yet, Charlotte. I don't know when I have felt so well. But please remember that, Charlotte. Another thing I wish is that the clergyman remind the listeners that I was the apostle who walked the roads to bring the message of heaven to the people in their daily lives, at leisure or at labor.'

Charlotte does not answer. She wonders whether Karl-Artur is mocking her.

He goes on talking in the same affected tone of voice.

'I think it would be fitting, too, for the minister to say that, like the Lord Jesus, I have also demonstrated my humility by eating and drinking with publicans and sinners.'

'Oh do stop carrying on, Karl-Artur! You and Jesus! Those words are blasphemy.'

A few minutes pass before Karl-Artur responds.

'I didn't much like that last remark,' he finally says. 'But I suppose it would be all right even if the minister didn't mention the publicans. It might be misunderstood. The rest would suffice to explain why I devoted my work to the roads, to the people of the roads, in spite of all the other opportunities I had to extend it to other places.'

Charlotte sits there horrified, wanting to scream. Is he serious? Or merely trying to impress her? Has he lost all his sense of judgment?

'Perhaps you will recall, Charlotte, a friend of mine who became a missionary?'

'Pontus Friman?'

'Exactly, Charlotte. He writes to me often, urging me time

and again to travel out to heathen lands and assist him. I have been sorely tempted. I do like to travel. Language studies interest me as well. I have always been a very fast learner. So, Charlotte, what do you say?'

'I am wondering, Karl-Artur, whether you are mocking me. But if not, I do think it an excellent idea.'

'Me? Would I mock you? I am always serious, Charlotte, as you ought to know from way back. But there is something about your reactions, Charlotte, that really does seem unsympathetic. I would not have expected that, as we have not seen each other for so long. I am afraid that this meeting between us will prove a disappointment.'

'That would be very sad, Karl-Artur,' says Charlotte, who is utterly bewildered, completely disconcerted by the incredible presumption and vanity of this poor, ragged creature.

'I know, Charlotte, that you are now very wealthy, and the wealthy easily become superficial and judge by appearances. Charlotte, you cannot understand that my poverty is entirely voluntary. I do have a wife, you know…'

When he mentions his wife, Charlotte attempts to intervene, to say something that might attract his interest.

'Now you listen to me for a moment, Karl-Artur! Have you heard that, during the last few years of her life, your mother did not want to hear anything but your letters from your university days read to her? Jaquette read them aloud to her, day after day. But she must have tired of doing so one fine day, and do you know what she did then? Well, she made the journey to Korskyrka and went to see Anna Svärd and your young son. She took them back to Karlstad with her, and showed the child to his grandmother.'

'Goodness, how lovely, how touching, Charlotte.'

'After that day, Jaquette no longer had to read those letters. Your mother wanted the child near her all the time. She played with him, she admired him, he preoccupied her entirely. She was inseparable from the little boy; your wife had to move to Karlstad. It is said that she won the affection of them all, particularly your father. Once your mother passed away, your wife moved back to Korskyrka. She and her brood of foster children are transforming your little cottage into a proper farmstead. But they say your son spends most of his time with Jaquette, who lives in Älvsnäs now. He is a charming child. Do you not long to see your son, Karl-Artur?'

'I know very well, Charlotte, that my wife is all but dying to see me, as are all the others as well. But it is no use, Charlotte, to plead their case. I want my liberty. I like life on the road. I like my little adventures.'

'He retains no sense at all of anything good,' Charlotte thinks. 'He gives me nothing but evasions. I cannot get a grip on him.' Still, she makes another effort.

'You sound so pleased with yourself, Karl-Artur.'

'How can I be anything but pleased now that I have found you again, Charlotte?'

'Have you no regrets whatsoever about having stolen away with the little girl? It did result in two deaths.'

'Two deaths,' says Karl-Artur, 'two deaths. Charlotte, you do say the strangest things. Why would I care if two people die? I detest all people. It is my greatest pleasure to gather them around me in order to chastise them, to tell them what disgusting swine they are.'

'Say no more, Karl-Artur. You are appalling.'

'Appalling? Me? Well, it is natural for you to say that, Charlotte. But it is the retribution of one who has been rejected. It is sour grapes. And yet, Charlotte, you must admit that anyone who can arouse as much devotion as I have… Goodness, Charlotte, I am amazed at her patience. I would have expected her to come and tear me out of your arms.'

'Oh, Karl-Artur, please say no more.'

'But why not? I am so enjoying our little conversation, Charlotte.'

'You're disturbing me. I am praying to God. I have been praying to Him ever since I met you this afternoon.'

'A most praiseworthy occupation. But what are you praying for, Charlotte?'

'To be able to save you from that woman.'

'From her! There is no point, Charlotte. Nothing in the world can alter her devotion.'

He leaned right forward and whispered into Charlotte's ear:

'I have tried every conceivable thing myself. But there is no aid. Nothing but death. *Nemo nisi mors*.'

'Well, then I shall pray for your death, Karl-Artur.'

'Oh, Charlotte, you have always been so objectionably honest. It is not pleasant to know that you are praying to God for my death, but of course I shall not disturb you further.'

For a long while they travel on in silence, as they had before Karl-Artur regained consciousness. Charlotte is trying to structure her thoughts, to figure out what to do about a man who has gone so much to ruin.

Then Lundman turns around in the driver's seat once more:

'Ma'am, can you hear that there are people after us? They're driving as fast as they can; they're whipping the horses and shouting "Now we've got 'em" to each other. D'you want me to get us away from 'em, ma'am?'

'No, Lundman. Certainly not. We must stop instead. They are welcome.'

A moment or two later their pursuers caught up with them. In the dark of night, Charlotte is able to discern two little vagrants' sledges as they pull up alongside her sledge. Dark figures move on the road. A couple of them move forward in haste, grasping her horses by the harnesses. A man and a woman approach her.

'Are you Charlotte? I mean: do I have the honor of addrething the ethteemed Mrs. Schagerström whose husband is on the Nathional Board of Trade?' asks a lisping voice. 'May I inquire as to whether you can provide me with any informathion contherning Karl-Artur, Madame? Before he ran down to the ice, we arranged to meet at the home of one of the smiths, where I waited for hours. In the end I went to the foundry office to find out what had happened, and wath told he had fallen ill and that you, Madame, had taken him along in your sledge. That wath exthremely kind and generous. What is it they say? "Firtht love never dies."'

'You outnumber us, Thea,' Charlotte remarks with perfect equanimity.

'Yeth, I had the great good fortune to meet two of our best

friends out on the road this very evening. They immediately offered to help me get Karl-Artur back. Ah, Madame, you cannot imagine how much good thervice Karl-Artur has done among the traveling people, and how well he is liked. They want him back at any cost.'

'I assume that you intend to take him by force if I refuse to let him go.'

'Not by force, Madame, that is not at all our intention. But we do want to feel assured that Karl-Artur is free to follow his own inclinations and come back to uth if he so wishes.'

'I have no doubts about his wishes, Thea. He has maintained polite conversation with me for the last hour, but he finds it dreadfully dull, and is delighted that you have arrived. Of course I will not detain him. So you may tell your friends that their drawn knives, so bright in the dark, will not be needed. You may have him.'

Thea Sundler, who must have anticipated fierce resistance, is so astonished she is at a loss for words.

'You go right ahead and take him,' Charlotte repeats loudly. 'Take him and finish him off! I thought I would be able to help him, but I find myself unable. He is beyond all reason. Here he sits with two human lives on his conscience, and is barely aware of it. Get him out of here! Take him back to lying and crime and misery! Down in the cesspool with him! He is pleased with what he has done this evening. It causes him no horror. He does not wish to mend his ways. He wants to go on living as before. Get him out of here!'

She leans over to Karl-Artur's side, pulls off his foot fur and turns down his cover, to enable him to disembark from the sledge.

'Get out! Go back to the woman who has made you what you are now. I am finished with you.'

Without a word, Thea Sundler moves around to Karl-Artur's side, and he gets up. But when she extends a hand to help him down from the sledge, he shoves it aside. He turns to Charlotte, sinking down at her feet.

'Help me, save me!' he cries in a voice suddenly ringing both honest and true.

'Karl-Artur, it's too late now.'

He clings to Charlotte's legs, hanging on for dear life.

'Charlotte, deliver me from her. You are the only person who can help me!'

Charlotte leans forward, trying to look him in the eye.

'You know what the price will be,' she says very softly but extremely solemnly.

'Yes, I know, Charlotte,' he answers, just as solemn, holding her gaze steadfastly.

'Lundman!' Charlotte shouts, her voice suddenly joyous. 'Crack your whip! Get going!'

Lundman, the coachman, rises up from his seat. He is a huge man with a heavy beard. He looks just as the coachman from a fine manor ought to look as he swings his long whip forward, backward, and to the sides. The dark figures run off, cursing, the horses rear up and take off. The men who were holding their harnesses try to hang on for a short distance, but the whip strikes them time and again, and eventually they let go. At a wild gallop, Charlotte and her companions head for Hedeby.

THE WEDDING RING

Who was she, to remember things everyone else had forgotten? Why should she sit thinking about the days when he traveled the markets like so many other vagrants? Why should she keep seeing, in her mind, that woman whose company he kept in those days?

She was quite certain that it was 1842 when he traveled out to be a missionary, and it was now only 1850. It had been no more than eight years since he left. And yet everyone seemed to think that all should be forgiven and forgotten. But surely she, who had been his wife, ought to be allowed to have her own opinion on that matter?

Just imagine that now that he had been back in Korskyrka for a while and was staying at Stora Sjötorp, her neighbors from the village kept coming to ask her if she planned to go back to Africa with him! Well, that's what people were like down in these parts: they were easygoing and inconstant; they rolled back and forth like the water in a trough. Should she go to Africa with him, now that she was sufficiently well to do and respected to have a farmstead of her own! Would she leave home now that her foster children had grown up and could fend for themselves and she finally had a bit of peace and quiet and was able to bring Mother Svärd to live with her, to make her old age more comfortable?

She had not seen him, although he had been in Korskyrka for a couple of days. He had at least had the sense not to try to impose on her. And now she only wished she hadn't gone to church a couple of hours ago and listened to him. People might take it that she was eager to see him again. But in fact she had not gone of her own volition. It was Mrs.

Schagerström who had come and collected her. And she was not an easy person to say no to.

Who was she, not to be able to stop thinking about everything that had happened? Mrs. Schagerström told her that he had been doing good work out there amongst the heathens. He had finally found his rightful place in the world, she said. God had driven and hounded him like a cornered animal, all roads had been closed to him except this single one, and it had proven to be the right one, the one he ought to have chosen from the start.

Mrs. Schagerström did not tell her outright that she ought to abandon everything and go out there with him. She had just mentioned that it wasn't easy for him out there among the savages and that it would have been good for him to have someone with him who could see to it that he had decent meals. And Schagerström, who had been supporting him financially out there all this time, would certainly not hesitate to pay a helper, if one could just be found.

Another thing she said was that he had now learned to love his fellow man. That was essential, and was exactly the ability he had been missing before. He had loved Christ and had demonstrated his ability to sacrifice his entire worldly life to follow him. But he had never possessed the right love of his fellow human beings. And anyone wishing to follow in the footsteps of Christ without loving mankind is bound to drag both himself and others into misery.

Mrs. Schagerström also told her that if she came along to church to hear him preach, she would see his great change for herself. She would hear that he truly loved the blackies he was striving to convert to Christianity. And that was the love that had made him a new man.

And, well, she didn't quite know how, but she had been enticed into going along to church.

When he stepped up to the pulpit she did not recognize him at first. He was bald, and his face was lined with great suffering. He was no longer handsome, and he had stepped up with great humility, and very quietly. She had felt the strangest urge to weep, upon seeing him. And yet he did not look sad. No, he had a gentle smile on his face, a smile that illuminated the entire church.

She couldn't really say that there had been anything very remarkable about his sermon. In her view, it had contained too little of the word of God. He had just spoken of what life was like for the people out there in the heathen lands; actually he had been invited to give not a sermon but a mission address. And certainly, she could see that he loved those people out there, since he was enduring it and intending to go back out. Of course life had been impoverished and difficult in Medstubyn, too, but that was nothing compared with those people. Their huts had neither proper floors nor proper windows.

And as she sat there looking at his gentle smile and hearing the heartfelt commitment to his every word, she remembered that this was the man who had insulted the crowds at markets, and been laughed at. That was the way she was. She did not come from Korskyrka, no, she came from Medstubyn, and she was Erik from Jobsgården's niece. She was single-minded and suspicious, just as he was.

When she left the church she noticed that they had put up a table by the door, with a brass plate where people donated whatever they could afford, to the conversion of the heathens.

Two gentlemen of the village were guarding the plate, and she felt that they stared long and hard at her as she passed by. She had no money with her, not having imagined that this preacher would put her in a frame of mind for giving. So, having nothing else, she had quickly removed her wedding ring from her finger and tossed it into the plate. He had given it to her, and he was welcome to have it back.

And now she sat at home alone in the kitchen thinking about whether there might be any consequences.

He might take it as a statement on her part that their marriage was dissolved and she never wanted to see him again.

And if he took it like that he would not come to see her, she knew. In that case, he would leave and that would be that.

But he might also take it as a reminder on her part that here in Korskyrka he had a wife waiting for him.

Well, she would have to see how he took it. It would depend on his own state of mind whether he took it in the former or the latter way.

But if he took it in the latter way and came to see her, what would her answer be?

So, who was she, what did she want? Did she know what she wanted?

She did feel her heart pounding harder. She was so peculiar. She was unable to forget that he was the man to whom she had once sent a message with the birds of passage.

Now there was someone passing by the window outside. Was it he? Yes, it was.

And now he entered the passageway. Now he was raising the latch.

What would her answer to him be?

Selma Lagerlöf

Translator's Afterword

In his address upon receipt of the 1991 Selma Lagerlöf award, author and Swedish Academy member Lars Gyllensten spoke of Lagerlöf as 'far more complex than her reputation would lead one to believe'. He also spoke of the Bachtinian 'polyphony' of her characters, describing individual person-alities as diverse and contradictory, mysterious and surprising, as if each of them was several characters in one. In this Afterword I relate to Gyllensten's comments by focusing on the thread of continuity binding together the women in the trilogy, and following it in *Anna Svärd*. This is only one of many other possible approaches, of course. The Löwensköld trilogy contains a myriad of interesting stylistic and narrative devices, shifts between first and third-person narration, from solemn, straightforward description to deeply ironic humor, and from pedagogical didacticism to bewildering ambivalence, each of which deserves an Afterword of its own.

Lagerlöf was not only more complex but also more modern than her reputation would indicate. In an interview on Swedish Radio in November 2015, best-selling Swedish author Lena Andersson answered a question in words which, I believe, Selma Lagerlöf might well have used about her own writing. The question was about what Andersson's own recent writing on the subject of love is really about, and she replied that it concerns 'breakdowns in communication, and people who meet but have utterly opposing views of what an encounter really is, what relationships really are, and what they are for.' Let us see how equally well these words apply to the characters in the Löwensköld trilogy, and specifically to Volume Three, *Anna Svärd*. In addition to love, other important themes include rings, clergymen and reconciliation.

In her general introduction to this series of new Lagerlöf translations, Helena Forsås-Scott writes that in the Löwensköld trilogy the author gives: 'prominence to a series of strong and independent female characters'. And according to Danish scholar Henrik Wivel, in the three books about the Löwensköld family Selma Lagerlöf uses her superb technique to pit the 'people' against the upper classes, women against men, and passion against its own distorted image.

This trilogy also brought Selma Lagerlöf's career as a writer of novels to a close. By the time of the publication of *Anna Svärd*, Selma Lagerlöf was seventy. Although she had projected a fourth volume, intended to describe what becomes of Karl-Artur, it was never completed. She devoted her remaining writing energy to her memoirs. And so we, her readers, are left with our own conjectures as to what the characters go on to do with their lives.

The Löwensköld trilogy begins and ends with rings. Lagerlöf's overtly fictional world begins and ends with a minister in the pulpit. Of course it is with retrospective construction that we raise an ironic eyebrow at the opening line of *The Saga of Gösta Berling*, 'At long last the minister stood in the pulpit,' knowing that the final chapter of *Anna Svärd* concerns just that, a minister who is finally back in the pulpit, coming full circle, closing a circle, or ring.

The theme of the first volume, *The Löwensköld Ring*, is the revenge exacted when a ring is stolen from its rightful owner. *Anna Svärd* concludes with a question concerning the rightful owner of Anna's wedding ring. *Anna Svärd* also begins with a query about forgiveness, and ends with another.

A brief recapitulation of the first two volumes is in order, to bring the reader back to the overview of the trilogy after reading *Anna Svärd*.

In *The Löwensköld Ring* the love between Marit Eriksdotter and her fiancé Paul Eliasson, both of peasant stock, is prevented from reaching fulfillment by the intervention of the wealthy and powerful, who insist on convicting three possibly innocent men, one of whom is Paul Eliasson, for the theft of

General Löwensköld's ring from his grave at Hedeby manor. Marit then pronounces a curse, although the reader does not hear it directly until close to the end of *Anna Svärd*, when a later baron and master of Hedeby explains to Charlotte – they are both Löwenskölds but only distantly related – that the story had it that Marit's curse was: 'Three members of my family suffered a sudden, violent death, and so shall three of yours, equally violent and sudden, because you have failed to keep your promise.'

At the end of *The Löwensköld Ring*, a full generation after the initial theft, young Baron Adrian Löwensköld, the descendant of the general, is deathly ill. Perhaps he will be the first of the three Löwenskölds to pay with his life in accordance with Marit Eriksdotter's curse? What may save him is love – but it is a love across class lines. The young housekeeper Malvina Spaak adores him from a distance, but when he seems to be dying she reveals her adoration. And Marit, who has lived her entire life loveless after the execution of Paul Eliasson, is able to help the young housekeeper find the ring and rescue her beloved, only for both women to find that he is, in fact, engaged to a young woman of his own class. So in *The Löwensköld Ring*, two peasant women are deprived of their beloveds, the opportunity to love and be loved is thwarted, and there are three lives outstanding in accordance with the curse.

In *Charlotte Löwensköld* it is Hedeby housekeeper Malvina Spaak's daughter, the physically unattractive and psychologically intriguing Thea Sundler, who becomes the vehicle for pursuing the curse. She is pitted against the beautiful, charming Charlotte Löwensköld, a distant relative of the Hedeby Löwenskölds. Both Charlotte and Thea love the young, handsome clergyman Karl-Artur Ekenstedt, who is also a Löwensköld on his mother's side. He lives under the powerful influence of his mother Beate, the wife of a colonel in Karlstad. Karl-Artur and Charlotte are betrothed, but Thea (who is married to the sickly church organist in the parish) is infatuated with him, and intervenes. Under the influence of Thea, Karl-Artur eventually breaks off his engagement to Charlotte, has a violent rupture with his mother, and vows to marry the first woman to cross his path. In the manipulative way of a man with power and influence, however, he ensures that the path leads to a pretty peasant woman, Anna Svärd. Lagerlöf contrasts these two women and the kind of love Karl-Artur has for each: Charlotte refined and intellectual, Anna robust and sensual. As the novel closes, Charlotte has broken free of the spell of Karl-Artur and married a kind, wealthy foundry owner whose background is diametrically opposed to that of her former fiancé. Karl-Artur and Anna Svärd are betrothed, Thea Sundler, the serpent in paradise, believes she will be able to maintain her hold over Karl-Artur, and he and his mother (who has many of the qualities of Thea, but whose basic relation to Karl-Artur is well-intended yet overbearing love rather than intrigue) are fatally at odds.

Thus we enter the world of *Anna Svärd*, having accumulated impressions of Marit Eriksdotter and Malvina Spaak in the first volume, and of Beate Ekenstedt, Thea Sundler, Anna Svärd and the eponymous Charlotte Löwensköld in the second.

The very first sentence of *Anna Svärd*: 'Whatever you may think about Thea Sundler, you must admit that she knew better than anyone else how to handle Karl-Artur Ekenstedt' throws readers familiar with *Charlotte Löwensköld* directly back into the essence of that text as well as drawing us into the story through the narrator's indirect implication of the reader, the 'you'. At the same time, the sentence awakens our suspicions. We know from our previous reading that Thea Sundler epitomizes the selfish and distorted side of love. How can *Anna Svärd* begin with a compliment to her? And why, if she is so important, is the final volume of the trilogy not entitled *Thea Sundler*? Thea Sundler is in many ways the central figure behind the scenes throughout both *Charlotte Löwensköld* and *Anna Svärd*, as is her mother in *The Löwensköld Ring*. Karl-Artur Ekenstedt is the male protagonist of volumes two and three, but it is Charlotte and Anna, the title figures, who give us Selma Lagerlöf's answer to the vision that all three volumes orbit around, as does much of her *oeuvre*: how can a woman satisfactorily spend the one life she has to live, and to what extent is love the key?

We also note that the first chapter of *Anna Svärd* concerns a journey, 'The Journey to Karlstad', while the two chapters leading up to the final one are entitled 'The Journey Out' and 'The Journey Home'. These journeys are also the journeys of life cycles, away from and back to oneself, for all the characters involved.

Just as Charlotte Löwensköld does not appear by name in the first chapter of 'her' novel, neither does Anna Svärd. She is not referred to until after several pages and then not by name, only as 'my fiancée'. Karl-Artur and his mother Beate Ekenstedt, the Colonel's wife, are the focus of the first chapters of both *Anna Svärd* and *Charlotte Löwensköld*. And if Thea Sundler is the manipulating figure, Karl-Artur is the figure in both volumes around whom the story revolves.

According to Lars Gyllensten, Lagerlöf's characters span the spectrum from the stylized heroes of the epics to Dostoyevskian multiplicity and built-in contradiction. Who, Gyllensten asks, is Karl-Artur Ekenstedt: a bigoted fool with his own perverse picture of God, or a potential saint? An egotistical braggart or a humble, bewildered seeker?

Was Thea Sundler, Gyllensten goes on to ask, merely a lying, vengeful intriguer – or was there some true, albeit damaged, love in her, love constantly gone astray, until neither she nor anyone else understood its real name?

And as for Charlotte Löwensköld herself, asks Gyllensten, that appealing, lovely young woman so fond of dancing, who had everything the young Selma Lagerlöf felt she lacked – was she lovingly loyal, stubbornly defiant, or both? Do we all contain these opposing forces?

The reader will recall that *Anna Svärd* is divided into three sections. Part I describes the time up to and including her marriage to Karl-Artur, how they settle into their new home and adjust to life with the ten children Karl-Artur had bought at a poorhouse auction to save them from being sent out to work for separate families. We then read about how the scheming of Thea Sundler results in Karl-Artur's resigning from his church position and leaving the parish, leaving Anna Svärd, pregnant, to fend for herself and the children.

In Part II Karl-Artur returns to Korskyrka and to his marriage, but Thea succeeds in destroying it and taking over his life. In an extraordinarily powerful scene after Anna Svärd has stormed out of her home and marriage, Thea is at hand, literally, to pick up the pieces (the deck of cards Karl-Artur has cut into tiny scraps after Anna has disobeyed his commandment not to play cards under his roof). At the apex of this scene, Thea responds to a vain effort on the part of Karl-Artur to show her the door: 'Strike me! Kick me! I will still come back. You will never be able to get rid of me. The things that frighten off the others are the things that keep me here.' Soon a new life begins, in which Thea and Karl-Artur travel the roads as itinerant evangelicals, he preaching and she singing. Thea's unconditional subordination awakens the very worst instincts in Karl-Artur, and after a few years he is on the brink of self-destruction. By the time the reader catches up with them, his once wonderful sermons have degenerated into hateful, accusatory ones, and her once beautiful singing voice has become harsh and dissonant. His body is skeletal, while hers is large and shapeless. The paradox of the novel is that the life he has longed for (and believed he might have with the peddler woman Anna Svärd), freedom on the road and walking in the footsteps of his Savior, becomes instead the most painful possible itinerant co-dependence between himself and Thea, entirely destructive and having nothing at all to do with saving souls. Nowhere does Selma Lagerlöf paint a more horrifying picture of how distorted and perverted love can become, and how much harm it can do.

At a key point in the middle of *Anna Svärd*, Charlotte's husband Schagerström has glimpsed an encounter between Charlotte and Karl-Artur which leads him to imagine that her professed love of him and happiness in their marriage are nothing but a pretense, and that she actually continues to be in love with Karl-Artur. The reader knows that this is not correct, but is powerless as Schagerström stands thinking about what he has seen, devastated. Charlotte approaches a few minutes later with a hug and a kiss. Lagerlöf writes that 'he could not have wished for a warmer welcome' but

Schagerström thinks 'what a good show she puts on'. There is a bit of conversation as the reader feels the build-up of Schagerström's misinterpretation of events. Their meeting ends in silence and 'Schagerström, of course, drew his own conclusions from this silence'.

This scene embodies Lagerlöf's masterful use of ambivalence. She constantly leaves the reader feeling uncertain about her characters in a way not unlike our reactions to encounters in real life. Have we misunderstood? Whose picture of reality determines the development of the plot/our lives? How and why? We draw our own conclusions from what we see, let our emotions cloud our judgment, and things go awry, in life as in literature. Breakdowns in communication, as Lena Andersson says.

In Part III the curse from *The Löwensköld Ring*, the revenge projected by Marit Eriksdotter, is fulfilled. The scene shifts to Hedeby manor, where *The Löwensköld Ring* was also set, where a new Adrian Löwensköld (descendant of the young man whom Thea Sundler's mother Malvina Spaak rescued from death) now reigns supreme, presiding over a wife and five daughters. This section is, in contrast to Part II, one of the funniest, most ironic pieces of prose Selma Lagerlöf ever produced. After describing Baron Adrian's misery and frustration at the bareness of his dull and seemingly meaningless life without a son and heir, she brings his vagrant brother back into the family fold, along with a son he is prepared to leave with Adrian, only for the reader to find that this now degenerate brother has played the ultimate practical joke on his wealthy, spoilt brother, the son actually being a little girl in disguise.

Selma Lagerlöf allows the baron's wife and daughters to share in our laughter, a grand, liberating laugh. If only that were the end of it! Thea Sundler reappears, however, accompanied by Karl-Artur, and engineers the last two of the three Löwensköld deaths threatened at the end of *The Löwensköld Ring*. In the final chapters, Charlotte Löwensköld attempts to rescue Karl-Artur from his ultimate ruin, and Anna Svärd strives to assert her independence and to liberate herself from Karl-Artur.

In contrast to *The Story of Gösta Berling*, where the women are never quite able to assert themselves over the male protagonist, the last time we meet Charlotte in *Anna Svärd* we find her (as she was at the end of *Charlotte Löwensköld*) responsible for a sledge, this one making its way home. Karl-Artur is at her feet, ill and a bundle of nerves, but instead of shouldering him as her burden, or making him the burden of his (still) wife Anna Svärd, she sees to it that he is separated from Thea Sundler and indeed from all of them, and sent to Africa as an evangelical missionary for several years. In the final chapter, 'The Wedding Ring,' Lagerlöf returns to a ring, but only to toss its significance into ambivalence. Anna Svärd, who has made a stable, strong life for herself in Karl-Artur's absence, goes to church to hear him preach in Korskyrka. Not overly impressed with what she sees and hears, she deposits her wedding ring in the collection plate as she leaves the church. Selma Lagerlöf continues to deprive us of a definite interpretation of this gesture by concluding the novel with a question mark, leaving the reader wondering whether Anna Svärd intended to indicate that she was giving up her husband once and for all, or issuing an invitation to return to their marriage. The novel ends that same evening, as Anna Svärd wonders how Karl-Artur will react when he finds the ring in the collection plate:

> He might take it as a statement on her part that their marriage was dissolved and she never wanted to see him again.
> And if he took it like that he would not come to see her, she knew. In that case, he would leave and that would be that.
> (…)
> Now there was someone passing by the window outside. Was it he? Yes, it was.
> And now he entered the passageway. Now he was raising the latch.
> What would her answer to him be?

What fantastic development of character Lagerlöf has undertaken in the journey from Marit Eriksdotter to Anna Svärd! Both are peasant women, and both are powerfully manipulated by the men and societies around them, but Anna Svärd is able to ask herself questions that require a great deal of independence and integrity to pose. Although we are left to speculate as to the answers, we see a woman fully capable of making her own considered choices, and a journey through breakdowns in communication and contradictory expectations to solid personal integrity of a kind that may well have inspired Lena Andersson as well as other late twentieth and early twenty-first century writers.

In her essay 'The Loathsome Woman from Korskyrka,' Ulla Torpe pulls together the strands of the three women and their orbiting around Karl-Artur Ekenstedt. She does so in a way that sheds useful light on the question of why Thea Sundler is allowed to take up so much space in a story clearly intended to highlight the creativity and strength of the two healthy women, Charlotte and Anna:

> Thea is the one who is ill and infected and whose intrusiveness makes her omnipresent…. Thea is so tightly shut into her female world, so unfree and invisible, that the only way for her to become visible is through destructive action. … The two other women, whom she has wounded and offended mortally, evade her grasp. They go on, thanks to their uninfected strength, to construct their lives with the building blocks they have been given. (My translation)

The late general editor of this series, Helena Forsås-Scott, read and commented on the first hundred pages of my draft translation. This was one of the last things she did before illness forced her to stop working in spring 2015. I will always be particularly moved by her having put her limited time and energy into my translation rather than other projects. Sarah Death, who has generously taken over the general editorship, read and commented on the entire draft, and her eagle eye and not least her kind and consistent pointing out of questionable uses of register are, as always, greatly appreciated. Thanks as ever to the Norvik Press staff members, Elettra Carbone and Marita Fraser for their supportive attitudes and prompt assistance, as well as to Janet Garton and my husband Robert for their careful readings.

Gothenburg, November 2015
Linda Schenck

References

All translations from Swedish reference literature are my own.

Gyllensten, Lars, speech of thanks when awarded the annual Selma Lagerlöf prize in 1991, in *Kära Selma*, Torsby, Heidruns förlag 2013, pp. 69-80.
Lagerlöf, Selma, T*he Saga of Gösta Berling*, translated by Paul Norlen, Penguin Books, 2009.
Torpe, Ulla, 'Den vedervärdiga kvinnan från Korskyrka', in Ingrid Holmquist and Ebba Witt-Brattström, eds., *Kvinnornas litteraturhistoria*, Vol. 2: *Nittonhundratalet*. Stockholm: Författarförlaget, 1983, pp. 57-72.
Wivel, Henrik, *Snödrottningen. En bok om Selma Lagerlöf och kärleken*, translated from the Danish by Birgit Edlund. Stockholm: Albert Bonniers förlag, 1990.
Interview with Swedish author Lena Andersson (interviewer Martin Wicklin), *Sveriges radios söndagsintervju*, 12 November 2015.
http://sverigesradio.se/sida/avsnitt/630398?programid=4772

SELMA LAGERLÖF

The Löwensköld Ring

Charlotte Löwensköld

(translated by Linda Schenck)

The Löwensköld Ring (1925) is the first volume of the trilogy considered to have been Selma Lagerlöf's last work of prose fiction. Set in the Swedish province of Värmland in the eighteenth century, the narrative traces the consequences of the theft of General Löwensköld's ring from his coffin, and develops into a disturbing tale of revenge from beyond the grave. It is also a tale about decisive women. The narrative twists and the foregrounding of alternative interpretations confront the reader with a pervasive sense of ambiguity. *Charlotte Löwensköld* (1925) is the story of the following generations, a tale of psychological insight and social commentary, and of the complexities of a mother-son relationship. How we make our life 'choices' and what evil forces can be at play around us is beautifully and ironically depicted.

The Löwensköld Ring
ISBN 9781870041928
UK £9.95
(Paperback, 120 pages)

Charlotte Löwensköld
ISBN 9781909408067
UK £11.95
(Paperback, 290 pages)

SELMA LAGERLÖF

Nils Holgersson's Wonderful Journey through Sweden

(translated by Peter Graves)

Nils Holgersson's Wonderful Journey through Sweden (1906-07) is truly unique. Starting life as a commissioned school reader designed to present the geography of Sweden to nine-year-olds, it quickly won the international fame and popularity it still enjoys over a century later. The story of the naughty boy who climbs on the gander's back and is then carried the length of the country, learning both geography and good behaviour as he goes, has captivated adults and children alike, as well as inspiring film-makers and illustrators. The elegance of the present translation – the first full translation into English – is beautifully complemented by the illustrations specially created for the volume.

Nils Holgersson's Wonderful Journey through Sweden, Volume 1
ISBN 9781870041966
UK £12.95
(Paperback, 365 pages)

Nils Holgersson's Wonderful Journey through Sweden, Volume 2
ISBN 9781870041973
UK £12.95
(Paperback, 380 pages)

Nils Holgersson's Wonderful Journey through Sweden, The Complete Volume
ISBN 9781870041966
UK £29.95
(Hardback, 684 pages)

SELMA LAGERLÖF

The Phantom Carriage

(translated by Peter Graves)

Written in 1912, Selma Lagerlöf's *The Phantom Carriage* is a powerful combination of ghost story and social realism, partly played out among the slums and partly in the transitional sphere between life and death. The vengeful and alcoholic David Holm is led to atonement and salvation by the love of a dying Salvation Army slum sister under the guidance of the driver of the death-cart that gathers in the souls of the dying poor. Inspired by Charles Dickens's *A Christmas Carol*, *The Phantom Carriage* remained one of Lagerlöf's own favourites, and Victor Sjöström's 1920 film version of the story is one of the greatest achievements of the Swedish silent cinema.

The Phantom Carriage
ISBN 9781870041911
UK £11.95
(Paperback, 126 pages)

SELMA LAGERLÖF

Lord Arne's Silver

(translated by Sarah Death)

An economical and haunting tale, published in book form in 1904 and set in the sixteenth century on the snowbound west coast of Sweden, *Lord Arne's Silver* is a classic from the pen of an author consummately skilled in the deployment of narrative power and ambivalence. A story of robbery and murder, retribution, love and betrayal plays out against the backdrop of the stalwart fishing community of the archipelago. Young Elsalill, sole survivor of the mass killing in the home of rich cleric Lord Arne, becomes a pawn in dangerous games both earthly and supernatural. As the deep-frozen sea stops the murderers escaping, sacrifice and atonement are the price that has to be paid.

ISBN 9781870041904
UK £9.95
(Paperback, 102 pages)

Selma Lagerlöf

Selma Lagerlöf